RAVE REVIEWS FOR J. F. GONZALEZ AND *SURVIVOR*!

"It pushes your eyes off the page and then pulls them back, forcing the kind of visceral relationship between writer and reader that the best horror writing can produce."

—*The New York Times Book Review*

"Fans of Jack Ketchum are definitely going to enjoy *Survivor*. You need to buy this book."

—*Cemetery Dance*

"Quite possibly the most disturbing book I've ever read in my life."

—Brian Keene, Author of *City of the Dead*

"J. F. Gonzalez is a writer to watch."

—Bentley Little, Author of *The Policy*

"[T]his is extreme horror, unflinching and uncompromising."

—Chiaroscuro

HER TURN IS COMING

Lisa tried not to watch, tried to drown out the sounds of what was going on, but she felt drawn to the scene as it was being filmed.

As the assault continued, Lisa had feigned unconsciousness for what felt like hours. Lisa had never heard anybody scream in pain the way Debbie screamed. The screaming went on for a while and was punctuated by wet slapping sounds.

Somehow, Lisa managed to suffer through the ordeal of listening to Debbie Martinez being brutalized while she cowered in the corner, trying to drown out what was happening. For the first time since her ordeal the thought of the fetus in her womb didn't come up. *It's never going to be,* she had thought, her heart heavy with sadness. *Brad and I aren't going to have our baby, we'll never get the chance to make a baby again because when they're finished with Debbie they're going to do the same to me.*

Lisa didn't know if Debbie was dead or alive until the three men left. She heard them packing the camera and lighting gear up, and she heard the blond guy ask, "Is it okay if we leave that one here until tomorrow or the next day?"

SURVIVOR

J. F. GONZALEZ

LEISURE BOOKS  NEW YORK CITY

For William Relling, Jr.
RIP Brother
I miss you

A LEISURE BOOK®

February 2006

Published by

Dorchester Publishing Co., Inc.
200 Madison Avenue
New York, NY 10016

Portions of Part One of this book were previously published in 2002 under the title *Maternal Instinct*.

ISBN 0-8439-5567-8

Printed in the United States of America.

ACKNOWLEDGMENTS

Thank you: Dave Nordhaus for taking the bait the first time with *Maternal Instinct*, and Shane Ryan Staley for pulling it off; to Bill Relling and Bob Strauss for the editorial support when I needed it. The biggest thanks go to Gilbert Schloss for coming to the rescue when nobody would step up to the plate.

The following people also need to be thanked for various reasons, primarily for their friendship and support during the writing of this novel; in some cases for sending me money when I needed it or for providing technical support; in others, for their sheer wonderfulness: Cathy and Hannah, Joe and Lucy Becker, Jesus and Glenda Gonzalez; Gary Zimmerman and Bonesaw; Sean Wallace, Mary Wolf, Brian Hopkins; Matt Schwartz, Del and Sue Howison; Ramona Pearce and Salpy Manjikian; Trish Chervenak, Wrath James White, and Khaled Hosseini, MD, for providing me with answers to my questions as they pertained to their individual fields (and I hope I didn't mess up too badly); the California Highway Patrol and LAPD; Andrew Vachss and the Zero; Monster.com; the city of Las Vegas and the Luxor Hotel; John Graff; Kevin Johnson, Gord Rollo, Garrett Peck, and Brian Keene for their support and friendship; to Coop for helping stage the first "anti-reading"; and for my readers who believe in me.

A tip of the hat to G. Hof, Zack Venable, and Buddy Martinez for inspiration they never could have imagined. And to Zack, Richard Long, Angel Garcia, Justin Grave, and William Smith—my longtime buddies and partners in crime. Your secret's safe with me.

SURVIVOR

Prologue

October 5, 1955
Lititz, Pennsylvania

Their neighborhood was deserted. Nobody had seen her get off the school bus at the corner of Lincoln and Elm on the outskirts of town, heading toward Rothsville Road. Bonnie Febray clutched her books to her chest, her skirt flapping against her shapely legs as she commenced her walk home. The autumn wind blew brittle leaves along the sidewalk, and she could sense the approach of fall as the skin along her arms rose to goose pimples at the sudden cold. She hugged herself. Football season was already well under way, and it was going to be a good year. She was head cheerleader this year at Warwick High School, she was dating Richard Swiegert, star quarterback of the team, and this was her senior year.

I'm on top of the world!

Traffic along Rothsville Road was light. There was a

small development about a half a mile from the White Swan restaurant, where Rothsville Road curved into Newport Road, and that is where she had gotten off. She lived just four blocks down Elm Street, the direction in which she was headed now. She glanced at her wristwatch. It was three-thirty P.M. Mom was supposed to be at Kenny's game this afternoon; they were playing Cocalico in the Middle-School Division. They would get home about the same time Dad arrived home from work at Armstrong, and by then Bonnie would be home, clothes changed, showered and fresh, the smell of sweat and sex scrubbed off her. She felt her skin flush with excitement and a rising sense of shame as she drew closer to her destination. She cast furtive glances around the neighborhood. Bobby Martin and his snot-nosed friends from up the street weren't playing on their front porch—that was a good thing. She paused as she approached her home, looking around to see if anybody was around. She was fairly confident no one was paying attention to her, so she quickly walked past her house and darted up the sidewalk, heading to the Smith house, a cute brick home with a porch swing on the covered porch.

She darted up the steps to the porch and knocked on the wooden screen door. Her heart was pounding. Her stomach fluttered. Nerves. She didn't dare risk glancing back over her shoulder. There was really no reason to be ashamed. If anybody asked, she would simply explain that Mabel wanted her to stop by and help her with the bake sale that the First Methodist church was having next Sunday. It was true; Mabel *had* asked her to help her prepare a batch of chocolate-chip cookies and a cake two weeks ago. Bonnie had run to the store for ingredients while Mabel took her kids, a son and a daughter, to the Lititz Recreation Center. That's how it had started.

Now they were lovers.

Footsteps approached from behind the door and Bonnie felt her stomach sink further into nervous despair. When it swung open, revealing Mabel's blond, slender figure, Bonnie smiled. "Hi! Um, I can't stay long, but—"

"Come on in." Mabel smiled as she opened the door, and Bonnie quickly scampered inside.

Behind closed doors, they embraced. Kissed. Tingles of quivery sensation raced up and down Bonnie's spine. She felt her nipples harden. *Why can't Richard make me feel like this?* she thought as Mabel's hands and tongue explored her mouth, her breasts.

Mabel smiled at her between kisses. "This is surprising. I wasn't expecting to see you today."

Bonnie smiled, the shame and embarrassment of what she was involved with—and with an older woman!—rising to the surface. "I was thinking about you at school."

"That's nice."

Bonnie kissed her. "I don't have much time."

Mabel took the girl's hands and pulled her toward the rear of the house, toward the basement. "You've come just in time. I've got something to show you."

"What?" For the first time, Bonnie noticed that beneath the red bathrobe Mabel was nude. Had she been playing with herself before Bonnie showed up?

"A new game." Mabel pushed the door to the basement open and smiled. "Come. You'll enjoy it."

Bonnie followed Mabel down the wooden stairs to the dimly lit basement. It was finished, but crudely so. The walls had been finished with rough concrete, wooden beams exposing bare insulation along the ceiling. The rear of the basement had a dirt floor, and it was here where Mabel was leading her. There was some kind of weird contraption on the dirt floor . . . it looked like a mishmash of black rope and silver chains.

Mabel led her to the strange contraption and smiled.

She motioned toward it. "Let's get you out of those clothes."

Bonnie began slipping out of her skirt and blouse, eyeing the bundle of leather on the floor. "You're not going to whip me again, are you?"

"No, silly! It's a bondage harness."

Bonnie slipped out of her bra, her perky breasts firm and supple. She kicked her shoes off and hesitated before pushing her panties down her legs. Mabel had slipped out of her robe and Bonnie saw that she had, indeed, been engaged in pleasuring herself. The skin along the back of the older woman's upper thighs and buttocks was bright red. Flagellation had been the first thing Mabel had introduced the younger girl to, and Bonnie found that she had actually enjoyed it.

"Let me help you slip into this," Mabel said.

Bonnie stood still while Mabel trussed her up. She wound the leather straps around her waist and hips, then around her legs, binding them together. Another strap was wound up between her legs to another series of crisscrossing straps that bound her arms up. Mabel raised Bonnie's arms above her head, securing them together. Then she attached a metal ring to a section of the strap that lashed her wrists together, and another that bound her ankles. She helped lower Bonnie to the dirt floor. Bonnie felt the cold dirt along her ass as she waited, her excitement rising as she watched Mabel secure both ends of the harness to metal hooks in the ceiling. Then she began hoisting her up off the floor.

Bonnie grinned as her body rocked to and fro. They had played a similar game before in the bedroom Mabel shared with her husband, only instead the older woman had tied Bonnie to the bed. "Are we going to—"

"Umm, hmmm," Mabel smiled. She inserted a red ball gag in Bonnie's mouth and secured it with a leather strap behind her head. "I'm going to eat you up!"

Bonnie felt the cool air at her puckered nipples. Mabel kissed each breast, chuckling as her teeth nipped lightly at the skin. Then she worked her way down her navel to her thighs. Bonnie sighed, eyes closed, the feathery, sensual feelings creating such a vertigo of feeling that it was like a whirlpool. And when she felt Mabel's hand part her legs, felt a finger work its way into her warm wetness, she sighed.

For a moment she was lost in the sound and sensation of Mabel's hands and lips. She felt herself getting wetter, felt her heart race, unmindful now of the shame she knew such a relationship would bring to her family should they find out. She didn't care. The way Mabel treated her made her feel a thousand times better than any boy she had given herself to.

Mabel's lips ran kisses from the hollow of her throat, up her face, and lightly kissed each closed eye. Bonnie opened her eyes as Mabel's working fingers reached her G-spot. Mabel leaned over her, her lips over her right eye. "You have such beautiful eyes, honey."

"Mmmm." Bonnie could taste the leather of the ball gag; it made her quiver in anticipation. She opened her eyes as her lover's warm breath brought more feathery sensations to her face as she licked at the tender area of her upper right eyelid.

Mabel's lips moved over Bonnie's right eye in a kiss as her fingers worked their way in and out of her pussy harder. Then, just as Bonnie felt the first shudder of orgasm, Mabel's mouth pressed down over Bonnie's open right eye and began to suck.

What the fuck? Bonnie instinctively flinched at the sudden pressure being applied to her eye and the feathery sensations of pleasure turned into a sudden about-face of panic and pain. She felt Mabel's tongue brush against the fluttery skin of her eyelid, heard the moist sucking sound grow more frenzied as she squirmed and her mind shot into panic mode. *What the fuck is she doing, what the—*

Then her right eye exploded into extreme pain.

Bonnie Fabray was beyond panic—now she was petrified. She struggled wildly in the bondage harness, rocking it in its secure straps as Mabel held her head in place between her hands, her mouth forming a perfect suction cup over her eye socket. Bonnie could feel the older woman's teeth and tongue pull at the orb as her mouth sucked at her eyeball the way a child will draw a thick chocolate milk shake through a straw. The pain exploded as Mabel jerked her head back in a spray of blood, a flap of skin between her teeth, and the vision in Bonnie's right eye went watery blurry.

She wasn't even aware she was trying to scream through the ball gag. Mabel spit the flap of skin—*my eyelid, was that my eyelid?*—onto the ground and went at her again. Bonnie howled through the gag, trying to flail her head as the older woman clutched her face in her hands. Warm blood spattered her cheeks. The pain rocked through her face, echoing to the back of her skull. Her panic reached overload; she wasn't even aware of Mabel's tongue and teeth as her right eyeball was simultaneously sucked and pulled out of the socket by the combined force of Mabel's mouth and teeth.

Another explosion of pain, this one so great that everything went black.

Then, sudden consciousness.

The first thing she was aware of was the ferocious pain in her right eye. Even opening her left eye brought fresh waves of pain through her face. She tasted leather on her tongue, felt the straps that bound her arms and legs together, and felt gunk in her left eye. She forced it open, agony rocking through her face, and through tear-blurred vision she saw Mabel Schneider standing before her.

Mabel Schneider's face was bloodied, but she was smiling. She was chewing something, and as Bonnie felt her gorge rise, Mabel stepped forward and swallowed something. "I just love your eyes," she said, as she leaned over Bonnie Febray again for seconds.

PART ONE

Maternal Instinct

August 2, 1998
Southern California

One

They had set off at noon that day, heading north from Aliso Viejo on Interstate 5 toward Cambria, where they were planning on visiting Hearst Castle in San Simeon. They stopped in North Hollywood for lunch around two P.M. at a Coco's restaurant that they spotted from the freeway. It was their first real vacation in over a year; they had been looking forward to it for two months, ever since Brad began to make the plans. Lisa was looking forward to it. She knew it was going to be a romantic weekend, and she was going to use the opportunity to tell her husband that she had just found out this morning that she was pregnant.

They had been married for five years and had been trying to get pregnant for the past two. After a year of no results from their attempts, they had sought the help of a fertility doctor. After a series of tests, it was concluded that: a) Brad had a low sperm count, and b) Lisa's irregular periods made conception much more difficult. So began a nearly yearlong quest to correct the problem with modern medicine. Numerous drugs and injections were undertaken, and then once a month, when Lisa ovulated, they both went into her ob-gyn for an IUI. Of course, they tried on their own every chance they had; for six months nothing happened, and then she had her last insemination two weeks ago. And with that came the news she had been hoping and praying for.

It was hard to keep the news a secret. She had taken a home pregnancy test Monday, and had gone into her doctor's on Wednesday for a more definitive test. The doctor's office had called this morning with the results. "Congratulations!" the receptionist had said. "You are definitely pregnant." When Lisa heard the news she allowed herself a small cry, and then quickly gained control of her emotions. Brad had gone into the office briefly to finish some paperwork on a case, and she decided to tell him over dinner tonight, in Cambria. She wanted to be with him when she told him, letting her emotions convey her happiness; she wanted the setting of a nice romantic dinner to relay this wonderful news.

As they made small talk at the restaurant, Lisa played out the scenario she had in mind for telling Brad, and reflected on the last few years of their married life. She had felt a sense of despair during the past year they had been trying to have a baby. There were thousands of women who had babies that didn't appreciate the life they had helped to create. She grew angry whenever she heard a news story about a baby being abandoned in a trash can. What the hell was wrong with people? There were thousands of couples that would give anything to adopt a child, and these selfish bitches dump their kids like so much trash. It was pathetic. And then there were children that grew up in disadvantaged homes. She knew that she and Brad would be able to provide for their child above and beyond providing food and shelter. As lawyers, they both had a combined yearly salary of just under three hundred thousand dollars; their child would never have to worry about being hungry. She knew that any child she and Brad had would be well taken care of, both in love and in security.

While Lisa usually didn't like to discuss personal stuff at work, she had let it slip to her coworker, Danielle, that she and Brad had reservations for Hearst Castle this weekend. "San Simeon?" Danielle had said, smiling. "How romantic!"

One of the senior partners had been walking to his office, and he'd turned to Lisa and Danielle. "Did I hear somebody mention San Simeon? If you're going to Cambria, may I recommend Bonito's? It's right on the main drag, across the street from the post office. It has a very elegant atmosphere and great food."

"I'll have to keep that in mind," Lisa said, grinning.

"When are you leaving?" The senior partner had approached her, his features open and friendly. He had been one of the partners responsible for her recent promotion to junior partner, and his office was directly behind hers. They usually traded good-mornings in the coffee room, and lately they'd been working together on a case. His name was George Brooks.

"Tomorrow morning," she said, looking up at George. "My husband and I had been planning this off and on for a few months. We finally locked in the reservations last month."

"Sounds wonderful," George said, his features sunny, carefree. He looked immaculate in his white shirt and blue satin vest. "You driving up 101? It's a beautiful drive."

"Yes, it is," Lisa had agreed. "We're going to take a nice, leisurely drive up."

"How long does it take to get up there?" Danielle had asked.

"Four hours," Lisa had said. "Brad has a few things to do tomorrow morning, then we'll probably leave from there, around ten or so."

"Sounds like you're going to have a good weekend," George had said, nodding at her. "Have a good time." He had turned and headed to his office.

Of course, Lisa had been bursting at the seams to tell Danielle about her impending pregnancy, but she didn't want to jinx it. So she had kept it to herself and somehow found the strength to not let that little secret out.

Thanks to George Brooks's suggestion, she made reservations at Bonito's in Cambria that afternoon for the following evening. She found out the restaurant had an elegant setting, with a fireplace, soft music, and candlelight. She was going to give Brad the news there. The anticipation she was feeling was nerve-racking. She knew Brad was going to be ecstatic. But she wanted the right setting to tell him; she wanted to surprise him.

When they were finished eating lunch, Brad paid the bill and Lisa went to the ladies' room. When she came out and joined Brad outside near the entrance, she found him talking to a tall blond woman dressed in blue jeans and a cream-colored blouse; both garments looked stained with dirt. The woman looked like she had been crying recently; tearstains had tracked rough furrows in the remnants of her makeup and made her mascara run. Resting on a small concrete ledge by the woman was a travel bag, a diaper bag, and a baby seat with an infant swaddled in a blanket. The infant was awake, its eyes staring upward, making cooing sounds. Brad turned to Lisa as she stepped out. "Do you have any change?" Brad said. "I've only got large bills and—"

"Sure," Lisa said, reaching to her wallet automatically. She looked curiously at the woman. "What for?"

The woman turned toward Lisa, her features pleading. "I'm sorry to bother you, ma'am, but . . . I . . . I asked your husband if he could spare some change. I'm . . ."

Homeless, Lisa thought. Her fingers closed over her wallet. She hesitated, her eyes meeting Brad's. She normally didn't give money to homeless people. All they did was buy booze or drugs with it anyway. Besides, there were shelters and organizations designed to help those legitimately in need. If this woman was really homeless, why didn't she just go to a shelter? "Let me see what I have," Lisa said, opening her wallet.

"I really appreciate it," the woman said. She looked defeated, ragged and tired. "I've . . . I'm so sorry to have bothered you . . ." She sounded on the verge on tears.

"It's okay," Lisa said, flipping through her bills. Something about the woman's tone of voice spiked through her emotions. The baby started to cry.

"Shhh, it's okay, Mandy," the woman said to the infant, crooning to her. "Mommy will feed you in a minute."

Lisa flipped through ones, fives, a few tens, and rested on a twenty. She glanced at Brad; she knew Brad had twenties, but knew he was apprehensive about giving homeless people such large sums of money, too. However, this woman seemed different. She truly looked like she was in a desperate situation.

Lisa pulled the twenty out and handed it to the woman. "Here. I hope this can help."

At the sight of the bill, the woman's eyes widened. "Oh, thank you! This is—I don't know how to thank you. I've . . . I've never . . . I never thought this would happen to me and—" She burst into sudden tears.

Brad shuffled awkwardly, looking uncomfortable. Lisa

felt uncomfortable, too. "Everything will be okay," she said. She sounded stupid saying it. Obviously, the way the woman was crying indicated that everything was *not* okay in her world.

"I'm sorry." The tears suddenly stopped and the woman pulled a ragged Kleenex from her purse and dried her eyes with it. She struggled to hold the tears in. "I'm sorry, it's just that . . . I never thought this would happen to me. Two weeks ago I wasn't homeless and I had a job and now . . ." Her features screwed up, threatening to unleash a flood of tears again, but she fought them down. She looked at them through tear-filled eyes. "I'm sorry. You don't need to hear my sob story."

"It's okay," Brad said, embarrassed. He reached into his wallet and rifled through it. He handed her another twenty. "Here, maybe you can get a motel room for the night."

The woman looked at the offered twenty, then slowly took it. "Thank you," she whispered.

Lisa couldn't help but be affected by the woman's plight. Homeless and with a small infant, she didn't appear to be the typical homeless person she encountered from time to time when she had to drive into downtown Los Angeles or Santa Ana for court appearances. The homeless people she encountered there were dirty, ugly, smelly, and lazy. This woman reminded Lisa of herself in a way; she appeared intelligent and headstrong. The fact that she mentioned that she had once held a job told Lisa that the woman had the ability to earn a living. She wondered if drugs had caused her downfall. She glanced at the infant, who had reduced her crying back down to simple mewling. The baby seemed fine, not the kind of baby she thought would have been born to a drug-addicted mother.

"There's YWCA centers all over the place," Lisa heard herself say. "We can help you find one if you want."

"No, that's okay." The woman shook her head. She had gotten herself under control now. She shoved the two twenties into her purse. "I've already tried them, but . . . they're all filled up. I've been doing okay, really. I've only had to sleep in my car for the past two nights. I was staying with a friend, but her husband told her that she didn't want Mandy and me to stay with them anymore, and I ran out of money three days ago."

"I'm sorry," Lisa said, softly.

The woman looked at Lisa with a strong resolve. "It's okay. I . . . he's a jerk anyway. He's friends with my former boyfriend. He's the one that kicked us out of the house and fired me. He was cheating on me the whole time I was pregnant with our daughter. I didn't find out until three weeks ago. When I confronted him with it, he got angry and had me fired, then he threw us out of the house."

"How could he have you fired?" Brad asked.

"Easy," the woman said, turning to Brad. "He was my boss at my job. It was stupid of me to fall in love with the guy who hired me, but I did. I thought we had a good thing going, especially when I found out I was pregnant." She sighed. "I was so stupid! He came across as so lonely and broke and . . . I helped pay his bills. I literally ran the limit of my credit cards up to help him out, and now . . ." She shook her head. "He took me for a fool."

"What about your parents?" Lisa asked.

"My mom died ten years ago and my dad disowned me not long after," she said. "He has his own problems. The chief one being he's a closed-minded, bigoted preacher. I was married once before and left my husband for the same reason that got me kicked out of Richard's house. My father sees marriage as this strict thing. If you leave your spouse, you're committing adultery if you remarry. I started dating right away and . . ." She shrugged. "He disowned me. We haven't spoken in seven years. I called him when Mandy was born, but he refused to speak to me."

Lisa felt heartbroken over the woman's story. She joined Brad, feeling awkward and embarrassed.

The woman turned to them. She looked embarrassed. "I'm sorry I burdened you with this. Thank you for helping me out. I promise you that the money will be put to good use. I've got a little one that is more of a concern to me right now."

"Are you sure there's nothing else we can do?" Brad asked.

The woman shook her head. "I'll be fine. I'm sure I'll be able to get work soon, even though I don't have a permanent address. My friend Christie told me I could use their address for a reference, and I'm sure she'll pick up whatever mail I get there. If I can do that, I'll be able to get a job—even a temp job—and move into a motel or something until I can get back on my feet."

Lisa offered the woman a smile. "I'm glad we could help. Good luck to you."

The woman smiled for the first time; it was a beautiful smile. "Thank you."

"Your baby's name is Mandy?" Lisa asked.

"Yes." The woman nodded. "Amanda Jane."

"That's a pretty name."

"Thank you."

"What's your name?"

"Alicia."

Lisa smiled. "I'm Lisa, and this is my husband, Brad."

Brad smiled and offered his hand. Alicia shook it. "Thank you," she said. "Both of you."

"Take care, okay?" Lisa said, taking Brad's hand.

"I will."

"Will you be able to get a place tonight?" Brad asked, glancing at the baby in the car seat. "There's a motel across the street, you know."

Alicia nodded. "I think so. For the past two nights, Mandy and I have been sleeping in my car. It's that blue Datsun over there." She pointed and Lisa saw it, parked ten feet from them, the back of it filled with suitcases and clothes. "I've been parking on Douglas Street off Ventura Boulevard. Its nice and quiet there. Thank God it's summer."

"Yeah, really," Lisa said. She smiled at Alicia again. "Well, good luck to you, and take care of your baby."

"I will," Alicia said. "Thank you."

Brad and Lisa turned and headed back toward their car.

They were silent on the drive back to the freeway. Once they had merged back into traffic, Lisa broke the silence. "That was so sad."

"I know."

"Part of me wishes that we had done something more to help her," Lisa said. "I felt so sorry for her."

"Me too. I almost didn't want to at first, but . . . well . . ."

"She really needed help. You could tell."

"Yes." Brad kept his eyes on the road ahead of him, hands on the steering wheel.

Lisa thought about her own baby that was now growing inside her. The minute she had seen Alicia and her baby, she immediately thought of helping and protecting the baby more than the mother. But then she saw that Alicia was truly a woman who was down-and-out, a woman who, through circumstances beyond her control, had been dumped on the streets with no support and a baby to take care of. She hoped the money they gave Alicia today would help. "I hope they'll be okay," she said.

"Me too," Brad said.

They headed north, and after five minutes the plight of Alicia and her baby daughter were forgotten.

Two

They noticed the van shortly after they pulled out of the rest stop.

They had pulled over at the rest stop just inside the Ventura County limits for bathroom breaks and a quick rest before heading on the road again. The hour-and-a-half drive from North Hollywood where they had met up with Alicia and her infant daughter had been spent mostly in silence.

The radio station they were listening to, alternative rock station KROQ, was now fizzling in static, so five minutes into arriving at the rest stop Lisa had put in a Blondie CD. Brad had thought about Alicia for about thirty minutes after leaving her and the baby, and for the last forty minutes or so had been thinking about the long weekend ahead of them. The bathroom breaks were a long time coming, and upon meeting outside the lavatories, they meandered over to a picnic area with tables and benches. They shot a couple of photos of each other for posterity, including one photograph of Lisa posing by a sign warning of the dangers of rattlesnakes, which were plentiful in the area. Then they got back into the Lexus and continued on toward their destination.

Brad switched lanes to pass a slow-moving car towing

a trailer in the slow lane. Lisa was consulting the map. "Looks like we've got another two hours."

"Piece of cake," Brad said, as they climbed the hill.

"It's so nice up here. I wonder if—"

"What the hell is this sonofabitch doing?"

Lisa looked over her shoulder. The entire rear window of their Lexus was filled with the metallic grille of a red van. Brad's grip on the steering wheel tightened. "What the fuck is wrong with people? I'm already doing seventy and this guy has the whole fucking road to pass me!"

"Let him pass us if he wants to get around."

"That's exactly what I'm going to do. I'm not speeding up for him."

They reached the crest of the hill, and Brad took his foot off the accelerator as they wound down Interstate 5. They picked up speed, creeping to eighty. Some cars continued whizzing past at ninety or faster. Brad checked his rearview mirror, saw that it was clear, and moved back into the slow lane, his foot tapping the brake to slow down a little. The van stayed on his tail, moving to the slow lane right on his back bumper.

"You motherfucker." Brad's foot was riding the brake. His heart was pounding rapidly as his eyes darted from the rearview mirror to the road ahead of him. Their speed dropped gradually to seventy, then sixty. The van receded slightly, then sped up and tailgated them again. It was hard to see the driver through the tinted glass of his windshield, but Brad already had a mental image of him: Judging by the vehicle, he was probably another repressed, thirtysomething hothead with an ax to grind because Brad wasn't going fast enough to suit his needs. *He can fuck off as far as I'm concerned.* Brad thought.

"What is this guy's problem?" Lisa wondered, craning her neck to look out the rear window.

"I don't know. You have the cell phone with us?"

"Yeah. Think we should call the police?"

"I don't know. Let's see what he does first."

"Maybe we should pull over."

"Why? So he can pull up behind us and shoot us or something?"

Lisa opened her mouth, then closed it. She looked scared. Brad was scared himself. His mind retraced the last few minutes frantically, trying to reconnect with something that might explain why this guy was dogging their every step. Had he cut anybody off? No. When he'd passed the slow-moving car a few miles back, there hadn't been anybody in the lane next to him at all, otherwise he wouldn't have made the move. But then the guy had almost seemed to materialize out of nowhere right after he made the lane change. He must have been flying along at a hundred miles per hour, which would explain why Brad wouldn't have seen him when he checked his rear- and sideview mirrors. The guy had been coming up so fast that he hadn't been in the mirrors when Brad checked, then he was there the minute Brad made the lane change. Which means now the fuckhead behind the wheel was pissed off.

"Christ," Brad muttered, his knuckles white as his hands gripped the steering wheel. "Just what I need is some enraged asshole on my tail because he feels slighted over some stupid traffic dispute."

"He's pulling back," Lisa said.

Brad glanced in his rearview mirror. Sure enough, the van had pulled back to a more respectable distance. The afternoon sun glinted in the sky, reflecting off the van's windshield. Brad released a long sigh and felt better. "As long as he stays back there," he said.

They were silent for a moment as they reached the bottom of the hill and continued on, Interstate 5 stretching out before them like a long, black snake. It was a three-lane highway, bisected by a median strip of grass that separated the north and southbound lanes. Traffic was moderate. Brad kept the Lexus at a safe and legal sixty-five and stayed in his lane. No sense trying to play speed racer now. As long as they reached the hotel in one piece, that was all that mattered.

Lisa turned the Blondie CD back on. Debbie Harry began singing about being an X Offender.

They were relaxed enough now to make small talk. Lisa started talking about a transgression that had occurred at the office. Brad listened, wondering silently how his wife put up with those incompetent assholes at the law office. "So all they want to do is complain about all the work they have—like nobody else does?—and then they sit around and file their nails and gossip all day, and then complain about all the work they have and how they can never get anything done. George Brooks doesn't even notice what's going on. He spends all day in his office. And meanwhile, I'm trying to hold the department together, and Amy won't do anything to pare the deadweight down, and—"

Brad was listening, but he was monitoring the traffic behind him. The van was still behind them at a good distance. They were drawing close to another slow-moving vehicle—an old Ford piloted by a little old lady with blue hair and thick spectacles, barely tall enough to peer over the dashboard. Brad signaled for a lane change, checked his mirrors, and swung into the next lane to pass the Ford. The van changed lanes also, still a safe distance behind them.

He's changing lanes because he sees the Ford is crawling at a snail's pace. Brad thought. He tried to reassure himself with this thought, but a small part of him suggested that wasn't so. That part suggested that the faceless driver of the van still had a burr up his ass and was trying to be discreet about following them.

When Brad saw that he was at a comfortable distance past the Ford, he signaled for another lane change and merged back into the slow lane. The van did likewise, still a respectable distance behind him.

"So I just don't know what to do anymore," Lisa was saying, looking out at the road ahead of them. "Sometimes I wonder if I should just go directly to Debbie and—"

He listened. And he nodded and responded at the appropriate times. And he watched the road ahead of him and monitored the van behind them. It stayed a good distance back, never retreating nor accelerating to catch up.

And every time Brad changed lanes to pass a slower vehicle, the van did likewise. After three times Brad began to get an eerie feeling that the driver of the van hadn't forgotten the minor transgression fifteen minutes back. It was a feeling that gnawed at him, creating a pit of unease in his belly.

Lisa appeared not to notice what was going on. *And I won't say anything*, Brad thought. *It'll just freak her out. Besides, it's probably just my imagination. I mean, why would—*

The van suddenly sped up, closing the gap between them. Brad expected it to tailgate him again, but it didn't. It crept up to one car length away and then eased up, widening the gap between them. Lisa, who had been talking about work, noticed the change of expression on Brad's face as the van accelerated, and glanced in her sideview mirror. "What the hell is he doing now?"

"I don't know. But he's been following us the whole way."

"Are you *serious?*" Lisa watched the van out of her sideview mirror.

"Yeah. Every time we change lanes, he does the same thing. I almost get the feeling he's . . . well . . . stalking us."

"Why don't we pull over?" Lisa said, turning to Brad now with a scared expression. "Let's just get off at the next exit, pull into a gas station or something, and call the police."

"What for? The guy hasn't actually done anything."

Lisa looked like she was at a loss for words. "Well, at least we could see if he pulls off the road, too. It's better than nothing."

Brad nodded, eyes on the road, glancing back at the van behind them. For the past twenty minutes or so, the van had kept a safe distance behind them, never out of their sight even when other cars were in front of it. That was what worried him.

"I don't know. It's probably nothing. I mean, it's not like I—"

"There's a cop up ahead."

Brad looked. Parked in the grassy median between the north and south lanes was a California Highway Patrol car, as if the officer was laying a speed trap. Brad self-consciously checked his speed—he was well within the speed limit—and then they were zooming past the police car. His eyes darted to the rearview mirror just in time to see the patrol car pull into the highway behind them. *It's just a coincidence,* Brad thought. *Surely he can't be lying in wait for us—*

Flashing blue and red lights danced along the dome on top of the patrol car as it tailed them, the twin beams of its headlights flashing. The officer activated the siren briefly. Brad felt a stab of fear in the pit of his belly. *Why is he pulling me over? I'm not speeding. I'm—*

"I don't believe this," Lisa said, glancing back behind her shoulder.

"I don't either," Brad said, as he signaled and merged to the right-hand shoulder and stopped.

He looked in the rearview mirror and saw that the patrol car had moved in behind him and was now parked, its lights still flashing. But that wasn't what made the pit of ice in his belly stab into him harder.

It was the van that pulled up behind the patrol car and parked behind it that sent his nerves twitching.

"Oh my God," Lisa said, her voice hollow. She looked at Brad, and her blue eyes were wide and scared-looking. "What the hell is going on?"

"I don't know," Brad said, keeping his hands on the steering wheel. He watched in the rearview mirror as the officer approached the passenger side of the car. Lisa rolled down the window.

The patrol officer was thin, in his mid-thirties, with thin, angular features, brown hair, and a mustache. Dark sunglasses hid his eyes. He leaned down and looked at Brad. "Can I see your license and registration, please?"

"Yeah, sure." Brad fumbled for his wallet, got the identification out, and handed it over. The officer glanced at them, then looked back at him. "Got a call that you were doing some reckless driving back there. Speeding up real fast, then braking suddenly, swerving all over the road, trying to cause accidents."

Lisa looked over at Brad, confused, then back at the officer. "You must be mistaken, officer. We weren't doing anything like that."

"I didn't say you, ma'am. I meant him." He motioned to Brad, his voice taking on a tone of condescending.

"I haven't been doing anything like that," Brad said. He could feel his hands shaking. His voice, when he spoke, was thick and guttural. He had never felt so nervous in his life.

"I don't really care what you say," the officer said. "The person that called it in saw it and requested a citizen's arrest."

Lisa's features went pale. Brad couldn't believe what was happening. "There's some mistake," he heard himself saying. "I wasn't driving the way you said I was. I was going the speed limit, I was—"

"Save it," the cop said. "The person that reported it saw it and wants to make a citizen's arrest. I'm going to run your ID, then I'm going to go back to the person that made the complaint to confirm that you're the person he saw committing the violation. When he called it in he sped up to get your license plate number, so I'm sure identification won't be a problem. When that's done, I'll place you in custody—"

Place me in custody? Brad's heartbeat slammed harder.

". . . then, depending on what time it is, we'll see if we can get you before the judge to arrange bail and then . . ." The cop looked at his wristwatch and shook his head. "Nope. It's a little after four o'clock. Courthouse is already closed. Anyway, it looks like you'll be in custody till Monday morning, when the courthouse opens again and bail can be arranged."

"*This is bullshit!*" Lisa's voice took on a high-pitched shrill. "We weren't *doing anything!* That guy—"

"Shut up," the cop said casually. "I don't really care one way or the other. It's your word against his, and he witnessed it. Wait here while I call this in and have a talk with him." Without another word, the officer walked back to his car.

Brad watched him go, feeling light-headed and dazed. He had never been in trouble with the law before, had never been guilty of anything except a parking ticket. For a moment he forgot his knowledge of California criminal law from law school. He was in private practice in family law, and hadn't been keeping up on criminal law much since getting his law degree. Surely this had to be some kind of mistake. His heart hammered in his chest as he watched the cop go back to his squad car and slide behind the wheel.

Lisa turned to Brad as he watched the cop type his information on the computer in his car. "This is fucking *bullshit!* That asshole is just trying to fuck with us. *We* should be the one calling the cops on *his* ass to make a citizen's arrest!" Lisa had turned from a confused, scared woman to a woman with seething, righteous anger. When Lisa got angry, she got explosive and cursed like a sailor. And when she got explosive, you didn't want to be around her.

"I didn't do anything," Brad said, still in a daze. "I—I—" He didn't know what to say.

"No *shit,* we didn't do anything." Lisa fumed. "And when that asshole cop comes back, I'm going to demand a citizen's arrest on *that* asshole in the van."

Hearing the venom in Lisa's voice injected some in Brad's own system, although now that he was thinking about it he realized that Lisa wouldn't be able to do that. It was all coming to him now: To assist in a citizen's arrest, the officer had to confirm that the violation in question was a felony punishable by at least a year in jail. If the guy was claiming speeding and reckless driving with intent to cause bodily injury, that would be enough for the officer to place him in custody. Lisa couldn't do a damn thing except represent him in court Monday. His stomach still churned, but he felt a sudden burst of adrenaline. "Let's see what that guy tells him," he said, watching the cop in his rearview mirror and the van parked behind it, its windshield a solid black screen.

"You're *not* going to jail," Lisa said, watching the scene from her side mirror. "I'm going to tell him I want to place a citizen's arrest myself. The guy in the van was stalking us and tailgating us. If that asshole wants to play at this game, that's just fine with me."

Brad's mind was racing. *Worst-case scenario, maybe Lisa could contact a local judge over the weekend, get him to look at the case. Maybe we can get this dismissed by tonight. Yeah, that's the ticket—*

"He's going to talk to the guy in the van now," Lisa said, watching from the sideview mirror. Brad watched from the rearview mirror. The cop stood at the passenger side of the van as he talked to the guy, who was still hard to make out due to the dark windshield. They were silent as they watched the conversation take place. *What is he telling him?* Brad wondered. *What are they discussing?* The few minutes that the cop spent talking to the faceless driver in the van felt like five hours.

Finally, the cop headed back to their car. Brad felt his gut tighten as the cop drew abreast of the Lexus, placing the driver's license in his breast pocket. His right hand went down to the grip of his firearm. "Would you please step out of the car, ma'am?"

Lisa cast a fearful, wide-eyed glance back at Brad. The cop leaned forward, looking directly at Brad. "And would you please place your hands on the steering wheel so I can see them, Mr. Miller?"

I can't believe this is happening, Brad thought as he put his hands on the steering wheel. His heart was racing madly. *I can't believe this fucking asshole is* doing *this!*

Lisa stepped out of the Lexus. "I would like to make a citizen's arrest of my own, officer—"

"Shut up." The officer leaned toward the open passenger side of the car. Speaking directly to Brad, he said: "I want you to open the driver's-side door with your left hand, keeping your right hand on the steering wheel where I can see it."

"Did you hear what I just said?" Lisa's tone of voice was taking on that righteous pissed-off anger that it tended to get when she was ignored. "I *said—*"

"I'm telling you to shut up now, or I'll be taking two people to the Ventura County Jail today." The cop glared at her, then turned back to Brad, the subject of Lisa's interruption dismissed as he tended to the arrest at hand. "Now I want you to step out of the car carefully with your hands over your head where I can see them."

Brad did what the officer told him, the adrenaline pounding in his veins. Lisa stood at the side of the road in shock. When he got out of the car, he saw the officer standing on the other side of the vehicle, his mirror shades black and menacing. Lisa looked helpless and angry. "Put your hands on your head and walk around the front of the vehicle and come toward me."

Brad put his hands on his head and walked around the front of the Lexus on wobbly legs. When his feet reached the side of the road, the officer stepped forward. "Turn around."

Brad turned around and the officer grabbed his wrists, jerking them behind his back. He felt the cold snap of steel around his wrists as he was handcuffed. "Now I want you to sit down while I go and get the person that issued the compliant. Stay here." He helped Brad to a sitting position on the ground, then walked back toward the van.

Lisa knelt down beside him. "Everything will be okay. When we get to the police station, I'll call contact the District Attorney of Ventura County. We'll get this taken care of."

Brad felt a lump in his throat; he felt like crying, but not out of fear. He felt a sudden outpouring of blinding, white-hot rage. "Call Billy, too." William Grecko was a friend of Brad's family and a criminal defense lawyer in Orange County. He was a brilliant, if annoying, criminal defense attorney. He was brilliant because he had a knack for getting some of the most repugnant people off with little more than a slap on the wrist. He was annoying because he was an alcoholic, one who was a pain in the ass to be around when he drank.

"I want to kill that fucking sonofabitch," Lisa said, her voice trembling. Tears appeared at the corner of her eyes, but her voice carried a tone of anger and loss of their weekend together being suddenly destroyed.

"Just be calm," Brad said. "We don't need you in jail this weekend, too. I need you to be calm to get us out of this, okay?"

"I love you," Lisa said. She kissed him quickly, and then the sound of approaching footsteps caused them both to look up as twin shadows fell across them.

The man standing next to the officer was of medium height, but overweight with a huge belly. He had sandy hair that was balding at the top and a scruffy, sandy beard. He was wearing a T-shirt with the word *Hawaii* on it in a tropical design, and a pair of faded blue jeans and white tennis shoes. He was wearing sunglasses. He grinned wide.

The officer looked at the driver of the van, then nodded down at Brad. "Okay, you can go ahead."

The man took a step forward, grinning at Brad. "I'm placing you under citizen's arrest for reckless driving, asshole. That'll teach you to fucking pull in front of people on the highway."

Lisa shot to her feet. "This man is *lying*, Officer. He's been harassing us ever since we pulled out of the last rest stop outside of Ventura. He's been tailgating us and—"

"I don't want to hear it," the cop said. He reached

down and pulled Brad to his feet, his hard callused fingers digging into the flesh of Brad's upper right arm. "And I ain't letting you make a cross-complaint, because this gentleman witnessed you make several felony driving violations. Your only recourse is in court when your husband goes up for trial. If the case is dismissed or he's found not guilty, then you can seek civil recourse against Mr. Smith, here."

Brad glared at the man the officer referred to as Mr. Smith, who smiled back at him. That smile seemed to say *I got you, you stupid fuck. Teach you to fuck with me.*

"I hope you have deep pockets, Mr. Smith," Lisa said, nearly spitting the words out. "You've picked the wrong people to fuck with; my husband and I are both lawyers, and when this is over we are going to sue you so fucking bad you won't be able to find a shopping cart to live in!"

Mr. Smith smiled at her. "My apologies for being a concerned motorist, ma'am." He turned to the officer. "Do I need to do anything else, Officer?"

"You need to follow me to the station to fill out some paperwork," the officer said. He began to lead Brad toward the patrol car. To Lisa: "Lawyers, huh? Looks like you'll be needing one yourselves, ma'am."

"I plan on having a word with your captain, too," Lisa said.

"Whatever." The cop opened the back passenger-side door of his cruiser and Brad slid inside. "Watch your head," the officer said.

Brad looked up at Lisa. "Call Billy, honey."

"I'll follow you to the police station," Lisa said. The officer slammed the door.

"Okay," the officer said, turning to Lisa. His face was expressionless, his features stony. "Let's get this show on the road."

Three

The Days Inn off the Interstate had vacancies. Lisa Miller was sitting on the lumpy queen-sized mattress in her room, her suitcase opened, phone book out. The curtains were drawn, the rays of the setting sun bleeding through and casting shades of orange across the table and part of the bed. Lisa and Brad had been looking forward to this vacation for the past six months; now it was shot to hell thanks to that Mr. Smith asshole.

Thinking about the situation again made Lisa want to smash something, preferably Mr. Smith's smug, self-righteous face. *The nerve of that man!*

She had seethed the whole time she was at the sheriff's substation. First she had to watch Brad be led back to the jail. Then she had to watch that prick of a cop come out with some paperwork and talk to that Mr. Smith numbfuck who had been standing on the opposite side of the lobby, pausing every now and then to grin at her. It was hard to ignore the man; she had to fight the urge to walk across the lobby and rip his smug face off his skull. *Just you wait,* she had thought as she watched the officer hand the paperwork to Mr. Smith and instructed him on how to fill it out. *When this is over, I'm not even going to wait for Brad to come to trial. I'm going to slap you with the biggest lawsuit you've ever seen. You won't know what hit you. You'll wish you had driven that fucking van of yours off a cliff.*

When the officer was finished with Mr. Smith, he had come to her. He wasn't wearing those stupid cop sunglasses anymore. His eyes were like cold flint. They were cop's eyes—cold, unemotional, uncaring. "I need to explain to you your legal rights and the ramifications of a citizen's arrest," he began. "The first thing I suggest is find yourself a motel room in the area. Your husband is going to be in a cell until Monday, when we can drive him to the Ventura County courthouse and have him arraigned. The bail will probably be low, but you can never tell what mood the judge will be in. I suggest getting a lawyer this weekend."

"I've already got one," Lisa huffed, arms crossed in front of her chest, looking boldly at the officer.

"You mentioned back at the scene that you and your husband are lawyers; what kind?"

"Family law."

"Then I'll explain to you what you may not have learned in law school. The reason I can't allow you to make a citizen's arrest on Mr. Smith is because one, your claim, if it's true, is a misdemeanor offense. Mr. Smith claims to have witnessed felonies. The minimum statute which a private citizen can file a complaint for a citizen's arrest is a felony punishable by up to one year in prison. That's just the minimum."

"And driving within the legal limits of the law is a felony," Lisa said with a hint of sarcasm. "I see. Thank you for clarifying that for me."

The officer ignored the remark and continued. "When I talked to Mr. Smith back at the scene, I explained all the legal ramifications to him. I don't know what happened back there because I didn't see it. Mr. Smith claims to have witnessed your husband driving in a reckless manner in a way that would have put other motorists in grave danger. His descriptions to the 911 operator amounted to that of at least two felonies, and that's when I was dispatched. Otherwise I wouldn't have made the arrest. I *did* explain to Mr. Smith the consequences he could face should the case be thrown out, or if your husband is found not guilty; that he could face a civil lawsuit. He was firm that he understood and that he wanted to pursue the complaint, so by law I was obligated to place your husband in custody."

"Should this go to trial, is he called as a witness?" Lisa asked, motioning across the room toward Mr. Smith.

"Depends on what the DA says. The paperwork Mr. Smith is filling out will require him to explain precisely what he saw, including information on where he lives and other contact information. In most cases, that is all anyone needs to do in making a citizen's arrest. In some cases, nothing further is needed of the witness. That isn't always the case."

"So all this crap that asshole says we did . . . speeding, and swerving dangerously in traffic and braking suddenly . . . that's a felony?"

"Reckless driving with the intent to cause grave bodily injury or property damage is a felony in the state of California," the cop said. "Like I said, the minimum for which a citizen—and that's *anybody*—can file a citizen's arrest is that the crime they witness has to be a felony punishable by up to one year in jail. That's why you don't hear about people making citizen's arrests on jaywalkers."

"What about witnesses?" Lisa asked. "Or physical evidence? Will the DA try to gather some?"

"Who knows?" The officer shrugged. "My guess is they won't. A case like this, it's you and your husband's word against Mr. Smith's. Personally, I think the DA will take one look at this case Monday morning and decline to file charges. I told Mr. Smith that I didn't think he had a very good chance in something like this, especially out on an open highway. Of course, if other people call in to say they saw it happening, then there might be a stronger case. But unless that happens, there isn't much to go on." The cop cocked his head and his features became softer. "If you don't mind me asking, did you notice this guy before this happened?"

Lisa had almost exploded with anger, but she held it in. *We're only told you eight million fucking times that this asshole was dogging us all the way from the last rest stop!* Instead she had said, "We noticed him just after we pulled out of a rest stop twenty miles or so back. There wasn't much traffic, and Brad made a lane change to pass a slow-moving vehicle. There was nobody, and I mean *nobody* in that lane, and then all of a sudden that guy," she motioned to Mr. Smith, "was right there on our ass, tailgating us like crazy."

The cop had actually listened. He had nodded as Lisa spun the story, his eyes darting over to Mr. Smith, then settling back on Lisa. Lisa had felt a little better that somebody was finally listening to her now, but she was still angry over the way she and Brad had been treated, especially at the hands of this cop. When she was finished, the cop nodded. "I'm sorry for what happened," he had said. "I'll be perfectly honest in saying that I really can't do anything about the situation. But I would like to say off the record that I think the judge or the DA is going to take one look at the complaint against your husband and throw it out. I know your vacation is probably all shot to hell now—"

"It is."

The cop had nodded, his features apologetic. "I explained to Mr. Smith the full consequences that could happen should the outcome be found in your favor. I explained that he would be fully opening himself up to a civil suit, and despite that, he wanted to proceed. Between you and me, I think the guy has a screw loose."

"I think he did this because he was zooming along at a

hundred miles an hour," Lisa had said in a hushed whisper. She had been facing the officer, but her eyes were fixed on Mr. Smith's back as he bent over the paperwork at the counter. "That's why Brad didn't see him in the lane, and it also explains why he was suddenly there right on us. He probably got pissed off because he had to slow down to avoid hitting us, and I'm sure it didn't make matters any better when Brad slowed down as we descended the hill. Brad got back into the slow lane, but he followed us, right on our tail."

The officer had nodded, looking across at Mr. Smith. "I think that might be a safe assessment."

There had been nothing left for her to do at the substation. They wouldn't even let her see Brad, but the officer did promise to relay a message to him. She would be checking in at the Days Inn and would be placing a call to his parents in Orange County, as well as his friend Billy. She would also try contacting the DA, or a local judge, to see what she could do in speeding the arraignment process up. If she couldn't get the wheels grinding tonight, she would cancel their hotel reservations in Cambria and remain in town until Monday morning. In fact, she would be waiting at the substation bright and early Monday morning when the paddy wagon showed up to transport him to the Ventura County Courthouse. She would be in court for the arraignment, hopefully with their lawyer. And the minute he was out they were going to have a little talk, the three of them, about filing a lawsuit against Mr. Smith.

She had left the substation and driven to the Days Inn five blocks east. There was a Denny's on the corner, which she supposed was where dinner would be eaten tonight. She had checked in and called his parents. Luckily, they had been home. Brad's father, Frank, was an executive at Farrar & Sons, an investment firm, and the cushiony salary and thirty years with the company had left him and Joan, Brad's mother, pretty well off. To devote more time to her art, where she excelled in watercolor, Joan had been able to take early retirement as a junior high school teacher after slugging it out for twenty years. Due to his position at Farrar and his years with the company, Frank had plenty of flex and vacation time. They had been very upset and alarmed by what happened. "Do you want us to come up?" Joan asked.

"Yeah," Lisa had said, sitting on the bed, twirling the telephone cord between her fingers. She would feel better if Brad's parents were here. She wouldn't feel so alone.

Joan asked if she would be okay by herself tonight, and Lisa said she thought she would. "We'll be up in the morning, then," Joan had said. "Between ten and eleven."

Lisa glanced at the clock on the nightstand. It was now closing in on six P.M. Her stomach rumbled. She hadn't eaten a thing since this morning and she was hungry. She stood up and began rummaging in her purse. The cop that had pulled them over—he had finally introduced himself as Officer Chris Lansing—said that Brad would be fine for the weekend. He was in his own cell, and he would be served three meals a day. Lisa's heart went out to Brad, who was a good man. He surely didn't deserve to have this happen to him, but at least he had his own cell and the jail itself was empty. "If we get anybody else for the weekend, they'll have their own cell. Don't worry, Mrs. Miller, he'll be fine."

She was reflecting on what a gentleman Officer Lansing had become the more he learned about what really happened, when her thoughts were interrupted by a knock on the door.

She whirled to the door, her heart leaping slightly in her chest. That couldn't be Joan and Frank, not this early.

Even if they had changed their minds about coming up tonight, it would still take them three hours or more to get up here from Huntington Beach. She went to the door and peered through the peephole. Nothing.

She opened the door and peeked out, and that's when the door slammed back violently and hit her above the left eye.

She fell back and hit the wall as the door slammed open. Her mind was spinning, trying to track what was happening, and then he was looming over her, his beard scruffy in his grin. "Thought you were rid of me, huh, bitch?" Mr. Smith said. Then he swung one hard, callused fist down onto her head and Lisa saw stars, then blackness.

Four

The next thing she was aware of was her head hurting.

Lisa came awake gradually, as if swimming up from the bottom of a pool. The darkness turned to gray, then a murky color punctuated by lights and muffled sounds. The lights grew brighter, but everything was blurry. A shadow loomed over her and hung there; she was frightened, thinking the shadow was going to descend and take her down into darkness again.

Then her blurred vision cleared and she blinked. She was lying on her back in the motel room's queen-sized bed. Her arms were tied behind her back, and the strain on her shoulders was what brought the pain to the surface. She shifted on the bed and then she saw him, sitting on a chair by the end table. He smiled and rose to his feet. Instinct took over and she kicked out with her feet, but she didn't get anywhere: he had tied her ankles together, too.

Mr. Smith laughed. "Now now, Mrs. Miller. No need to get antsy."

"Let me out now!" Lisa screamed. The sound of her scream was loud, even to her ears. She let loose another loud, piercing scream and tried to lunge off the bed at Mr. Smith.

Mr. Smith's cocky grinned disappeared. He swarmed over the bed, his body pinning her down as she screamed and flayed on the bed. *"You cocksucking motherfucker, I'm gonna kill you—"*

"Now now, let's not have any of that." He clamped one large, meaty hand over her mouth to shut her up. Lisa clamped her teeth over the fleshy part of his thumb and bit down hard. Mr. Smith yelled and jerked back, holding his thumb. Lisa squirmed violently and tried to scream again, but managed only a slight croak. "You bitch!" He held up his bleeding hand to Lisa, his features seeming to say *I-can't-believe-you-bit-me!*

Lisa took a deep breath and yelled at the top of her lungs. Her back arched as she lifted her upper body off the mattress. Mr. Smith fumbled in a small bag she saw on the nightstand, and he extracted a handkerchief. He picked up a small bottle resting by the bag, poured something in the handkerchief, set the bottle down, and advanced toward the bed. Lisa's eyes widened in shock, and she struggled. Mr. Smith approached her and Lisa opened her mouth to scream again, but the handkerchief was stuffed into her mouth, the wet part clamped down over her nostrils, and then she was breathing in a heavy, acidic stench and she saw stars. The room was spinning, and she barely had time to recognize the looming figure of Mr. Smith over her as her mind reeled from the scent of whatever it was he had given her, and then her last thought was *Oh my God, the baby—*

When she woke up again, she had a splitting headache. She tasted something in her mouth and ran her tongue along it. It was a cloth rag, wedged into her mouth and tied around the back of her head. She was gagged.

The sun had dropped outside and it was darker in the room now. She lay on the bed, her heart pounding, letting her eyes grow accustomed to the dark. She heard him before she saw him, from the chair at the writing desk opposite the bed. "You're awake," he said. "You don't have to lie there and pretend to still be out. I know you're awake."

She almost let out a sob of frustration and fear. She felt tears at the back of her throat; her face felt hot and flush. She was no longer hungry, but there was an empty feeling in her belly anyway—the empty feeling of fear.

The dark shape sitting at the chair rose to its feet and walked over to the side of the bed. Lisa could barely make out Mr. Smith as he stood over her. "I had to gag you," he said, "because you were being unreasonable. There's no need to be unreasonable. It's a good thing for you nobody heard you. If somebody had heard you and come to investigate, you wouldn't have woken up, little lady. No sirree."

Lisa began to cry.

Mr. Smith leaned over her and she could make his features out more clearly through tear-blurred eyes. He was grinning. "Everything's going to be fine," he said. "You got a nice little bump on your noggin, but it's barely noticeable, which is good. We're just going to wait until it gets dark, then we're going to hit the road. That's why I had to tie you up and gag you. Once it's dark and the coast is clear, I'll move you to my van and we'll head off."

Head off to where? Her mind screamed. She tried to control her sobs, but couldn't. The tears flowed freely and her breath was harsh. *Why are you doing this?*

As if he had heard her silent question, he smiled. "I know you're probably wondering why I'm doing this. If it'll make you feel better, I've never done this kind of thing before—kidnapping people, that is. I'm not some psycho or some serial killer. I'm not going to hurt you."

So why are you doing this?

Mr. Smith leaned over her. "You guys presented yourself to me so perfectly. The citizen's arrest? That was just my way of getting you separated from your husband. By the time he gets out of jail Monday morning, you and I will be over the hills and far away."

Lisa felt a sudden weight of fear in her belly. *Oh my God, he's going to kill me!*

Mr. Smith leaned closer to her. She could smell his breath; it smelled of onions. "So your hubby gets to spend the weekend in jail—and you?" He chuckled and straightened up, rising to his full height. "You get to spend the weekend in my company. We're going to have a good time together." He walked to the window and parted the drapes, peering out at the darkness.

Lisa's heart raced. What was he going to do with her? She felt a sinking sense of dread. It wasn't just her anymore—there was the baby to think about now. She was almost paralyzed with fear at the thought of the fetus in her womb being hurt, but somehow she barreled past that. Her hands moved to and fro behind her back, testing the bonds. He had trussed her up pretty tight. It would take a miracle to untie herself, and unlike the heroes and heroines of novels, she didn't think she'd be able to free herself.

Mr. Smith turned back to her. "You might be wondering what I'm going to do to you. Like I said, Mrs. Miller, I've never done this before. I ain't no serial killer, and I ain't no rapist, either. It's just that, well . . ." He shrugged. "Maybe I'll tell you later if you behave. How's that sound?"

He grinned wide again, his teeth gleaming in the darkness. "We'll leave when it gets dark. We have a good three-hour drive ahead of us."

Lisa's breathing became quick and labored as Mr. Smith stepped closer to her and leaned over her prone, trussed-up form on the bed.

Five

When Joan and Frank Miller pulled into the parking lot of the Days Inn the next morning at ten-thirty, they saw the kids' Lexus parked in front of room 6. There were four other cars in the parking lot: a black Camaro, two SUVs, and an Accura Legend. Frank pulled in next to the Lexus and turned it off. "Here we are," he said.

"I wonder if she was able to talk to Brad this morning," Joan said, grabbing her purse and sliding out of the passenger seat.

"If she hasn't yet, maybe the three of us will be able to this morning," Frank said, shutting the driver's-side door and stretching his back. The three-hour drive had begun very early for them. They had been out of the house by seven o'clock.

Joan crossed over to room 6 and rapped on the door. They stood there for a moment, waiting for Lisa to answer, and then Joan knocked again. "Maybe she's in the shower," Frank suggested.

"Maybe." Joan rapped harder on the door and they

waited, spending the next three minutes knocking every twenty seconds or so, trading puzzled looks. Joan put her ear to the door and frowned. "I don't hear anything."

"She couldn't have gone anywhere," Frank said, motioning to the Lexus. "Her car is still here."

"Do you think she might have walked to the police station?" Joan shaded her eyes with the flat of her hand as she gazed down Rim Road. "The police station is only five blocks that way."

Frank shrugged. "It's possible. She might be at the Denny's having breakfast, too. Why don't we take a little walk and find out?"

Their little walk took them to the Denny's, then to the Ventura County Sheriff substation. Once at the substation, they inquired at the front desk about their son. The desk clerk, a young woman with black hair carefully pinned back, consulted a computer. "He's in the jail's holding and receiving area," she said.

"Has he had any visitors this morning?" Joan asked. It had been warm this morning in Orange County, and she had dressed in a pair of white slacks and a blue blouse. It was a little chilly in Ventura, and she pulled a white sweater over her shoulders.

The clerk shook her head. "No, he hasn't. Are you family?"

"We're his parents," Frank said. "Can we see him?"

"Let me check." The clerk picked up the extension on her desk, punched a number, and got somebody else on the line. "Mr. Miller in 4D? His parents are here. Can he have visitors?" She paused. "Okay, thanks." She hung up and turned to Frank and Joan. "The jail warden will be out in a minute."

Five minutes later, a door opened and a young officer looked out. "Mr. and Mrs. Miller?"

As they followed the officer down the hall to the rear

of the building where the jail was, Frank asked again if Brad had received any visitors this morning. "None," the officer said.

"Are you sure?" Joan asked. "We were thinking our daughter-in-law might be here already."

"You're the first to see Mr. Miller this morning," the officer said. He inserted a key into a large metal door and opened it, ushering them inside. "Last cell on the left. Press the buzzer outside the door when you're finished."

"Thanks." Frank took Joan's arm and led her through the door and down the hall.

Brad was waiting for them at the front of the cell, his hands gripping the metal bars. His hair looked ruffled and there were dark circles under his eyes. He smiled when he saw them. "God, am I glad to see you guys!"

Joan went to her son and reached through the bars, grasping his hands and pulling him closer. She kissed his cheek. "We're glad to see you too, son."

"You okay, Brad?" Frank asked, taking Brad's hand and squeezing it affectionately.

"I'm tired. I didn't get any sleep in here last night."

Joan was nervous, not just for the situation at hand, but because they hadn't seen Lisa. "Lisa hasn't been by this morning has she?"

"No," Brad said, his face strained. "I thought she would have been here by now. She called you last night, didn't she?"

"Yes, she called us last night from her room," Joan said, casting a worried glance at Frank.

"She gave us her room number last night when we talked to her," Frank said. Joan could tell her husband was trying to appear calm. "We got here fifteen minutes ago and went to her room, but she wasn't there."

Brad frowned, worry creasing his features. "That's weird."

"Her car was there," Joan said, as if to reaffirm to her son that everything was okay. "Maybe we just missed her at the Denny's or something."

"Why don't I head back and see if I can find her," Frank said, looking from his wife to his son. "Maybe we did miss her."

"You do that," Joan said. "I'll stay here."

Frank nodded, gave his son a smile, and pressed the buzzer at the end of the hall. The door opened and he stepped through, pausing briefly to talk to the officer on the other side. The door closed and then it was just mother and son, alone in the jail.

Joan turned to Brad, trying to not appear so worried. "Have they been feeding you in here?"

"Yeah," Brad said, dangling his arms over the bars. "The guards are really nice. As you can see, I've got the entire block to myself." He tried to muster up a smile, but it came across as half-assed and forced.

"Dad got ahold of William last night around eleven," Joan said. "He said that most likely, from what Dad described to him regarding what happened, the judge will probably dismiss the case."

"That's what I thought," Brad said, his features worried. "The cop that arrested me said the same thing. He said he explained the legal ramifications to the dickhead that started this whole thing, but the guy wanted to go ahead with it."

"What a creep," Joan said, fiddling with her purse. "I hope there's some way they can arrest him for filing a false police report."

"I don't think they can do that," Brad said slowly, looking more nervous. He licked his lips. "So, Lisa wasn't at the motel room at all when you showed up?"

Joan told him the story again, telling her son that she thought Lisa might have been in the shower but she hadn't heard anything. Brad nodded. Joan reached through the bars and took her son's hands, patting them reassuringly. "We probably just missed each other," she said. "Your dad will find her."

They spent the next ten minutes talking about what had happened yesterday. Brad told her everything, starting with the lane change and Mr. Smith's van being suddenly on top of him, tailgating him all the way down the hill, to finally dropping back. Joan felt more nervous as the story spun out, and she tried to tell herself that she was overreacting when Brad was finally finished. "I'm sure everything will work out," she said. "When this is over—"

The sound of the door opening interrupted her and they both turned to the sound. Frank came down the hall alone, his features creased with worry. Joan felt a flutter in her stomach, and she heard her voice give a sharp squeak as she asked her husband, "You didn't find her?"

Frank shook his head, his dark eyes wide and scared. "I retraced my steps all the way back. Even asked the hostess at the Denny's if Lisa had been in. She hadn't been in at all, even last night. The front desk clerk at the motel says they haven't seen her since she checked in. I tried knocking on her door again, but there's still no answer."

If Brad looked scared before, he looked petrified at this news. His face went pale. Joan felt light-headed with worry. She reached through the bars again and took her son's hands. "I don't like this," she said. "Maybe we should—"

"Go back to the motel and ask them to open the door for you," Brad said, his voice wavering. "Tell them what's going on, and if they won't open the door, come back here and talk to the police. In fact, ask for Officer Lansing. He's the guy who arrested me yesterday."

"I'll be right back," Frank said, turning to head back down the hall. Joan watched him go, feeling light-headed and dizzy. Frank had looked ashen as he told them what he'd found, and as she turned back to her son she suddenly saw how Brad would look in thirty years: he would be an exact carbon-copy of his father.

"Everything's going to be okay," she said, forcing a smile and squeezing his hands through the bars.

Brad nodded, not meeting her gaze. "Yeah." But the tone of his voice suggested that he didn't believe her.

Frank had to threaten legal action if the front desk clerk didn't get off his fat ass now and accompany him with a passkey to room 6 and open the door. The clerk sighed, rolled his eyes, and moved himself off the stool behind the desk with a groan. "I'll probably get fired anyway for doing this, so let's go." He pulled the passkey to room 6 off the wall and swung around the counter. "Be right back," he called to somebody in the back room.

Frank felt his limbs grow heavy with trepidation as they approached the room. The desk clerk paused in front of the door, inserted the key, and opened the door, stepping back to let Frank pass. "Be my guest," he said.

Frank stepped into the room, the darkness seemingly sudden and final. He felt for a light switch, found it, and turned on the light. He stood at the threshold for a long time, not sure what he was seeing. He had almost forgotten about the front-desk clerk when he heard his voice behind him. "Well? Satisfied now?"

Room 6 was fine. The bed was neatly made, with no signs that it had been slept in. There was no sign of a struggle; no overturned furniture, no broken glass. Frank stepped into the room, his eyes sweeping around it. Lisa and Brad's Lexus was parked right outside the front door, but there was no sign of their luggage or any other personal belongings anywhere. He headed to the bathroom and turned on the light, inspecting the sink and countertop, the unused bathtub, the clean white towels lined up on the iron rung of the linen ring. He turned to the clerk who had followed him into the room. "Are you sure you haven't seen Lisa Miller? *Think!*"

The clerk shrugged. "Only time I saw her was last night when she checked in." He glanced around the room. "Are you sure she even spent the night here? Looks like she didn't even use this room last night."

Frank glared at the clerk. "What a brilliant deduction! What are you, employee of the month?"

The desk clerk's features went sullen. He shuffled on his feet nervously. "Listen, I have no idea if she was here last night. I got off at six-thirty, thirty minutes after she checked in. For all I know, she could have left right after I got off work."

Frank turned back to the empty room. "Stay here," he said. "I'm getting the police."

"Whatever," the desk clerk said, following Frank out of the room.

Frank glanced at the Lexus as he headed outside. He peered inside the car—it looked normal, no sign of luggage anywhere. Of course, they would have put their luggage in the trunk, and he didn't have the key to open it. With a sinking sense of dread, Frank hightailed it back to the Ventura County Sheriff substation, wondering how he was going to tell his son that his wife was gone.

Six

Lisa Miller was very afraid.

She lay naked on a narrow spring mattress, her wrists and ankles tied to the bedposts, her mouth gagged. It felt like she had been trussed up like this for days, but the shrinking part of her rational mind told her that it was probably only twelve hours or more. She had long stopped crying; crying made her throat hurt and made her more tired. It also made it hard to concentrate and sapped her willpower. And if she wanted to get out of here, she was going to need all the willpower she had.

She had been so overcome with anger when Mr. Smith had barged into her room *(last night?)* that she hadn't even thought about what she had been planning to tell Brad this weekend. This was supposed to have been a romantic getaway. A second honeymoon of a sort, punctuated by romantic dinners, cuddling together on the bed and making love, sightseeing, and just spending quality time together. Lisa had something else she wanted to do as well; she had wanted to tell Brad that he was going to be a daddy.

The thought of her pregnancy hadn't come up when Mr. Smith came into her room; what *had* come up was her sudden anger, and then the instinctual fight-or-flight mode. It wasn't until Mr. Smith was getting ready to carry her outside to his van that she thought of the baby.

She had feigned unconsciousness as Mr. Smith deposited her in the back of the van. For a time she must have passed out, because the next thing she remembered they were moving. She had been blindfolded, but she could sense that Mr. Smith was somewhere in the front driving. She had lain on the floor in the back, trying to calm herself down. The more agitated she became, the more her head hurt. Her mouth was dry, and the sweet, almost pleasant-smelling liquid he had knocked her out with was still in her nostrils. He had trussed her up more tightly this time, securing her wrists together tighter than before. Likewise, her legs were tightly bound together, as were her ankles.

But she wasn't gagged.

Lisa had waited until she felt calm and her throat was well moistened before she ventured communication. "Where are we going?"

"I was wondering when you were going to talk," Mr. Smith said, keeping his eyes on the road. "I could tell when you woke up; your breathing changed. How do you feel?"

"My head hurts," she said, saying the first thing that came to her mind. She decided that the best way to approach her predicament was to be calm and controlled. To let her rage take over was to invite more trouble from Mr. Smith. If she turned combative again, he might see fit to pull over and gag her again. Or knock her out.

Oh my God, did him knocking me out with that stuff—was it chloroform?—did that hurt the baby?

"If you promise to behave and not cause a scene, I'll give you some water and aspirin at the next rest stop. How's that sound?"

"Okay."

He drove silently for a while and Lisa debated whether or not to ask where he was taking her again when he answered her question. "As to where we're going, I'm taking you to a cabin near Big Bear. In fact, if you want, I can pick up some food for you at the next rest stop and whip something up for you once we get there. You must be hungry."

She was starving. "I could eat something," she said. Her mind was racing: *Be calm, don't do anything to set him off. If he was going to kill you, he would have done it by now.*

And on the heels of that: *Why is he taking me to this cabin?*

She wondered if she should tell him she was pregnant. She had heard from would-be rape victims that telling your attacker that you were pregnant was a possible deterrent. Would it work with Mr. Smith? She was just about to mention it when he started talking. "I don't want to hurt you," he said, eyes on the road. "In fact, if I didn't need the money I wouldn't be doing this. That whole scenario that happened back along the interstate? Like I said, that was just to separate you from your husband. My name's really not Mr. Smith, and this van isn't even registered to me. Nobody will know what happened to you. I cleaned up at the motel, wiped everything down, even used gloves after I knocked you out. I took your luggage and your purse—they're in the back with you somewhere. I left your car at the motel because that will be the first thing they look for, and a stolen car is easy to trace. This is going to work out." It sounded like he was saying this aloud to reassure himself that what he had planned was going to work, rather than attempting to explain to her his intentions.

He's going to rape and kill me, she thought, a sudden lump rising in her throat. *That's why he's taking me to this cabin. That's why he didn't take my car. When he's done, he'll bury me somewhere in the woods and nobody will know. Nobody will ever find out.*

And on the heels of that: *But if he was going to rape me, why did he say that he wouldn't be doing this if he didn't need the money? Is he kidnapping me for some kind of ransom?*

"I'm pregnant," she said, not really knowing if this revelation would be an influence. It wasn't; Mr. Smith laughed.

"If you think that's going to get you out of this, you're a bigger fool than I thought. But I admire you for trying anyway. I know what it must feel like."

"You have no idea how I feel. And I'm not lying about being pregnant, either."

"You don't look pregnant."

"I just found out early this morning."

"Really?" He paused for a moment. "Have you told hubby yet?"

She didn't know what to say. "No," she said in a whispering tone.

"But you were gonna tell him, weren't you? This weekend?"

Lisa felt the anger and hate come boiling back. She could picture his cold gray eyes watching her in the rearview mirror. "Maybe I was. What is it to you, anyway?"

"Just that I want to know what I'm dealing with. I can understand now why you were so feisty back there at the motel. Your maternal instinct kicked in. You weren't just thinking about saving your own skin, you were thinking about the unborn baby in your womb. Weren't you?"

Trying to push the anger down, she nodded. "I guess you could say that."

Mr. Smith sounded like he was considering this. "If what you're saying is true, then they might actually like this."

Those words had a chilling affect on Lisa. She felt a pit of ice creep into her belly. "What do you mean? Who are *they?*"

"Later," he said, dismissively. "The rest stop is coming up and I'll be pulling over. Remember: One peep out of you and you are one dead bitch. Got that?"

She had been forced to remain silent, struggling silently with her tears as he gagged her, then exited the van. The few minutes he spent in the AM/PM mini-market felt like hours, all the while safety and freedom only a shout away as other travelers pulled up beside them and people walked past the van to the convenience store. She had tried maneuvering around in back of the van in a vain attempt to see if she could chance opening the door and making a run (or a stumble) for it, but she was bound so tight that she could barely move. If she screamed, there might not even be a chance she would be heard. She would have no way of knowing where Mr. Smith was because she wouldn't see him until he opened the front driver's-side door of the van, and he would surely know she had been screaming for help. She believed he really would try to hurt or kill her. And she couldn't do anything that would jeopardize herself or the baby. She had to wait until she saw a better chance to escape and then take it.

When he came back, he had a bottle of Evian water and some Anacin. He crawled in the back and helped her sit up. Then he popped two Anacins in her mouth and held the bottle up for her to drink. She thanked him, and he managed a faint smile. "Got some ready-made sandwiches for you, too. You'll eat one when we get to the cabin."

He kept his promise. They had arrived at the cabin a little under an hour later, and he got her into the bedroom through a side door. She could tell they were in the mountains by the brief scent of pine and the brisk, cool air as he ushered her through the door. Ten minutes later, he took the blindfold off and he was patiently feeding her as she sat up on the narrow bed, holding the Evian bottle up for her to drink. When she was finished, he instructed her to lie down on the bed, and then she felt him struggle with the knots he had used to tie her up. "You'll feel some of these loosen up, but don't move or try to do anything. You try anything, I've got a hammer right here that I'll use to smash your skull." She had lain down, fighting the tears as he practically untied her. Then he quickly peeled off her clothes, then told her to turn over. When she turned over, she saw that he indeed had a hammer. She was almost tempted to try rushing him again; she could surprise him, try to claw out his eyes or something, but he had that hammer, and he was holding it in his right fist, ready to swing. She couldn't risk it. He told her to lie down on her back, and then he slipped the rope he had tied around her arms down to her wrist and tightened it with one swift tug. He had her wrists and ankles tied to the bedposts within a minute, and then he stepped back and surveyed his handiwork. "You'll be fine for the night. If you gotta piss, go ahead and piss on the mattress. I'll be up in the morning to change it and bring some other things."

"What are you going to do?" Lisa was sobbing, and now her emotions *did* gain the upper hand. All she could think about was how this man was destroying all her hopes of having a baby with Brad, a dream she had been working to achieve for the past two years. All she could think about was saving herself so that her baby might live. "You sonofabitch, why are you doing this!"

"I told you," Mr. Smith said calmly, a look of indifference on his bearded face. "It's nothing personal. I need the money, okay? I'm not going to hurt you."

"I don't understand!" she wailed, trying to sit up in the bed. "*Please* let me go! I *swear* I won't say anything. I won't tell anybody—"

"It's too late for that now," Mr. Smith said, looking down at Lisa calmly. "Look, it's nothing personal. The people I'm working for . . . well, the *clients* they're working for, they wanted somebody just like you. They were getting tired of using runaways, drug addicts, and vagrants, the kind of girls they had been using all along. They wanted somebody who has a clean, wholesome image. Somebody who actually has a *life*. It took me two days to find you." He grinned down at her.

She still didn't understand; Mr. Smith said that he wasn't going to hurt her, but what he was implying suggested that somebody else *was*. She sobbed hoarsely, her vision blurred with tears.

Mr. Smith leaned forward. "The . . . clients who we're doing this for . . . they've got some real expensive tastes. They've got a taste for . . . well, let's just say they have a taste for some pretty hardcore shit."

"What are you talking about?" Lisa wailed.

"They're into extreme hardcore and snuff films," Mr. Smith said, once again indifferent. "Surely you've heard of snuff films, haven't you?"

Lisa shook her head, feeling her flesh break out in goose pimples. She had never heard of extreme hardcore or snuff films, but she instinctively felt that whatever they were, they were bad.

Mr. Smith leaned forward slightly. "Extreme bondage . . . S&M . . . surely you've heard of those, haven't you? You don't strike me as being *that* naive."

Lisa nodded, a shudder running through her body. She was going to be raped! Raped and tortured for some pervert's private porno film collection. She began to sob again. "Well . . . yeah . . . but . . . I still don't understand . . . bondage . . . isn't that like . . . I thought . . . I thought . . . that was just . . . regular porno people doing that!"

"The clients that my associates and I are working for have tastes of a more brutal nature," Mr. Smith said, indifferently. "It's a very small circle of people, really. They gather at various intervals throughout the year in the privacy of their own homes, and buy and sell various tapes that my associates, and others, produce; mainly extreme hardcore S&M films, sometimes snuff films. Regular porno people don't associate with this stuff. You'd have to be crazy or a fool to want to appear in one of these things. Unless you're a complete sadist like Animal." Mr.

Smith's features were grim. "Of course, there are some hardcore freaks—masochists—who get off on that kind of shit. Some of them appear in the hardcore S&M and torture flicks, but the others? Snuff films? Like I said, our clients were getting tired of watching the same chicks and butt boys time and time again and wanted something different—something fresh." Mr. Smith grinned slightly. "It's nothing personal, really."

"You're going to kill me," Lisa whispered, looking up at Mr. Smith with fear.

"I told you that I'm not going to kill you," Mr. Smith said. "And I'm not going to hurt you. I'm supposed to take care of you to assure my associates that you are in the best physical appearance as possible for our shoot. Then when Al and the Animal get here sometime tomorrow or the next day—"

"The Animal?" Lisa said, dread suddenly filling her even more at the sound of the name.

Mr. Smith cocked his head at her. "Yes, Mrs. Miller. I was telling you the truth when I said that I wasn't going to hurt you or kill you. But your costar in the snuff film we'll be shooting . . . the Animal . . . he will."

Lisa's hands were shaking, and when she spoke her voice quivered with fear. "Please. You don't want to do this."

"I'll be back tomorrow," Mr. Smith said. He turned and exited the room.

She found her voice and let loose with a wail. "*Please let me go! Pleeeaaase!*"

Her wail fell on deaf ears. Mr. Smith exited the cabin, and a moment later, amid her heavy sobs, Lisa heard him start the van up, back down the gravel path, and head down the highway.

Seven

The three nights and two days Brad Miller spent in the Ventura County slammer were the longest of his life.

Fueled by his anger over the initial road rage incident that sparked his incarceration, he got little sleep that first night, and when he found out that Lisa was missing, his nerves went on a frenzy. He continually paced the length of his cell while his mother stood by, helpless as he drove himself deeper and deeper into worry. "I don't like this, Mom, this just isn't like her, I don't like this, why aren't they *doing* anything!"

That first day, Frank Miller succeeded in getting ahold of Officer Chris Lansing, the patrol officer who had placed Brad in custody Friday. When he told Officer Lansing that Lisa was now missing from her motel room, with no clue as to where she could have gone, Officer Lansing grew concerned. "And Brad hasn't seen her since his arrest?"

"That's right," Frank had said. He had cornered the officer as he strolled in to begin his two-to-midnight shift. "And everybody I've talked to in this fucking building says they can't do anything about it because she can't be considered missing yet!" He spat that last sentence out with an air of contempt. "Fucking *bullshit*, if you ask me."

"Come with me a minute," Officer Lansing said. He led Frank through the office to a desk where a young officer with a crew cut was at a desk in front of a computer. "Can I borrow your computer for a moment, Doug?"

"Sure." Doug moved aside, and Officer Lansing sat behind the terminal.

"In my right-hand drawer there is an arrest file on a citizen's arrest by a Mr. Caleb Smith. Can you pull that for me?"

Doug retrieved the file and Officer Lansing flipped through it. He entered Mr. Smith's name and address in the system, hit a key, then waited. A moment later, a message appeared on the screen: NO MATCHING RECORDS FOUND.

"Shit." Officer Lansing retyped the information as Frank peered over his shoulder at the screen. The query returned the same message.

Officer Lansing turned to Frank. "This system hooks up with the DMV's central database. I should have gotten Mr. Smith's DMV record, which would have included any outstanding warrants or other records, but there's nothing."

Frank looked at Officer Lansing. "You saying this guy gave you a false address?"

"I'm not saying anything yet." Officer Lansing handed the file to Doug. "Run a complete check on Mr. Caleb Smith, then run a DMV check on his vehicle. When you're done, bring the printouts to me. I'll be in Ken's office." He rose from the desk and began heading toward an office at the rear of the building. "I'll have to get back to you, Mr. Miller. Will you have a seat in the waiting room for me?"

That had been the longest wait in Frank's life. When Officer Lansing came back, he was accompanied by a lieutenant. The lieutenant appeared to be his age, with salt-and-pepper hair and ruddy features. "We're sending a pair of detectives to the Days Inn now, and another to talk to your son."

Frank had risen to his feet. "Does this mean you can let him go?"

For the first time, he realized that Officer Lansing looked embarrassed. Lieutenant Young gave Officer Lansing a cursory glance, then looked back at Frank. "Unfortunately, because your son was placed under citizen's arrest in pursuant of a felony, we can't release him until Monday morning."

"Christ!" Frank ran a hand through his thinning hair.

"We're doing everything we can to find Lisa," Lieutenant Young said, trying to muster a positive smile. "We'll find her. Don't worry."

Frank relayed all this to his son that afternoon, trying to break the news as gently as possible. Brad could only listen with a growing sense of dread; he didn't know how, but somehow Mr. Smith had something to do with this. He could feel it in his gut.

Brad's parents stayed with him at the jail until five P.M. By then a search had been conducted at the motel room, and no signs of foul play had been found. Officer Lansing had remained at the station to ferry the news back to the Millers and comb through the files for any information on Mr. Smith. He broke the news shortly before five o'clock. "Something happened to her," Brad said, his voice threatening to break. "Find this Mr. Smith guy and—"

"We're working on it," Lieutenant Young said. "Believe me, we want to find this guy ourselves."

"What's his story?" Frank asked. "Did you run his license plate? Was that fake too?"

Officer Lansing looked grim. "The DMV check we ran on his plate came up reported stolen six months ago. The plates belonged to a Chevy Suburban in San Diego. I didn't get a PIN number on Mr. Smith's vehicle at the time of your arrest because . . . well . . ."

"I was the criminal yesterday, not him," Brad said, feeling the cloud of anger return.

Officer Lansing ignored the comment. "Every check we've done through the DMV has resulted in a dead end.

I've got a sketch artist coming up with a composite now, and we'll put that over the bulletin by this evening. Don't worry, we'll catch him."

"What do we do till then?" Brad asked. His eyes were bloodshot and he was exhausted.

Officer Lansing sighed. His face had an empty, haunted look. "There's only two things we can do. Wait and pray."

Eight

The sound of a car engine pulling up in the driveway woke her up.

Lisa snapped out of a light sleep, her senses alert. She heard the slam of a door and then footsteps. The sound of a door opening and then a rattling sound. Her heartbeat quickened. *He's back, and this time he's with those other guys, that Animal and whoever else, and then they're going to start. They're going to rape me and kill me and my baby and film it and—*

The footsteps sounded across the gravelly driveway and up the front walk of the cabin. She held her breath as a key was inserted in the lock of the front door, and then the door was opened and the footsteps were clicking across the hardwood floor of the cabin. "Hello?" Her heart leaped in her throat, because at first she didn't recognize the voice. Then the man said "Hello" again and recognition flooded in: It was Mr. Smith.

He walked into the bedroom bearing something in his arms. He bent down and set it on the floor with a clanking of metal and stood up, smiling. "How are you this fine morning?"

Lisa opened her mouth to answer, but all that came out was a dry hiss. Her throat was dry. Mr. Smith nodded. "Want some water?"

Lisa nodded. "Yes," she rasped.

"Coming right up." Mr. Smith disappeared into the kitchen and returned a moment later with a glass of water. He held the glass to her lips while Lisa sipped at it slowly. "Better?"

Lisa nodded. "Yeah."

"Good." Mr. Smith glanced down at the mattress. "I see you couldn't hold it last night."

Lisa felt the tears spring to her eyes again. The pain in her bladder had grown unbearable by late last night and she had been forced to void it. The smell and dampness that had spread under her buttocks and settled into the mattress had kept her awake the rest of the night.

"Don't worry. There's a spare mattress in the next bedroom that fits this bed frame just fine. We'll replace it. And you won't have to worry about making wee-wee in the bed anymore. I've found a solution to your problems." He picked up the thing that had made the metallic clanking sound, holding it up for her to see. It was a piece of chain.

Lisa started to cry.

Mr. Smith ignored her as he went about his work. First he attached a device on the windowsill, screwing it on with heavy-duty screws; it looked like a pulley. Then he payed out the heavy line it was attached to and fastened a metal ring to it. A piece of short, heavy chain was attached to that, and another device was attached to *that*. Then he drew out two pairs of handcuffs, one which he attached to her wrists, the other to her ankles. He attached a piece of chain to the thin but sturdy chain of the handcuff and ran that length of chain to the heavy pulley on the larger chain. He did the same thing to the handcuffs attached to her ankles. When he was finished, he untied the rope that secured her ankles and wrists to the bedposts. Lisa was barely aware of what Mr. Smith was doing; she lay on the bed crying uncontrollably, hysterical in her fear.

Mr. Smith tested the strength of the chain by tugging on it. Lisa felt a sharp bite of steel in her wrists and ankles and stopped crying. Mr. Smith smiled. "There. Why don't I help you stand up now."

He helped Lisa sit up by moving her shoulders and upper body into a sitting position on the mattress. Then he helped her move her legs over the side of the bed. "Stand up now and let's see you walk." She did so, and Mr. Smith kept a close watch on her, grinning and nodding. Lisa's cries had reduced to sniffles, and she walked around the room, testing the new contraption that would keep her prisoner in this room. The shackles around her ankles were barely a foot apart and forced her to shamble along like a prison inmate. She stumbled as she tested the limits of it. Mr. Smith reached out to help her up. "Whoa, watch out there! I can't lengthen the chain on the cuffs down there. Wouldn't want you trying to kick me or Animal."

Lisa glared at Mr. Smith but said nothing. "How far can I move in this thing?"

"Let's head to the bathroom and find out." He held his arm out, as if escorting her like a gentleman. He led her to a door she had barely noticed before that was set against the wall. He opened the door, and she saw that it was a small bathroom, complete with a tub and a sink. Lisa walked into the bathroom. "Can you sit down at the john? Let's try it."

Lisa turned around and sat her naked buttocks on the lid of the toilet. The payout of the line attached to the pulley grew taut. Mr. Smith smiled. "Wonderful! Just like I thought. You have enough line to reach the toilet, which means you probably have four feet beyond the bedroom door and that's it. I'll board up the window to keep you from smashing it and trying to escape, but then I've got you pretty well trussed up."

Lisa looked at Mr. Smith, feeling defeated and beaten. She had been doing some thinking last night and resolved herself to not even try to plead with him. He had told her last night that it wasn't personal, he was only doing this for the money. He had picked her up because she was what his unknown clients were looking for to be the star of a snuff film. She had been thinking about that last night, and while the implications of what was going to happen to her were petrifying, she had a thousand questions to ask him. She had been debating on whether to try to draw him into some sort of conversation. Part of her felt that she needed the human contact of conversation to keep from going crazy, while another part of her held the dim hope that perhaps if she evoked enough compassion in him, Mr. Smith would let her go. She seriously doubted that, but it was worth a try.

"How did you get into what you're doing?" She asked him, her voice submissive but not pleading. "You know . . . the whole snuff film thing."

Mr. Smith shrugged as he worked at the window. He had gone into the living room and come back with several five-by-twelve pieces of wood, which he proceeded to erect across the window and nail to the wall, boarding it up. "I never really *got* into it. It's just something I do for money."

"But you had to fall into it somehow."

Mr. Smith turned to her. "Why do you want to know?"

Lisa shrugged. "I figure as long as I'm going to . . . you know . . . I might as well know more about it."

Mr. Smith turned back to the window and continued

boarding it up. "I admire that. You'd rather face up to things than run away from them. I like that."

Except for the pounding of nails as Mr. Smith boarded up the window, there was silence for a moment.

"I was a producer for a while," he said, finishing up the window. "I produced a lot of hardcore porn back in the seventies. That's how I met Al, one of the guys you'll meet later. He's a director. He shot a bunch of films for me. I specialized in a lot of extreme hardcore S&M and bizarre shit—golden showers, fisting, bestiality, blood sports, scat films, rape films, a lot of kiddie porn—you name it. I had an audience that ate that shit up."

Lisa listened, feeling disgusted with Mr. Smith. He looked, acted, and sounded like the stereotypical pervert. Middle-aged, balding, overweight, glasses, small beady eyes. It was easy to picture him sitting his girth on a director's chair, pulling his pants down, and telling the naive teenage giggleboxes who came to Hollywood with dreams in their eyes that, sure they could have a part in his film, but first they had to get down on their knees and show him how much they appreciated him.

"So how did you come to be a part of making snuff films?" Lisa asked, hiding her revulsion.

Mr. Smith was finished boarding up the window. "I don't *do* just snuff films. I *do* a lot of stuff on commission. Al and I, we do a lot of extreme hardcore S&M shit. And I ain't talking your everyday, run-of-the-mill slap-and-spanking shit that bored yuppies and trendy goths are into, either. All that rope bondage and whips and chains shit that people are into? Forget that. You can get crap like that at your neighborhood video store. The stuff I'm talking about that Al and I deal in is extreme, sick shit. Most of it is near-death stuff: mutilation, a lot of asphyxiation. Al's tapped into the extreme hardcore community real well. Some of the people he shoots for privately, they're into this kind of shit. Whenever we get a job, he comes to me and I . . . well, I sort of comb through the girls I know of that would fit perfectly."

"What kind are those?"

Mr. Smith looked at her. "Not like you, that's for sure."

"Why's that?"

"You're not like them, that's why. You got a life. A career. You're a lawyer, right?"

Lisa nodded.

"The chicks I usually get for extreme hardcore films and snuff films," Mr. Smith said, regarding her calmly, "they've got nowhere to go but down. Sometimes we get a request for a guy, and they're just as easy to get because they fall into the same shit. Most of them are hardcore druggies; runaways, hookers, people that aren't immune to turning some pretty sick tricks, you know what I mean? I find them, take them out, buy them clothes, show them some money, they fall all over me. Turn them on to a bit of blow or smack—most of them are already fucked up on drugs anyway—and they'll keep coming back for more. Once they get a taste for a shitload of money and free drugs, they'll do anything. They'll even come back for more. Shit, some of them are so fucked up when we use them for an extreme hardcore film, they actually like it! Can you imagine that? Getting off on somebody cutting your tits or burning you with cigarettes? Well, some of them get off on it, and those are the ones we use for the films. Like I said, they got nowhere to go but down, and they don't give a shit what happens to themselves anyway. Shit, most of them are too fucked up to care. And most of them have the same sob story to tell: Daddy abused them, or they ran away from a shitty home life or some other shit. It don't matter where they come from as long as they're on the way down. Long as they been on the street for a while and they got nowhere to go, no mommy and daddy to go to, no boyfriend or husband that will give a shit about them, they're the ones we use. Long as nobody misses them, that's all that matters."

Lisa was disgusted, but she tried not to let it show. "So why me?"

"I told you. The guys that commissioned this film, they got tired of watching a bunch of junkie cunts being raped and sliced up. To tell you the truth, a lot of those chicks get so fucked-up-looking they look real skanky by the time we use them. The clients wanted something fresh. Shit, they woulda used a bitch like that Britney Spears chick or Heather Locklear if they could get away with it.. They wanted somebody that was pretty and healthy-looking, somebody that didn't look like they had been shooting dope for the past five years, or who had too many fucking scars on their bodies from S&M mutilation or size-fourteen assholes from too many fisting sessions."

So in other words, I'm nothing to them and to you. Lisa thought, digesting the information slowly. If she had heard this yesterday, she would have gone into hysterics. Now she merely processed the information and shifted gears. "I'll be missed, though," she said. "My husband . . . my parents, our friends. I'm *not* just some *nobody*. People will want to know what happened to me."

"Maybe." Mr. Smith shrugged and headed toward the entrance to the bedroom. "But who gives a shit? What matters is that nobody will know afterward. That cop that pulled you over yesterday? He's got nothing on me. And when this is all over, this here," he pointed to his scruffy beard, "gets shaved off and I wear my contact lenses for a while. Maybe lose a few pounds. Trust me, we had this planned for a while. The van I used last night is already in Mexico, the driver's license I used was fake. In short, the cops got nothing on me. And this place?" He swept his hands around the cabin. "It's so far off the beaten track nobody will know anything. Nearest neighbor is a mile away, and—"

"Nobody will hear me if I scream," Lisa finished.

"If they do, they'll think it's just the coyotes howling at the moon." Mr. Smith grinned. "And besides, you'll be too fucked up to do any screaming. The shit Al will shoot you up with . . . you'll be conscious, but you won't be able to scream."

Lisa was silent. Mr. Smith watched her for a moment, then bent down to pick up his toolbox. He started heading outside.

"What about the people who are into this?" she asked. Mr. Smith stopped at the doorway and looked back at her. "The people that . . . pay to watch. I mean . . ." She gestured vaguely. "What kind of people are into this? Why? Why do they do it?"

Mr. Smith appeared to ponder the question before he answered. "More than fifty percent of the people that watch snuff films are weak, inadequate, high-profile people with high-profile jobs, mostly people in the business community: corporate executives and CEOs, bankers, people like that. Some of them are high-priced lawyers. The others are participants in the extreme hardcore scene just looking for something they haven't seen or done. As to why they do it . . ." He paused, stroking his chin. "It's a power trip," he said, looking directly at her. "It's a rush for them. It gets them off. Extreme hardcore and snuff isn't just about sex. It's about owning someone, making them beg for mercy, deciding whether or not they're going to give it. It is the ultimate power over someone. When the . . . people who are into this kind of stuff . . . when they watch a snuff film, they like to imagine what it's like . . . what the killer feels. They like to pretend *they're* him, doing the things *he's* doing. They get a tremendous sense of power, knowing they orchestrated the torture and death of another human being."

The thought terrified her, but she tried not to show it. "What about the guy that will be doing it . . . the Animal? Why does he do it?"

Mr. Smith grinned. "I guess you'll have to ask him." He turned and left the room.

Lisa sat on the bed, all hope draining away. She had no idea what time it was now. There was no clock in the bedroom, and the sun had been up for how long? Two hours? Three? All sense of time was a blur. She had barely slept last night, especially after being forced to pee on the mattress she slept on. She had started crying after soiling her mattress, and the next thing she remembered, the sun was coming up. She supposed it could be anywhere between eight and eleven o'clock in the morning by now.

Her bladder felt full again and she stood up, walked into the bathroom, lifted the toilet lid, and sat down. She peed, then flushed the toilet. The urge to wipe came, but then she thought, *why should I?* Mr. Smith was bringing the Animal to rape and kill her anyway. Why clean up for him? She stood up and moved to the sink, sobbing quietly as she washed her hands. Even though she had just found out she was pregnant, she was already picturing what her and Brad's baby would look like. And now it was all going to be snuffed out. She took a deep breath and hung her head over the sink, trying to calm herself down. When her sobs trickled down, she looked in the mirror at her reflection. There were large, dark circles under her eyes, the whites red. Despite not sleeping much last night, and everything else she had gone through, she didn't look that bad.

She walked back into the room just as Mr. Smith was replacing the mattress. The old pee-stained mattress was resting on its side against the bedroom wall. He patted the new mattress. "Have a seat. I'll be outside nailing up that window." He exited the room and she stood there for a moment, her mind numb and reeling. After a few minutes, she sat down.

She heard him clomp outside to his vehicle, then a few minutes later she heard him at the side of the cabin outside the bedroom window. She heard the sound of pounding along with his mutters, and then he began putting the wood up, securing it over the window. She sighed and tried to drown out the sounds of Mr. Smith hammering nails in the wood that would secure it to the windowsill. The room was dark from the boards already blocking the sun from the inside. She looked up at the ceiling, feeling her eyes grow heavy with tears again. The sound of those boards going up over the window was like nailing the lid of her coffin.

She sat on the bed and tried not to cry as Mr. Smith worked on boarding up the window to her prison. Her mind retraced yesterday's nightmare quickly: leaving the rest stop, the van's grille suddenly filling up the rearview mirror, Brad's panicked voice as the van dogged their every move for the next mile or so down the highway, then the whirling lights and sirens of the Highway Patrol. She had known the minute she saw those lights appear in the rearview mirror that it had something to do with the van, that the driver had pulled some kind of stunt. And when that cop had pulled them over with his holier-than-thou attitude and told them it was *Brad* that was driving around like an asshole, she'd felt an impending sense of doom. She had felt a sense of disbelief as the officer told her why he had pulled them over, and why he couldn't really give a shit about them—*after all, the law is the law, and I'm only doing my job*. And now as she sat naked on a bare mattress in a small cabin somewhere in Big Bear in the San Bernardino mountains, her mind flashed on something she had almost forgotten.

They had still been at the rest stop. They had stopped for bathroom breaks, and as usual Brad had finished first. Lisa had exited the women's restroom and joined Brad at a little scattering of picnic tables. There was a yellow sign with a blocky-looking drawing of a snake on it, a warning to tourists that rattlesnakes were in the area this time of year. Lisa had stood by the sign with a wild grin as Brad snapped a photo of her, and it was then when she had seen him walking by, casting his gaze on them.

She closed her eyes and tried to remember, summoning the image in her mind. Yes, she was positive it had been Mr. Smith. He had been wearing sunglasses, and the more she thought about it, the more the picture came to her mind. He had been standing by a large tree that overlooked the rest stop. She didn't remember him being there when they had pulled up, but she surely remembered glancing over at him when she left the ladies' room. She had quickly dismissed him, figuring he was just another tourist waiting for his wife or significant other to exit the ladies' room. There had been four other women in the restroom besides her, and she had dismissed it from her mind until she and Brad were shooting photos and horsing around, and then he had walked past them slowly, casually, and then Brad had said something that distracted her and then they were laughing over something and the guy was forgotten as they gathered their stuff together and headed toward the Lexus. He was gone anyway, both physically and from her mind, when they climbed into the Lexus and backed out of the parking space to hit the Interstate.

But hadn't there been a red van parked at the rest stop? Now that she thought about it, she could have sworn that there was. She could picture it now: him sitting at the rest stop, carefully but unobtrusively watching as tourists came and went, waiting for just the right people to come along. And then she and Brad had dropped in. How did Mr. Smith pick them? Did he overhear a scrap of conversation they might have had as they walked to the restrooms together? Some bits of information that told him everything he needed to know? Did that information—talking about their vacation plans this long weekend—give him what he needed to know to convince himself that he would have at least two days to do what he needed to do before any alarm was raised about her disappearance?

The feeling of dread settled in her belly further. Now she was more terrified than before. The story he'd told the officer was bullshit. The thought of actually feeding her to this guy he called the Animal for a snuff film, all for the satisfaction of a faceless group of perverts, was more frightening the more she thought about it. He didn't appear to be bothered by the fact that he was playing a key role in her murder. He didn't seem to care when she told him she was pregnant. All he had been concerned about was the money he was being paid.

There was no question about it. She had to get out of here at any cost. She would run through the woods naked if she had to. She didn't care. What mattered more than anything was getting out alive. She didn't have just herself to think about anymore—the life of her unborn baby was at stake.

A thought suddenly came to her as she remembered being knocked out by Mr. Smith: *Did the chloroform he gave me yesterday . . . did that hurt the baby?*

Oh God, please no, please let my baby be all right!

The sound of Mr. Smith working outside became background noise as she sat on the bed and thought about what to do. When Mr. Smith left later today, she was going to have to do some roaming around the room to see if she could find something to help her escape with. She inspected the bed she was sitting on. Maybe she could take a piece off of it, use it to batter down the boards he had nailed over the window. Surely if she was able to do that and wriggle out the window she wouldn't get very far because she was chained up, but if she stood outside and yelled long enough, wouldn't somebody hear her? Even if the closest cabin was a mile away, surely somebody would hear her during the day and—

"Hey, Tim? Jeff? Anybody here?"

Lisa's heart froze. For a moment she thought it was Mr. Smith, but then she heard the sound of nails being hammered into the wood outside the room. Mr. Smith was still outside boarding up the window. Which meant that—

Footsteps clumped from the back of the cabin and grew closer. "I was wondering when you would be coming back up. I saw your van and—" It was a woman's voice, and now Lisa looked up just in time to see her stop in the middle of the living room, silhouetted against the rays of the sun that streamed in through the half-boarded-up window. The woman looked like she might have stepped out of the pages of a fashion magazine. She was tall, with dark hair that fell to her shoulders. She had high cheekbones and a sharp nose, with full lips and dark eyes. Now those lips were open in a round O of surprise, her eyes wide with shock as she looked through the doorway at Lisa sitting naked on the bed, her ankles and wrists shackled together. "Oh my God!" she said.

Lisa was so stunned by the sudden intrusion that she didn't know what to do. Her brain was frozen. She thought the woman standing in front of her was an illusion, a wishful thinking of her imagination. The woman took a step closer, her face still frozen in that *I-can't-believe-I'm-seeing-this* expression, and said, "Are you okay? What the hell is—"

Mr. Smith suddenly appeared in the living room, grabbing the woman from behind, one arm locked around her throat in a chokehold, the other around her waist. The woman struggled, her eyes going wider, and Lisa watched as Mr. Smith tried to wrestle the woman to the ground. The woman tried to scream, but all that came out were muffled, strangled sounds of fear and anguish. Lisa watched, her stomach in a tight ball.

For a minute it looked like the woman had a fighting chance. She had a good six inches on Mr. Smith, and she used her height to its full advantage, throwing herself around, trying to offset the balance and throw him to the ground. But Mr. Smith managed to knee her in the kidneys and the woman went down with a muffled *woof* of pain, and then he had her. He brought her to the ground and, planting his knee on her back, he held her down. "Goddamnit, why did you have to barge in like that? Oh goddamn, goddamn . . ."

The woman had been stunned by the blow to her lower back, and tears welled up in her eyes. Mr. Smith hit her again, and the woman screamed and curled up into a ball. The sound of the scream curdled Lisa's blood. She drew herself up on the bed in a protective gesture, not even aware she was whimpering.

Mr. Smith stood up, looking anguished as he ran a hand through his thinning hair. "Oh Christ, this is a mess. *Shit!*" He turned to the remaining chains on the floor, and Lisa watched as he trussed the woman up with them. "Debbie, why the fuck did you have to barge in like that, huh? Why the fuck did you have to stick your nose in my fucking business?" He repeated similar mantras as he trussed her up. By the time he was finished, the pain from the two blows to Debbie's kidneys seemed to have subsided. Now all Debbie did was sob loudly. She didn't resemble the woman who had stumbled into the cabin a few minutes before. Mr. Smith had reduced her to a quivering, blubbering thing.

Mr. Smith tested her bonds. "Shit!" He turned and clomped outside. Lisa watched, breath held as she heard him rummaging around in his van. Then he returned a moment later with some rope. Mr. Smith tied Debbie up with the rope, trussing her up more securely than he had with the chain. When he was finished, he stood up and surveyed his handiwork. Debbie lay on the floor, arms tied behind her back, wrists tied together, her legs and ankles lashed together. No way was she going anywhere. "I'm sorry I have to do this, Debbie," Mr. Smith said. He looked around nervously. "You up here alone? Did Neal come with you?"

Debbie only cried.

"*Fuck!*" Mr. Smith stomped outside. Lisa heard him get into his van and start it. He backed it down the driveway and sped down the road.

Lisa waited, her stomach doing slow flips in her belly. If Neal was up here as well, he might be her chance to escape. That is, unless Mr. Smith didn't kill him first.

The wait for Mr. Smith to come back was torturous. Debbie cried the whole time, and shortly before Mr. Smith returned, her crying slowed down to trickles. Her eyes were puffy, and they glanced around the room, wide-eyed with terror. Lisa looked down at her. "What's your last name?"

"Martinez," Debbie said, hiccupping. "Who are you?"

"Lisa Miller. Is Neal up here with you?"

"No." Debbie's face screwed up and she began sobbing again, heart-wrenching cries that tugged at Lisa's gut.

Mr. Smith stomped back in. He looked somewhat relieved to find Neal not at the cabin. "Is Neal coming up this weekend?" he asked the crying woman on the floor.

Debbie shook her head, trying to calm her crying down. "No . . . *please don't hurt me!*"

"I'm not going to hurt you." Mr. Smith was agitated. He bobbed back and forth on unsteady legs. "When is Neal coming up?"

"I don't know!" Debbie cried.

"Shit." Mr. Smith ran his hand through his hair again. He looked at Lisa, then turned away and headed back outside. A minute later, he resumed his work at the window.

Lisa sat on the mattress, her mind racing. Surely, whoever Neal was, he would grow worried when Debbie didn't come back, or when he couldn't reach her at her cabin. Debbie was most likely a neighbor and was acquainted with whoever Tim and Jeff were well enough to feel relaxed around them (*Was Mr. Smith, Tim? Or was he Jeff?*). If Neal wasn't around this weekend, how long would it take him to get worried and try looking for her?

Would he think of looking for her at Mr. Smith's cabin?

And if he did, would Mr. Smith—or worse yet, would the Animal—be here to kill him?

Lisa couldn't think of that now. To do so would be courting defeat. Neal was her only hope. Debbie lay on the floor, her crying trickled down to sniffles, and now the darkness in the room was like a permanent thing. Mr. Smith finished boarding up the window.

He trumped back inside the cabin. He looked in at the two women, his eyes darting to Debbie, then to Lisa. "I'm leaving, but I'll bring you some food. Are sandwiches okay?"

"Yeah."

"Okay." Mr. Smith disappeared, and a moment later she heard him in the kitchen.

Lisa looked down at Debbie. "Crying only wastes your energy," she said in a whisper. "We're going to need all the energy we can get, girlfriend. You better believe it if you want to get out of this."

Debbie lay on the floor, her eyes wide and staring. "Why is he doing this?"

"I'll tell you later," Lisa said. She turned away from Debbie and waited on the bed for Mr. Smith to return. Several times Debbie whispered up to ask her what was going on—why had Tim tied her up like this? Why did he attack her and tie her up?—but Lisa didn't answer her. "I'll tell you later," was all she said. "When he leaves." And then Tim—Mr. Smith to Lisa—was back with four sandwiches, a bag of potato chips, four bottles of Evian water, and several pieces of fruit. And then he was gone.

When the sound of the van's engine receded in the distance, Debbie asked Lisa again. Lisa looked down at the woman. "How well do you know Tim? And what's his last name?"

Debbie opened her mouth, closed it. "His last name is Murray. I . . . I don't know him that well, I guess. I mean, we're neighbors, I see him and his friend Jeff and their other friends up here every so often, but—"

"Listen to me very carefully," Lisa said. "And try not to freak out. I know that will be hard to do. It took all of my willpower to not collapse, and if we're going to get out of this we're going to have to work together. You and me. Okay?"

Debbie nodded, her face stony. And then Lisa shuffled closer to Debbie and told her, and Debbie *did* freak out.

Nine

"You people are a real piece of work, do you know that?"

"Ma'am, we're doing everything we can. Now, if you'll please—"

"Please *nothing*. My daughter-in-law is missing, and you not only refuse to believe that, but you've been holding my son now for two days without a legitimate cause for—"

"Ma'am, we've been through this before." The officer on the other side of the desk was trying hard to remain calm, but was clearly becoming agitated the more Joan Miller kept arguing with him. "There's nothing we can do until Monday morning when Brad is arraigned. I know Officer Lansing has been helping you and your husband through this, but—"

"That's enough, Officer," Frank Miller said. He grasped his wife's elbow firmly, pulling her away from the reception desk. "Come on, Joan."

"But—" Joan looked torn between wanting to leap over the desk and throttle the officer and breaking down in tears.

"It's okay. They're doing everything they can. All we can do is wait." Frank looked like he had aged ten years in the past twenty-four hours.

"Wait for *what?*" Joan's voice was full of anguish. The tone of it caused several people in the lobby of the sheriff's station to turn their way. "For that *scum* Caleb Smith to—"

"Enough!" Frank grasped his wife more firmly and led her away from the reception desk and got her outside.

Once outside, Joan turned on her husband. "Goddamn it, Frank, don't you *dare* do that to me again!"

"You listen to me," Frank said, holding his ground firmly. He grasped his wife's shoulders, his eyes boring into hers. "The facts are, these people are doing everything they can already. To release Brad from custody would not only be a violation of California law, it would get them in a hell of a lot of trouble. Like it or not, there's legal protocols they have to follow. As for the accusations against Caleb Smith—"

"Accusations my ass! That bastard has done something with Lisa! Don't you see it?" Joan's voice practically screeched. Her hair was in disarray, her eyes puffy from lack of sleep.

It was late Sunday afternoon, over a day and a half since arriving to keep Lisa company for the weekend while they tried to get Brad out of jail. In that time the situation had grown from bad to worse. The sketch of Caleb Smith had been put over the wire and so far there had been no word. The police were searching for the van and it hadn't turned up. Their lawyer friend, Billy Grecko, had called at the hotel room this morning, and when confronted with Lisa's disappearance told them he was going to put in a call to the Federal Bureau of Investigation. He knew an agent there whom he was on good standing with, and he was sure he could convince him to get a missing-persons investigation started, at least give the Ventura County Sheriff a good kick in the ass to get going quicker. Meanwhile, Brad was still sitting in a cell, getting by with little sleep and food. The more the hours passed with no word on Lisa, the more frantic he was becoming behind bars.

"They are accusations right now," Frank said, his voice firm. "Mind you, I have just as strong a feeling as you have that he has something to do with all this. The only thing we have going for us right now is the fact that this Caleb Smith guy doesn't appear to be who he is. If it wasn't for that . . . if they had actually found him and discovered he has a strong alibi, we wouldn't have a leg to stand on."

Joan was crying now. She sank into her husband's arms and he held her, paying no heed to those who were coming in and out of the sheriff's station casting them curious looks. Joan hadn't cried like this in years—hell, Frank had never seen her cry like this before. He just hoped his strength didn't sap away nearly as fast as hers did. He was now the rock that held them together.

"*Why is this happening to us?*" Joan sobbed against Frank's chest. "*Why?*"

"I don't know, honey," Frank murmured, holding his wife close. "I don't know."

They remained that way for a while, and Joan calmed down. Finally, she broke away from him and wiped her eyes with the back of her hands. "Look at me. Blubbering like an idiot."

"It's okay. You needed that cry. It's been long overdue."

Joan looked at her husband; she looked lost. "I'm sorry. I've been trying to hold it all together. It's just . . ." She threw up her hands in despair.

"It's been too much. I know."

"I'm sorry that I caused such a big scene in there," Joan said. "I don't want to cause any trouble for them. I know they're only trying to help us."

"I'm sure they realize you're upset. I think we both know what it feels like to be an officer now: to feel helpless and bound by the law against doing what you feel in your gut is right."

Joan nodded. She reached into her purse for a tissue and wiped her nose with it. "What do we do now?" She put the tissue back into her purse.

"Let's go back inside and tell Gary where we'll be for the rest of the night." Officer Gary Fraser was the officer Joan had just yelled at; since Officer Lansing had gone off duty late last night, Fraser had been their main contact at the station. "Then we'll go see Brad. We'll tell him that he'll be out tomorrow morning. Billy should be at his hotel by now, and he may even have word on getting an investigation going on finding Lisa. Then the only thing we can do is go to our room and wait until tomorrow."

Joan sighed. "Tomorrow. That seems like such a long time from now."

"I know." Frank put his arm around Joan's shoulders. "I know."

They walked back to the station together.

Ten

On the morning of Brad Miller's arraignment, his parents followed Billy Grecko in his silver Mercedes as it sped down Interstate 5 toward Ventura. Visible three cars ahead of the Mercedes was a white van with a Ventura County Sheriff's logo on its side. Joan and Frank caught a brief glimpse of Brad as he was led to the van, and when he saw them he waved. Joan and Frank waved back. Brad tried to smile, but it looked forced. He looked tired and defeated.

In Judge Kurt Plummer's chambers, the bailiff escorted Brad to the defendant table. When the judge got the papers that were filed on the charges, he cast a glance out at the court. "Case 498736, people of California versus Brad Miller." His eyes found Brad's, locked in on him. "Are you Mr. Miller?"

"Yes, Your Honor," Brad answered. For some reason, the judge reminded Brad of the actor Ossie Davis; his voice was deep and commanding, his graying hair giving him a dignified appearance.

"And do you have counsel?"

Billy Grecko rose from his seat at the defense table. "I represent Mr. Miller, Your Honor."

"And your name?"

"William Grecko, Your honor."

Judge Plummer looked over the paperwork, his eyes magnified from behind the thick glasses he wore. He scowled. "This is a citizen's arrest." He looked across at the prosecution table as an African-American man in a dark suit and a power tie stood up. "What is the nature of this case, counselor?"

"The County of Ventura would like to decline to file charges against Mr. Miller at this time, Your Honor," the lawyer for the DA said.

"On what grounds?"

"Lack of evidence, Your Honor."

"And you wasted my fifteen minutes this morning just to drag this young man into my courtroom for that? I should fine you, Mr. Carr."

"I'm sorry, Your Honor."

Judge Plummer pounded his gavel. "Case against Mr. Brad Miller dismissed, by request of the prosecution."

Five minutes later, Brad was walking briskly out of the Ventura County courthouse, his parents and William Grecko trailing him. His eyes were wide with fear. "We've got to find Lisa!"

"Brad!"

He stopped and turned around as his parents and William Grecko caught up with him. William Grecko was panting, sweat dotting his forehead. He smelled faintly of rum.

"What? We can't fuck around. It's been, like, three *days*—"

"Brad." Billy was suddenly in front of him. He took

Brad by the shoulders, his eyes locked with his. "Listen to me very carefully."

Brad's eyes suddenly went wide with fright. *"What happened? You found her! Please tell me you found her—"*

Billy paused, his eyes flicking from Frank to Joan, then back to Brad. He looked nervous. "Brad, let me explain this to you."

"Will you just tell me what's going on!" Brad's voice cracked. Joan almost broke down at the sight of her son.

"Son, there's not much to go on," Frank said. He looked nervous and scared, and he traded a glance with Billy, who stepped back from Brad. Brad turned to look at his father. "Billy has a friend with the Bureau. He was able to get a couple of detectives over at the hotel and . . ."

"They couldn't find anything," Billy finished. He looked dejected. "They talked to all the employees at the motel. Nobody saw or heard anything. There's no sign of a struggle in the room. Your car is still in the parking lot, your luggage is still in the trunk, but Lisa's stuff . . . her purse and suitcase . . . they're gone—"

"What do you *mean* there's no sign of a struggle?" Brad cried.

"The police have been unable to find Caleb Smith anywhere," Bill continued. "The Bureau ran a list of aliases and checked them all out against the composite that was done back at the station. Neither man they came up with was Smith. It's almost like he just vanished into thin air."

"You've got to be kidding!" Brad cried, his hands going up to his face. He looked absolutely panic-stricken.

"I'm trying to push this down the pipe as fast as I can, but my friend at the Bureau says that we need more to go on," Billy said, and now he did look defeated. It was in his eyes, his posture, the way his shoulders slumped. It seemed to permeate the air around him, much like the smell of rum that was seeping out of his pores. "We have nothing at the motel, no reasonable cause for suspicion on Caleb Smith, whoever he may be . . . we have no witnesses, no—"

"You've got to *try!*" Brad said, grabbing the lawyer's suit with weakened fingers. His eyes searched the lawyer's face, then lighted on his parents. He could feel himself breaking down. "Please, you've got to try."

"We'll try," Billy said, taking Brad's hands and squeezing them tight. "We'll do everything we can."

Brad could do nothing else but stand in the parking lot of the Ventura County Courthouse in the clothes he had worn for the past three days, not even aware of his body odor as his mother took him in his arms, not even aware of his own warm tears coursing down his cheeks.

Eleven

Noon.

Lisa tried to ignore the stench of vomit, piss, excrement, and blood that now permeated the room, but with the window boarded up and the cabin now locked up good and tight, that was hard to do.

She sat cross-legged on the floor just outside the bedroom, still in shackles. Aside from yesterday, Caleb Smith—a.k.a. Tim Murray—had only been in one other time since Saturday morning, and that was later that afternoon to deliver another series of chains and a pulley to truss up Debbie Martinez in a like fashion. *Wouldn't want Debbie to shit her pants now, would we?* he had said grimly as he worked. Debbie had been reduced to a quivering thing that could only moan as Mr. Smith came near her. She had burst into tears the minute he entered the room. "Please let me go . . . *pleeeaaassseee!*"

Lisa had told Debbie what happened to her and Brad, starting with the road rage incident and ending Saturday morning when Mr. Smith/Tim Murray had shown up to truss her up more securely. Debbie's eyes had grown wide at the mention of the snuff film and Tim's involvement. "I don't believe this . . . this is some kind of sick joke . . ."

"I'm afraid not," Lisa had said matter-of-factly.

Debbie couldn't believe that Tim Murray was capable of what Lisa was telling her. She couldn't believe that somebody so sweet—so *normal*-looking—was a bona fide weirdo. She had still been puzzling over the revelation when Tim returned to truss her up more securely, and that was when the implication hit her—why else would Tim be keeping her prisoner like this? That's when she had begun to plead for her life. It fell on deaf ears.

When Tim finally left for the night, Lisa set about to find a way out. She tested the length of chain she was tied to and found she could only exit about four feet out of the bedroom before the chain pulled tight. There was a small closet in the bedroom, which yielded nothing. Aside from the single bed in the middle of the room, there was a small dresser and a nightstand. The bathroom was bare bones, too; just a bar of soap, a couple of towels, and a dusty medicine cabinet. Lisa flipped on the light switch; the bedroom light came on.

Debbie had sat on the lumpy mattress and watched as Lisa stormed around the perimeter of their prison, trying to find a way out. Debbie was just as pretty nude as she had been fully clothed. Lisa's first impressions of the woman were that she could have passed as a model. With her flat tummy, her full, perfect breasts, and her long legs, she looked like she could pose for a *Playboy* centerfold. Lisa scowled as she searched frantically for a way out, casting glances back at Debbie, who sat on the bed still in shock. *"Bambi" better get her head out of her ass if she wants to stay alive,* she thought. Then she silently chastised herself. *Stop it. She's a victim as much as you are. She doesn't deserve this any more than you; she's just handling it differently. She's not as tough. You've got to help her toughen up. If you can help her find the strength she needs, she'll be an incredible asset.*

For a while, Lisa thought that's exactly what would happen. They had talked, and after a while Debbie began to relax. Sometime later that night, Debbie became a different person. She was still scared, but now she was angry as well. She told Lisa that her husband Neal was probably worrying about her right this minute. "I thought I could hear my phone ringing a while back," she had said. "Sound can sometimes carry pretty well out here."

Did that mean that if they screamed loud enough somebody else might hear them? Debbie shook her head. "Nobody up here now except us. The closest cabin is the Hamptons' about two and a half miles east of here, and they might not even be at their place this time of year."

It was a start. They grew tired as the night wore on, and after eating a sandwich and some chips they went to sleep, both of them lying together on the narrow bed. Lisa had never slept with another woman before, and sleeping with Debbie wasn't sexual for her in any way, but it was comforting. The feel of the other woman lying beside her, feeling her breathe next to her, feeling her skin touch hers, was comforting. Having somebody with her helped make the night more bearable.

They had inspected their room further the following morning, Sunday. Lisa emptied out the drawers of the nightstand and removed them, moving them and the nightstand to the blind side of the door. When Tim—or the Animal—came through this door, she or Debbie could conk him on the head, get the keys to the handcuffs, and free themselves.

It was a good plan if you weren't pregnant.

Lisa couldn't bring herself to go through with it. What if something happened and the baby was hurt? Then she would just be killed anyway.

They were arguing about this, trying to come up with a feasible plan, when they heard a vehicle pull up outside the cabin.

There was a pause, low voices outside, more than one person. Then slow footsteps mounted the porch, and then a key was fumbled into the lock and the door opened. "Yoo-hoo?" a voice called out, and the minute she heard that voice a shiver of ice went down Lisa's spine. "Anybody home?" He chuckled, and then the footsteps grew closer.

Tim Murray stood in the living room looking into the bedroom. Flanking him were two other men, one in his early forties with thinning, dirty-blond hair, bearing lighting and video-recording equipment. The second man was tall, wearing black leather pants, and a black leather vest over his bare chest.

His head was completely covered with a black bondage mask, holes cut over the eyes, nostrils, and mouth.

For a moment they stared at each other. "That one's the one I picked up outside Ventura," Tim Murray told the man with the camera. He pointed to Debbie. "And that's the one that brought her nosy ass in yesterday, the one I told you about last night."

The guy with the thinning blond hair nodded. "What do you think, Animal?"

Animal stood there and stared at them. His breathing

was harsh and heavy. He was staring at Debbie; he raised a finger and pointed. "Debbie," he said.

Debbie screamed.

It was done quickly. Tim grabbed Lisa and gagged her quickly, trussing her up even tighter and throwing her in the corner. Lisa watched with numb fear as Debbie was overpowered by Animal and the blond guy. The blond guy gave her some kind of injection in her arm and Debbie quieted down, her eyes growing droopy. Lisa's heart beat a mile a minute; it was beating so hard it felt like it was going to burst out of her rib cage.

After that it was simple. The mattress was moved aside so Tim could lay down some plastic tarp on the floor. The blond guy joined him in nailing the tarp up along the walls, and then the bed was moved back into place. Tim helped the blond man with two sets of lights, got them set up, and then they went to work.

She tried not to watch, tried to drown out the sounds of what was going on, but she felt drawn to the scene as it was being filmed. It was strangely mesmerizing and soul-destroying.

The blond man filmed Debbie Martinez being raped by the man in the black bondage hood as he held a knife to her throat. Lisa would realize later that the reason Debbie didn't cry out louder was that she was doped up with something that left her conscious but incapacitated.

As the assault continued, Lisa had feigned unconsciousness for what felt like hours. When the man in the hood was finished raping Debbie, he turned her over and did something to her that seemed to shatter the effects of the drug. Lisa had never heard anybody scream in pain the way Debbie screamed. The screaming went on for a while and was punctuated by wet slapping sounds. When Debbie began to vomit, the hooded man left the room and the blond man stopped filming and the three of them left. They returned some time later—thirty minutes? An hour? Two hours?—and resumed the rape and torture session. All of their attention was riveted on Debbie Martinez; they seemed to have totally forgotten that Lisa Miller was even there.

They hardly spoke at all during the ordeal. The few times words were spoken was the blond man instructing the man in the hood—Animal—to perform various sex acts on Debbie or hurt her in some way—bite her tits, cut her with that knife, burn her with that cigarette, fist-fuck her ass, strangle her just short of passing out then let her breathe—whatever. Tim said nothing during the ordeal; his sweaty features were riveted to the scene, his breathing harsh and panting.

Only once did Animal speak. He told Debbie that he had been wanting to "fucking torture her ass and stick it to her" for a long time now. Ever since he had laid eyes on her.

Somehow, Lisa managed to suffer through the ordeal of listening to Debbie Martinez being brutalized while she cowered in the corner, trying to drown out what was happening. For the first time since her ordeal, the thought of the fetus in her womb didn't come up. *It's never going to be,* she had thought, her heart heavy with sadness. *Brad and I aren't going to have our baby, we'll never get the chance to make a baby again, because when they're finished with Debbie they're going to do the same to me.*

Lisa didn't know if Debbie was dead or alive until the three men left. She heard them packing the camera and lighting gear up, and she heard the blond guy ask, "Is it okay if we leave that one here until tomorrow or the next day?"

Tim answered: "Yeah, she'll be fine. I left some food for her."

Then they left.

Lisa waited until the sound of the engine had receded down the dirt driveway, and then she got up and went to check on Debbie.

Debbie was unconscious; her face was horribly bruised and swollen. Her nose was crushed, flattened against her face amid a gout of gore; her bottom lip was split by a great gash that would scar badly even if it was treated correctly. A great amount of blood had spurted from her nose and drenched her face and upper body, mixing with the blood from the other wounds Animal had ravaged on her. Carved into her belly were the words SLUT and CUNT. The blood had clotted, making the words one jumbled mass. Lisa had put a hand to her face to stifle a cry, but had been unable to. The tears sprang fresh and unbidden from some untapped well deep within her. She knelt down beside Debbie's tortured body and cried.

Debbie was alive at least, but it was hard to make out the damage. From what Lisa could tell, there were the wounds to her face and stomach, as well as further cuts to her breasts, back, and thighs; most of the cuts needed stitches. She had numerous bite marks on her body, some bad enough to pierce the skin and draw blood, and it looked like her left nipple was almost chewed off. Her vagina was swollen, bruised, and bleeding; her anus was dilated horribly and was bleeding steadily, clotted with feces. The mattress was drenched with blood, vomit, saliva, feces, piss, and semen. Probably the most damaging wounds were those that Debbie would suffer in her mind. Lisa tended to Debbie's wounds in a daze, knowing that she needed professional medical attention. Somehow she cleaned Debbie up as best she could and stopped the bleeding.

When Debbie came back to consciousness later that night, she screamed so shrilly it chilled Lisa to the bone.

By sunrise this morning, Monday, Debbie was catatonic. She had lain on her back on the bed, her once beautiful brown eyes now reduced to a muddy, vacant stare as they gazed up at the cracked ceiling. Her lips were dry and chapped, and she didn't even try to wipe away the snot that pooled out of her nose. Animal's attack had shattered her; the next one would probably kill her.

Lisa had inspected herself in the bathroom mirror. Aside from the shocked expression on her face and the red in her eyes, she looked fine.

She hoped that taking it easy last night would calm the sick feeling in her stomach, and it did. This morning she felt better, and she was able to think more clearly. After cleaning Debbie's wounds with a towel and some warm water this morning, she had eaten one of the sandwiches and a banana, drank some water, then tried to get Debbie to eat something. The woman ignored the food, her eyes staring somewhere past her. Maybe later.

She had spent the next two hours in the living room, as far as the chain would allow her. She sat on the floor, her back against the wall, watching the sun rise higher in the sky. She checked on Debbie occasionally, and for a while briefly debated another escape plan. She looked at the nightstand and once again thought about whether to use it as a weapon the next time they came back. She had nothing to lose.

She sighed and looked at the food, which she had placed just outside the bedroom. They were down to one sandwich now and half a bag of chips. Lisa had eaten a sandwich for breakfast and had tried to get Debbie to eat something, but the woman wouldn't eat. She wondered how long Tim intended to keep her and Debbie prisoner here. The next time they came would probably be to film the completion of Debbie's torture and murder. Would they commence filming her own murder shortly after? Or would she get another short reprieve?

Lisa went into the bedroom and tried to get Debbie to eat again, but she still refused. Debbie Martinez was still in a dazed, catatonic state, her muddy brown eyes staring vacantly at the wall. Lisa checked her wounds, then went back to her spot outside the bedroom. She ate the rest of the potato chips and chased them with the rest of the water from her Evian bottle. They were down to five bottles of water now, enough to last a while, but not forever. It was the food she was more worried about now.

Just then, as if in answer to her concerns, the sound of a van pulled up in the driveway.

Twelve

They didn't venture immediately into the cabin.

Apparently, on the drive up a heated discussion had commenced.

"So what the fuck are we supposed to do with this Debbie bitch?" It sounded like the blond guy. "I mean, Animal went fucking nuts on her, so yeah, of course I'm gonna film the shit. That was the best shit I've gotten on film in a long time, and we can probably finish it today. What I want to know is what are you gonna do when the bitch is dead?"

"I'll get rid of her," Tim said. They were slowly walking up the walkway to the front door. "Don't worry. I found a new spot two weeks ago. We can get rid of her easy there. But we got to do it soon, like tonight. Neal hasn't cruised by yet, so as long as he don't come up, nobody will know."

Lisa listened, her heart pounding hard as she listened. Debbie moaned on the bed, raising gooseflesh along Lisa's arm. The men had stopped outside the front door, their voices lowering somewhat, but still audible. "What about this fucking place?" The blond guy was saying. "When you told me you had a new place, you didn't tell me it was in the center of where every fucking California yuppie flocks for their summer homes. What is this shit?"

"Nobody will know anything," Tim said, trying to calm the blond guy down. "Sam Bash made the arrangements. His name isn't attached to it at all, and neither is ours. Nobody will know anything. We'll just use the same tarp we rolled over the floor and roll both bodies into it when we're done and dump them. Then we got two films ready to go. That's some extra cash there."

"You sure Sam and his boys will be in the market for a second one?"

"You better fucking believe it. He told me himself that they were tired of all the fucked-up-looking junkies and whores I been getting them. Debbie's gonna really please them. And that other bitch? She may not be no fucking beauty queen like Debbie, but she's got a nice wholesome image, you know? They'll like that—that's what they asked for anyway."

Lisa shuddered at the conversation. She felt her limbs go numb. *It's going to be tonight,* she thought. *Oh God, not tonight, please help me get through this—*

"Fine," the blond guy said. Then the sound of the door opening rolled through the cabin and they stepped inside.

"I'm fucking starving," the blond man said as three pairs of booted feet stomped into the cabin. "All that arguing made me hungry. Animal, you hungry?"

A muffled, throaty "No."

"You?"

Tim: "Nah. I'm gonna go outside and take a walk around the grounds to make sure everything is cool. Why don't you go on ahead."

"Okay. I'll be right back." The blond man stomped back outside. A moment later she heard a car door open and close and then the sound of the engine starting.

Tim: "You want to come with me and check things out?"

"No." At the sound of Animal's voice, Lisa felt her skin tremble. His voice sounded so normal, so unassuming. "I think I'll stay here."

"Well, don't fuck with them," Tim said, walking to the door. "You want to fuck with them, wait until Al gets back so he can film it."

"Okay."

Tim left the cabin, and she heard his footsteps on the porch for a minute, then click down the front steps and around to the side of the house. A second set of footsteps slowly approached the bedroom, and Lisa felt her skin crawl as they grew closer, a large shadow materializing in the doorway, and then Animal was standing in the threshold of the room.

They stared at each other for a minute. Lisa couldn't tear her eyes away from him; her mouth went suddenly dry. She couldn't believe what she was seeing.

Standing before her was a tall, slim, nice-looking man in his mid-thirties. He was dressed in a clean pair of faded blue jeans and a green polo shirt. There was no trace of bondage apparatus anywhere on his person. Without his bondage hood, Animal could have passed for a young executive at a large corporation, or maybe a lawyer at the firm she worked at.

His features were angular, his jaw strong, his cheekbones sharp. He had mesmerizing green eyes that danced and complemented his smile, which was now cracking his boyish features. His mouth was fine, framed by sensuous lips, clean, even, white teeth. His hair was black and wavy, cut short and stylish. He looked like an All American Boy.

They looked at each other and for a moment Lisa was too stunned to say anything. *This is the man they call Animal. This is the man that almost killed Debbie yesterday. This is the man that is going to kill me either today or tomorrow in a snuff film.*

Her mind was reeling; she couldn't get over how *normal* he looked.

"Why?" The question came unbidden, her voice sounding strong to her for the first time in days.

Animal blinked; he seemed surprised by the question. *He's probably expecting me to beg for my life right now,* she thought.

"Why . . . what?" he asked, his lips curling upward slightly in a grin.

"Why do you do it?" She gestured at the room; the bloody tarp, the bed with the worn mattress, Debbie lying in a bloody stupor. "Why do you do this? Snuff movies . . . kill people . . . ?"

"Why do you want to know?"

Lisa looked at him, meeting his gaze. "As long as you're going to kill me, I think I would like to know the reason why before you do it."

For a moment, Lisa didn't think Animal was going to answer her. He looked at her in silence. Then he glanced behind him into the living room—the sound of Tim's footsteps had receded—and then took a step into the room. For the first time since laying eyes on him, Animal looked human—he looked like the kind of guy that she would pal around with at the office. "You really want to know?"

Lisa nodded, trying not to appear too desperate. "Yeah, I would."

Animal shrugged. "Guess it can't hurt." Then he stepped into the room and began to tell her how he acquired the taste for hurting and torturing other human beings.

"I used to work for a large, international consulting firm," Animal began. "It was through my employment there that I met a woman who I became involved with. She introduced me to the scene. Even then, to look at her you wouldn't have guessed she was into the painful arts. She looked like she could've been a cheerleader in high school. She was pretty and incredibly sexy. At work she had a bubbly personality—lively, free-spirited, fun to be with. But she was sharp. When it came to her work, she was a real professional.

"It started innocently enough. We became lovers. We had a good time, but I could sense that for her she was just going through the motions. At first I thought that perhaps she didn't want to get emotionally involved with me, that she only wanted me for a fuck toy or something. That was the furthest thing from my mind. I only wanted her for the sex. See . . ." He began pacing the floor, his brow furrowed in concentration as if he were trying to think of a way to express himself most clearly. "I was never much of a ladies' man. I'd always had an inferiority complex around women. I'd only lost my virginity two years before and I was pretty much racing to catch up, if you know what I mean."

Lisa nodded, accepting his confession but finding it hard to believe that a man as handsome as Animal would have lost his virginity well into his twenties. Physically, he was a hunk. But the more she watched him, the more she listened to his speech, the way he carried himself, the more she began to get the sense that he was something far different.

"Anyway," he said, stopping his pacing to look at her. "It was a sexual thing. It always was. And the more we got into it, the more she started . . . demanding certain things."

"What kind of things?"

"It started with biting," he said. "We were having sex one night and she begged me to bite her while we were fucking. I was so into it that I did, and she loved it. At first I thought I had hurt her . . . my teeth had actually broken the skin and drawn blood, but she'd been ecstatic. She actually *came*. It was like that night was the happiest day of her life. And it was then that I learned the first lesson in the painful arts." He took a step forward, regarding her as a teacher would a student. "Pain and pleasure are two sides of the same coin. Pain tolerance goes up during sexual arousal. The brain also produces endorphins during sex to compensate for pain. It gets you high. It's the same rush you get while eating chili peppers. It comes from that same center in the brain where pain and pleasure come from, and that's what makes it enjoyable for S&M players being whipped or spanked or whatever. It isn't pain to them. It's pleasure." He smiled.

Lisa felt a shudder run through her body, along with a slight stab of guilt. The mild bondage she and Brad had participated in—tying each other up, slipping into the role of the naughty girl and begging Brad to spank her—was nothing compared to this.

"That was the first step toward my initiation," Animal said, still smiling. "When I first saw her naked body, I was shocked. The skin along her back and her torso and breasts was like one big puckered scar. It was so bad she looked like a burn victim. I thought she had been in an accident. When I learned that they were self-inflicted or from others, I felt . . . a combination of revulsion and attraction. And the more we talked about it, the more she told me that she really enjoyed pain and being abused, the more I saw that she was serious. And seeing that she was serious, that she was willing to put herself through such scenes, turned me on."

"I don't understand," Lisa said, choosing her words carefully. "What does being a willing participant in an S&M scene have to do with what you're doing with me?"

"It has a lot to do with it, if you'll listen."

"I am listening."

"No, you're not." He was standing in front of her, menacing even in his Gucci loafers and polo shirt.

"Okay," she said, shifting gears. "Okay, I'm listening."

"You're just like all of them," Animal said, looking at her with a sneer of contempt. "All the whiny, pitiful little yuppie fucks who think they can be hip and cool by dressing in rubber and leather at underground fetish clubs at night and be corporate rats by day. You don't know shit. You don't know the first thing of what it's like to feel power over another human being."

"Then tell me!" Lisa said, trying not to sound too demanding.

Animal stepped forward, and at first Lisa thought he was going to strike her. Instead, he hunkered down so that he was looking at her eye to eye. "Let me give you a little bit of my background. I may look like a yuppie fuck to you, and maybe in a way I am. I came from a normal WASPish family. My mother was Miss Susie Homemaker; Daddy worked his nine-to-five like a good boy and came home every night to a home-cooked meal. Mommy and Daddy were also repressed shits who did their best to repress their children. All I heard from them was that sex was wrong, that it was only for procreation. Hearing that warped me, especially when I saw the exact opposite happening at home. My dad coming home drunk after having gone out with the boys from the office, getting fresh with my mom and her slapping him away, and then hearing them fighting over it. The fucking bitch wouldn't put out for my dad, and it pissed him off, you know? Then at the same time both of them are telling me that sex is wrong no matter what, even if it's between two people who love each other."

Lisa didn't know what to say. She met his gaze, not daring to drop it.

"Don't get me wrong," he said. "They never beat me, they never physically abused me in any way, but they did have their way with getting their message across. They were also both extremely domineering. I could only wear the clothes they wanted me to wear, have the kinds of friends they approved of, choose the kind of career path only they approved of. Anything I did on my own, from the people I chose to associate with, to jobs I've had, if they didn't like it they would let me know they were disappointed in me. It was beat into my head at an early age that disappointing my parents was something that was unacceptable with not only them, but to society at large. To disappoint those that had given birth to you, who had created you, was the worst thing a child could do to their parents. For them to be disappointed in me created such a feeling of guilt. And when it came to sex, it was hardwired in me to not disappoint them in that area. Could you image what it would have been like if I had gotten a girl pregnant? My God, they'd go off the deep end and I couldn't live with myself! It was that fear of disappointing my parents, of getting a girl pregnant, that kept me from indulging in whatever normal sexual feelings I had." He snorted back a laugh. "As you could probably imagine, I jerked off a lot through high school."

Lisa didn't laugh; it really wasn't funny to her. If anything, it scared her.

"I never felt in control of anything in my life," he resumed, standing up. He turned around and began pacing the room as he talked. "I let all this frustration bottle up inside me, and it wasn't until I began my relationship with Susan that I realized I could let them out. I was with somebody who was encouraging me to act on my fantasies. She didn't disapprove. In fact, the more I told her about them, the happier she got. They were fantasies I wanted to indulge in for real."

"What were they?"

"I thought you'd never ask," he replied. He turned to her, counting them off on his fingers. "Let's see . . . dominating every single woman or girl that had ever turned me on in high school or college or in the few years after obtaining my MBA. Sometimes I had fantasies about doing similar things to men, but men don't excite me sexually the way women do; the only way I get turned on by homoerotic thoughts is if I'm torturing another man."

Torturing another man. Obviously torturing women, too. Lisa licked her lips and swallowed, her throat dry, and nodded.

Animal continued. "I tried to deny I was having these thoughts. I thought I could never act on them—normal people don't give in to such urges, much less have them. So for ten years I would occasionally think about what it would be like to strangle the head cheerleader of the high school football team, or castrate the homecoming king and stuff his cock down his throat, or cut my secretary's fingers off with a paring knife and force-feed them to her. And then I would deny that such thoughts excited me. I didn't realize that inflicting pain on these people would be like music to my ears.

"Obviously, when Susan found this out our sex life become more intense. She encouraged me to get rougher with her, to hurt her. She enjoyed being tied up and whipped. She enjoyed having her ass slapped with a leather belt until I drew blood. She was with me the whole way, and I knew that as long as she was there I could do it. I knew I was safe with her, that our secret would only be between us. I later learned that this is what true S&M is: It is the complete surrender and trusting of your body and emotions to another person. I no longer saw it as something deviant practiced by perverts. Of course, what I'm going to describe to you . . . if a regular S&M practitioner were to hear this they'd be horrified. Basically, the entire extreme hardcore scene is a very brutal, very underground subculture that lurks within the S&M world. Most S&M participants are either ignorant of the more forbidden aspects of the extreme hardcore world or they don't want to admit it exists. But it's there. The more you get into S&M, the more you get into a local scene in a big city like New York or LA, the more you dig into its various subcultures, you'll soon start finding some people that are into some pretty extreme shit."

He paused, his features appeared reflective, then he continued. "In a way, I guess we loved each other. We were the perfect partners for each other. We were friends and lovers in the extreme sense. Our sex life accelerated into something I had never experienced before and never knew existed. Previously, I was merely content to play my part in a wham-bam-thank-you-ma'am role. I suppose most guys are. With Susan, I was becoming more confident in myself in dealing with my fantasies; she encouraged me to act on them. Our sessions accelerated rapidly until we were getting into some heavy stuff, things I wouldn't have even imagined participating in. She demanded that I hit her harder, bite her harder, whip her harder. And I complied. The harder our sessions became, the more I would feel that I shouldn't be doing this, that what I was doing was wrong, but then Susan would encourage me." He looked at her. "And the more she pulled me in, the more I found myself liking what I was doing to her."

Lisa looked into his eyes, and what he said next made the skin along the back of her neck erupt in gooseflesh. "We began having regular intercourse less and less. It never really did much for me anyway." He stepped closer to her. "But what we did together? Me playing the sadist to Susan's masochistic fantasies? That's what got me off. It's what *still* gets me off."

Lisa swallowed, and tried not to look away as Animal stared at her. His gaze was penetrating, cunning, predatory. She forced herself to meet it head-on, even as she fought to control her rising fear.

"She introduced me to the underground extreme hardcore scene," Animal continued, not breaking his gaze from hers. "It was at such functions, usually held in private homes, where she told me she often had to go to be completely satisfied sexually. I was a little nervous at my first party, but that didn't last long. As soon as I saw that there were others who shared my fetish, I relaxed around them. Susan introduced me to an underground hardcore porn filmmaker named Alex Pressman—he's the guy that filmed yesterday—who sometimes filmed the parties for private video collections. He asked us that first night if he could film Susan and me in a scene, and . . . well . . . I suppose he recognized talent when he saw it." He grinned.

Lisa could only imagine what it must have been like . . . Animal abusing his consenting girlfriend, getting off on it, Alex filming it, recognizing something in Animal that he could use . . .

Animal continued the narrative, shattering the image

in her mind, replacing it with something more gruesome. "Her first earth-shattering orgasm with me was when she introduced me to blood sports. We were at her place one night, and she opened a slim mahogany case that was lined with red crushed velvet and showed me a scalpel. She told me exactly what to do, coached me exactly how to cut through the top layer of skin on her lower back. First I tied her up, then I inserted a ball gag in her mouth. I flogged her back and she got wet instantly even as she bled. Then she cried out for me to cut her. I drew the blade across her back and finger-fucked her. She had the most earth-shattering orgasm I'd ever seen anybody have before. She actually cried afterward, and at first I thought I'd really hurt her. I actually *apologized* to her! Can you imagine that?

"Of course, I didn't have to apologize for anything. She wasn't crying because I had hurt her . . . she was crying out of sheer joy! Sheer ecstasy! And even better, what we'd done together had really turned me on more than I ever imagined! I actually *came!* It was the first time I had come without having my dick stroked or sucked or stimulated by a clenching pussy."

Animal began pacing the room again, and Lisa watched him, hands tied behind her back, legs lashed together, sitting on the bare mattress in the shabby little room. She took in what Animal was telling her, and she supposed if she hadn't been in the position she was in now, that if this were a scene in a movie and she were watching it, she'd turn the TV off, unable to watch any more. Not able to listen to the atrocities this man was claiming to take part in. But now she listened intently, part of her deeply afraid, another part of her searching for a way to escape, to find a way out of her predicament.

"That cut on her back was the first I put on her, but it wouldn't be the last," Animal continued. "Susan told me later that she had been into the pleasures of pain for as long as she could remember. Her family background was similar to mine. Her parents didn't abuse her, Daddy never tried to have his way with her, she never had abusive boyfriends. She just liked pain. She told me about the people she met at the underground parties like the one she took me to. That they were just feeding off of each other, like they were willingly carrying out this symbiotic relationship. She had to get what she needed from the more hardcore freaks, though, the people that were into mutilation. The more she played out scenes with them, the more hardcore it got for her. She showed me this huge scar that ran from her belly to just below her breasts; it was from a burn. She told me that most people who are into heat playing won't burn the skin due to the medical consequences, but she wasn't getting anything out of a simple first-degree burn. She said she had to actually scream at her partner to hold the flame to her skin until she orgasmed." Animal smiled. "Aside from the night I first cut her, that had been her most intense sexual experience."

Lisa thought about some of the S&M imagery she had seen in the kind of magazines one found among the fetish racks at newsstands; images of men and women in skintight black leather or rubber clothing, their faces and heads covered in black leather masks, only their eyes and nostrils exposed slightly, a small opening along the mouth with a zipper to allow for closure; half-naked people in leather and chains and bondage harnesses; women tied up to racks with ball gags in their mouths, their eyes wide open and pleading, *No don't, please don't hurt me,* but at the same time saying, *Yes, do it to me, do it to me doittome—*

Use me, hurt me, abuse me. Do whatever you want with me.

"I thought about the people I had met at the underground parties we attended." Animal stopped pacing; he stood by the boarded-up window, peeking outside between the nailed up two-by-fours and strips of plywood. "I thought about the scenes I had seen them play out. I remember watching a man in a black leather hood draw blood from his slave with a syringe and then feed it to her. I fantasized about being him at that moment, wielding such incredible power over this person. I remember watching a gay couple, the dom cutting his slave with a scalpel and then sucking the blood from the wound as his partner writhed in pleasure, and I wondered what the blood tasted like. I got hard watching all these scenes being played out before me. I thought about the extreme hardcore films that were screened at these parties, watching women and men scream in pain as their doms pulled at pierced labias and scrotums, stretching the fragile skin to the point that it began to bleed and they began begging for mercy. I imagined myself doing that to those people, and the more I thought about it the more excited I became. I thought about the first snuff film I saw at the last party Susan and I attended, in which a young black girl who looked like a homeless junkie was fucked to death with a baseball bat in an abandoned warehouse. I remember watching it with bated breath—I don't think anybody breathed while we were watching that thing. I couldn't take my eyes off the screen. All I could do was imagine myself doing what her killer was doing, working the fat end of the baseball bat in and out of her as she screamed in pain and died."

Animal turned to her, and Lisa felt her stomach crumble into crushed ice. There was no sense of guilt or sorrow in his face over what he had witnessed, no sense of horror at watching other human beings being tortured and abused, thrown away like trash. She didn't know what to say—how does one respond to somebody who relates such things as pleasurable, who now has your life in their hands?

"Do you understand what I'm telling you? When I cut her skin and she screamed in a mixture of pain and pleasure, it made me *feel* good. When I branded my name into her flesh with a piece of hot metal and she passed out from the intensity of the orgasm, I felt an extreme sense of *power.* I'd never had power over anything in my life before, and with her giving me blanket permission to indulge in her freely, knowing it pleased her so much, gave me a sense of empowerment I never thought I would have. Susan changed me, and at the same time what we did during the last month of our relationship was to spell the end of it as well."

He stopped, turned toward the boarded-up window as if he was looking outside. Lisa waited, heart thumping in her chest, her stomach churning in grave anticipation to what was coming next.

"She finally told me what her ultimate fantasy was," he whispered. "She told me because she could tell that I was ready to hear it, and she felt that I was the only man who could give it to her. She could tell I was ready. When she told me . . ." He paused, as if trying to search for the right words to continue. ". . . at first I didn't want to do it. I thought we . . . that she . . . was going too far. She tried to convince me that it was okay, that it was what she really wanted, and I got angry. I got dressed and she chased after me in the apartment, pleading for me to stay. What she was asking . . . I never thought I could do it, especially to her. I thought if I went through it that it would be over for me, that I would no longer have an outlet for my pleasure."

Lisa couldn't take it anymore. "What did she want you to do?"

Animal turned toward her, his features pensive, reflective. "She wanted to be tortured and killed in a snuff film," he said, the words rolling off his tongue as nonchalantly as if he were telling her about a family get-together or a weekend golf game. "She wanted me to be the one to do it to her, to share with her what was to be her ultimate pleasure. . . . her greatest orgasm ever, achieved at the instant of death. Eros and Thanatos, sex and death. And she wanted it captured on videotape so that her greatest pleasure would live on."

The crushed-ice feeling in Lisa's stomach churned. She could tell from Animal's tone of voice, from the look in his eyes, that the story was true.

"I wouldn't do it," he said, walking back to her casually. "In a way, I suppose you could say I was afraid to cross that line. But then I did some thinking. I did love Susan, in a way most people don't seem to understand that word. And I realized that turning her down had hurt her in a way most people would never imagine. Knowing I had turned her down, rejected her, hurt me. Yes, I didn't want to lose her, but I realized the only reason why I didn't want to lose her was because she brought me so much joy, so much pleasure when I ravaged and mutilated her. I'd have no outlet for this again—at least that was my thought. But then I realized that perhaps introducing me to the scene was her way of showing me that there were others out there like us. She had opened up a whole new world for me. Yes, there were more like her. And if I liked what I did to her for her final pleasure, there were more outlets for me to . . . indulge in, shall we say." He grinned. "After all . . . that snuff film I saw had to have come from somewhere, right? I made a call to Alex Pressman first and casually asked him where he had gotten it. He wouldn't tell me, and I don't blame him. When I asked if there was any way for me to appear in his next production, his voice changed. He became excited. He told me he could always use people like me.

"That decided it for me. I knew of a place in Orange County, a mental facility that had been abandoned for years. I did some discreet investigating and got a very detailed map of the hospital. I also did some more checking, found out when security was more apt to be absent, which was most of the time. Then I called Alex back and offered him a job. When I told him what it was, he agreed immediately, especially when I named my price. We settled on a date, and I gathered together some tools, then called Susan and told her to meet me at such and such a time, at such and such a place for her birthday present. I think she could tell by the tone of my voice what I had in store, and she showed up like I knew she would." Animal smiled, the memory of the incident replaying in his features. "When she saw me in that large run-down room in a dilapidated wing of what had once been a mental hospital, she smiled. I was wearing a pair of black leather chaps, my ass exposed to the wind. I wore a black leather vest over my shirtless body, a black leather bondage hood over my head. There was an old mattress placed in the center of the room, laid out on top of a large roll of plastic tarp. I had set up a table with knives. Alex was waiting with his camera and lights. And when she saw us standing there, she smiled. And she thanked me."

Lisa looked up at Animal. "You killed her."

"Yes." Animal looked triumphant; proud. "I still have that tape. Her final, most pleasurable orgasm ever. I paid Alex ten thousand dollars for his work and his secrecy. I take the tape out every once in a while and watch Susan and me play out our scene. And the more her screams of pain echo in my ears, the more I realize that she was responsible for my breakthrough. Without her I would have lived in torment. Now? I live for nothing else but fulfilling my desires. I still have my job, though not with the same company. It's mostly to maintain a front for sheep like you, society at large. Susan's life had been similar. After we disposed of her body, I went to her apartment and found her letter of resignation on her computer and knew that she had prepared it in the hopes that her fantasy would someday come true. I printed it, dated it, forged her signature on it, and mailed it to corporate headquarters. Then I took care of her things. To everybody at the office, she had just suddenly quit for no reason and moved to the Midwest. To her parents, she moved and left no forwarding address. In a way, wiping out her existence was great preparation for what we're going to do with you." He grinned.

Lisa forced herself not to look scared, wondering if Susan's parents still missed her. Or did they even care?

"As for me," Animal said, shrugging his shoulders and walking toward the doorway that led to the rest of the cabin. "I became hooked. Alex saw that I had the kind of potential that he and his clients needed. Finding somebody like me in our circle is always hard; the majority of people in the S&M scene are what you would think of as good, decent people. Everybody consents to what they do. But the extreme hardcore scene? It's run by ruthless people who don't give a shit about anything except money and getting their dicks sucked every now and then. They don't know the meaning of the word *consensual*. Finding people like me to appear in extreme hardcore films and snuff films, that's even tougher. Nobody wants to get caught, for one thing. That's why it's so closed, so insular. I assured Alex that as long as we kept things within the circle, we were safe. Six months later, they received another job. Somebody in Virginia commissioned a film, something basic. Alex tapped into his contact, whom you've already met in the form of Tim, and he gave us a sixteen-year-old runaway. She was perfect; a heroin addict from a broken home. Nobody would miss her. The woman that commissioned the film paid a nice fee for it."

"Woman?" Lisa felt her stomach sink.

"Oh yes," Animal said casually. "It's not just men that get off on watching the suffering of other human beings, although they do outnumber the women. Females get off on it, too. Ever been to a boxing match? The audience for boxing is primarily made up of men. Most of the women in attendance are there because their boyfriends or husbands are into it, but there is a sizable portion who are into it as much as their male counterparts. They get off on the violence and bloodlust in the same way. Of course, the analogy between a so-called civilized and legal sport and the snuff underground is extreme, but in a way the same rules apply.

"Anyway, where was I? Oh yes! The first snuff film I did after Susan. Tim brought us a worthless piece of shit that had run away from her foster home. She was a prostitute, a junkie. Tim's good at finding talent from the ranks of losers like that. He has contacts all over the country that give him insights on the background of some of these people. That first one was a local girl . . . or I should say, she had run away from home somewhere in the Midwest and come out to sunny California, Hollywood to be exact. She got hooked up with the wrong crowd, started doing drugs, started walking the streets, and the rest is history. Tim had hired her for some bondage sessions with one of his private clients to get her initiated; he does that to let them think that when they come on my set they're going to be in just some regular porn film. If they're already junkies, he lets them get high on the set so they don't resist when we tie them up, and they're almost always junkie fuckups. He brought her to the location I had done Susan in, and I let loose on her as she came off her binge. I raped that bitch until she was bleeding out of orifices you wouldn't even think of. I kept her alive for a full hour before she finally expired." He laughed. "It's only gotten better since then. Now, thanks to Alex and Tim and our contacts among the more financially secure in the circle, people who live all over the world, I'm in big demand. I make good money doing this. And I get immense sexual satisfaction from doing what I do. I also get something else." He stepped forward, his grin wide, evil. "I get a strange sense of . . . *power.*"

Thirteen

When Animal was finished Lisa was too stunned to say anything. She could feel Animal's stare, like that of a hungry beast, and she immediately met his gaze and asked the first question that popped into her mind. "How many snuff films have you been in since then?"

Animal shrugged. "I don't know . . . over the last five years I'd say eighteen or so, as well as numerous extreme hardcore films."

Eighteen or so snuff films. Eighteen or so bodies. Used and discarded like trash.

"I still don't understand why you do it," Lisa said, Animal's story pulsing in her brain. "You told me how you got into it, but . . . I still don't understand."

"I do it because I like it," Animal said, and the simplicity of his answer chilled her to the bone. "I get extreme pleasure from inflicting pain on other people."

"Pleasure . . ." Lisa was looking at him, trying to understand. "Sexual pleasure? What, do you come? Does your dick get hard? Is it like sex? What is it?"

Animal shrugged. "I haven't had normal sex in five years. What I do here . . ." He gestured at Debbie's prone, bloodied form on the bed. "It's the most ultimate pleasure I've ever felt. That's the only way I can describe it. When I . . . when I don the mask and wield the knife, I feel like a god. I get to choose whether they live or die. They cower at my feet, they beg me for mercy. I completely rule them. I have power over their lives . . . their death. It . . . fuels my fantasy and then . . . then I can go to work on them." He looked so calm explaining this to her. "Then when I cut them with a knife . . . it's like ecstasy. Feeling the blade slice through their flesh, hearing them scream as I cut them, seeing the expression on their faces as the knife slices through . . . it . . . it's even *better* than sex."

The sound of footsteps returning from the side of the cabin interrupted her thoughts, and Animal turned toward it. Lisa's breath was shallow, her mind racing. Al and Tim were coming back; she could hear them talking. Then they would finish what was started yesterday and then it would be her turn. Her turn at a starring role in the grindhouse of death.

"Debbie and I are the first, then," Lisa said, the question coming unbidden. "We're the first people who aren't junkies or homeless people. Right?"

Animal nodded as he stood up to his full height. "Yeah."

Lisa's mind was racing. Tim and Al entered the house, and as they crossed the living room into the bedroom the idea sprang to Lisa's mind full-blown; she was desperate. "Listen," she said, looking up at Tim. "Please let me go. If you let me go, I can get you somebody that could take my place—"

Tim traded glances with Al and laughed. "Who you kidding, lady?"

"Please, just listen to me! Before Brad and I stopped at that rest stop, we stopped for breakfast in North Hollywood. There was a woman there that we gave money to. She had just been kicked out of her home and—"

"They ain't looking for homeless chicks," Tim said, scowling. "I thought I told you that yesterday? That's why I was scoping that rest area out. The group we're shooting this film for, they were gettin' tired of the same kind of chicks. That's why—"

"But this one's *different!*" Lisa said, her nerves on edge. "She's only been on the streets a few days and she's *gorgeous!* She's—"

"Forget it," Tim said, dismissing her with a wave of his hand. "I don't give a shit if this chick's a supermodel. I ain't—"

"But she's *beautiful!* She's a . . . a *professional*, and she's *intelligent*. She's really pretty, she's not a drug addict or a prostitute and she'd fit perfect!" Lisa glanced back and forth from Animal to Tim. "*Please* . . . I'll even help you find her. I know where she is and—"

Al and Animal laughed. Tim chuckled, shaking his head. "You're a riot, lady. Why the fuck should I go out and risk my neck in getting this other bitch? I already got *you*. For all I know, this chick is probably just another whore like all the other ones, or she doesn't even exist."

"I'll pay you!" The adrenaline was flowing through her veins, making her feel light-headed. She could feel the clock ticking on her and her unborn baby's life. "I'm a lawyer—I was just made a partner in my firm. I can give

you whatever these clients of yours are paying you. I can get you the money immediately!"

Al looked intrigued. He looked at Tim. "Money talks, Tim."

Tim stroked his chin nervously.

Al turned to Lisa. "You can match it, huh? You sure?"

"Yes," Lisa said, her heart thumping. "I can not only match it, I can find the woman for you. Please, just take me down there with you and I promise you that—"

"You can come up with ninety grand cash?" Al cocked a questioning glance at her. "You got that kind of money?"

"*Yes!*" She and Jeff had around sixty thousand in their joint savings account, and another sixty grand or so in their IRAs. She was fairly certain she could cash out her IRA quickly if she hit her bank at the right time. She also had her wedding ring—there was five grand right there. "I can get it," she said, straightening herself up. "Hard cash."

The three of them were glancing at each other, and as Lisa watched the exchange she realized she'd struck a nerve with them. She'd hit the gold mine. With the exception of Animal, the only reason they were engaged in this was for the money. Hadn't Tim told her that over and over again on the drive up after her abduction?

"I don't know," Tim said shaking his head. "I can sure use the extra money, but . . . I got a product to deliver in three days."

"I can help you get her by the end of the day," Lisa said, desperate now. "If we leave now, we can be in LA by two or three, and I can have the money to you by four. Please, I'll do all that and—"

"And lead the cops right to us," Tim said, angrily. "No fucking way."

"N-no," Lisa said, her voice cracking. "No police. I swear to *God*, I won't tell anybody."

"What about your husband?" Al said, an irritated grimace on his face. "He's gonna call the cops, you know they're gonna be involved anyway."

"I won't say *anything*!" She said, pleading now. "*Please* . . . I don't know your names, I don't know what you look like, I've never seen you before in my life. You're four black men, but you may have been Hispanic or Samoan or something. I don't know, it was too dark and I couldn't see, and you had me blindfolded and you knocked me out and . . . *please, I won't say anything!*"

Al looked at her for what seemed an eternity. He turned to Tim and shrugged. "I can sure use the money, Tim."

"No, man," Tim said, shaking his head. "I don't like it. I mean, I got orders—"

"Fuck that shit," Al said, turning to Tim. "You telling me you'd be willing to throw another ninety grand down the toilet? You shittin' me?"

Animal had been standing in the corner during the exchange, fists clenched at his sides. He was silent as Tim shook his head. "I don't know, man, I don't like it. I mean, I did my part, but . . ."

Al turned to Animal. "What about you, Animal?"

"The money would be nice," Animal said, his features suddenly darker than they had been when he'd just seemed like another young professional. "But the itch is gettin' strong. Frankly, I could tear into this bitch right now if you let me. I don't give a shit who I do. Long as I get mine."

Al turned to Lisa. "Well, that settles it for me. Animal's ready, and we already got you and the other bitch. I say we just do them both tonight and—"

Before Lisa could stop herself, she let it blurt out. "The other woman has a baby!" They stopped and turned toward her. The atmosphere in the room got heavier, as if cold water had just been dumped on everything, setting the flames to sizzle and steam. Lisa could feel the blood pounding in her veins. "She has a baby girl," she heard herself, instantly hating herself for saying it. "Probably not even a month old. You can have her, too. Please . . ."

The three men were silent. Animal's breathing grew heavier. Al shrugged at Tim. "Well . . . Animal's always wanted to do a baby. It might be . . ." He shrugged, a mixture of unease and anticipation on his features. "Hold on a sec." He pulled a cellular phone out of his jeans pocket and stepped outside, dialing a number. Lisa watched him leave with a growing sense of dread.

Oh God, what did I just do!

Tim and Animal stood in the corner of the room, regarding her with cold stares. Lisa couldn't look at them, the dread solidifying in her belly. She drew into herself, head down, trying to staunch the flow of tears that threatened to burst forth. *Oh my God, what did I just do? I just . . . I just . . .*

I just want to have my baby! Please let me have my baby!

She didn't know how long Al was gone, but it felt like an eternity. When he came back she refused to look up, not knowing if she would be able to look into his face. "We're on with the other chick and the baby. Get this bitch in the van and find them pronto."

Lisa looked up, the surprise of the verdict stunning. Al had a satisfied look on his face. Tim looked stunned; Animal looked excited. "You sure?" Tim asked Al.

"Sam just said they'll pay double if we have a baby in it." Al folded the cell phone up and replaced it in his pocket. "Let's get going though. Get rid of this bitch and find this other chick and the kid."

"Did you tell him about this one?" Tim asked, motioning to Lisa.

"No." Al turned to Lisa, his eyes cold. "This woman . . .

you said she's only been homeless a few days, right? What's she look like?"

Lisa fumbled for the right description. She felt numb with shock. She couldn't believe this was happening. "Sh-she's about six inches taller than me. B-blond hair . . . shoulder length . . . real pretty. N-nice body . . . n-nice l-le-legs . . ."

"Fine." Al leaned close to her, his face dark. "If you don't find this chick and her baby, Tim will bring you back here, and then we're going to film you getting fucked to death, and I can guarantee you that Animal will make it the most vicious, most painful fuck you have ever had in your life. Do you understand me? He'll put a hole in your belly and fuck the wound while you're still alive. We don't call him the Animal for nothing, you know what I'm saying? That's why he's in such demand for our little group. We've used other doms, but Animal's special. He'll cut your fingers off and make you eat them if he wants to. He'll keep you alive for the next week if he wants to. Shit, he'd pop your left eyeball out and fuck the socket while you're still alive if he could. He's never been that lucky, though. Usually, they die the minute Animal sticks his dick in the eye socket."

Lisa was sobbing, the images washing over her, turning her stomach. Al leaned closer to her, his breath sour. "And if this is a scam, or if you don't find this chick and the baby, your ass is going to be tortured so bad that you're going to *wish* you just opted for the quick way out. You got me?"

Lisa nodded, tears silently spilling down her cheeks. She was shaking, paralyzed with fear.

"You find the chick and the baby, Tim will take care of everything," Al continued. "You find them, and once he's got them, he'll take you to your bank and you'll both go in and get the money. You won't try anything in there, you got it? If Tim ain't back up here by nine o'clock this evening . . ." He reached for her purse, which had been sitting in the corner since being dumped in the room, and rummaged through it. He extracted her wallet, took her driver's license out, then rifled through it until he found some photos. He found the one he wanted and took it out. He held it up for her to see: It was Brad. "I take that back. If I don't hear from Tim by five o'clock on my cell phone, I'm going to pay your hubby a visit myself. And then maybe we'll take him somewhere nice and safe and film ourselves a homosexual snuff film. Animal, he has no fucking sexual preference, so long as he mutilates and tortures people. Don't you, Animal?"

Animal nodded and grinned. "I've done men before. They can be fun, too."

Al turned back to Lisa. "After you've given Tim the money, we don't want to so much as be reminded of you. You got me? And if I so much as get pulled over by a cop for a traffic ticket, I will find you, got me? If you say *anything* to the cops about this and they come looking for us, I'll know where to find you." He held her license up, grinning. "Tim tells me you told him you were expecting a kid yourself? That true?"

Trembling, Lisa nodded slowly, trying to control her crying.

"I'll keep tabs on you," Al said, his grin wicked. "And if the cops come nosing around, I'll know where to find you. And I'll wait until you're well along in your pregnancy. I'm sure the guys in the group will love to watch a flick of a pregnant bitch getting it." He grinned sickly.

Lisa was unable to control herself now. She felt weak from the terror of her ordeal and she felt nauseated, but she also felt as if a huge burden was being lifted from her shoulders, as if she had just been given a reprieve. *My baby gets to live, my baby gets to live!*

"And if I don't get you then, I'll get you later, after you've popped the kid," Al said. "Then we'll make ourselves a nice little sequel to the film we'll hopefully be making tomorrow." He tipped his head back and laughed, and then the tears came fresh, bursting out of her.

Please don't hurt my baby, she almost said, but held it in. Instead, she nodded and said, "I won't tell anybody. I promise."

If he understood her through her sobs, Al gave no indication. He nodded to Tim. "I'm sending Animal with you." To Animal: "Tie this bitch up and get her in the van."

Animal stepped up to Lisa, his grin wide, and Lisa felt herself go limp. She didn't put up any resistance as Animal gagged and blindfolded her. The last thing she saw before she was blindfolded was Al talking in low tones to Animal as the young sadist nodded seriously. Then, with Tim's help, she was carried outside to the van.

Fourteen

Tim delivered the news to her five minutes into the ride to Los Angeles. "We're going by your bank first to get the money. Where is it?"

She felt a stinging burn as the duct tape that had been slapped over her face was ripped off, removing small facial hairs and an upper layer of skin. Her blindfold had been removed a moment before, and now she sat propped against the side panel, blinking up at Animal as he hovered over her, his green eyes predatory and cold.

She stole a quick glance at the front of the van where Tim was driving; he met her gaze from the rearview mirror.

"Well?"

"Bank of America, Huntington Beach branch." She gave them the nearest cross street. "It's right off the 405."

"It's off Beach Boulevard, you said?"

Lisa nodded. "Yeah."

"I can get to Beach from the 22," Tim said, turning his attention back to the road in front of him. "That goes right through Little Saigon."

"Where's the homeless chick and the baby?" Animal asked, and hearing him ask this sent a shiver of ice down her spine.

"North Hollywood," Lisa said, the feeling of dread rising in her again. "Off Burbank Boulevard. There was an IKEA right off the exit."

"I know where that is," Tim said.

They were silent for a while as Tim meandered down winding, twisty mountain roads. Animal sat across from her, sizing her up occasionally, mostly looking out the windshield. Lisa tried to ignore him as they headed down the mountain, but it was hard to do. Every time his eyes lighted on her, she felt like a mouse being sized up as a potential meal for a snake; it was a cold, impersonal feeling. It made her want to draw into herself more.

Once they reached the main highway that would take them to Interstate 10, Animal moved to the front seat. Lisa slumped back against the side panel and almost let out a sob.

Omigodwhyisthishappening!

She cried silently, the tears squeezing out of her eyes to roll down her cheeks. She didn't care if Tim or the Animal heard her or not. They would probably think she was crying out of fear anyway, but she wasn't. She was crying out of shame.

What have I done?

Well, let's see, Lisa. In order to save your own hide and your's and Brad's unborn child, you willingly turned this trio of murderous psychopaths on to a woman you not only don't know, but you also told them they could rape, torture, and murder her infant daughter. Gee, that's a really nice thing to do to somebody, don't you think?

What else could I do? They were going to kill me? They were going to kill me knowing *I'm pregnant?*

Yeah, and in the process, you've managed to sell a woman you don't even know and a baby to them. Your own baby isn't even born *yet and Mandy's, what, a month? Two months old maybe? And Alicia? What about her? You'll be helping kill two people here, Lisa.*

But they were going to kill my baby! They were going to—

Can the save your baby crap. You just want to save your own skin. Isn't that right?

No! That's not true! That's—

Bullshit! Why else would you do what you just did? Oh please don't torture me to death in a snuff film! I don't want to die! I know somebody else you can kill instead. And while you're at it, you can have her baby, too! Just don't kill *me*.

And as the tears spilled down her cheeks, she realized that the part of her that was telling her this was right.

And that only made her feel more ashamed and disgusted with herself.

Tim's voice cut through the din of her sobs. "Shut your fucking trap back there!"

She hitched in a breath at the bark of Tim's command and tried to hold back the sob that threatened to spill forth. *Don't fall apart now,* she thought. *You've got to be strong if you want to get through this. You're going to need a clear head if you want to save not only yourself, but Ali-*

cia and her baby. Because you owe it to her—you owe it to them. You know that, don't you? You are going to get out of this and you are not going to let them take Alicia and Mandy.

And as the van sped down Interstate 10, she began to try thinking of a way out of her predicament.

They were on the 57 Freeway breezing by Anaheim Stadium when Animal popped back into the rear of the van. He held a nasty-looking knife in his hand. "Hold still," he said. "I'm just cutting you loose so you can get dressed."

"And don't try anything," Tim warned from the front seat. "Animal's killed eighteen people. You try anything, he'll gut you faster than a rat can shit."

Lisa's skin tightened as she felt Animal cut the rope that bound her wrists together. She felt him work the lock that held the handcuffs together and then she was free. Then he was in front of her, holding the knife to her menacingly as he held her clothes out to her. "Put your bra and shirt on first, then I'll uncuff your ankles."

Lisa rubbed her wrists, then did what she was told. She dressed slowly, her mind racing. She had been thinking about a thousand possible scenarios for the past hour and none of them appeared promising. In the first she saw herself enter the bank, most likely with Animal, then suddenly making a break for it and diving over the teller's desk. That would cause a scene; Animal would surely get the hell out of dodge. And she would be safe . . . but not for long. Al had her and Brad's photographs. He had her address and phone number, which he had taken from one of her bank slips. Hell, he had her social security card. With all that information, he could probably find her pretty quickly.

Another scenario saw her getting the money, then

making a run for it out the front doors. But then that would end the same way.

She tried playing different scenarios out all the way till the end, to their final destination in Burbank. What would happen? Suppose Alicia and Mandy were gone? How would Tim and Animal get them in the van without attracting unwanted attention? The more she thought of it, the more volatile Alicia's abduction would be. Lisa had the feeling Tim knew this, which was why they were going after the money first.

The only scenario she really liked had her lunging for the armed security guard at the bank. If she could surprise him and get his gun, she could maybe shoot him (in the leg, of course; she didn't want to kill him), then maybe shoot Animal (again, in the leg; she wanted him alive to confess to the police. On second thought, maybe she'd shoot his balls off. Shooting a man's balls off wouldn't kill him, would it?), then rush outside and surprise Tim in the van, holding him at gunpoint until the police arrived.

There were several problems with that scenario. Suppose there was another guard at the bank and she was shot first? Suppose she couldn't get the gun, and in the struggle for it Animal escaped? Suppose the police arrived too quickly and shot *her*? All these problems flashed through her mind in seconds as she slipped into her bra and shirt.

"Slap some makeup on your face," Tim said. "We're almost there."

Lisa looked out the front windshield. They were on the 22 Freeway heading north. They were getting close to their exit. *Let's take this one step at a time,* she thought as she put her shoes on.

By the time they reached the bank, she had put some makeup on and inspected herself in her compact. Despite all she had gone through in the past three days, she didn't look that bad. Tired maybe, but not that bad.

Tim swung into a parking space near the bank's entrance, cut the engine, and turned around. "Animal's goin' in the bank with you. If you try anything like screaming or something, Animal will just dash out here and me and him are off. You won't know when we'll get you next, but we will. And we'll get you and your whole fucking family, and we'll film Animal torturing and killing all of you, you got me?"

Lisa nodded stoically.

"Is this savings account a joint account?" Tim asked.

Lisa nodded. "Yes."

"Do any of the tellers in there know you and your husband?"

"No."

"So they won't know Animal here from Adam, right?"

She nodded, straightening herself up. "They won't know him."

"Good. Animal will play hubby for today. Animal, give your wifey here a kiss."

Animal grinned, leaned toward her, and licked the side of her face. She grimaced as his tongue lapped up her chin, across her cheeks, then over her lips, pausing at her nose. She felt her revulsion rise, fought the urge to gag and push him away. Animal's teeth nipped the tip of her nose playfully, like a lover. "Mmm. Tastes good. Never tried ripping a chick's nose off with my teeth before."

Tim laughed. "Remember . . . you fuck up, Animal will do it next time we get together."

"I won't fuck up," Lisa said, slightly defiant as Animal moved away from her and began inspecting his looks in the vanity mirror.

"Do you need both parties to sign to take money out of your account?" Tim asked.

"No." Lisa wiped Animal's saliva off her face with her palm in disgust and wiped her hands off on her jeans.

"Good. You are very lucky, my friend. Very lucky. What about your IRAs?"

"They're individual IRAs, from our own separate retirement accounts," she said, reaching for her purse, checking to see if she had everything in place.

"Then what you're going to do is go to the teller and withdraw the money from your savings account, then you're going to tell them you want to cash out your IRA. They'll probably have you fill out a bunch of forms and shit, so that may take a while. Make sure you get everything you can out of the IRA; don't have them take any taxes out of it. You can eat that later. Just take your cash out of your savings account, fill out whatever forms you need for the IRA, get the money, and get the fuck back out here. How much is in your IRA?"

"Thirty grand."

"They'll probably hold back a few grand for penalties and shit. That only leaves us with eighty-five grand or so. What about your ring?"

Lisa looked at her wedding ring and began to pull it off her finger. It was a five-carat diamond ring, the stone set in a nice gold band. It had cost Brad almost six thousand dollars when he bought it for her three years ago, and she later had diamond studs embedded in the gold band. She pointed this out to Tim as she handed the ring to him. "You could probably get ten grand for it if you sold it on consignment."

"Or half that if I just outright sold it to a jeweler." Tim inspected the ring, then pocketed it. "If you come out with the cash, we'll call it even. How's that sound?"

"Fine." What else could she say? Especially when it was her and her unborn baby's life at stake?

"I expect you out of there in twenty minutes," Tim said.

"If you aren't back by then, I'll know there's trouble and then I'm gone. If—"

"But wait! What if—" Lisa protested, feeling her nerves rise.

"Don't interrupt me," Tim said, glancing at Animal. "If there's a big line, Animal will give me a ring on my cell phone." He tapped his index finger on a small cellular phone in his breast pocket. "He'll do that within a minute of the two of you walking in. But if I see anything funny going on, I'm gone, you understand me? I ain't waitin' around for Animal. He knows the protocol should he get picked up by the cops; he'll be clean."

Lisa listened in dread as Tim continued. He extracted his cellular phone from his shirt pocket. "Animal's got one of these babies." Animal grinned and patted his jeans pocket, indicating the bulk of a small cell phone. "Animal knows that we're to be out of here in twenty minutes. If it looks like things are legitimately going to take longer, Animal will call me at the nineteen-minute mark to tell me that. If I don't get that phone call, you and your family are dog meat, you got me?"

Lisa nodded, swallowing a dry lump. "I got you."

"Just be cool, don't tip off the teller, pass her a note that you've been kidnapped, or any of that shit. You do, and Animal will know and he's out of there. You might not want to admit it, but having Animal by your side for the next thirty minutes is going to be very beneficial to you. Because you know what will happen if I see him come out of that bank and you aren't with him?"

"I know," Lisa said.

"Say it."

Lisa glared at Tim, her stomach churning. "Me and my family will be dog meat."

Tim chuckled. "Not just dog meat. *Movie stars!*" He

laughed sickly. Lisa trembled at the sound of his laugh. It was the laugh of a man with no conscience.

"Okay!" Tim clapped his hands together. "Let's get this show on the road."

Animal slid open the door of the van and Lisa followed him out, her heart accelerating as she tried to appear normal while at the same time trying to seek an avenue of escape that wouldn't end disastrously.

Fifteen

When they walked through the double glass doors into the cool interior of the Bank of America on Beach Boulevard in Huntington Beach, Lisa felt her gut clench when she saw that the line to the tellers wasn't very long. Tim's threats weren't really getting to her now; if she had still been tied up, she might have been scared. Being untied and walking around was beginning to work on her self-esteem and at chiseling the fear away. Fuck Tim and his idle threats! So what if Animal ditched her and they left! So what if they had her address. She and Brad could go into hiding; she could identify all three of them; she could funnel money into getting an investigation started. She could have them caught quickly, she was sure of it. And just to play it safe, she would use her own connections in the legal profession to have her and Brad's identities changed. Nobody would find them. They would be safe.

When they entered the bank, Animal surveyed the interior then reached for his cell phone. He pressed a speed-dial button and said, "Twenty minutes tops." Then he hung up. He replaced the phone in his pocket. They walked together to the line that fed to the bank tellers, her mind working on overdrive. She knew exactly what she was going to do now. Forget the heroics. She was going to stand calmly with Animal in line. And when it was their turn, she was going to walk calmly to the next teller and tell him or her point blank that the man she was with had kidnapped her and was robbing her and *please,* would you press that silent alarm button *now!* Animal would probably fake a look of surprise—*Whatever are you talking about, dear?* And Lisa was going to let her instinct take over. She knew the teller would be able to see what was happening was the real deal, that this wasn't a joke. And then Animal would probably make a dash for the door and maybe security would stop him, maybe the police would arrive quickly and they'd get Tim. and then—

They were the next customers up, and Lisa felt a sudden rush of adrenaline pour through her. This was going to work. She was sure of it. Everything was going to be fine. She allowed herself one small glimmer of courage, and then she felt the blade of a knife in her back as Animal put his arm around her from behind.

"Let me give you a friendly warning," he whispered casually in her ear. "I won't have this knife on you the entire time we're in this bank, but I will be at your side like the ever-faithful husband. And at the slightest sign of you making a break for it or calling for help, this knife comes out and I sever your spinal cord." She felt the blade pierce through her skin and she winced at the pain, feeling warm blood run down her back from the wound. She felt Animal's lips on her earlobe, his warm breath on her cheek. "And then I'm out of here before your body even hits the floor. And if you live, I'll know. And then the next time we see each other, we'll both be on Al's set and

I'll be jamming this knife up your cunt. Do we have an understanding?"

Lisa nodded, trembling. She heard the female teller call her over, and then suddenly the blade was gone and she was walking toward the teller, Animal at her side and slightly behind her, his arm around her shoulders casually, a smile on his pensive, handsome features.

"How can I help you?" The teller was a small woman, maybe five feet one with delicate porcelain features, shoulder-length black hair and big brown eyes. She smiled at Lisa. The name on the badge pinned to her blouse identified her as Trish Lynn.

"I'd like to make two withdrawals, please," Lisa said, pushing the withdrawal slip she had filled out a moment before to the teller. Her voice sounded like it was coming from another dimension. "One from my savings account, the other from my IRA."

The teller looked at the withdrawal slip and her slim fingers danced on the keyboard of a computer terminal at her station. The teller's fingernails were impeccable; it looked like she'd had a manicure recently.

"You wish to close out your account with us at this time, Mrs. Miller?" the teller asked.

Lisa started; her mind was in a funk. The small of her back still stung from the knife wound, and she could feel the back of her shirt and her panties grow sticky with blood. She looked at the teller and blinked. "Excuse me?"

"Would you like to close out your account with us, Mrs. Miller?" The teller frowned slightly.

"Yes," Lisa said, trying to smile. "Yes, I would."

She felt a hand enfold hers and saw that it was Animal's; he was smiling at the bank teller. "We're both a little nervous about this, Ms. Lynn. My wife and I are relocating back east, and we plan to bank back there."

Trish nodded, seemingly indifferent. "You wanted to withdraw funds from your IRA as well?"

"Yes," Lisa said, forcing herself not to let her voice tremble. "Yes, I would."

"Do you have the account number?"

"Right here." Lisa fumbled for her purse and, with Animal's help, she presented Trish with the appropriate account number.

"You'll have to fill out some paperwork," Trish said, looking at her computer screen, then back at Lisa and Animal. "I can close your savings account here, then I'll have to direct you to our special accounts person for the IRA withdrawal. In fact, if you like, I can direct you to Mr. Walsh now. He'll help you fill out the appropriate paperwork, and when you're finished with him he can walk you back up here and I'll close out your accounts."

Lisa nodded as Trish stepped around to join them in line, leading them to the Special Accounts Desk. It seemed that the room was spinning as she was introduced to George Walsh, the special accounts person, and then she was sitting down at his desk, listening to him give his spiel regarding the early-withdrawal penalties that were incurred when you withdrew your money from an IRA too early. She nodded and told him she understood, then after asking her a few more questions he pushed some forms toward them, and she gave Animal a quick glance before she turned to fill out the forms. Animal smiled and gave her an encouraging nod. Playing the ever-faithful husband.

She filled out three different forms as Animal called Tim again to give him an ETA, declined to have federal and state income taxes withheld, signed the forms, and handed them back to George Walsh, who looked them over quickly and tore copies out for her. "Right this way, Mr. and Mrs. Miller," he said.

They followed George Walsh back to Trish's window and waited while Trish finished tending to a customer. When the customer left, George nodded. "They're ready," he told her.

Trish smiled. "Great." Lisa and Animal approached her window again while the teller consulted the paperwork George gave her, and Lisa's original withdrawal slip. "Will you excuse me for a moment?" she asked, leaving her post before Lisa could respond.

She's going to call the police! Lisa thought, her heart hammering wildly. *She sensed something and she's going to call the police, they're going to catch Animal and Tim and this nightmare will be over and then—*

Trish returned with another woman, this one in her late forties, probably a bank manager. She stood by as Trish reached into her cash drawer. "What denominations would you like your money in, Mrs. Miller?"

Lisa opened her mouth to answer, stunned that they still hadn't caught on. She tried to tell the woman how she wanted the money, but she couldn't. Then she heard Animal beside her, saying, "I think we'll take hundreds, Ms. Lynn."

And as Trish Lynn began counting out her and Brad's life savings and her entire IRA contribution minus penalties into Lisa's hands, the whole experience was becoming more and more like some strange nightmare that wouldn't go away.

Lisa didn't remember much of the ride to North Hollywood. She spent the first thirty minutes or so crying as she sat in the back of the van and Tim piloted them along the 405 Freeway, heading north. Animal sat across from her, eyeing her occasionally as he counted the money. He counted the money twice before transferring it to a small duffel bag that Tim had produced from the front seat. All Lisa could think about was a lifetime of work that had just been pissed away, a lifetime of work that she had handed to these two monsters because she'd been stupid enough to—

She wasn't going to go down that train of thought. She sniffed, ran her hand across her face, brushing the tears off her cheek. Traffic was already getting heavy as people began to get off work. Tim turned the radio to a classic rock station; Kansas blasted from the radio, followed by Journey and Boston. Tim turned the dial and found an oldies station specializing in R&B. Al Green's smooth tenor crooned from the speakers and Animal smiled, humming along. "Al Green . . . what a beautiful voice that man has," he said.

Lisa looked at him. The idea that Animal found beauty in something was mind-boggling to her. She couldn't understand it—he was moved by the music of Al Green, thought it was beautiful, yet he was anticipating raping, torturing, and murdering a woman and her infant daughter. What was wrong here?

The drive to North Hollywood took close to an hour, but it felt like four. Through it all, Lisa thought about what could soothe the savage beast that lay within Animal's soul (*Jeff,* she thought, *his name is Jeff*), and possibly Tim's. She also tried to think of a way to stave off the inevitable: the abduction of Alicia and Mandy.

Thinking of a way to save them fared no better than her plans to foil Tim and Animal at the bank. She still couldn't come up with anything plausible. There was still the possibility they wouldn't find Alicia. If that happened, Lisa was fighting tooth and nail to escape and stay alive. In fact, if they didn't find Alicia at the restaurant or along the street she claimed to have parked her car to sleep in, she was going to make a break for it. Come to think of it, why even go that far? Tim and Animal had no idea where

Alicia was; they were depending on her to lead them to her. She could lead them to some other restaurant and then, as they circled the parking lot looking for her, she would take that opportunity to make a run for it.

Animal was watching her from the other side of the van, his green eyes studying her. Lisa refused to meet his gaze; it felt penetrating, as if he could see what she was thinking. *It's probably written all over my face,* she thought.

One of her scenarios had her telling them where Alicia was, then finding her, then screaming bloody murder as she accompanied whomever it was she was going to be helping lure Alicia to the van. She saw Alicia make a run for it, carrying her baby as Lisa ran after her, urging her to *run, goddamn it, run!* She saw them being chased and then either a) Animal and Tim catching her and taking her down, but not before being rescued by bystanders, thus spoiling their murderous plans, or b) having Animal and Tim turn tail and run back to the van, escaping back to Al. In both cases, she saw them trying to carry out Al's earlier threat of tracking her down, but she already had plans for that. She and Brad were going to change their identities as she had planned back at the bank. That was the ticket.

She tried to stay calm as Tim reached Interstate 5. She was just going to have to play this one by ear. But she was damned if she was going to let them take Alicia and Mandy without a fight. "You said Burbank Boulevard near the IKEA, right?" Tim asked.

Lisa knew she couldn't lie; she had already told them where she and Brad had run into Alicia. Part of her had hoped Tim had forgotten this. "Yes," she said, with a sinking sense of dread.

"We'll be there in fifteen minutes," Tim said.

They were silent during the remaining fifteen minutes

of the drive. Lisa felt her body go leaden as they approached the exit, felt the dread solidify and become a hot, squirming thing in her gut as they exited Burbank Boulevard and headed west. Animal was looking out the windshield, and he pointed ahead of them. "Coco's is on the right," he said. Tim nodded and merged to the right lane, slowing down to enter the restaurant's parking lot. Lisa felt her heartbeat speed up, felt her face grow flush with adrenaline as they cruised through the parking lot. She was trying to look out the windshield to see if she could catch a glimpse of Alicia, but she couldn't be sure. There were people all over the place; the restaurant was housed in a busy strip mall that also included a supermarket, a drugstore, and several smaller businesses. Tim drove the car to the rear of the restaurant and slid into a parking space. He killed the engine. "I thought I saw a woman standing near the restaurant who looked like the woman we're looking for," he said. "I'm going to back up and cruise by slowly so you can get a look at her. If that's the chick, tell me. And don't lie to me, 'cause I'll know. Shit, I don't even know why I'm telling you to ID her for me. She'll probably have her kid with her."

Lisa didn't say anything. Her mind was racing a mile a minute. *It's going to be now. It's going to happen now, and I'm going to have to put up the fight of my life.*

Tim motioned to Animal. "I want you to go with her. And we'll do what we talked about, okay?"

Animal nodded, his face showing no emotion.

Tim turned back to Lisa. "You and Animal are going to go out to see if the chick I saw standing outside the restaurant is Alicia. If it is, Animal will know—she'll most likely have her kid with her. If it's her, you and Animal are going to go up to her and this is what you're going to tell her." He told her, and Lisa felt nervous. It sounded so perfect, a plan masking altruism at its best. She held her emotions in and nodded as Tim regarded her. "We'll take care of the rest. Got it?"

Lisa nodded. She looked out the windshield. "And what if the woman isn't Alicia?"

"We'll drive around," Tim said. "We'll drive down that street you mentioned, then we'll hit the YWCA. If we don't find them at either place, it's over." He smiled at her. "The game ends."

Lisa heard what he was saying but didn't feel the implications. She understood them—they would take her back to that lonely mountain cabin by force and kill her slowly in front of the camera—but she didn't let their threats affect her. She had gone beyond that. She had gone beyond feeling scared.

"I'll be right here," Tim said. "And remember what I said before: If you scream or cause a scene or make a break for it, we'll find you and we'll kill you later. Only we'll kill you slowly. And we'll get hubby and baby, too. You got me?"

Lisa nodded. The threat echoed in her mind; it didn't seem real anymore. Nothing did. "Let's do it."

Animal opened the side door of the van and stepped out. Lisa followed him and began to lead the way to the front of the restaurant where, just three days before, she and her husband had stopped to help a woman in despair.

Sixteen

Lisa was cursing herself the entire time for being too chickenshit to do anything. The only thing she could think of was that line of thought part of her conscious mind kept whispering to her a few hours before: *You were only thinking about saving your skin. You weren't even thinking about your unborn baby, were you? You just wanted to save yourself!*

It was that thought that kept running through her mind, as well as her general fright, that kept her from doing anything. It wasn't until they were back at the van and Tim emerged to make the capture that Lisa sprang into some kind of action. And what triggered it was Animal—who had been walking behind her as the three of them walked to the van (while Alicia carried Mandy, who was strapped into her carrier)—as he clamped his hand over her mouth and attempted to shove her in the van.

No! her mind screamed, and then she fought. Something deep and primal awoke within her and she struggled hard, more ferociously than she'd struggled when Tim had abducted her back at that motel a thousand years ago. Animal's left hand found her left wrist and attempted to bring it behind her back in a choke hold, but Lisa moved with it, thwarting him. Animal panted. "Thought we were just gonna let you go after this, huh? Think again, cunt!"

She screamed but nothing came out of her mouth, and then she saw the glint of steel and her eyes grew wide. He pulled her toward him, hand pressed down over her mouth, and he brought the knife up, and she could dimly hear movement in the van as Tim tended to Alicia and Mandy and she tried to forget the look Alicia gave her when it all happened. She pushed all that out of her mind and burst through it, fueled by a sudden explosion of adrenaline that seemed to give her extra strength. The knife came up toward her throat, and then she bit down hard on Animal's palm.

She felt her teeth pierce through his skin, and suddenly the hand was gone and she heard a yelp of pain. His grip on her loosened, and she took this small window of opportunity to drive her elbow into him. She felt it connect solidly with his solar plexus and she felt something hit her shoulder, then heard the clink of metal as it hit the ground at her feet. Animal's grip on her loosened to the point of letting go as he doubled over, the breath knocked out of him, and now she *did* scream. She let loose with one motherfucking *wail* of a scream, and then she was running. She screamed and ran toward the front of the restaurant, ignoring the surprised looks of entering restaurant patrons as they froze to look at her, and then she was in the restaurant, screaming at the twentysomething hostess to call the fucking police, and then she collapsed on the floor in a shaking fit of sobbing, not even aware of the commotion around her and the excited voices that accompanied it, not even aware of the van as it peeled out of the parking lot and set off down Burbank Boulevard heading for the freeway.

Brad Miller sat in the Lexus as the garage door opened to his and Lisa's home, feeling a numbed sense of detachment.

The day had gone by in a blur: the brief arraignment and dismissal of his case; filing a missing persons report with the Ventura County Sheriff's Department; then a late breakfast at some restaurant with his parents and William Grecko as they all tried to console him. *We'll find her, don't worry. She'll be all right. We'll get to the bottom of this.*

Brad had told William Grecko that if they wanted to find Lisa they needed to do one thing: find Caleb Smith. He had something to do with this. Brad knew it. But Grecko told him it was going to be tough. *As far as any-*

body knows, Caleb Smith doesn't exist. It's probably an alias of some sort and the guy's long gone by now. For all we know, he might not have had anything to do with Lisa disappearing.

Brad had wanted to leap over the table and throttle the smug sonofabitch, but his parents were there, and then they were joined by one of the detectives Grecko had called. They had talked some more, and Brad had mostly listened to the conversation, simmering in his anger at the lawyer and the detective, silently screaming at them to *get the fuck out there and find her!* Then they had driven back to Orange County with Brad's father driving the Lexus. They had gone to his folks' house first, and that was when Brad knew he had to get some kind of plan going. If the police weren't going to do anything about finding Lisa, then *he* would. He would hire a private detective if he had to. But he would find her.

He felt a little better after coming to this realization, and he had told his folks he was going to go home. His mother had been against it—she seemed to think he was on the brink of a nervous breakdown and might harm himself. Brad dismissed it. "I'm tired, Mom. I haven't showered in three days and I'm tired. I want to go home and take a shower and go to sleep. Maybe if I get some rest, I'll feel better."

His father had felt that was for the best too, so both parents had escorted him back to the car and helped him with his things. They watched as he drove away.

Now as he pulled the car into the garage he realized that for the first time since this whole nightmare started he was actually starting to think in a positive manner. First things first: Get a shower and a good night's sleep. Take a Valium if you have to, but get a good eight or more hours of sleep. Then tomorrow we'll tackle this thing from all ends. Maybe he would do some calling around and find a good private detective. He would spare no expense. Thank God he and Lisa had been made partners in their respective firms this year, because the extra income they'd been throwing into savings was going to be dearly needed.

The garage door whirred closed behind him. Brad sighed and got out of the car. He retrieved both bags from the trunk and trundled them through the laundry room and the kitchen. He'd get them both upstairs and then he'd—

He was just crossing the living room with the suitcases when the telephone rang.

He rushed to the phone after dropping the bags in the entry hall. "Hello?"

"Brad?" It was Lisa. She burst out sobbing.

"Lisa!" Brad's voice broke. *"Oh my God, Lisa, what happened—where are you?"*

"Oh Brad, thank God you're home." Lisa was crying hard, and Brad could hear voices in the background over the line. It sounded like she was calling from an office or something.

"Lisa, where are you?" Brad's own nerves were on edge at the sound of her voice, and he thought, *Thank God she's all right.*

"I'm in Burbank," Lisa said. "At the police station . . . I don't know . . . near . . . *I don't know where this fucking police station is!* It's in the valley—"

"Stay right where you are!" Brad said, his mind racing. "I'm leaving right now!"

"Oh Brad!" She started crying again. Hearing her voice, hearing her break down like that, broke Brad's heart.

"I love you, Lisa," Brad said, his throat choking up. "I'm leaving now."

Another voice came on the line. "Mr. Miller? I'm detective Morse. Your wife is fine. We're having her transferred to USC Medical Center to have her checked out, but physically she looks okay. She's been through a terrible ordeal, though, and . . ."

The minute the conversation was over, Brad hung up and was racing back to the car, then peeling out of the garage and down the street to the freeway, his heart racing with anticipation at seeing his wife.

He couldn't get to USC Medical Center fast enough. What would have normally been a forty-five-minute or more drive took Brad less than thirty minutes. It was a miracle he made it to the hospital at all; his mind was completely focused on Lisa and reuniting with her—seeing her, touching her; holding her close to him. He barely paid attention to his driving. When he arrived at the hospital, he pulled into the first available spot and leaped out of the car, racing toward the hospital with bated breath.

When he burst into the lobby, he went directly to the receptionist desk. "My wife Lisa was just brought here! She was kidnapped and—"

A uniformed officer who was standing near the receptionist desk stepped forward. "Brad Miller?"

Brad turned to the officer. "Yeah. Is Lisa okay, is she—"

The officer nodded at the receptionist and a security guard who had approached. "She's fine. Come with me."

Brad barely noticed as the officer gave him a visitor's badge and led him through a seemingly endless maze of corridors. He could hardly keep his emotions in check. He'd cried briefly on the drive over; the thought that he had almost lost her had hit him hard. He still couldn't grasp the concept that she had been given a second chance, that she was safe. He had to see her.

They reached the emergency ward and the cop nodded at a nurse who was standing at the nurse's station. "This is Brad Miller," he said. "Lisa's husband."

The nurse held out her hand and smiled. Her features were calm and reassuring. "Mr. Miller, I'm Candace Thorton. Come with me."

Brad followed Candace on trembling legs. She opened one of the doors to a triage unit and Brad's eyes fell on the figure lying in the lone bed in the center of the room. "Lisa!"

The figure looked up, and at first Brad thought he had it all wrong, that it wasn't Lisa dressed in a white hospital smock lying in the hospital bed. The woman who looked at him from across the room was too pale, heavy dark circles under her eyes, her blond hair a stringy mess, the skin stretching tightly over her bones, her face weathered. This couldn't be Lisa. Maybe they had it wrong; maybe the men who had kidnapped her had tracked her to the hospital and snuck off with her, replaced his wife with this wraithlike stick figure who looked like she had been through hell and back and—"

"Brad!"

It was hearing the sound of her voice that confirmed it for him. The minute he heard it, he knew. The face, still pretty but bearing the emotional and physical strain of the past few days, the dark circles under her eyes from lack of sleep. It was Lisa, all right. There was no question about it.

Nothing else mattered to Brad at that moment—not the nurse or the cop that he barely noticed, who was sitting in a chair near the bed, not even the cop who had met him at the receptionist desk or the doctor that came in to talk to him. All that mattered was Lisa, the confirmation that she was alive. He didn't care about anything else at that moment; those people did not exist for Brad as he quickly crossed the room to Lisa's bedside and swept her into his arms, the tears coming so strong and so sudden that he didn't even bother trying to stem their flow. He let it all out, let the tears come, let himself cry his heart out as he held her close to him, not wanting to let her go, not wanting to lose her ever again, and Lisa cried against his chest and he let her, everything outside of their little world nonexistent right now as he held her and told her he loved her over and over again and that everything was going to be all right.

Seventeen

They had just finished filming when the shit started going down.

Tim had thrown up at least twice during the shoot. He couldn't help it; he'd never seen anybody get done like that before, and he had never seen a *baby* get done before, either. That was the worst. They'd actually kept the baby's mother alive and tied up while Animal did it, too. Her hands tied behind her back, legs lashed together, her mouth gagged tight, she'd been forced to watch in anguish as Animal . . . even thinking about what Animal had done to that baby made him sick.

Tim took a deep breath, closed his eyes, trying to gain control of himself. He had to keep telling himself that in the grand scheme of things, he didn't give a shit. Nearly a quarter of a million bucks was riding on this gig, split three ways between him, Al, and Animal. That was a lot of dough for one night.

But then, every time he tried to tell himself that, Alicia's terror-stricken eyes, her anguish, stabbed into his conscious. He had watched her as she watched helpless, powerless to do anything, and in doing so was transported back to when he had been in her shoes.

The rabbit's name had been Binky. Stupid name for a fucking rabbit, but Tim had loved it anyway. The rabbit had been a gift from his mother, for Easter, and he had doted on it the way most boys fawn over dogs. He'd built a little hidey-box inside its cage, fed it, made sure it had water. And he played with it every chance he got. When he came home from school, Binky was always there waiting for him. Tim would lose hours in a single afternoon playing with the creature, absorbed in his own world.

Tim had loved Binky. And he was sure that Binky had loved him.

He must have forgotten to do a chore or something—playing with Binky made him forget a lot of things, made him neglect stuff around the house. His mother went after him about it constantly, and he would quickly perform whatever task had needed to be done before Dad came home. But one day he hadn't been so quick about it and his father had come home early. And when Dad saw that the garbage hadn't been emptied and that Tim was lying on his stomach in the backyard, laughing and talking to Binky as they played, he had stalked across the yard and plucked the rabbit up by its ears.

Tim had protested, quickly sensing the error of his ways. *Please*, he had beseeched. *I'm sorry, it won't happen again.*

How many times have I told you, his father had said, grasping the rabbit's body with one meaty forearm, *that chores come first?*

Tim had begged his father not to do it, but he knew the begging would be in vain. Dad had done the same thing to his brother Doug's cat two summers ago, to teach him a similar lesson. There was no reason to suspect he would change his method of operation now.

Dad had pushed Tim on the ground and said, *Now you watch and you think about the inadequacy of your ways which has caused this great and terrible injustice to be done.* And then, as Tim had watched, helpless and horrified, unable to do anything to intervene lest he receive the whooping of his life, his dad had grasped the rabbit's head between his meaty hands and pushed them together. Binky's little red eyes had bugged out in terror and pain, his hind legs had kicked frantically, his little body wriggled as a horrible mewling cry rose deep from within him; that cry had sounded like the scream of an infant. Blood had spurted from the rabbit's eyes and nose and then the head just exploded in a watery pop that sent brains and thick red blood gushing everywhere. And all Tim could do was stand there helplessly while his father killed the only thing he had ever loved.

Tim blinked, trying to chase the memory from his mind. The agonizing screams of that baby, seeing that same look in Alicia as she'd watched her daughter being torn apart by Animal, had brought the memory of what Dad had done to Binky rushing to the surface, making him feel helpless. The feeling was so great that Tim turned away from the scene, throwing up and crying.

Jesus motherfucking Christ! What the fuck are we doing?

He'd forced himself to watch the rest of it. Forced himself to watch as Animal had ravaged the infant in front of its mother, who screamed and moaned and strained against the ropes binding her to the floor as she tried to break free. Al had remained silent, catching it all on film. When Animal started in on Alicia, it got a little easier to watch; Tim was used to watching Animal torture and kill adults. Even then, watching this scene was harder than all the others. He had thrown up a second time as the memory of Binky's death rose in his mind, and he'd had to fight back the sudden unmistakable feelings of regret he was now beginning to feel. *Jesus fuck, I never thought it would be this bad. Christ, I never thought it would be this bad.*

Animal was standing in the center of the room over the worn metal bed frame, naked and covered in blood and pieces of flesh. Even the black leather bondage hood he wore for the shoot was drenched with it. He stood rigid, hands held out at his sides, clenching and unclenching his blood- and flesh-stained hands. Tim stood up from the pool of vomit on the floor and saw with a sickening sense of horror that Animal still had an erection. His dick was covered in semen, blood, and red gooey flesh.

What was left of Debbie Martinez was huddled at the foot of the bed. More of her was on the floor and walls.

There was virtually nothing left of the infant. Just pieces, really.

In his frenzy Animal had even *eaten* parts of the infant. Another first. Tim wondered if they could get more money for the film now that it had cannibalism in it.

"Goddamn," Al said, packing away his camera equipment. "Goddamn, but wasn't that some shit. Jesus Fucking Christ!"

Tim was panting, trying to catch his breath. He felt hot and sweaty. His eyes felt hot and moist; he felt the unmistakable dampness of tears on his cheeks. He didn't think he would react this way, that he would actually weep the way he did. He had watched Animal torture and mutilate people before. He had watched Animal stick his prick in places of the human body not designed for phallic objects as whatever junkie whore or butt boy he was doing wailed and screamed in pain before passing out and going into convulsions. Probably the grossest scene he had witnessed was the first time Animal had skull-fucked one bitch while she was still alive. The bitch had been unconscious, yeah, but Animal didn't give a shit. He was *paid* not to give a shit. Animal didn't even use his knife to gouge the woman's eyeball out; his thumb and forefinger had sufficed perfectly, and the woman was still screaming when Animal guided his dick into her blood-spurting eye socket. Tim had watched that one in morbid fascination, not even aware that he had thrown up at that shoot, too. By the time Animal was pumping his cock in and out of the woman's eye socket, she was beginning the shuddering dance of death, hemorrhaging out of both eye sockets, her nose, and her mouth. She had even shit blood when Animal came.

Until tonight, that had been the most extreme flick they had ever shot.

"Hey, Tim. *Tim!*"

Tim looked up. Al was grinning at him. His lean features were sweaty. And even though his hazel eyes danced with glee, Tim detected something else in them. Something that suggested that even Al had been disturbed by this latest shoot. "We did it, man! We fucking *did* it!"

"Yeah," Tim said, turning back to Animal, who appeared to be gaining control of himself. The body of the baby's mother, Alicia, was lying on the plastic tarp floor at the foot of the bed. Her sightless eyes stared up at the ceiling. Her face was a mass of contusions and cuts. Her torso was sliced open, the flesh spread apart like a dressed-out deer to show her inner works. Animal hadn't dragged them out like he usually did when they filmed a snuff flick; he'd merely jacked off over them and come inside her body cavity.

Tim looked at Debbie's horribly violated remains, then back down at Alicia's corpse, still in a sense of awe at Animal's performance tonight. Three times was the most Animal had ever come during a shoot, and tonight Animal had come at least five times. Five orgasms, three dead bodies.

The sound of Al packing up his camera gear snapped Tim back to reality. "We gotta get the fuck out of here," Al said. "Animal, go take a fucking shower and wash that shit off of you. Brush your teeth, too. I can't have you looking like a fucking horror-movie serial killer all fucking evening."

Animal turned around, and for the first time Tim was struck with cold fear as the dominiatrix's muddy eyes fixed on him from behind the leather mask. It was the first time Tim had ever felt this way about Animal; mostly he liked Animal just fine. The guy was witty, smart, funny, nice to be around. And he was good-looking, too. He really did look like an all-American boy. He certainly knew how to put the charm on around the women. When he wasn't playing the role of a dom, he was a financial consultant for a large international firm. He made good money, surely more than enough so that he didn't have to partake in the role of a sadist for the snuff and torture films he starred in. But then, as he had explained to Tim one afternoon after they'd dropped off a film to a buyer who had commissioned it: "I like pain, and I enjoy inflicting it on others." There was no arguing with logic like that.

And as for his stage name, well, when he donned the mask and slipped into the role of a dom for one of his and Al's films, he was . . . well, an Animal.

Animal's eyes flicked from Tim to Al, then back to Tim again. He rubbed his hand over his sweat- and blood-drenched naked torso. The room they were in was splattered with it. The plastic tarp they had rolled onto the floor was slick with blood; it was also running down the tarp they had nailed up along the walls. It was on the ceiling. Al would have to get in here tomorrow and paint the ceiling. Getting rid of the bodies was going to be easy. All that needed to be done was to move the bed frame, roll the bodies into the tarp, and stick them in the back of the van. Tim had found a nice secluded dumping spot a few weeks ago. It was in a remote area; no one would think of looking for them out there.

"Time's a-wastin', people," Al said, winding up cable.

Animal turned and walked into the small bathroom off the bedroom. A moment later, the shower came on. Tim wandered outside for a breath of fresh air; the smell of blood, puke, and shit was too much for him right now. He had produced eighteen snuff films over the past ten years, and he had never gotten used to the smell of death.

Tim looked up at the star-filled night, breathing in the fresh mountain air. Despite that bit with the baby, it had gone good tonight. Debbie and that Alicia chick were perfect; those in the circle had been itching for something different in the flicks he produced. They had wanted something new, something fresh. Tim could surely see where they were coming from. Watching the same breed of whores and bun boys getting raped and sliced up was getting old. But it was definitely safer. Nobody ever missed the kind of kids that sold their asses on the Hollywood streets when they turned up missing. Christ, they were from all over the fucking place. They came from the cornfields of Nebraska, the deserts of Arizona, the heavily wooded areas of Maine, the swamps of Louisiana. Fuck, one guy they'd used had come from Alaska! That guy had been a real masochistic freak. He had gotten off on some pretty heavy shit. Animal had only been too happy to oblige.

But these two women . . . that was a different story. Both of them had been good-looking as hell, much better-looking than the homeless chicks they usually used. They looked as if they had just stepped out of a *Vogue* shoot or something. That was one of the requirements the client wanted for this shoot; he'd even had somebody in mind and had provided Sam with a physical description and a license-plate number. It had been risky, but Sam said the client would double the money to match the risk and Tim had taken it. And then he had gotten even more lucky with Alicia and her kid.

Tim frowned. He didn't doubt Al's claim that Sam would double the price a third time due to the fact that they'd found a baby. He'd heard of a pedophile group in the Pacific Northwest that was rumored to be interested in a snuff film with a baby in it. What he was worried about was letting Lisa Miller get away. He'd had strict orders, down to the make and license number of her car and her physical description, to grab her and bring her to the cabin by Saturday. Al and Animal were to do the rest. Tim didn't give a fuck—he was being paid double for the risk, and the plan he'd formulated *had* worked perfectly.

Then everything had fallen to shit.

First that Debbie Martinez bitch wandering into the cabin. Stupid cunt. That had been a minor annoyance, but he'd taken care of it. He'd mentioned what happened to Sam, and while Sam hadn't been pleased he'd grudgingly agreed to find a buyer and encouraged Tim to have Animal finish her quickly. Tim assured Sam he'd do that, and the three of them had driven to the cabin to do just that. Animal had managed to draw it out, though, which was fine in some ways, but they'd stopped production midway through. Animal was spending a lot of time with the bitch—he really must've been wanting to fuck this bitch up for a long time, because he was really enjoying it. Al had wanted to resume the next morning, and Tim had seen no reason to disagree. Debbie surely wasn't going anywhere, and Lisa Miller was tied up tighter than a gnat's ass. So they'd left.

What had fucked things up . . . what really fucked it up was Lisa Miller selling this other chick and her kid down the river for her own life.

The minute Al heard Lisa say she could get ahold of an infant, Tim had seen the dollar signs in Al's eyes. There was no arguing with him after that. If Sam wanted to change his mind, that was his business. He understood business. And as they transferred Lisa to the van for the drive to Orange County, Al had pulled Tim and Animal aside briefly and told them that the minute they grabbed Alicia and the baby they were to grab Lisa's skinny white ass too and haul her back in the van. They weren't letting her go, and as far as the original job went that was still on the agenda. Let Lisa think they were letting her go; ignorance was bliss, right?

As it turned out, the money didn't matter to Animal. He'd been wanting to do a baby for some time.

What hadn't been in the script was Lisa Miller escaping. Bitch had slammed Animal pretty good in the solar plexus. Must have been a lucky shot. But there was no way Tim was hanging around to chase after her. Animal had climbed back in the van and Tim had sped off back to the cabin. Al had been pissed as donkey shit, and he was flying off the walls. He'd been indulging in the face Drano while he and Animal were gone, too. Tim had spotted the mirror and razor blades and Al had kept rubbing his nose and sniffling, his pupils dilated as he yelled at them for letting Lisa go. Animal had had to hold Al back as Tim told him he'd take care of it. "We'll get her," he'd said. "I know where she lives. When we're done tonight, I'll take my cousin's truck and cruise by her place and scope it out. We'll get her, don't worry."

"Jesus *fuck!*" Al had thundered. He'd twisted out of Animal's grasp. "What the hell am I going to do now that she's gone? Shit!"

"Tell Sam we got the film," Tim said, the ruse springing into place perfectly. "Tell him we got it all. When are you supposed to make the delivery?"

"In two weeks!" Al said, running a shaky hand through his thinning hair.

"Piece of cake," Tim said, exchanging a glance with Animal. Alicia and the baby were still in the truck, and Tim remembered hearing the infant cry as he'd tried to calm Al down. "She doesn't know us, she doesn't know where this place is, and she doesn't know you."

"But she saw Animal's *face!*" Al had almost screamed the words.

"Yes, she did," Tim said. How do you argue with logic like that? "But we're going to get her. Trust me on this. Besides, I think right now we got something else on our plate we gotta take care of."

That had broken the spell. Al had huffed dramatically, then motioned for Animal to bring Alicia and the baby in, and Tim had spent the next few hours watching in horrified fascination, then disgust and fear and sickness, as they worked. And as the gut-wrenching scenes unfolded, Tim had felt those old feelings from years ago erupt to the surface of his psyche.

And now they had it. Three snuff films, one that of an infant. Ready to roll and bank on.

Tim extracted a cigarette from the pack he kept in his breast pocket. He lit it with shaky fingers, dragged in deep. Fuck, but this had been an intense shoot. Animal had just been . . . watching him and that baby had just been . . .

No, Dad, please don't hurt Binky!

The look in Alicia's eyes that screamed *No, my baby! No, please—*

Remembering the anguish he felt, seeing it on Alicia's face.

He felt the tears again. "Oh fuck, what've I done?"

Al stepped outside, lugging camera equipment. He was no longer paranoid and seemed to be his old self. He glared at Tim. "Quit fucking around and help me carry this shit to the van."

Tim struggled to rein his emotions in. He took a deep breath, struggling to hold back the tears. Time to focus; time to get through this night. He took a drag off his cigarette. "Yes, boss," Tim said, as he helped Al dismantle the camera equipment.

It was closing in on three A.M. and they had just rolled the last tarp containing the body of Alicia and the remaining scraps of her baby daughter into the van when headlights lit up the cabin.

Tim looked up, his heart leaping in his throat.

"Who the fuck do we have here?" Al said.

"Where's Animal?" Tim asked, suddenly feeling scared. He had insisted they clean up as much as possible at the cabin, including removing the boards he had nailed up on the back bedroom window, and he was glad they did.

"Here." Animal stepped up behind them. He was dressed in blue jeans, a white chambray shirt, black loafers. His brown hair was combed and styled perfectly. He was carrying a briefcase that contained the tools he used for shoots. He smiled, his eyes gleaming. "Don't worry," he said. "We can handle this."

When the vehicle pulled up, Tim saw that it was one with the words BIG BEAR P.D. painted on the doors. The driver turned the engine off and the passenger door flew open. A tall man with angular features and short brown hair leaped out. He looked frantic. "Tim! Hey, Tim, you seen Debbie around?"

"No, I haven't, Neal," Tim said, trying to calm his nerves. He'd had a feeling this might happen, and he was hoping they could get the hell out of here before Neal showed up. Neal had probably shown up at his cabin and freaked out when he saw that Debbie wasn't there.

The cop stepped out of the vehicle. He was wearing a light windbreaker. "Are you the owner of this cabin, sir?"

"No, Officer, I'm not." Tim offered them a smile. "I'm just renting it from the owners."

"You sure you haven't seen Debbie?" Neal was suddenly looming in front of him. He could feel the panic washing off the man in waves. His eyes were frantic.

"I'm sorry, Neal, I haven't." Tim feigned a look of concern. A sudden sense that he had the upper hand burst through him. It made him feel better, in control of the situation. "Is there anything wrong?"

"She's *gone!*" Neal said, his voice a fast clip. "She was supposed to be at the cabin when I came up yesterday, and she was gone!"

The cop was calm and professional. "Mr. Martinez reported his wife missing earlier today. He'd been looking for her and calling us all day, and we got involved this evening. Are you sure you haven't seen her recently?"

"No." Tim shook his head.

"Can I ask who your two friends are?" the cop asked.

Tim turned back to Al and Animal, who had been listening with interest. Al turned on the charm, instantly transforming from snuff pornographer to a guy who looked like he might be a contractor or a cabinetmaker. "I'm Al Pressman," he said.

"And I'm Jeff," Animal said, turning on the charm as well. "Jeff Scott."

"How long have you been up here with Mr. . . . ?"

"Murray," Tim said. "Tim Murray."

"How long have you been with Mr. Murray today?" the cop asked.

"All day," Jeff answered.

"And you haven't noticed anything unusual?"

"No."

"Did the three of you come up for the weekend?"

"Yes," Al said. "We've been up here since late Saturday."

"Are you sure you haven't seen Debbie?" Neal asked frantically. Tim could see that the man was imploring them for help. His eyes were wide and frantic with panic. "She just walked out of the cabin. She left her car, her purse, everything at the cabin. I thought maybe she might have taken a walk by here or—"

"I haven't seen her all weekend," Tim said. He was feeling the pressure mount again.

The cop nodded. "Mr. Martinez says he called yesterday and his wife didn't answer the phone. And she never returned his calls."

"I was working this weekend," Neal said, pacing back and forth in front of the jeep. "I couldn't get off. We were going to meet up here today. And when I got here, she wasn't there!"

"What does she look like?" Al asked, his features masked with concern.

The officer described Debbie Martinez to them, and as he did, Al and Jeff frowned, shaking their heads. "No," Al said. "I haven't seen anybody looking like that. We haven't really been out much."

"Can I ask what's in the van?" the cop asked.

Tim felt as if he had been punched in the stomach.

"Camera equipment," Al said.

"Camera equipment?" The cop looked at him.

"My friends and I," Tim said, attempting to explain as

his mind raced. "We're amateur filmmakers. We've been up here all weekend working on a film project."

The cop was looking at the van, as if trying to see through it. Tim felt the lead in his belly grow solid. He glanced at Al quickly and saw that Al was watching the cop, trying hard to look casual. Only Jeff bore the slightest trace of normalcy; he looked both concerned for Neal and curious as to why Debbie Martinez could disappear.

"When was the last time you saw Debbie Martinez?" the cop asked, turning back to Tim.

Tim shrugged, trying to come up with the right answer. "I don't know—few weeks ago maybe?"

"And you two?" The cop nodded at Al and Animal.

"I've never seen her," Al said.

"I was up here a few weeks ago with Tim," Animal said. "That was the last time I saw her."

The cop turned to Neal, who was hugging himself in the brisk coolness of the Big Bear night. "Why don't we try the Harper place and Keene's shack down 772?"

"Okay." Neal headed to the passenger side without looking at Tim or the others.

"Sorry to have troubled you folks," the officer said.

"No problem, Officer," Tim said.

Al lifted the last carrying case containing the camera as the officer started the Jeep's engine. The headlights popped on and the Jeep pulled away, heading down the road.

"That was a close one," Tim breathed, watching the taillights recede.

"Don't just stand there watching them leave!" Al barked. "Help me pack this shit up and let's get the fuck out of here!"

And Tim turned to do just that.

They got the hell out of there.

Eighteen

Lisa had been feeling a little sick the past day or so, and this morning it had been worse. She was curled into her favorite chair by the sofa, trying to ignore the pain. Brad could tell there was something wrong, but every time he asked if she was all right she said she was fine.

It had been two weeks since what they were now referring to as "their vacation that went to hell." Since that time, both of them had been questioned numerous times by the LAPD, the San Bernardino County Sheriff's department, and the Ventura County Sheriff's Department, and Lisa had been examined at USC Medical Center. She had been taken to the hospital, where a thorough examination had been performed. Aside from a few bruises and scratches and dehydration, she was fine. The surprise she had hoped to tell Brad on their vacation was revealed that day, and Brad treated the news with a mixture of joy and relief. The medical personnel questioned her thoroughly about her attack, trying to determine if penetration occurred, and Lisa assured them that, no, they didn't rape her. They did other things to her, but they didn't rape her that way.

Brad was so happy she was alive that he seemed to brush off the story she told the police: She had been on her way to the Denny's near the motel when a van pulled up and she was grabbed. She was pulled into the van and somebody knocked her out with a rag drenched in chloroform. The next thing she knew, they were driving up to the mountains. They kept her in the van the entire weekend, slapping her around a little, forcing her to perform oral sex on them, and doing drugs, probably coke. Maybe it was crystal meth. Whatever it was, they were snorting it, it made them hyper, and it made them horny, but no matter how much they forced her to perform oral sex on them they never got hard. The first time she told this story, the detective nodded. "Speed freaks become impotent after a while. If they hadn't been, the attack probably would have been worse."

She couldn't describe her assailants, no matter how much she was questioned. It had been dark, but she was certain there were four of them. They were big, they might have all been black, but they could have been Hispanic or Samoan or something. They were big and dark-skinned, and some of them had kinky hair, and some of them were speaking a funny language that sounded like it could have been Spanish, it all happened so fast that she just didn't remember. They asked her repeatedly if Caleb Smith had anything to do with this, and at first her mind had drawn a blank until one of the detectives reminded her of the road-rage incident that had landed Brad in jail. She shook her head. "No, it wasn't him. The van these guys were driving was white, with no windows. It wasn't Caleb Smith at all."

The detectives who had been questioning her traded glances with each other and said nothing.

She had been a nervous wreck throughout the whole ordeal, and after a while they eased off on the questioning. They had vague descriptions of suspects and a description of the van, and that went out over the bulletin. They tried questioning her more in the days that followed, but every time they did Lisa could offer them nothing new. Besides, every time they took her down that line of questioning, she would start crying, becoming hysterical. It was obvious to the detectives working the case that she had been emotionally traumatized by her abduction, and she was, only it wasn't the way they thought.

Her parents, who had flown out to Orange County from Iowa, had broken down and wept at the news that she had been found. Brad's parents had been equally happy—his mother had displayed her relief the same way both of Lisa's parents had. His dad took it the way he usually took good news; all the weight of stress and worry that he had been carrying seemed to ease off his shoulders, and he wandered around the hospital while Lisa was being examined, looking tired, then relieved, then happy for Brad, then worried again. "I just hope she's going to be all right," he said when Brad asked how he was. Father and son traded smiles; Dad's looking a little bit more worn for the wear after being awake for the past two days.

During the past two weeks, she had been brooding and silent. She went back to work after a week, but managed only one full day of work before asking for a one-month leave of absence. She was still traumatized by the incident, and she needed time to get herself together. Her boss, George Brooks, had been absent from the office on a business trip when she returned, so the request had gone to one of the other partners. The leave was granted and she spent her days in front of the television, watching talk show after talk show, her mind always elsewhere. Her nerves were always twisting and turning in on themselves, her mind weighing heavily on what she had done to save herself and her and Brad's unborn baby.

Brad was looking at her from across the living room. "Are you sure you don't want me to call that therapist Detective Morse recommended? I can make an appointment for the both of us."

Lisa stared blankly at the television. "I don't know," she said morosely. "Let me think about it."

Brad regarded her silently. In the days that had followed the nightmare, Brad had been overwhelmed with joy at having her back. He was also overwhelmed with joy at the news of her pregnancy. He had been so happy that he'd gone bustling around the house rearranging things, making plans to turn the spare bedroom into a nursery, talking to her about starting up a college fund. Lisa hadn't told Brad yet about the money she had taken out of their savings account and her IRA; she had intercepted both pieces of mail from the bank verifying the transactions, and she supposed she would have to tell him something eventually. After all, he *would* notice. She just wasn't sure when she should tell him about what *really* happened. She had to make sure that if she did he would abide by her wishes and not tell anybody. He would have to agree that they go away, that they pack up and leave and start a new life somewhere far away.

Become new people, with new identities. They could do it.

"Are you sure you don't want to talk to me?" Brad asked, scooting closer to her on the sofa. His features were soft and open. "You look like you have a lot on your mind you want to talk about."

She looked up at him and forced a smile. "I'm fine . . . really, I'm fine. It's just . . ."

"It's still on your mind? Isn't it?"

Lisa nodded, mouth set in a bloodless grimace. Her stomach rolled in her belly and the nausea returned. *Morning sickness,* she thought, as the next wave hit her deep, making her cringe. *It's just morning sickness that's making me feel so bad, that's all, just—*

If it was morning sickness, she had been having it since the day Brad picked her up at USC Medical Center. If it was morning sickness, it hit her strongest whenever she thought about what she had done to save herself and their unborn baby.

The guilt was weighing down heavily on her more and more as the days went by.

And with it came the pain in her abdomen.

The only reason she was alive today was that her abductors had found another to take her place. To spare her life, and the life of the unborn baby growing in her womb, she had offered Alicia and her baby girl Mandy as ritual sacrifices. The image that stayed in her mind the most was the look on Alicia's face when Lisa had surprised her near the entrance of the same restaurant she and Brad had met her. That look of surprise as Alicia recognized her, the look of hope flooding her features as she swallowed the story Animal told her—that he was a friend of Lisa and Brad's, and that the three of them had done some thinking and decided to put Alicia and her baby up in a motel until she could get on her feet. All she needed to do was follow them this way—Brad was waiting in the car—and then the look of utter surprise as they got to the van and Tim popped out from behind the door as Animal ushered Alicia inside, clamping the chloroform-drenched rag over her mouth and nose, pushing her inside the van, Lisa grabbing the handle of the baby's car seat before it could crash to the ground. For a brief instant, she glimpsed the expression on Alicia's face and her eyes seemed to light on Lisa's, terror-stricken and asking *Why?*

It was that look she had to ignore as she'd fought Animal for her life outside the van.

That look on Alicia's face was on Lisa's mind constantly now. It chased her into the night, keeping her from sleep.

"Are you sure you don't want to talk about anything?" Brad asked again.

Lisa shook her head, fighting back the tears. She

wanted so much to tell him everything, but she was afraid.

If you tell anybody—and I mean anybody—I will fucking find you, and you and your family are going to wind up as playthings for Animal in a film. You got that?

I just wanted to save my baby . . .

Lisa felt the tears coming. "No . . ." she said, her voice trembling. "No . . ."

The look in Alicia's eyes before the chloroform rendered her unconscious. *Why?*

The screaming of Alicia's infant daughter, Mandy, growing dim as Lisa ran away from the van . . . the thought of that baby crying as Tim drove away, the sound of that baby's cries still lingering in her haunted mind.

Lisa began to cry, deep sobs that burst from her gut. She doubled over from the force of them. She had only wanted to save her own baby. She had only wanted to save the wonderful life she was building with Brad. She had only wanted to give her own unborn baby—a baby she and Brad had sacrificed so much for and had gone through hell to conceive—a chance at life. Thinking about this, thinking about the fact that she had so easily turned Tim and his murderous group onto an innocent woman and her infant daughter, all to appease the faceless group of perverts who paid big money to satisfy their sadistic urges, was more devastating to her than she had ever expected.

"Lisa." Brad's voice was filled with concern. He knelt down beside her, touching her knee gently. "Hey, it's okay, honey. You're safe now. Everything's going to be all right."

Lisa shook her head, the tears flowing more freely now. The sobs were coming from deep within her, pouring from the depths of her soul. "No, it's not." She felt another sudden pain in her abdomen, this one more penetrating, and she began to cry harder. It was a cry of loss. "No, it's *not* going to be all right. It's *never* going to be all right."

Lisa Miller was beginning to bleed.

After they returned home from the hospital to deal with the miscarriage shortly after midnight, Lisa Miller told her husband what *really* happened.

Everything.

PART TWO

Down with the Sickness

Nineteen

"Please don't say anything!" Lisa was crying. She had been crying for the past thirty minutes as she spun the narrative out.

Brad hadn't been able to sit still through Lisa's sudden confession. He had paced the floor of the master bedroom where Lisa was lying in bed, feeling his shock, fear, and anger grow as the story went from its harrowing beginnings to its desperate conclusion.

"Please don't hate me!" Lisa cried. She buried her face in her hands, bawling.

"Honey," Brad said. He went to her bedside and tried to take her in his arms as she sat hunched over. "I could never hate you."

"I *killed* them!" she cried.

"Lisa," Brad began. He didn't know what to say. He was at a loss for words.

"I killed them!" Lisa said. She pounded the mattress

with her fist over and over. "I killed them and our child is dead and it's *my* fault!"

"It is *not* your fault!" Feeling a sudden burst of anger at the man who had been responsible for the near murder of his wife, Brad gripped Lisa's shoulders. *"Look at me!"*

Lisa raised her tear-streaked face to his. She had been crying for days, and her face was red and damp. Brad looked into her eyes, gripping her upper arms firmly. "You did not kill them. *They* killed them, not you. You tried to save Alicia and Mandy. Okay?"

"But I *failed!*" She broke down sobbing. She collapsed into his arms. "I failed and they died because of me, and I still couldn't . . . still couldn't save our baby!"

"I know," Brad said, holding her, just wanting to protect her and love her. "I know, honey. But the important thing is that you saved yourself. You got yourself out of there. That's all that matters now."

They remained that way for a while. Lisa sobbed and Brad held her, stroking her hair. He told her he loved her. He told her he was glad that she was safe and sound and in his arms.

In time, Lisa's sobs trickled down. She wiped her upper lip with the back of her hand. Despite the long day, Brad didn't feel the least bit tired. Their day had started at seven A.M., and it was now well past two A.M. He had taken Lisa to the hospital shortly after three P.M. and she had been discharged at eleven-thirty. The doctor had instructed them that Lisa needed three days of bed rest, and had prescribed a mild sedative to help her sleep. Lisa had taken one but had been unable to sleep. All she had been able to do was cry.

"I feel so bad," Lisa said. She looked up at Brad. Her eyes were red. "Do you understand how I feel? I feel so . . . so *violated.*"

Brad nodded. "I understand."

Lisa leaned into his embrace again. "I feel worse than a rape victim," she said, her voice muffled slightly through his shirt. "Even though they didn't . . . didn't do anything to me . . ."

"I know," Brad said, holding her.

"And I'm so *scared,*" Lisa said. "And I feel so *guilty.* That's . . . that's one of the reasons why I had to tell you. It was just . . . just eating me up inside."

Brad held her, just listening. As much as he wanted to help her, he knew that what she was feeling would have to be sorted out by her.

"I just don't want you to hate me for what I did," she said, her voice a low whisper. "Please don't hate me."

"I don't hate you," Brad said. He kissed the top of her head. "I would have done the same thing."

"You would've?" A sharp intake of breath, as if she were surprised.

"Yes." A sharp pang of guilt and shame stabbed him in the gut; *would he have done the same thing? Would he have done something so . . . so* harsh? *So* cruel?

She sniffled. "So you don't think I'm a monster?"

"No. If anybody's a monster, it's those men." Brad felt his anger return. And with it came fear.

"I had to get it off my chest," she said. "But I also don't want you to . . . to say anything. I don't want them to come after us."

"They won't."

"Please don't say anything," Lisa said. She looked up at him again, her face pleading.

"Everything will be okay." Brad kissed her. "You need to get some sleep." He glanced at the clock. It had been more than four hours since she had taken a sedative, so it would be safe for her to have another. In fact, she could take two of them, the doctor had said. "Why don't I get you your pills and some water so you can sleep."

Lisa leaned back against the pillows. For the first time since they arrived home from the hospital, she looked tired. "I could use maybe one pill. All of a sudden, I feel so tired."

"Talking probably helped," he said. He caressed her hand. "I'll be right back."

He went into the master bathroom and drew a cup of water for her and got her a pill. He returned and handed the pill to her. She drank it down with a swallow of water. He replaced the glass on the bureau. He drew the covers up over her and turned off the bedside lamp. "Try to get some sleep," he said. "I'll be in a little later."

"You don't hate me?"

"I don't hate you."

Lisa let out another small cry. "I'm so sorry."

Brad kissed her and held her close. "It's okay," he whispered.

Lisa cried for a little bit, then quieted down. The last thing she said before she drifted off to sleep was "Please don't say anything. Please don't . . ."

Brad knelt beside her and held her hand, watching as she descended into a deep sleep. When he was sure she was sleeping soundly, he exited the master bedroom and went into the living room to call William Grecko.

William Grecko answered the phone on the third ring. " 'Lo." His voice was groggy.

"Billy, it's Brad."

"Brad." William's voice perked up. "What's up? Christ, it's . . . it's after two in the morning. Is everything okay?"

"I need to talk," Brad said, resisting the urge to blurt everything out to Bill now. "Can you come over?"

"I . . . yeah, I guess I can. What . . . what's going on?"

"Please, just come over. I need to talk, Billy, I really need help. You're the only person I can trust."

"Is it Lisa? Is she all right?"

"We lost the baby."

There was silence for a brief moment. "Oh, Brad." Billy's tone was sad. "I'm so sorry."

"There's more to it than that. I can't talk about it on the phone because I think I'm going to lose my mind if I do. Please come over."

"I'll be there in thirty minutes."

When he hung up, Brad went into the kitchen and found a bottle of Jim Beam and two glasses. He poured the whiskey into both glasses, then brought them to the living room. He turned a lamp on in the living room and sat down to wait for William Grecko to arrive.

And while he waited, he drank.

And thought.

William Grecko arrived thirty minutes later, right on schedule.

Brad ushered him inside. "Want a drink?"

William had thrown on a pair of blue jeans and a white polo shirt. His hair was uncombed. His eyes were red, his features still puffy from being woken out of a sound sleep. "Um, yeah," he said, licking his lips. "I guess I could. Um, you know I'm trying to quit, Brad . . ."

"Have a drink," Brad said, handing Billy the glass he had poured for the lawyer.

Billy took the glass. He looked nervous. "Really, Brad, um . . . I know I'm a fuckup, but I really am trying to quit. I'm an alcoholic, for God's sakes."

"We both know that six months from now you'll be back to drinking again," Brad said, pouring himself another glass. "One drink isn't going to hurt you. Besides, you're going to need it after hearing what I have to tell you."

William hesitated, then took the glass.

"I have something to tell you," Brad said, walking into

the living room. He sat down in his favorite easy chair and motioned for William to sit down. "It's something Lisa told me this evening, when we got home from the hospital. It . . . it has something to do with some of the . . . inconsistencies of her story."

"Yes?" William leaned forward, looking both curious and afraid of the look on Brad's face. A week ago, the detectives handling the case had mentioned to Brad that there were some inconsistencies in Lisa's story that had them concerned. Brad had responded angrily, telling the cops that Lisa had been fucking *kidnapped* goddamnit! She was the fucking *victim!* Billy had been present during the brief meeting and had calmed Brad down. Later, the lawyer had met with the detectives and told Brad what had them concerned. "They think her story doesn't add up," he'd told Brad. "They say it's highly unlikely that they would have let her live. That they would have killed her."

Brad had responded angrily and the detective on the case, a guy named Paul Orr, had backed off, saying he'd be in contact again the following week. Now that Brad had had time to think about Lisa's story and what she'd told the police originally, he could see the holes in her official statement on the crime. "Lisa told me everything," he began. "It . . . it's very similar to what she told the original officers, but . . ."

He told William. And as Brad spun the story out he could see the color drain from Bill's face. The lawyer set the glass down, his mouth agape as Brad told him what her original kidnapper's purpose was. "Oh my God," he said.

"There's more." Brad quickly told the lawyer about Debbie Martinez, the arrival of Animal, and the cinematographer, Al. He told Billy about the long night Lisa had spent with Debbie, wondering if she was going to be next. When Brad got to the part about Lisa's desperate plea for her life and her bringing up the homeless woman they had run into on the first day of their trip, Billy's hand went up to his mouth. His eyes were wide with terror. "Oh my God, please don't tell me what I think she . . . she . . ."

"She told them she'd lead them to this woman and her baby," Brad said. His voice sounded dead. He *felt* dead. He drained the rest of his drink. "She said they could have this woman and her baby in exchange for her own life. And she offered them money. All the money in our savings account."

"And . . . and they *went for it?*" William's face was damp with sweat.

"Yes. They took her in their van and she got the money. Then she . . . led them to . . ."

"Oh fuck," Billy said. He hadn't taken another sip since Brad had begun, but now he drained the entire contents of the glass. "Where's the rest of that bottle?"

Brad got up to retrieve the bottle. When he brought it back, William took it and refilled his glass. Billy's hand shook as he poured the whiskey. He looked like he had just seen a horrible car accident. "Jesus Christ, Brad," William said, drinking down half of the glass's contents. "Jesus *fucking* Christ!"

"They were going to renege on their deal," Brad said. "They tried to abduct her in the parking lot of that Coco's, probably to take her back to that cabin. But somehow—I don't know how she did it—she escaped. She got the hell out of there and screamed at the top of her lungs and they split."

"And they got that lady, right? And her baby?"

Brad nodded. He poured himself another glass of Jim Beam.

"Fuck!"

The two men were silent for a moment. William drank down the rest of his whiskey and quickly poured himself a refill. Despite already drinking steadily for the past forty minutes or so, Brad didn't feel the least bit drunk. He was sweating it out as rapidly as he was pouring it down.

"Billy, I need your help," Brad finally said, his voice low and shaky.

William looked at him. "What do you want to do? Go to the police?"

"I don't know," Brad said. "I want to do something, but . . . I'm confused and I'm scared and . . ."

"Are you afraid these guys will come after you?"

Brad felt like he was going to collapse. He struggled to contain his emotions; he could feel his limbs shaking. He nodded, the tears springing to his eyes. "Yes."

William leaned forward. He set his hand on Brad's knee, looking directly into his face. "Listen, buddy, there's nothing to worry about. I'm going to help you, okay?"

Brad nodded. His throat hurt. He wiped his eyes with the back of his hands. "Yeah," he said, stammering. "I'm sorry, Billy," he said, choking back the tears. "It's just . . . I'm just so glad she's back and . . . and I had no idea what she went through and to . . . to think that . . . it was much worse than she let on . . . God, no wonder she's been acting this way!"

"I know," William said. He took Brad's hands in his own. Billy was acting more like a fatherly figure to him than a friend. Billy was twenty years Brad's senior, but he looked thirty. "But now we know, and that means we can do something about it."

"I don't know what we can do, though," Brad said. He took a deep breath. He took a peek down the hall where his and Lisa's bedroom was, then looked back at Billy. "She didn't want me to tell anybody. She's scared that they'll make good on their threat. I know she is."

"Thankfully, Lisa has a good memory," William said. He had gained a lot of composure, and his stature was making Brad feel good about calling the lawyer over. "She got names. Tim Murray, Al, and Jeff. No last names on the other fellows, but I'm sure that shouldn't be too hard to get. We do have one full name of a victim, though. Debbie Martinez. That should be easy to trace. If she and her husband own a cabin in Big Bear, we can probably find the place Lisa was taken and locate the deed."

"Do you think we should go to the police?" Brad asked.

"You're goddamn right we should go to the police," William said. Now Billy was looking more angry than confused or frightened.

"I'm scared," Brad said. He looked at William, feeling suddenly flush with adrenaline. "I'm scared of what might happen if we go to the police. These guys have our address, and they have her social security card, for God's sakes!"

"Don't worry about that," William said. "I can get you and Lisa whisked away into a protection program. They won't be able to find you."

"Shit." Brad broke down and cried.

He felt hopeless.

When he gained a little bit of control over himself, he looked up at William. "I don't know what to do," he said, wiping his eyes. "I feel like . . . such a helpless idiot."

"Leave it to me," William said, gripping Brad's knee with his hand. "I'll take care of everything. I'll talk to Detective Orr. He'll probably want to talk to Lisa again. We'll have to talk to her when she wakes up tomorrow. She might not like it, but we'll have to reassure her that the two of you will be safe and we'll catch the people who did this. We're gonna get these bastards, Brad. I'll hunt them down myself if I have to."

Brad gripped his friend's hand. "Thanks. Thanks a lot. I don't know what I'd do without you."

William offered Brad a smile of encouragement. "I'll take care of everything."

Twenty

The Seagram's Business District in the City of Industry comprised rows of industrial buildings that circled the perimeter of a large lot in a U shape. Twin rows of identical buildings flanked this structure. The majority of the businesses that operated in the thirty or so spaces fell on the industrial side: commercial printers, T-shirt manufacturing plants, auto-body shops, glaziers, electronics shops, computer hardware manufacturers. The office Al Pressman was visiting this evening bore the legend Mark and Sons, Printers, and it was at the end of the lot. He pulled in front of the sliding door of the garage into what would have been the print shop but which had since been turned into a makeshift film studio. Al turned the car off and sat in the front bucket seat, listening as the engine cooled. He hated this fucking car. It was a Porsche, and it had a great engine, but he hated it anyway. It was too goddamned tiny. Like driving a roller skate on the highway. When he got his check for the latest job he was going to get a Corvette. He'd always liked 'Vettes. They were not only strong, they were durable and wouldn't crumple if you sneezed on them.

Al sat in the car for a moment. It wasn't every day he got called to Rick Shectman's place of business. He usually dealt with Sam Bash, who gave out the orders for jobs. Most of the time it was routine blood-sport shit. The last job—the one that had turned into quite the gold mine thanks to the Miller woman selling that homeless woman and her baby down the river—had been arranged by Sam. Al had been told to shoot footage that was to include Animal and a woman that Tim Murray brought. That was it, no questions asked. Al had been surprised to see two women at the cabin, but when Tim explained what had happened he'd shrugged it off. Since they had to get rid of the other bitch anyway, might as well film the shit, right? He was paid to operate a camera and catch the right angles and provide the right amount of lighting, then edit the shit down. That was it. And Animal was paid to do what he did best: rape, torture, and then kill people. They didn't care who they did it to, as long as they were paid.

Except this job had been different. Sam Bash had been quite explicit when he told Al that the woman Tim brought was a special job, that there was double money involved in it. Fine. No big deal. So when the bitch mentioned the homeless woman and the baby, of course it attracted their attention. There were plenty of pedo freaks out there who got off on the prepubescent scene, but infants were another league altogether. You just didn't find many of them in the extreme hardcore underground. Al had known of junkies who sometimes sold their babies for crack and the kids usually wound up dead from whatever freak they'd been sold to. Al knew there was a thriving pedophile underground that got off on this shit, and he knew some of them had money falling out of their assholes. He'd seen the dollar signs immediately, so he'd gone to another part of the cabin and made an executive decision. He'd pretended to call Sam with the news, and Tim just about shit his pants when he came back and told him that the Miller bitch was out and the other woman and the baby were in. Later, while Animal was putting Lisa in the van, he'd pulled Tim aside and told him the real deal: get Lisa Miller's money, get the homeless woman and the baby, and get back to the cabin pronto. They were still going to do the Miller bitch as planned. That had made Tim feel better, but then the cunt had escaped. Tim had been fucking paranoid—hell, Al had been paranoid too and had had to indulge in some blow to cope. He'd just about had a fit when Tim came back sans the Miller bitch, but he eventually calmed down. "We'll get her," he'd told Tim. "Don't worry. They want her, we'll get her, but I think right now they're going to be pretty happy with what we got now."

He'd explained that to Sam Bash the day after he made the delivery, when Bash called and asked in an icy tone why he had not carried out the job he'd been paid to do. "You paid me to shoot a scene that included Animal and whatever woman Tim Murray brought me," he'd explained. "That's all I did, no questions asked."

It was clear that Bash had been pissed, even though he conceded that they already had two buyers willing to pay two hundred and fifty thousand dollars for the tape with the infant. That was more than double what he'd get for a normal snuff film. They'd exchanged a few more words and Sam had rung off with a "you'll be hearing from me," then he'd hung up. Al hadn't heard from him since.

In the last week, though, he'd talked to Tim. They'd been paying close attention to the news and there'd been no media coverage of Lisa Miller's abduction. Tim had even done an Internet search and had come up with nothing. Tim told Al he'd been yelled at by Sam too, and he was nervous. You didn't fuck with these people; Al knew that, and he assured Tim they'd be fine. "You got her address. I can hold Sam off for another week until the money for these films comes in. That'll be a nice pacifier for him. Then, say in two weeks, me and you pay a surprise visit to Ms. Miller. Get yourself a white panel van and I'll have a shot of morphine all fixed up and ready for her. It'll be a nice quick abduction, and this time we'll just do it. She'll be dead and disposed of within a few hours after we pick her up, and the next day Sam'll be happier than a pig in shit. How's that sound?"

That had sounded fine to Tim, and Al had lain low for the rest of the week. He didn't hear from Tim or Animal, and he tried to keep a low profile. He didn't even call Sam to check on where his money was. Then this afternoon he got a phone call from Rick Shectman telling him to get over to his print shop for an evening meeting regarding the next job. Rick and Sam were acquainted, and from the brief conversation he had with Rick, Al surmised that Sam had gotten over his anger regarding the last job. The money the organization had just made must've sweetened them up.

Al reached under his seat for the coke vial he kept in a compartment he had gouged into the seat. He opened it, reached a pinkie in, and scooped some blow out with his fingernail. He took a snort up his left nostril, dipped his nail back in for seconds, snorted that up his right nostril, then rubbed the residue over his gums. He replaced the vial under the seat and checked himself out in the rearview mirror. Might as well get this over with. He opened the door, swung his long legs out of the Porsche, and headed to the office. He felt amped up and ready to do business as he entered and paused for a moment at the threshold, letting his vision get adjusted to the darkness. "Yo," he called out. "You here, Rick?"

"In the back," a voice called out.

Al made his way through the office to the rear of the establishment.

Mark and Sons Printers had originally been a commercial printer that operated a four-color press. The back room was a darkroom where paste-ups were shot and converted to plates for printing. There had once been two presses, but one had been sold and the other sat against the rear wall under a layer of dust. The remaining floor space of the shop had been cleared away from other printing machines and was now used as a makeshift studio for some of the hardcore S&M loops Al shot. Rick Shectman, the guy who had inherited the printing business from his father, only did business as a printer occasionally. Mostly he used the press to generate child pornography or other illegal underground smut. He also ran drugs and stolen jewelry through the shop. And he leased space to Al for the production of some milder hardcore S&M. "As long as they don't get blood and shit all over my floor," Rick had told Al one day a few years ago in that thick Slavic accent he'd inherited from his father. "You can use my shop. You use big-titty women, you tell me so I watch, yes?" He'd smiled a gap-toothed smile.

Rick Shectman was a man who conducted himself in a casual manner, but Al knew he was a heavy key player in the illegal hardcore community. He was one of the money people. He knew the clients. And he knew the talent. Al, Tim, and Animal had worked for Rick five times in the past three years, and Al knew Rick to be a fair man, but a hard one. Rumor had it that he'd once beaten a customer who had commissioned a torture film with a lead pipe after the customer failed to come up with the fee for the finished product. The beating had been so bad that the victim had lost both eyes. Al had heard of worse crime bosses. The guys back east in New York and New

Jersey, they didn't fuck around. They usually had a goon squad get medieval on your ass if you fucked with them, and you wound up at the bottom of New York Harbor with a pair of cement boots.

When Al rounded the corner where the darkroom flanked the rear of the print shop, he saw that Tim Murray and Animal were there. They were leaning casually against the printing equipment. Rick was seated on a skid of computer paper that had been carted back there for storage. He smiled at Al. "Nice that you could join us." His teeth were very white, and Al felt his limbs go numb. There was something about the look on Rick's face, which was usually happy-go-lucky, bright and cheerful, that was sharply different. Now Rick's Slavic features were dark, with a hint of menace swimming beneath his blue eyes.

"What's up?" Al asked, trying to sound casual.

"We need to talk," Rick said.

Al glanced at Tim quickly. He couldn't tell if Tim was nervous, but he guessed the man was; he could tell that last job had been too hardcore for him, and during the drive to Los Angeles Al had soothed whatever worries Tim might have by telling him how much money they were all going to make. That seemed to work at lifting the man's mood. Now Tim wouldn't meet his gaze. Only Animal looked indifferent. He looked bored.

"Okay, let's talk," Al said.

"What did Sam tell you to do when he gave you this last job, Al?" Rick asked.

Al felt the blood drain from his face. He looked from Tim to Animal, who refused to meet his gaze. "He said that . . . that . . ."

"When Sam called and said that Tim had our star, I related this news to the client," Rick said, smiling calmly. "He was very pleased. *Very* pleased. Then, when Sam called a few days later and gave us the news about the other one and the baby and what had happened, well . . . I wasn't happy, but I saw the potential. I ran it by our client. Personally, he wasn't interested in a baby. But I knew some in the group would be. I knew they would pay a lot of money for it. I made the arrangements for it not knowing . . . what?"

Al was mortified. He swallowed a dry lump. "I don't understand. Everything—"

"No." Rick leaned forward and smiled. He looked like a Great White Shark; his teeth were white and long, his eyes dull and emotionless, like a predator's. "You replaced the star of our film with a baby. You let her con you into giving you money and you let the bitch go."

"I gave those two fuckheads orders to bring that bitch back when she led them to the homeless chick and the baby!" Al protested, his voice rising. He was getting pissed now.

"Bullshit," Tim muttered in a low voice.

"You fucking me?" Al turned on Tim, feeling himself grow hot with anger and agitated from the cocaine he had snorted a few minutes ago. "You back-stabbing fuck, you fucking with me?"

"Who instructed Mr. Murray to release the star of our film?" Rick Shectman grinned casually at Al.

"This goddamn sonofabitch—" Al pointed at Tim.

"You made the call to Sam," Tim said, trying to look casual. He looked nervous, and Al knew immediately that the fat fuck had squealed the minute Sam began sniffing for holes in the story he'd told him. "You told him we'd gotten hold of that homeless chick and the kid—"

"And I told Sam that there was the potential for more money and—" Al protested.

"And Sam told me he never received a phone call from you," Rick replied. "Bad move, Mr. Pressman."

Al turned to Rick. He was instantly sober. "Now wait. This—"

Tim interrupted. "You said that it was a go. I thought you'd talked to Sam and the plans were changed. You told me to take Lisa and drive her to her bank and make her find the chick and the kid. And I did."

"And I also told you to bring that cunt back!" Al yelled.

"That's not what you told me," Tim said quickly.

"Bullshit!" Al felt hot with anger. Tim Murray was lying to save his own fat ass. He'd been called on the carpet by Sam and Rick, and now he was backpedaling to save himself. He knew he had fucked up by letting Lisa escape, and he was doing everything he could to shift the blame to Al.

Rick hopped off the skid casually. He looked at Animal. "I don't know." He shrugged. He looked at Tim and Al. "I don't know what to make of this shit, personally. All I know is, my client is fucking pissed. You know how much business I get from this guy?"

Al opened his mouth to respond, then closed it. He had no idea how much money Rick made from this faceless client, whoever the fuck he was. Probably just another closet pervert like the rest of them, but what did he care? Closet perverts usually had money falling out of their assholes. That's all that mattered to Al.

"You know what matters the most in all this?" Rick was addressing Tim and Al. He took a step forward. Tim automatically retreated back, his face showing the slightest registration of fear. Al forced himself to stand his ground. Let that fat-ass fuck Tim Murray cower with his tail between his legs. He was the one that fucked things up.

"You deaf?" Rick asked, taking another step toward

them, leaning forward as if he were straining to listen to them. "What the fuck did I just say?"

"You asked if we know what matters most," Al said.

"Bravo!" Rick Shectman clapped his hands, applauding. "Al Pressman *does* have acute listening skills! Let's put them to the test. What did Sam tell you three weeks ago when he gave you the job?"

"Shit," Al said. He felt his limbs grow tingly. He knew where this was leading.

"Wrong answer," Rick said, and then he hit Al so hard and so fast that Al didn't even see it coming. He caught a brief flash of the fury in Rick's face, felt the sudden whoosh and saw the flash, and then he felt a freight train crash into his face and he knew no more.

It was the pounding headache that brought Al Pressman back to consciousness.

The cool air prickled gooseflesh on Al's bare skin. He groaned. His head felt like a sledgehammer had split it open. He was almost afraid to open his eyes.

He was lying on something cool. Concrete? Steel? It was hard to tell.

The cool air against his skin told him he had been stripped of his clothes.

He opened his eyes. A wave of pain broke out across his forehead and eyeballs.

"I think our star is waking up." Rick's voice.

Fuck. Al struggled to open his eyes. *Fuck no, fuck no, fuckno—*

He got his eyes open and tried to sit up, but the rope binding his arms to his sides prevented him from doing so.

At first he couldn't see much; his vision was blurred and doubled. He blinked and the first thing that swam into his vision was Rick Shectman, leaning forward, grin-

ning at him. "Well, well! You're awake! Good, good! Now maybe we can proceed further, yes?"

A wave of nausea washed over Al and he felt the urge to vomit. He could hardly breathe; his nose was clogged with mucus and dried blood; it felt broken, too.

Rick turned to his right. "Tim?"

Tim stepped forward and headed to Al's feet. He wouldn't look at Al. Tim reached down and picked up Al's feet by the ankles. Al saw that his legs were bound, too.

"What . . ." Al croaked.

"Save your voice and your energy," Rick purred. He leaned over Al's head as he gripped him under the armpits. Rick and Tim hoisted Al up and carried him to the other side of the print shop and laid him down on a sheet of black plastic.

"What . . ." Al started again, realization setting in. "No . . . what . . . what's going . . ."

Then Al saw Animal.

While Al had lain unconscious, Jeff had slipped into the role of Animal. He had shed his casual attire and now stood in the corner, completely naked except for his black bondage mask.

And the tremendous strap-on dildo that he had fastened around his waist at the groin.

With the seven-inch steel blade affixed to the plastic phallus.

Al sucked in air and began screaming, wiggling like a fish out of water as he tried to escape. His throat was dry, so his screams came out sounding like raspy squawks. Rick and Tim held him down while Animal stepped forward. Al's eyes bugged out of their sockets. *"No, please don't, please don't do this, nopleasedon't-dothis—"*

"I just have two questions for you, Mr. Pressman," Rick Shectman said. He stood up and planted one booted foot on Al's chest. He pressed his weight down, pinning Al to the floor.

Al didn't hear him. All he could see was Animal standing behind Tim, who held his feet down. Animal's eyes were indifferent, without compassion. It was almost as if he didn't even know the man behind the mask anymore, as if five years of working together side by side had all been obliterated.

"Two things," Rick said, peering down at Al. "The woman." He pressed more of his weight down on Al's chest. "She left vital information: Social Security card, driver's license, credit card, checkbook, wallet, photos of her husband and family. Her purse, perhaps. Where is it?"

"My bag," Al said quickly, huffing for breath. "Front seat of my car."

Rick turned to Tim. "Get it."

Tim left his position and went to get Al's bag.

Al ceased struggling for a moment and tried to make eye contact with Rick. "It's there," he said. "I can get her easily. Animal and me, we'll get her."

"I'm sure you will." Rick smiled.

Al's thoughts were racing. He swore to God that he would never fuck up again. Christ, when this was all over he was never going to work for Rick Shectman and Sam Bash again, period. All he had to do was stay calm and when Tim came back with the purse he would show Rick. The Ruskie would see that nabbing Lisa would be easy. Shit, he'd do it tonight if Rick wanted him to. He'd go down to Orange County and snag the bitch himself. He didn't care if anybody saw him or not. He didn't give a fuck if he had to face jail time—doing time was preferable than facing Animal.

"When Tim comes back, I'll go down and get her," Al said, putting a plan to action. He licked his lips. "Let Animal come with me, we'll get her. She's probably still traumatized by what happened anyway. We'll go down there, case the place out, break in this evening when her and her hubby are asleep. We'll kill the husband first thing, get him out of the way and then—"

Tim returned with the bag. "Here it is," he said, handing it over to Rick, who opened it and began rifling through the contents.

"Ah," Rick said, smiling as he lifted a yellow bulky wallet out of the bag. He flipped through it. His features beamed. "Ah! Wonderful! Driver's license, credit cards, pictures, the whole works! Wow!" He peered at Lisa's photo on her driver's license. "Pretty lady."

Tim retreated out of Al's line of vision for a moment as Rick looked at the contents of Lisa's wallet. Al didn't know what he was doing, but he could hear the fat man fiddling around with something. Animal stood in front of him, looking psyched up for bloodshed.

"Wonderful!" Rick set the wallet down on a workbench. The room grew brighter and Al felt the temperature grow slightly warmer. He immediately recognized the source of both the light and the rise in heat; Tim had turned on the lighting equipment he used during shoots.

Al craned his head around, trying to see where Tim was. His panic was rising. "Hey, come on! I told you where the wallet was—"

"One more thing," Rick said, ignoring him as he stepped into Al's line of vision again. "What were the instructions Sam gave you?"

Al felt his stomach muscles clench; his balls wanted to crawl up into his groin. He licked his lips and tried to keep eye contact with Rick. He wanted to show the man that he was beat. He had learned his lesson. "He said to film Animal doing whatever bitch Tim brought, then get rid of the body and deliver the tape."

"Exactly!" Rick said, leaning forward. "And what happened?"

"I fucked up," Al said, admitting his mistake. Maybe if he admitted his mistake and took responsibility for it, Rick would give him another chance. "I know I fucked up. I shouldn't have done it. What I did was stupid, but I was thinking of how much we would all benefit from it. I wasn't thinking. I should have. I'm sorry I fucked up, and I'll not only make sure it doesn't happen again, I'll do whatever it takes to fix it."

Rick nodded, seemingly satisfied with Al's confession. "Good for you. I admire a man who admits his weakness."

"It won't happen again, I swear!" Al reiterated.

"I'm sorry, Al," Rick said, kneeling on the floor in front of him, "but I can't take the chance anymore. You're lazy. You're a weak link. I can't afford laziness."

"I told you it won't happen again!" Al's voice rose in panic.

Rick shook his head. "How many times have you told me that, Al?"

"This is the only time!" Al said, feeling his panic rise. His eyes darted from Tim to Rick, then rested on Animal, who had taken a step forward. The steel blade affixed to the dildo jutted out like a cruel penis. "I swear to God, it's the only time!"

"You are right about that," Rick said, standing up. "This *is* the only time. And it *won't* happen again."

"I know it won't happen again," Al said, trying to sweet-talk Rick again to convince him that he should be released. "I swear to God it won't happen again, so—"

"Unfortunately, one slip is all it takes for the whole

scene to collapse," Rick said, now towering over Al. "Do you know what could have happened if Lisa had been able to lead the police to you? That would have led directly to *me!* Do you understand?"

"No!" Al protested, his heart hammering in his chest. "I swear to God, I won't say anything!"

"Bullshit! You'd fuck your own mother over. I know you too well, Pressman."

"No, no, I swear to God, I won't say anything!" Al was frantic now. He began wriggling again and Rick stepped on his chest, driving Al down to the floor with his weight. "Please," Al begged. "Please, I swear to God I'll make it up to you! I won't—"

"Sorry, Al," Rick said. He turned and nodded to Animal. "But I can't afford to have a weak link in the business. If I don't deal with it, my clients will."

Animal stepped forward and Tim loomed in front of him. He was holding a syringe. He depressed the plunger and liquid squirted out of the needle. Tim's eyes were indifferent as he bent down and sank the needle into the side of Al's left buttock. "No!" Al yelled, eyes bugged out in stark fear. "Noooo!"

"Relax," Rick said, smiling. "This isn't going to knock you out. It'll just . . . how shall I say it? Immobilize you for a moment."

Al struggled, fighting madly as Tim and Rick held him down, trying to yell and scream. Animal stepped forward and rammed a piece of cloth in Al's mouth as he screamed, stifling him. A minute later, Al felt the effect of the drug slow his movements. Thirty seconds later, he was unable to move. *Oh God no!*

Tim and Rick grabbed Al's legs and spread them apart. *No!* Al began to sob as Animal took position between Al's legs. *No, please!*

And as Tim stepped behind the camera, Animal began to work the blade in, partaking in the work that he liked best.

Twenty-one

The following twenty-four hours was a whirlwind for Brad.

William Grecko spent the night on his sofa. When Brad woke up the next morning, Lisa was still asleep. Brad walked in the kitchen to the smell of perking coffee. Billy was still dressed in the clothes he had worn last night. His hair stuck out like tufts of horns behind his ears. He looked like Dilbert's boss in the Scott Adams cartoons.

"Coffee smells great," Brad said.

"Thanks." William searched through the cabinets and found two mugs. He poured them coffee and set Brad's mug on the table. They sat down at the table. "I've been doing a lot of thinking," he began.

"So have I," Brad said. He took a sip of coffee.

"I'm going to go home real quick and shower and change," William said. He took a sip of coffee and sighed. "Then I'm going to the office. I'm going to call Detective Orr and tell him everything you told me last night. Then I'm going to arrange to have him come here today to talk to you and Lisa."

"She's not going to like this," Brad said, clutching the mug with both hands.

"I know, but we have to do it." William's eyes were red from lack of sleep. His stubble looked rough on his cheek. "I'm going to be here when Orr comes over. I'm going to emphasize that you and Lisa are under my protection until the guys that did this are caught. I'm going to arrange to have you and Lisa flown out of the city by this evening."

This surprised Brad. "Billy! Isn't that—"

"A little drastic? Maybe. But I don't want to take the chance. You have to get out of town."

"What if Orr has other ideas?"

"I'll handle Orr," William said. He took a hearty gulp of coffee. "In the meantime, you're going to have to get ready to be away for a while. It may take a few weeks or so to find these guys."

"It could take months, too," Brad said.

William frowned. "True."

"Suppose Orr doesn't believe us?" Brad asked.

"If Orr doesn't believe us, I'll enlist the services of a private detective."

Brad sighed. He rubbed his face. "Christ, Billy, I don't have that kind of money anymore. All the money in our savings is gone!"

"Don't worry about it," Billy said gently. "I'll bear the costs myself."

"Shit." Brad felt powerless. He hated to have other people pay his way, and the situation he and Lisa were in now made him feel like they were in a bind. He wondered what would happen if he didn't know Billy. He and Lisa would be nowhere. They would have to pick themselves up and run, try to go underground and hide on their own. Brad wouldn't know a thing about living on the lam.

"Where are we going to go?" He asked.

"I'll think of a place," William said.

"What if you can't find these guys?"

"We'll find them."

"No, I don't think you understood me." Brad faced William, feeling desperation rise in him. "I did a lot of thinking about this whole snuff-film business, and the thing I kept thinking was that something so underground and taboo must be hard to crack. Shit, I never thought things like this existed. It has to be so far underground that the average person wouldn't even hear about it. We're average people, so how the hell are we going to catch a group of guys that, by all accounts, even the police can't catch?"

"Leave it to me," Billy said again, and Brad could tell by the look in his eyes that the lawyer didn't know how they were going to find the men responsible for Lisa's kidnapping and near murder.

Brad drank his coffee, at a loss for words. He felt helpless. He supposed that the best thing to do was to place his and Lisa's lives in the hands of his friend, William Grecko.

When they were finished with their coffee, Billy stood up. "I've got to go. I'll call you in about an hour."

Brad refilled his mug. "I've got to get somebody over here to look after Lisa. I should probably dash out and run a few errands before Detective Orr comes in. Maybe I'll call Lisa's assistant at the office and see if she'll come in."

"Fine," William said. Brad walked him to the front door. "Try not to be too long. If you want, I could have somebody come over."

"I'll be fine," Brad said.

"Okay." William shook Brad's hand. "We'll get through this, buddy. Leave it to me."

When William Grecko left, Brad turned and headed to the bedroom to check on Lisa.

Lisa was still in a sound sleep when Brad checked on her. He glanced at the clock on the nightstand. The red digital numerals read five minutes after seven. She had only been asleep for nine hours. She might sleep at least another hour, hopefully. Brad left the door to the bedroom open and went to the second bedroom, which they had converted to a study, sat down at the desk, and turned on the computer.

He sipped his coffee as the computer booted up, thinking. He hadn't been able to sleep at all last night. All he could think about was the story Lisa told him, and the men who worked in the snuff-film business. And the question that kept popping into his head was *How could people do this kind of thing?*

He found it hard to believe that money would be the primary factor. He knew of some greedy people, but it was hard to believe that people would actually pay to watch somebody being tortured to death for sexual gratification. *But then I've heard of equally weird things,* he thought. *Pedophiles exist. That's a fact. Some people like to fuck dogs and sheep. That's sick as all hell. I guess if that kind of sickness exists, others do, too.*

When the PC was up, Brad connected to his Internet service provider, then launched his Web browser. When the browser came up, he typed "snuff films" in the search engine and hit the ENTER key.

The search engine spit out two hundred and fifty-six Web pages dealing with snuff films. The first entry was an article called "Snuff Films: Urban Myths or Grim Reality?" Brad clicked on the hyperlink and brought the page up.

The article in question was on a Web site called APBnews.com, which looked like a news service about crime and law enforcement. Brad read through the article slowly, reading each word as he digested the information. What he read was disturbing and frustrating.

According to the article, the FBI had been looking for snuff films for twenty-five years and hadn't found evidence of a single one. It also revealed documents the FBI had been maintaining about their search, reporting that despite widespread tales of rape, torture, and murder being committed in front of the camera for monetary gain, the leads all eventually fizzled to nothing.

Brad found the article riveting. According to the story, rumors of snuff films began circulating as early as 1969 when it was suggested that the Manson Family had filmed a murder. A few years later, snuff films were mentioned by a group called "Citizens for Decency Through Law," who claimed that young women were being raped and killed for the pornography industry. The Bureau's Special Crimes Unit, which investigated violations of interstate trafficking of obscene material laws, investigated and found no truth to the story. The rumors of snuff films continued. An FBI memo from February of 1975 showed that an unnamed source tipped the Bureau to the existence of twelve or so snuff films shot on 8-millimeter film. The informant's story fell apart when he later admitted to the Bureau that he had never seen the films himself.

Rumors continued from Atlanta, Chicago, New York, Los Angeles, and Cleveland. The stories were similar. The films were usually rumored to originate from California or Mexico. The victims were always described as being runaways, drifters, or smuggled immigrants.

Then, in 1976, one of the greatest hoaxes ever to be perpetrated in the film industry capitalized on the snuff-film rumors. A low-budget film that had been shelved three years previously was resurrected by its producer with ten minutes tagged on at the end of the original print. Dubbed "Snuff," its tag line on promotional posters read "Made in South America . . . where life is *cheap*!" The poster depicted a screaming woman cowering from a knife. The film premiered first in Indianapolis, then in

New York. "Snuff" purported to tell the story about a sinister satanic cult roaming the country slaughtering people. The producers also claimed that it was the "bloodiest thing to ever happen in front of a camera."

In the last segment of the film, separate from the movie's plot, the supposed real murder takes place. On the screen, a male member of the film crew tells a previously un-introduced woman, "You know, that last gory scene really turned me on." Other members of the crew then restrain her while the man proceeds to slash the woman with a knife, amputate two of her fingers with bolt cutters, and, finally, reach into her body and pull out her heart. The film runs out and voice-over says: "Did you get all that?" The response is: "Yeah, let's get the hell out of here."

End of credits.

Feminists protested the original theatrical release of the film, and the media hoopla over it caught the attention of law enforcement. Pathologists viewed the film and concluded that the staged murder was a theatrical production and not real. The FBI got interested, and the actress who was killed in the last scene revealed herself to be alive and well. So much for the great snuff-film conspiracy.

Brad shook his head as he read the article. *Weird,* he thought, as he scrolled down. What he read next chilled him. He read it to himself aloud. " 'There is legislation currently pending in the California Assembly that would outlaw snuff films along with crush videos, which graphically depict small animals being crushed to death.' What the fuck?"

Then he remembered something from a news item a few months before that he and Lisa had seen on television one evening after work. A woman had been tried and convicted of cruelty to animals after videos depicting her stomping mice to death were discovered. The video had been shot by another party, a male, for a thriving "crush film" industry, which were S&M porn films that depicted actresses in spiked high heels crushing small animals to death. Brad remembered watching that segment with Lisa, making a comment to her along the lines of, "Guess there's not much a pervert will find taboo, huh?" If only he could have foreseen what was to come.

Brad clicked on the back arrow button of the search engine and scrolled down the list of Web pages. He saw another link that grabbed his interest. This was a definition of the term *snuff-films*, from a site called "The Encyclopedia of Unusual Sex Practices." It defined a snuff film as one that portrays the actual murder and mutilation of one of the actors. Brad hit the back arrow button again and continued his search. The next item that caught his eye froze him. *Cops: Snuff films found among child porn.* He clicked on it.

It was a Reuters story about a recent raid in Italy. As he read the article, he quickly realized that the APBnews piece had been published a year previously, and that this piece was only a month old. As he read the article in shock and disgust, the words of an FBI agent quoted in the APBnews article kept coming back to him: "Despite 25 years of searching, I have yet to find hard evidence that snuff films exist." *Wonder what this guy thinks now?* Brad thought, feeling a pit of dread in his stomach.

The news item was about eight Italians who were arrested on charges that they used the Internet to traffic in child pornography, with most of the children coming from Russia. The material, ordered over the Internet, cost anywhere from $300 to $6,000, with the images being burned on CD-ROM. The more horrific the sexual acts the customer wanted, the more costly the price tag. The most gruesome products were coded "Necros Pedo," in which children were tortured and raped until they died.

"Jesus," Brad said. He couldn't take it anymore, but he had to find more information, as disturbing as it was. He clicked on another link and read on.

The story in question was in direct relation to the Italian case, this one involving a British man belonging to the same international ring. British police reported that Italian detectives, after a lengthy investigation, raided 600 homes and had evidence against 500 people ranging from businessmen to public employees. Many of the suspects were married and had children of their own. One suspect, accused of producing child pornography, was found with a client list that included people from America, England, Germany, and Italy.

Finally tired of the research, and depressed by the subject matter, he turned off his Internet connection, then shut down the computer. He sat in front of the computer, his mind running a mile a minute, everything clicking into place.

Lisa and I are in danger no matter what we do, Brad thought. *They know where we live, they'll be able to find us. We've got to get the hell out of here.*

Brad rose to his feet and headed to the master bedroom to wake Lisa up.

The only thing Lisa could think of as Detective Orr sat in front of her in the living room was that Brad had betrayed her. After pleading with him not to tell anybody what she'd done, he had gone ahead and done it anyway.

Lisa clutched a tear-sodden handkerchief in her hands and refused to meet Detective Orr's gaze as the detective sat in the chair opposite her. Brad was sitting in another chair; she had shot him a menacing look when he tried to sit on the couch with her, so he'd retreated to give her space. And with Brad in the room, there was no way she could deny the truth to Detective Orr. Brad would simply say, "You didn't deny it to me last night, Lisa. Tell Detective Orr what you told me."

The *bastard*.

Detective Orr listened calmly as she told him the harrowing account of what really happened. She thought he would be incredibly angry with her. Instead he listened to her calmly, taking notes as she told her story. When she broke down briefly, he waited till she composed herself, then urged her gently to continue. He was never condescending or accusatory, even when she exclaimed that she had been responsible for the deaths of Mandy and her mother. Then she started crying again because she couldn't remember the name of Mandy's mother.

Brad's friend Billy Grecko was present during the questioning. He hovered near the doorway to the kitchen, dressed in a pair of black slacks, a white shirt, and a black tie that was loose around the collar. When she was finished, she looked up at Detective Orr briefly, then looked back down at the floor again in shame. "I'm sorry I lied to you the first time," she said, her voice barely audible. "I was just so scared."

Detective Orr closed his notebook, then looked up at Brad and William. Then he looked back at Lisa. "I'll be frank with you, Lisa. I didn't believe your original story one bit. I've heard too many stories like that, and they're all the results of drug binges. That's why I kept hounding your husband, asking him if you had a substance-abuse problem. He kept denying it. I thought that either he was blind to it or that you really didn't have a problem and something else had happened that you were trying to cover up. I knew I would get the truth eventually."

"I'm sorry," Lisa said. She wondered if the police had

picked up anybody matching the descriptions she had given in her original confession.

"Lot's of times, somebody will go on a drug binge and be gone for days at a time," Detective Orr explained. "They'll turn up eventually. Either the police find them or they turn up somewhere disoriented. And to hide what they've been up to, they'll claim they were kidnapped and beaten up or that they were robbed and had been lying unconscious somewhere. It's hard to get them to admit otherwise, especially if drugs aren't found on their person or their vehicle. We do some preliminary investigation, but if nothing pans out and no serious laws were broken, we usually chalk it up to what I've just described and it isn't pursued further."

"Do you believe me?" Lisa asked.

Detective Orr looked open and frank as he thought about it. "I guess I have to. It sounds horrible, but . . . it's certainly more plausible than your first story."

"Will you be charging Ms. Miller for making a false criminal statement to the police?" Billy Grecko asked.

"No." Detective Orr replaced his notebook in his coat pocket. "No need to do that. I should, I've got a perfectly legal right to arrest her for providing false information, but . . ."

"You're going to try to catch these guys, right?" This from Brad, who had been sitting in the chair opposite Detective Orr, fidgeting nervously.

Detective Orr looked up at William and Brad. "I'd like her to make another statement downtown," he said. "Something more in depth. Then, yes, I'd like to start an investigation."

"What do we need to do?" William asked.

"Well, I guess we should go to the station," Detective Orr said, rising to his feet.

And with that, they left the house and went to the station. Lisa didn't even have time to shower or do her hair. She simply washed her face, brushed her teeth, applied deodorant, brushed her hair a little bit, changed into fresh clothes, and they were off. She said nothing to Brad on the drive to the Orange County Sheriff's Department, still angry at him for betraying her secret, and scared more than ever for what might happen to them should Al and Tim and Animal find out she'd told the authorities.

Twenty-two

When Lisa Miller was questioned a second time, it was with Detective Orr and his partner, Detective Hank Sanchez. William Grecko was present. Brad waited outside, in the lobby.

It all seemed so monotonous to Lisa. The detectives took her down the same path she had led them two weeks ago, starting with her and Brad leaving home for the drive to Cambria. Only this time she told them about meeting up with the homeless woman and her baby, Amanda. She finally remembered the woman's name, too. "Her name was Alicia," she said. "She didn't tell me her last name." She gave the detectives a description, willing herself not to cry. Then she continued her narrative. When she got to the confrontation on the highway and Brad's arrest, the detectives asked her to describe Caleb Smith. "He was about five eight, big belly—pear-shaped, I guess you could say. His hair was sandy-colored and thinning, and he was wearing glasses and had a thick, bushy beard."

When she told them about the kidnapping she was expecting to break down again, but for some reason she didn't. She had relived the abduction a million times and now it only made her mad. She told them about the conversation she had with Caleb, how he told her he was going to have her killed in a snuff film. "I had never heard of such things before," she said, feeling herself start to cry but forcing herself to stay calm. "I couldn't believe what was happening."

Then she told them about Debbie Martinez. Detective Sanchez asked her several poignant questions. "Debbie was beautiful," Lisa said, now starting to cry. "She was so beautiful and . . . what he . . . what he did to her!" She broke down sobbing, trying to erase the memories of the sounds Debbie had made as Animal tortured and raped her.

Detective Orr and Billy Grecko calmed her down as Sanchez left the room. When he came back, Lisa's sobs had trickled down. "I called the San Bernardino Sheriff's Department," he said. "A missing-persons report was filed on a Debbie Martinez almost two weeks ago by her husband. They're suspecting foul play."

"Is the husband a suspect?" Detective Orr asked.

"They wouldn't tell me," Detective Sanchez said, sitting down in front of Lisa. He was an intense man, with black hair and a large, bulbous nose set square in the middle of his face. He looked at Lisa. "They may want to talk with you, though."

Lisa nodded. She felt a sudden sense of relief that her story was being verified. She still felt bad about everything that had happened, but she felt a sense of vindication that the authorities were taking her seriously. They were already looking for Debbie, and she would do anything possible to speed up the investigation. "I'll talk to them," she said. "Did you tell them that Debbie's probably dead?"

"I told her she might be the victim of a homicide and that we were talking to a potential witness," Detective Sanchez said. He traded a glance with Orr. "Why don't you tell us the rest?"

Lisa tried to wrap it up without crying too much. She only broke down twice—once when she told them what she had done ("I . . . I sold that baby and her mother for my own life!" she sobbed), the second time when she broke free and escaped. Both detectives nodded sympathetically and took notes. They asked for physical descriptions of Al, Animal, and Caleb. Lisa provided that and more. "When Debbie came in, she referred to Caleb as Tim," she said, looking at them with watery eyes. "Tim Murray. I didn't get Al's last name. And Animal, she called him Jeff."

Detective Orr jotted this down. "They took you to your bank, right?"

Lisa nodded.

"Do you remember which teller you spoke to?"

Lisa shook her head. "I don't remember her name. She was little . . . black hair maybe."

"That's okay," Detective Orr said. "I'm sure once you see her you'll remember."

When Lisa was finished, they asked her to start over and tell them the story again, right from the beginning. Lisa protested. "I've already told you twice!" she exclaimed to Orr.

"We just want to hear it one more time," Detective Orr urged. "You might remember something else."

Lisa didn't want to live through the nightmare again by repeating it. She looked up at William Grecko, who nodded. "It's okay," he said. "One last time."

So she relived the nightmare again. Nothing new was revealed in the narrative. Detective Orr nodded when she finished, then glanced at his partner. "Would you be adverse to taking a ride with us up to Big Bear?"

"Big Bear?" Lisa asked, curious. "Why Big Bear?"

"Debbie Martinez and her husband Neal have a cabin there," Detective Sanchez said. "That's where this Tim Murray guy took you—Big Bear, that is. We're hoping you might be able to recognize the cabin they took you to."

Lisa felt her stomach revolve in her abdomen. "I don't want to go back there," she said, her throat drying up.

"We'll be there with you," Detective Orr said gently. "It'll be okay."

"I . . . I don't know if I can recognize it." Lisa's heart was pounding. Her hands were shaking. As much as she wanted to help the police catch these bastards, she did not want to go back to that house. "I mean, Tim had me blindfolded during the drive. And . . . when they carried me out to the van to . . . to get Alicia and Mandy—" She choked back a sob. "—they had me blindfolded. They had me blindfolded all the way to Garden Grove."

"Let's just try, okay?" Detective Orr asked.

Lisa took a deep breath and tried to compose herself. She felt so nervous and scared. *What if they're back there, waiting for me?* "They'll find out," she said, hearing her voice crack. "They'll find out I told you and then . . . then they'll—"

Detective Orr moved to her side of the table. He took her hand. His voice was soft and soothing. "You'll be under our protection. Nobody will see you. We'll ride up in an unmarked car with tinted windows. Nobody will see you in the car. You won't even have to get out."

Lisa was looking down at the scarred table. "I don't know," she said, her voice cracking.

"Lisa Miller is afraid that the people who did this to her will come after her and her husband," William Grecko said, clearing his throat. "They stole her purse, her identification, her credit cards. She's afraid they'll track her down."

"You'll be under our protection the whole way," Detective Orr said, his voice urging but gentle. "Just a quick trip up, we'll whisk you in to the San Bernardino Sheriff's Station to talk with some people there, then we'll drive you by the Martinez cabin. We'll cruise around the surrounding area. If anything seems remotely familiar to you, tell us."

"But I didn't *see* anything!" Lisa protested. Her eyes were filling with tears again.

"It could be anything," Detective Sanchez said. "Sounds you may have heard. The sound of the tires on asphalt or a dirt road maybe. Turns you may have made. All that can help in determining the location of the cabin."

"Debbie said that the cabin we were in . . . where Tim had us . . . prisoner . . . was the closest one to them," Lisa said, looking up at Detective Orr.

"Apparently, the San Bernardino Sheriff's Department talked to the residents nearby," Detective Orr said, looking from Lisa to William. "They didn't get anywhere." He leaned forward, the urgency clear on his face. "Please, Mrs. Miller."

Lisa saw the look on Detective Orr's face. He was serious. She looked up at William Grecko, who nodded. Trembling, Lisa turned to the detective and nodded. "Okay." She sniffled. "Okay."

"I'd like to accompany my client," William Grecko said.

"You can come," Detective Orr said, rising from his seat. He motioned to Detective Sanchez. "We're on! Let's go."

They made the drive up in two hours. Lisa sat in the backseat of a blue sedan with William Grecko. Detective Orr drove, while Sanchez rode in the front passenger seat. Brad hadn't wanted her to go. He had protested as they were led down corridors to the parking lot outside. She hadn't wanted to go either, but she didn't know what else to do. Fortunately, William had calmed them both down, saying he would take care of everything. Then he had turned to Detective Orr and told him in no uncertain terms that when they arrived back in Orange County he was having Brad and Lisa whisked out of the state to a safe house for their protection. "I don't know if you can do that," Detective Orr had said.

"Lisa is a victim," William Grecko had replied. "She is not a suspect, nor is she officially a witness to a homicide. She saw some pretty horrible things and she herself was the victim of a kidnapping, but that's all you have. In fact, you have no physical proof that Debbie Martinez is dead yet, and I hardly think that the Orange County Sheriff's Department is going to place my client in protective custody until you find the men responsible for Lisa's abduction and attempted murder."

"Don't give me any of that—" Detective Orr looked pissed.

But William had remained firm. He'd raised his hand, his features stern. "Will you guarantee that my clients receive twenty-four-hour-a-day protective custody, starting right now?"

"I can't commit to that and you know it! And besides, I don't have the authority to—"

"Then until you do, you deal with me and my rules." Lisa and Brad had watched the exchange with a sense of numb detachment. Lisa felt her confidence in William Grecko's abilities as an attorney blossom; previously, she hadn't had much regard for him, but now she could see why he was one of the most sought-after criminal defense lawyers in Orange County. "You need to talk to Lisa, fine. You give me twenty-four-hour notice and I will make sure that she is available to you here in Orange County. Until then, as long as the perpetrators who committed these crimes are free, Lisa and Brad are in danger. This means they will be under *my* protection. My protection, my rules."

"I don't have time to deal with this shit now," Detective Orr had muttered, leading the trio to his vehicle. "I'll deal with you later."

William turned to Brad before they left with Detective Orr. "I'll go with Lisa; she'll be safe. Go home and start packing some things. I'll make arrangements on the drive up to Big Bear. I'll call you with the details. When Lisa and I get back, be ready to get on a plane."

They spent the majority of their drive to Big Bear in silence. William Grecko made several phone calls on his cellular. One was to his office to ask his secretary to check airline departures out of Irvine to Las Vegas. He gave his secretary Lisa and Brad's names. "Vegas?" Lisa asked, looking at him questionly. "Why Las Vegas?"

"Why not?" William punched the disconnect button, then flipped through his personal phone book. "It's close enough to get back here quickly if you have to, and I've got contacts there. You'll be safe."

Lisa settled back in her seat and listened as William made the arrangements. She listened as he connected with somebody on the other line and explained, in vague terms, that he was "sending a young couple out your way who need physical protection twenty-four seven. Think you can set me up?" Lisa knew that Detective Orr was listening in on the conversation too, but what was he going to do? William hung up, called his office, jotted down flight information, then called his contact in Vegas again, relaying all this information. "They'll be getting in on Flight 817 on Southwest Airlines." He gave the contact a brief physical description of Lisa and Brad, hung up, then called Brad at home, giving him the information. "Have your bags packed and ready," he said.

"You know, this is crazy," Detective Orr said after the round of phone calls had been made. They were in San Bernardino, heading east toward the mountains. "I mean, we're on it. We'll probably have these guys in custody by tonight."

"I'm not taking any chances," William Grecko said.

"We'll get Lisa to look at surveillance video at the bank and get some blowups of the suspects," Detective Orr said. "We might come up with a match somewhere. The FBI has gotta have heard of these guys by now, from what Lisa says they're into."

"Maybe," William Grecko said. "But like I said, I don't want to take chances."

Detective Orr was silent. After a minute, he asked Lisa, "Would you be available to look at some video when we get back to Irvine?"

Lisa looked at William, who nodded. "Yeah. Her and Brad's flight isn't until ten-thirty tonight. Long as we can get them on the flight, sure."

They were silent again as they drove through San Bernardino County and made their way to the foothills and began the ascent into the mountain range. When they reached the Lake Arrowhead city limits, Detective Orr broke the long silence. "I'm going to call ahead to the San Bernardino substation at Big Bear and give them our ETA. If there's anything you remember, don't be afraid to tell me."

Lisa met his gaze in the rearview mirror. "I won't," she said. The minute they had begun ascending the mountains, Lisa had tried to piece together what she could remember from her trip up with Tim, but she couldn't. She'd been blindfolded! Weren't they fucking listening to her?

William squeezed her hand. "You'll be fine."

Lisa turned to him and made a halfhearted attempt at

a smile. She *did* feel better that William was with her and taking care of her. But the closer they got to Arrowhead, the closer they got to Big Bear. And with that realization came the sinking sense of dread she felt the last time she was up here with Tim Murray. Knowing they were on the same road was creating a sense of fear in her that was churning in the pit of her stomach.

The Big Bear substation was small, about the size of a small-town real estate office; with a closet-sized waiting room, two or three offices, and a holding cell in the back, it bore all the necessary requirements for a small-town police station. They were seated in Sheriff Dean Sweigert's office, and Lisa was beginning to feel claustrophobic.

She had begun to panic the closer they got to the station, and William had rummaged around in his briefcase for some antidepressants. Lisa gulped two of the capsules down and put her head between her knees, eyes closed, willing herself to calm down. By the time they arrived at the station she was feeling a little better, but she was still nervous.

The first thing Dean Sweigert had done when Lisa sat down was pull up a chair in front of her. He looked into her eyes, his features grim, serious. His brush-cut hair was gray, his face weathered, tanned, features sharply chiseled. She pegged him to be in his mid-forties. "You are a very lucky lady," he said, his tone soft yet strong. "And we're going to find the people that did this, so help me God."

Lisa nodded, not wanting to meet his gaze.

"Detective Orr told me everything on the phone a few hours ago," he said. "I can't believe that people can be capable of such barbarity. And in such a place as Big Bear." He shook his head. He reached for a file on his desk and pulled something out, which he now held up in front of

Lisa. It was a photograph. "He told me about what happened to Debbie Martinez during the time she went missing. Is this the woman you saw?"

Lisa looked at the photograph and choked back a sob. It was Debbie Martinez all right. Debbie was seated on a stone ledge with her back to a small canyon, smiling at the camera. It looked like the photo was taken at a natural park—Yosemite, perhaps. She was wearing a white cotton shirt, blue jeans, and a red scarf around her neck. Her black hair fell to her shoulders. She looked beautiful.

"Yes," Lisa said, nodding as she held back the tears. "That's her. That's Debbie . . ."

Dean Sweigert placed the photo back in the file. "Her husband filed a missing-person report on her nearly two weeks ago. We've combed the entire area looking for her." He looked up at Detective Orr and William Grecko, then back at Lisa. "Do you think you can help us? Do you think you can remember the cabin you were held in?"

"I don't know," Lisa said, dabbing at her eyes. "I was blindfolded during the trip up here, and they blindfolded me when they took me out!"

"There's three cabins within a mile and a half of the Martinez place that might be where you were taken," Dean said. "We've spoken to the owners already. Two of them deny having seen her, and the third cabin is owned by a corporation that's involved in multimedia or something. They use it for weekend retreats. They claim it was being rented the weekend Debbie disappeared."

"Were any of these cabins within easy walking distance from the Martinez place?" William Grecko asked.

"One of them was," Dean said, leaning back in his chair. "She could've walked to the other two pretty easily. Debbie ran three miles every day. A mile walk or so would have been nothing to her."

"Tim boarded up one of the windows," Lisa said, suddenly remembering her ordeal. She looked up at Dean, then at Detective Orr and Billy. "Right before Debbie showed up, he was boarding up the window to the bedroom I was in so I wouldn't escape. Maybe—"

Dean moved toward his desk and reached for his radio. "I'll have somebody check it out."

"Does the name Tim Murray mean anything to you?" Detective Orr asked Dean.

Dean shook his head. "His name isn't on any of the deeds to the properties we checked out."

"What about Jeff?" Lisa asked. She shuddered at the thought of calling him Animal. "No last name. I never did learn his last name."

"I'm afraid not," Dean said. He was just about to speak into the radio when a tall uniformed ranger poked his head in. Dean looked up. "Yes, Glenn?"

"Sorry to interrupt, Mr. Sweigert," the ranger said, looking nervous, "but I couldn't help overhearing. Um . . . I think I know what cabin you may be referring to."

Dean Sweigert set the radio down. "Okay . . ."

Glenn cast a nervous glance at Lisa. "You said one of the guys that abducted you was named Tim? And another called himself Jeff?"

Lisa nodded.

"Was there a guy named Al with them?"

Lisa nodded vigorously. "Yes."

Glenn looked pale. "Tall, thin guy? Thinning blond hair, looked like he was in his late thirties maybe?"

Lisa nodded. "That's him. That's Al."

"And Tim . . . kinda dumpy-looking guy with glasses? Bushy beard, sandy-colored hair, big beer belly?"

"Yeah," Lisa said. Her heart pounded.

Dean's eyes widened in surprise. "You saw these guys?"

"The other guy, Jeff," Glenn said, ignoring Dean. "Nice-looking guy, early thirties maybe, dark hair. Kinda yuppie-looking."

"Yes." Lisa felt her stomach sink as Glenn described the man she could only think of as Animal. A monster.

Glenn turned to Dean Sweigert. "The night Neal phoned the report in on Debbie, we canvassed the area south of the Martinez cabin. We pulled up to the Golgotha cabin and came across these guys. They looked like they were leaving and they were packing camera equipment into a van. Neal knew Tim, asked him if he had seen Debbie around, and Tim said he hadn't seen her. I . . . I didn't think anything of it at the time—"

"You really *saw* these guys?" Dean sounded surprised and angry.

Glenn nodded. He licked his lips nervously. "Yeah. Like I said, Neal looked like he knew this Tim Murray character. I questioned all three of them. One of them claimed it was the first time they'd been up here. Tim said they were using the cabin for the weekend to shoot a low-budget film." He looked nervous, scared, and sick. It was obvious that word of the crime had traveled around the station. "I . . . I had no idea that these guys . . . that they . . ."

"It's not your fault," Detective Orr said softly, sighing in obvious frustration.

Glenn took a deep breath and bowed his head for a moment. Lisa could tell that the ranger was having a hard time dealing with this. He took another deep breath, then looked up at them again. "Christ, I feel so sick about this. I had no idea *they* were the guys. I mean, at the time I questioned them we were dealing with a missing-person thing and . . . *shit!*"

"It's okay, Glenn," Dean said, looking grim.

"What's this Golgotha cabin?" Detective Orr asked.

"It's owned by the Golgotha Publishing Company," Dean told him. "They're some kind of multimedia corporation. Self-help books and videos, CD-ROMs, corporate training shit. They're apparently financed by one of the big churches in Orange County. The cabin itself is owned by the board of directors and sometimes they come up here for retreats."

"I asked Neal about this Tim guy after we left," Glenn said, looking nervous. "He said that Tim rents the place out from somebody, but he never told him who owns it. Neal never asked."

"You questioned these guys? The Golgotha people?" Detective Orr asked Dean.

Dean moved over to the filing cabinet and began rummaging through it. "Yeah, we did. I got on the phone with one of them a few days after Debbie disappeared. One of their board members claimed the cabin was rented that weekend. That a film crew was making some kind of student film for a Christian University."

"I don't believe it," Lisa said. Hearing that the perversities that had been carried on in that cabin were being hidden by the guise of organized religion was making her sick.

"Did you get the name of the person you spoke to?" Detective Orr asked.

"Yeah." Dean found the paper he was looking for. "Oliver Gardenia." He looked at Lisa. "Ring a bell?"

Lisa was trying to remember. "I don't know. I . . . I think Al might have mentioned somebody named Sam at some point during the weekend, but . . ." She didn't remember an Oliver Gardenia.

"Even though the corporate name is listed on the deed, Oliver's name and signature are on some of the other paperwork, so that's who I called."

"Make me copies of everything you got," Detective Orr

said, moving to another desk and picking up the phone. "Mind if I use your phone?"

"Go ahead."

And as the investigation kicked into high gear, Lisa could only sit back and let William Grecko comfort her as she sought to retreat from the madness.

Twenty-three

Brad was at home packing clothes for him and Lisa into a single suitcase when the doorbell rang.

He had gotten a call from William Grecko an hour and a half ago telling him to pack and to be ready to leave when he and Lisa returned. William said he had set them up at an undisclosed location in Las Vegas and that they were leaving this evening. When Brad asked how Lisa was doing, William said she was fine. "There's more, but I'll tell you everything tonight." Billy's tone of voice told Brad that things were brewing and that he couldn't talk about it on the phone. He would find out soon enough.

Brad moved through the house to the front door, wondering who was at the door. It couldn't be Lisa's parents, who were still in town. He had talked to them already and they were waiting by the phone per his instructions. He had talked to his parents this afternoon, telling his dad, then his mother, everything. His mom had gasped in shock, then had given the phone to his father; Brad had heard her crying in the background as he told his father. Dad had been silent, his voice shaky. He'd sounded shocked. He'd asked Brad if there was anything they could do and Brad told them no, not yet, Billy was taking care of everything. He'd call later.

He looked through the peephole, couldn't see anything at first due to the brightness of the porch light, and then a face swam into view.

Brad sighed and unlocked the door, opening it. "Danielle," he said.

Danielle Kwong stood on the porch, dressed in a black conservative business suit. Danielle was Lisa's partner at the law office, and she and her boyfriend often accompanied him and Lisa to the movies or to dinner on sporadic Friday evenings. "I'm sorry I can't talk, Danielle," Brad said. "I was just getting some stuff packed up."

"That's okay," Danielle said. Her tanned oval face was bright and inquisitive, and despite her smile Brad could read a sense of concern in her exotic features. "I was just on my way home and thought I'd stop by to see how Lisa was doing."

"She's better," Brad said, not bothering to step aside to let her in, which he normally would have done. "But she's not here now."

"Oh." A hint of disappointment in her voice.

"I'm sorry," Brad said, feeling awkward in his treatment of her. Billy's words echoed in his mind. *Pack your things and wait for me. Don't tell anybody where you're going.* "It's just that I'm short on time and I'm already running late. When Lisa gets home, we're leaving straight for the airport."

"Where are you going?"

Las Vegas is a big place, he thought. *It's not going to hurt to say we're going away for the week, is it?* Brad decided it wouldn't hurt to tell Danielle at least that much. After all, she was a close friend and she'd been concerned and shocked at what happened to Lisa. She had volunteered to run errands for Brad and told him numerous times that she was there if they needed help or just wanted somebody to talk to. Danielle Kwong was the definition of the word *friend*. He could trust her. "We're going to Vegas for a week. We need to get away and just . . . relax. You know?"

Danielle smiled. "I know. And you guys need the vacation. Well, tell Lisa I stopped by and that I hope she's feeling better. Maybe you can have her call me at the office?"

"Of course," Brad said.

"Okay." Danielle stepped off the porch. "Thanks. Bye!"

"Bye." Brad closed the door after her.

When the door was closed, Brad leaned against it. *I didn't fuck up by telling her where we're going, did I?* Billy's paranoia was starting to rub off on him. Whom could Danielle tell that would alert the murderous scumbags who had almost killed Lisa? Danielle and Lisa worked in Family Law, not Criminal Justice. Lisa spoke highly of her colleagues; he was certain that if William Grecko wasn't a loyal and trusted friend and ally, they could rely on a number of lawyers in Lisa's firm to help them. Danielle Kwong maybe, or Kyle Bennett. Hell, Lisa was friends with George Brooks, one of the senior partners. There was no end to the resources they could tap into if they hadn't been blessed with Billy's friendship. Besides, Billy Grecko was getting them out of town as a precaution. As he'd told Brad on the phone this afternoon, "I don't think these guys will be coming after you, but I want to play it safe. Most likely they're lying low right now. They won't be stupid enough to try to go after you this quickly. If we can get some solid leads in Big Bear, we'll be on their trail quickly and then we'll have them in jail where they belong."

We'll be fine, he thought as he checked the lock on the front door and retreated to the bedroom to resume packing. *By eleven we'll be on a plane to Vegas and Billy will have somebody there to meet us and take us to wherever it is we're staying. Even if somebody finds something out through Danielle—which is impossible—they'll have a hard time finding us in Las Vegas. Billy is probably going to have us in some safe house or a hotel under assumed names or something. We'll be safe.*

Brad finished packing and waited for Billy and Lisa to come home.

"So talk to me."

"Al's body'll never be found." Tim Murray grinned. The minute he entered Rick Shectman's office, he had settled his bulk down on the lime-green chair in front of the cluttered desk. He had only been awake for two hours. Last night had been an intense whirlwind. "Remember the movie *Pulp Fiction*?"

Rick Shectman looked indifferent. "Vaguely."

"A buddy of mine owns a scrap-metal yard in San Fernando," Tim continued. "I gotta key to his place. It's way the hell out in the middle of an industrial center. Me and Animal went out there around four in the morning. The best thing about it is that his shop is right next to an airport." Tim laughed. "There ain't no houses or anything anywhere near this place. And he runs so much shit through that yard, junked cars and shit. In fact, I've done some work for him . . . set him up with a few films. Anyway, he'd made it clear to me a while back that if I ever needed his services for disposal I could count on him. I called, and he agreed to meet us there bright and early at six-thirty when he opened up shop. Animal and I got there early and I found a vehicle on the premises that was set for destruction. Animal cut Al up . . . you know . . . dismembered him and shit before we threw the pieces in the trunk of the car." Tim tried to hide his revulsion as he remembered what else Animal had done before wrapping Al's headless torso in a dirty blanket and placing it in the trunk. He'd seen Animal cut holes in people's sides before and fuck them during torture sessions, but he'd never thought of a neck stump as a sexual orifice before last night. Animal's excuse had been *Might as well fuck another hole before we crush him up like a pancake. Besides, who'll know?* Strangely enough, Tim hadn't gotten sick watching Animal stick his dick down the gray tubing of esophagus that was sticking out of Al's bloody neck stump and pumped away. He *had* gotten sick, however, thinking about what Animal had done to that infant; those images came to him unbidden now, and they had come last night while watching Animal violate Al's headless corpse. It had taken all of his willpower to not throw up. "Anyway," Tim continued, looking at Rick, trying to fight back the images, "we just cut him up and put him in the trunk and waited for Mark to show up. When he came in he didn't ask questions, just moved the car in for destruction with a bunch of others and we watched as he and the first-shift supervisor mashed those cars to little chunks of metal. The car we put him in wound up being mashed with four other cars into a metal cube about four by four feet."

"I surely hope no offending bodily fluids leaked out of this metal cube," Rick said.

"Nah!" Tim said. "Whatever leaked out looked like oil. And Mark, he don't give a shit. He owed me a favor, and something tells me he's done this kind of thing before."

Rick nodded. "What about Al's vehicle?"

"We left it in East LA," Tim said, chuckling. "Left the keys in the ignition. Al'd shit if he found out his precious Porsche is probably cut up into spare parts now by a bunch of wetbacks."

"Good." Rick leaned back in his chair and appeared to

be thinking. He stared at the ceiling. Tim tried to relax but couldn't. It was hard to relax in Rick Shectman's presence. *After all, that could have been me last night,* he thought. *It* could *be me sooner than I'd like if I fuck up again*.

This train of thought was one of the reasons why he was getting out. After this next job, he was over the hills and far away. The incident at the cabin had been the last straw. It wasn't so much his own fuckup of not putting his foot down when Al had told him Sam changed his mind about the Miller bitch—Sam had been pretty explicit when he gave Tim the job, and he realized now he shouldn't have let Al manipulate him. He should have questioned Al more thoroughly. Al should have just fucking done his job, no questions asked, but he was a greedy fuck. No, it wasn't that narrow escape. The real reason was that ever since watching what Animal had done to that baby, and Al and Rick's indifference to it all, he realized that he wasn't wired like they were. Those guys were fucking ruthless; they didn't give a shit about anything. Tim wasn't like them; sure, he didn't care if some homeless junkie fell under Animal's knife—they were going to die anyway from alcoholism or AIDS or pneumonia, right? But that last job had affected Tim in ways he never thought it would. At first he'd been okay with it; it had been simple. Find this Lisa Miller bitch, separate her from hubby, and get her to the cabin and have her all nice and pretty for Al and Animal. No problem. But then Debbie Martinez had come along and spoiled things, and then Lisa had manipulated them by dangling that homeless chick and the baby in front of them. The way Animal's eyes had lit up at the mention of the baby, the way Al had nonchalantly agreed . . . it had bothered Tim in a way none of the snuff jobs had bothered him before. And Rick . . . well, that bastard would have his own children slaughtered for money. Tim knew the douche bag forced his son into some of the child pornography he churned out. Shit, the fucker had tied the kid down and had him sodomized by a Doberman for a bestiality film. Kid was ten years old and was a fucking loony now because of all the shit he'd been through. The woman Rick had him with had been a crack head and was probably dead, and Rick's current girlfriend, who normally took care of the kid during the day, didn't give a shit about him. She spent most of her time drinking in bars and fucking anything with a dick. Tim wouldn't be surprised in a few years if Rick used the kid in a snuff film after the poor little bastard started spiraling into drugs and alcohol. It would be just like him.

That's why it was getting to him. Previously, Tim Murray hadn't given a shit about the people they'd used. The difference was that they'd been adults; well, most of them had been. Those who hadn't had been confused, scared, fucked-up runaways who were on their way down. That's why Tim always chose them—they were going to die anyway or wind up as some dirty, shit-smelling, pee-stained-clothes-wearing, rotten-teeth, motherfucking homeless sad excuse for a human being that you always saw nowadays cluttering up big cities. Who the fuck needed them? He'd never felt bad about using people like that, procuring the dregs of society for the torture and snuff films he, Al, and Rick produced.

But this last one . . . a fucking baby! That was just too much. The homeless chick they'd picked up . . . yeah, he could see that, although as time had gone by he had come to disagree with it. Tim Murray had done some thinking about what had gone down the past two weeks, and if he'd had to do it over again he would have shut that Lisa Miller bitch up with a good blow to the head, then waited till she woke up and let Animal have her. He wouldn't have let her whine and plead the way she had, wouldn't have let her manipulate them into turning Al and Animal's attentions on the homeless chick and her kid. That homeless chick wasn't like the others he'd gotten.

Homelessness was just a temporary displacement for her; he could tell the way she'd fought them in the van on the drive to the mountains, the way she'd been dressed when they'd picked her up, the way she'd pleaded for them not to hurt her baby. She wasn't a fuckup, her mind wasn't blasted by drugs. She'd been coherent, sane, and totally aware of what was going on.

And the only thing she'd been worried about was her baby. The look on her face as she'd cried and pleaded with them not to hurt her daughter . . . it had brought that long-buried memory of what his father had done to Binky rushing to the surface, and he knew that he was dealing with people who were so ruthless, so brutal and cold, that even the death of a baby wasn't enough to satiate them.

"I've decided to use somebody else in getting Ms. Miller and her husband," Rick mused, breaking Tim's thoughts.

"Oh?" He looked up, feigning normalcy. This was new to Tim. He had been gearing himself up for staking the Miller place out with Animal and making a move within the next few days. Ever since Rick had begun talking to him about finishing the job, Tim had been mentally preparing himself for it to be his last.

"Lisa will recognize you if she sees you," Rick Shectman said, glancing at Tim. "Even though you've shaved and cut your hair and everything, she'll recognize you. If anything went wrong and she got away, that would be the end of it. I can't afford to have you caught."

"I understand," Tim said. He felt a little let down about the decision. He was actually looking forward to getting back at Lisa for escaping and putting him through this shit. If she hadn't manipulated them like this, that homeless chick and the baby would still be alive and Tim wouldn't be contemplating a move that might get him killed. Then again, if this *hadn't* happened, Tim wouldn't have seen Rick and Al for what they were: rustless motherfucking scum who didn't give a shit about life. "Is there anything I can do to help?"

"You're certain Lisa saw Animal?" Rick asked.

Tim nodded. "Yeah. He wasn't wearing his mask the afternoon we went there to make the film. They even talked a little bit." He laughed. "Bitch wanted to know what he got out of torturing people. Like she wanted to fucking understand how a guy like Animal works."

"Do you understand how Jeffrey works, Mr. Murray?" Rick Shectman wasn't smiling.

Tim's laughter faded. The image from last night and the last job flashed through his brainpan. "No. I'm afraid I don't. I don't understand how a guy gets off by fucking dead people's neck stumps and tearing babies apart with his bare hands."

Rick raised his eyebrows. "Fucking dead people's neck stumps? You don't say."

"Yeah." Licking his lips, Tim told Rick a simplified version of what Animal had done before Al's corpse was turned into sheet metal. Talking about it seemed to lessen the grotesque nature of it.

"Well, what do you know," Rick said, leaning back in his chair and stroking his chin. "I had no idea Jeffrey was a necrophile as well as a sadist. I've got a client who's been bugging me about getting him some necro stuff. Animal might come in handy with that, don't you think?"

"You better believe it." What was the world coming to? First snuff films, now necrophilia videos? What was next? Cannibalism films?

The image of Jeff tearing a chunk of that infant's flesh from its body and stuffing it into his mouth, chewing it as he tore it apart in front of the camera, came to mind and he shook his head. Fuck yeah, cannibalism films were next. That was a no-brainer. Shit, no wonder he had to get out of this business. It was getting sicker and sicker. It wasn't enough to have some gimp like Animal torture and slice up some homeless junkie for some faceless pervert. Now they were getting into using people who would be missed and babies, and Rick was seriously considering having Animal perform cannibalism. *Fuck!*

"You know as well as I do, Tim, that I don't give a fuck what my customers are into." Rick leaned forward, his pale features bored. "People are into all kinds of weird shit . . . fucking little kids, letting chimpanzee's fuck 'em in the ass, watching coke whores in high heels stomp on mice and kittens, watching people getting off on being tortured and shit . . . eating shit and drinking piss . . . sticking their heads up horses' asses and eating the shit while they jack off, watching somebody get cut up, getting off on somebody getting murdered by somebody like Animal. I'm not into the shit myself, but what the fuck do I care if some rich pervert wants to get off on this crap? Know what I mean? Long as they're discreet and have the money, I'm willing to . . . help them out. Know what I mean?"

Tim nodded. He'd been in the illegal pornography industry long enough to know that the core audience of this stuff paid a lot of money to obtain it. *Show me a man or a woman who works hard at wearing a veneer of respectability and I'll show you somebody with a dirty secret.*

"As much as I would trust you and Animal to do the job right in securing our loyal subject again," Rick said, leaning back in his chair, "I'm afraid I can't risk it. She's seen both of you. I *do* want you to be a part of the production of the film, though. In fact, the client has specifically requested Animal to be the . . . ah, how shall I say it? The method of execution?" Rick grinned.

"So we're going through with it, then? This guy really wants to see this particular bitch get done?"

"You bet he does."

"Fuck!" Tim couldn't believe it. What kind of sick fuck wasn't satisfied with two good-looking bitches getting done? Hell they'd delivered not one, but two snuff films with some pretty hot-looking chicks getting the shit fucked out of them by Animal, and that still wasn't enough. "What, this guy's got money falling out of his asshole or something?"

"Consider it picking up where we left off," Rick said, his features cold, predatory.

"Huh?"

"We fucked up the first time. We're going to deliver the second time."

Tim Murray looked at Rick, feeling his skin grow hot from the implications. What Rick was insinuating was that there was no additional money involved, that he and Animal were to do a job for free. "We're doin' this for free?"

"It's not for free."

"Bullshit it ain't!"

Rick flinched at the sound of Tim's voice, and Tim felt his stomach roll in his belly. He could tell by the look in Rick's eyes that he had pushed his limit. "Just shut up and listen. We're doing her, and we're doing this my way. I don't need to explain to you why we have to, but—"

"This motherfucker's got us by the balls, doesn't he?" Tim asked, trying to connect with something that would appeal to Rick's basic instinct. "We didn't deliver the bitch he wanted, and now he has us. He's trying to blackmail us, right?"

"Blackmail's the least of our problems right now," Rick said, leaning forward, jabbing a finger at Tim. "It's personal, Tim. The bitch got the best of you and she fucked me. I want her. I want to see her suffer. My client is rightly pissed, and he's scared shitless. If the bitch tells the cops and they start chasing down trails and even get one whiff of who I am, the whole fucking operation falls apart. You got me? It's not only about covering our asses, it's about getting the bitch who fucked us and making sure we shut her fucking trap."

"In that case," Tim said, feeling the tension ease. "We'll be ready whenever you are."

"This has to be done right," Rick said, drumming his well-manicured fingers on the desktop. "Let me speak to my contact. I'll call you tomorrow. What I'll probably do is arrange to have Lisa abducted. That's already in the works, and I'll need you to assist."

"Is there any news on the Golgotha cabin?"

Rick shook his head. "It's off-limits after Al fucked up."

"That's what I thought."

"I'll have a plan ready by tomorrow. I'll phone you tomorrow morning with details and hopefully a new location. I'll also have all the equipment you'll need for shooting. I should have Lisa in twenty-four to forty-eight hours."

"What about the husband?"

"What about him?"

"What if he causes trouble?"

Rick shrugged. "He'll be dealt with."

"Oh." Tim knew not to question him further. Rick was probably going to hire one of his goons to snatch Lisa in a stealth move. There was no doubt that she was being not only extra cautious, she was probably too scared to leave her home. Rick was pretty good at employing guys that could snatch anybody—businesspeople who had cheated him, lawyers that had not gone to bat for him the way they said they would, suppliers that skimmed from the top. Rick had a way of getting to people who were cautious and always looking for danger. Whatever it was Rick did, it worked every time.

"Don't worry, Tim," Rick assured him, grinning as he leaned back behind his desk. "It'll work out fine. I've got tabs on the Millers. I'll make a few phone calls and *poof!*" He waved his hands like a magician. "She'll cease to exist. Next thing you know, she'll be before your very eyes screaming for mercy as you capture her final moments on film."

Tim smiled as he rose to his feet. "I'll be waiting for your call, then." Then he went home and prepared for the upcoming shoot.

Twenty-four

Brad Miller woke up late the following morning. He knew he was sleeping in, but he allowed himself the luxury. After all, Lisa was sleeping soundly beside him and they were in a plush hotel room, twenty floors above a sprawling casino in the Luxor in Las Vegas.

Brad lay in bed, his mind tracing the events of last night. Lisa and Billy had returned late last night before nine-thirty. Brad had thrown the suitcase he had packed into Billy's car and the lawyer had driven them to John Wayne Airport, explaining to him what had happened in Big Bear. "We should have a search warrant by tomorrow morning," he'd told Brad. "Big Bear P.D. and the FBI will be searching that cabin. Golgotha Multimedia has threatened to file an injunction to prevent the search from happening, but I don't foresee that happening."

The police had informed Golgotha of the intent to search based on the testimony of the victim of a kidnapping and attempted murder who alleged she had been held at the cabin and that she'd witnessed a second attempted murder there. She also hinted at the possibility that two homicides had been committed at the residence. A lawyer representing Golgotha had politely informed Big Bear that they would petition a higher circuit judge to circumvent a search warrant being issued. Meanwhile, the FBI had been contacted and was working with them on the case. Lisa had been driven to the Golgotha cabin, and despite being unable to identify the cabin by sight, she thought she could identify it as the place she'd been held captive. "She said she remembered a dip in the driveway," William had explained as they drove to the airport. "There's a noticeable pothole in the driveway. Plus we poked around and saw evidence that the windows to one of the rooms on the south side had been boarded up. There were fresh nail holes in the shutters consistent with this."

They had tried peering through the windows but had been unable to catch much of a glimpse of anything; the curtains had been drawn over all the windows. There were also spatters of fresh paint dotting the porch, indicating that the place had been fixed up rather hurriedly within the past two weeks. Sheriff Sweigert had tried the front door, but it had been locked. "There wasn't a damn thing we could do without a proper warrant," Billy had said wearily, shaking his head. "We sat there and waited for word to come down, and an hour later it did in the form of a phone call and the arrival of a representative from Golgotha, who ordered us off the property." William had glanced at Brad as he drove. "The search warrant was suspended by a higher-court circuit judge, and the appeal is being heard tomorrow."

After dropping them off at the airport, William had told him whom they would meet in Vegas. "His name is John and he used to be a professional wrestler. He's worked security for a bunch of people. You'll like him. He's already got you set up. And don't worry about the money. We'll have you temporarily set up at the Luxor until John can find some other digs for you in another part of the city."

"The Luxor?"

"Yeah." William had grinned. "Hey, it's the best I could do under short notice. It was either that or some fleabag piece-of-shit hotel off the strip where there's no security. John's hooked up with the security at the Luxor, and he's gonna have them keeping an eye on things. Trust me." He'd clapped Brad on the shoulder. "You'll be under not only tight protection, but well-armed, twenty-four-hour protection. Know what I mean?"

The flight had been short. Lisa had dozed, and when they arrived in Las Vegas he had helped her out of her seat and escorted her down the walkway. Their contact, John Panozzo, was waiting for them. He'd recognized Brad, nodded, then approached them casually. "Got a car waiting outside," he'd said. John was in his mid-forties, with an olive complexion, long black hair, and a black goatee. He was about six feet tall, probably tipped the scales at two-fifty, and his fingers bore silver rings with skulls and bats on them.

John didn't talk much on the drive to the Luxor, but then Brad and Lisa hadn't been in the mood for conversation. John drove them to the strip in a Ford Explorer. When they reached the massive hotel and casino, he led them past the lobby to the elevators. Lisa temporarily snapped out of her dazed expression and looked around at the dazzling lights and explosions of activity at the casino. "Got you a room in the pyramid itself," John said as he ushered them into an elevator. "You're registered under the names of Brian and Katherine Hopkins. You're in room twenty-seven twenty-seven. Everything's all taken care of. If you want to leave your room and walk around the casino, press this button and dial star nine eight." He'd handed Brad a cellular phone. "That will get you directly to me or a member of my staff. We won't be hanging all over you, but we will be watching you quietly in the background. I'd suggest that you lay low the first day you're here, though, just to play it safe and until I hear from Billy."

They'd crashed almost immediately upon arriving at the hotel. Brad had made a quick call to his parents to tell them where they were, and had spoken to his father. "We're at the Luxor," he'd said, quickly giving him the room number. "Billy's got us hooked up here and we're safe. He's got a bodyguard looking after us, and I don't know how long we'll be here." Naturally, his father was worried, and his mother had come on the line and begun asking him a lot of questions. "I can't talk too much about it right now," he'd said. "Look, I'll try to call you tomorrow, okay?" Then he'd placed a call to Lisa's parents and given them the same brief message, giving them the same information on where they were staying before hanging up and going to bed for a mostly sleepless night.

Brad stood in front of the window, looking out at the Las Vegas morning. This was the weirdest hotel room he'd ever been in. Being in the pyramid of the Luxor meant that one side of the room slanted upward at a forty-five-degree angle. That side of the room was composed almost entirely of windows. Such an angle made it nearly impossible for anybody outside to see their suite. The interior of the room was decorated with hieroglyphics;

they ran along the walls and doorways, were imprinted on the tiled floor of the large bathroom. The bed sat along one wall in the middle of the room. The carpet was light beige and felt deep under his bare feet. In short, he and Lisa were hiding out in relative luxury.

Lisa yawned and sat up in bed. Her eyes blinked open, puffy in sleep. Brad smiled and went to the bed. "Hey," he said, sitting down beside her. "How ya feeling?"

"Tired," she said, yawning. She had slipped into a pair of boxer shorts and a tank top and tumbled into bed the minute they'd entered the room.

"Want some coffee?"

"Yeah." She looked around groggily. "First I need a shower. I probably stink."

"You go for it. Want some breakfast?"

"Yeah." The mention of the word "breakfast" perked her up. She stopped on her way to the bathroom and looked back at him. "Gimme some French toast and scrambled eggs."

"French toast and scrambled eggs it is."

Lisa went into the bathroom and Brad picked up the phone and ordered a pot of coffee, French toast and scrambled eggs for Lisa, and pancakes and eggs over-easy for him. As an afterthought, he also ordered orange juice. By the time he was finished, the shower had already started. As well as Lisa's crying.

Brad paused, listening. The shower wasn't on full-blast. He could hear Lisa sobbing quietly, as if she were trying to hide it. Brad's heart sank at the sound of it. She really wasn't doing so well, and he couldn't blame her. There wasn't a day that passed when she didn't mention Alicia and her infant daughter and how guilty she felt. For the first few days of Lisa's return home she had been quiet about it, holding it in. Then, when she'd begun to break down suddenly and without warning, Brad thought she was reacting to the ordeal she had been through—and what he still thought was her reaction to what she had originally told him and the investigating officers. Now that the truth had come out, he was realizing what a terrible burden she had placed upon herself. Holding all that guilt in for over two weeks, agonizing over it every day, thinking about it over and over.

Lisa's crying cut through the din of his thoughts. He wanted to go in and comfort her, but at the same time he felt incredibly awkward. Two nights ago, when she had broken down and confessed to what had really happened, he had been frightened by her state of mind. He had never seen her—or anybody—so depressed. *I killed them,* Lisa had cried. *I killed them, I killed them!* Those words packed such a powerful accusation that it was hard to argue with them. Oh, he knew she hadn't *really* killed them, hadn't really slashed them to death with a knife or pointed a gun at them and pulled the trigger. But from a subjective point of view he knew Lisa was blaming herself for the murders of Alicia and her daughter, as well as Debbie Martinez. He suspected she was really berating herself over the murder of the baby. *Because let's face it,* he thought. *She dangled that baby up as bait. And they went for it. Oh, they still tried to back out on the deal and Lisa was lucky enough to get away. But she hadn't been lucky enough to save Alicia and her daughter. And now she's beating herself up over it.*

When Brad had first heard the truth, he didn't know how to react. He'd been shocked. Then a strange numbness had set in. He began looking at Lisa in a different light, seeing her through new eyes. Thinking about what she'd done was making him question who she really was.

And one of the foremost questions was, *I can't believe Lisa would stoop so fucking low!*

Followed closely by *Don't think that about her! She's your* wife! *What would* you *have done?*

Brad didn't know the answer to that question. It was a question he thought of often.

He had no idea *what* he would have done.

Brad approached the door to the bathroom, hesitating. He could hear Lisa crying in the shower. "Lisa," he said, softly, knocking on the door before he opened it. "Lisa?"

Lisa didn't answer. All she did was cry.

"Lisa." Brad stepped into the bathroom and approached the shower. The curtain was drawn, but he could make her out behind it, standing under the spray of water, probably hugging her arms to her sides, head down, sobbing.

"Hey, do you want to talk?" Brad stepped up to the shower.

"No." She hitched back a sob, her voice a hiccup. "No, I'm okay, I'm just . . ."

"Just . . . what?"

She didn't answer him. She cried, her sobs loud and so ferocious that for a moment she couldn't answer. Brad waited outside the shower until Lisa calmed down somewhat. "Lisa?"

"What?"

Brad hesitated a moment, wondering what to say. He had never seen her so depressed. "Lisa, let's talk."

"I don't want to talk, I just want to die!" More sobbing.

"Lisa," Brad said, doing his best to remain strong, but inside he was breaking down. He felt so alone and so scared for Lisa and her sanity. For the first time he felt weak, unable to do anything to make it all better. "Lisa, don't say that."

"It's true," Lisa sobbed. Brad opened the shower curtain so he could see her. She was standing with her back to the spray. She looked up at him with haunted eyes, her face puffy and red. "I just want to die. If I could kill myself now, I'd do it. I can never forgive myself for what I did."

"Lisa . . ." Brad made an awkward attempt at taking her in his arms. Lisa shuffled back.

"No, don't *touch me!*" she cried. "Just don't touch me! *Leave me alone!* I'm a *murderer!* I'm a *monster,* and I just . . . I just . . ."

"Lisa . . ." Brad felt helpless, unable to offer a word or gesture of support. It felt like he was watching her drown in a rough sea that he couldn't calm.

"You don't understand what it's like," Lisa said, sobbing so uncontrollably that it was sometimes hard for Brad to understand her. "You just . . . don't understand how I feel . . . to know that I . . . I . . . I helped them kill this poor innocent baby. I led them to her . . . I . . . I . . . *fed* her to that . . . that . . . *monster!*" She broke down completely. "I fed a defenseless baby to a man who killed her! I just can't help thinking what . . . what . . . what she probably went through . . . how they . . . how they . . ." Lisa couldn't finish; she broke down sobbing.

Brad wasn't even aware that he was crying, too. Lisa's accusatory tone toward herself was like having a spike penetrate his guts. "Lisa, please," Brad said. He reached out and tried to grasp her arm. She didn't resist this time. He gripped her upper arm gently. "Please come out and let's talk."

"I'm *stupid!*" And then Lisa drove a fist into the center of her forehead so suddenly and so ferociously that it caught Brad by surprise. The blow rocked her head back. "I'm *stupid, stupid, stupid!*" Each *stupid* was punctuated by another blow to her forehead, right above the bridge of her nose.

Brad grabbed her arm before she could hit herself again. "Lisa, *stop it!*"

"Let go of me!" She struggled to free her arm from his grip.

"Not until you stop hurting yourself!"

Lisa went limp and sank to the floor of the bathtub, crying. Brad turned off the shower, then knelt down beside her, trying hard to keep his own emotions under control. He held her clumsily while she sobbed into his chest.

Brad sniffed back his own tears. His throat burned. He felt a heaviness in his chest. Hearing her say that she wanted to die, watching as she hit herself, hurt him in ways he never would have imagined.

They remained that way for a while, Lisa huddled on the floor, crying, Brad holding her awkwardly. Her tears slowed to a trickle, and when they did she was able to talk a little more coherently. "You don't know how much it hurts," she said, still averting her gaze from him, keeping her face pressed against his chest. "You just don't know . . . as a woman . . . putting myself in Alicia's shoes . . . as a mother . . ."

"I know," Brad whispered.

". . . it just hurts to know what happened to them. And to know that I *helped* make it happen. That if it wasn't for my own . . . *greed,* that—"

Something burst inside Brad. "Greed had nothing to do with it, Lisa, it was survival."

"How can you say that?" She pulled back from him, her features anguished.

"You were acting on instinct," Brad said quickly, hoping what he said would calm her down and help her see the error in her way of thinking. "You were pregnant yourself, Lisa. You were acting on . . . I don't know, a maternal instinct. Your number-one concern was protecting yourself so you could save our baby. You didn't know what you were saying when you—"

"But our baby died!" Lisa screamed, sobbing again.

"Yes, our baby died." Brad grasped Lisa's shoulders, forcing her to look at him. "But there's nothing we can do about that now. It's not your fault our baby died, and it's not your fault that these men killed Alicia and her baby. *They* killed them, Lisa, not you. *They* did it!"

"But I led them to Alicia and Mandy! I traded my life for theirs. *And that makes me just as much of a monster as . . . as . . ."* Lisa couldn't continue. She started sobbing again.

It broke Brad's heart to hear the guilt in Lisa's voice. Lisa was his life, his rock. He loved her more than anything in the world and had been so happy when she was found safe. When she had told him what had *really* happened, he still felt the same way. He'd been shocked, yes; disgusted by what these men had done and the activities they participated in. He still had uneasy feelings about what Lisa had done. He'd been horrified at the consequences—he wouldn't be human if he hadn't been. But he didn't hate her. He loved her and he wanted to protect her, and more than ever now he wanted to find the men responsible for what had happened and kill them.

Lisa leaned into him again, totally broken in mind and spirit, Brad held her, whispering to her, trying to soothe her as best he could but knowing that anything he said was falling on deaf ears. He felt dead inside. Part of him wanted to break down and cry, too, but he couldn't. It was as if his body wouldn't let him, as if it had turned that part of himself off so he could be strong for Lisa and support her, be her rock for her to lean on.

"I'm so tired," Lisa said after her sobs trickled down. "I'm just so tired . . ."

"Come on," Brad said. He helped Lisa to her feet and out of the shower. For the first time since yesterday, she looked awful. Her skin was white and pale. She was trembling, and Brad draped a towel over her shoulders. "Let's get you in and lie down. Maybe some food will—"

Lisa had been looking ahead with a fixed stare, her pupils dilated, fixed on nothing. Suddenly, she turned a whiter shade of pale, put a hand to her mouth, and bolted back into the bathroom and fell in front of the toilet. Brad turned away at the sound of her retching. God, he hated it when people threw up. He closed his eyes and took a deep breath, trying to drown out the sounds of Lisa throwing up, trying to summon the courage to be there for her. He made his way into the bathroom and knelt down beside her as she gagged and retched into the toilet. She hadn't thrown up much, just bile. A thin line of saliva drooled out of her mouth. She wiped it away with the back of her hand, gasping for breath. "I'm sorry," she said.

"It's okay."

"I don't think I can eat anything."

"That's okay. You don't have to."

Lisa sat up, trying to catch her breath. She closed her eyes. It looked like she was fighting off another wave of nausea. "I don't think I'm going to be able to handle the smell of food, either," she said hoarsely. "Do you think you can send the room-service stuff away?"

"Yes," Brad said. "I'll send it away."

"Thanks." Then she turned over and retched into the toilet again and Brad felt his own stomach churn at the sound. He waited by Lisa, patting her shoulder while she dry heaved, and then he helped her into the bedroom, where he eased her into bed and pulled the covers over her.

When room service knocked on the door, Brad hustled outside quickly and closed the door. "Listen," he said, slipping the room-service attendant a ten-dollar bill. "My wife suddenly got sick and I'm going to have to send this away. I'm sorry."

"No problem, sir." The bellhop was young, with a blond crew cut.

The door to the room opposite theirs opened and a huge black man with a shaved head peered out. He caught Brad's eye and nodded. Brad caught a brief glimpse of John Panozzo, the guy who had picked him and Lisa up last night, just beyond the door, and he nodded back. Security. The door closed, and Brad stepped into the room and closed his own door to the world of the Luxor.

Lisa was still huddled in bed. She had stopped crying, and she lay with her eyes closed, the covers pulled over her. "Will you be okay for a while?"

"Where are you going?"

"Just out for a while."

"I'm sorry!" Her voice broke, and for a minute Brad thought she was going to cry again.

"It's okay," Brad said quickly. "I'm just going to head out for a quick bite and I'll be back. John Panozzo is watching the room from across the hall with a partner, so you'll be safe."

"He is?"

"Yeah." Knowing that John and his men were watching over them made him feel a hundred percent better. As long as they stayed at the hotel, they would be okay. As long as somebody was around to watch Lisa, he could just slip out quickly and grab some breakfast and hightail it back. Plus, he had to call Billy and see if there was any news. "I'm going to get dressed and then I'll be gone. I'm leaving the cell phone John gave us in case you need it."

"Okay," Lisa mumbled, closing her eyes again.

Brad drew the shades, darkening the room. Carrying his travel bag, he went to the bathroom and quickly slipped out of the clothes he had slept in last night, washed up, brushed his teeth, applied deodorant, and dressed in a pair of shorts, a fresh polo shirt, and socks and shoes. He made sure he had his wallet and the room key, checked on Lisa one last time before he left, then slipped out of the room.

He knocked on the door to the room across from theirs and it opened. John Panozzo peered out at him. "Any trouble?"

"None, except Lisa's feeling sick," Brad said. "I'm going to go downstairs real quick for a bite to eat. You guys going to be up here?"

"Yeah. Hold on a second." He disappeared for a minute, then emerged. "You want somebody to come with you?"

"Nah, I'll be fine."

"Okay. I'll let hotel security know." John had explained to them last night on the drive over that if they wanted to walk around the casino to let him or his partner, Titan, know so they could alert security. Luxor security had been briefed on the situation yesterday afternoon, and they'd have plain-clothed security guys watching them discreetly, as well as be under the watchful eye of cameras. "Be back as quick as you can."

"I will."

Brad Miller headed down the hall to the elevators, trying to put some order to the thoughts that were running through his head. Under normal circumstances, the slot machines and card tables would have beckoned and he would have been playing roulette by now. But with a sick wife (who was also in danger of losing her sanity), Brad was worried not only about the investigation, he was worried about Lisa. If she kept beating herself up over what had happened, she might fall into a stage of such deep depression that she could become withdrawn, suicidal. He had to think of a way to help her. Therapy would obviously be the best option, but he couldn't very well look in the Yellow Pages in Las Vegas for a shrink, could he? They were on the run, in protective custody. They were supposed to be hiding out from the bad guys. He had to talk to Billy pronto. The more Brad knew what was going on in the investigation, the better he would be able to make a decision on what to do.

And what to do? That was a question that deserved much pondering, which he did downstairs in one of the restaurants over a hasty breakfast of scrambled eggs, sausage, and lots of coffee.

Twenty-five

William Grecko was in his office putting the finishing touches on a case file so he could turn his attention back to the Miller matter, when his secretary forwarded a call to his personal line.

He picked up on the first ring. "Yeah, Becki?"

"George Brooks is on the line," Becki said. "He says he's the senior partner of Peterson and Dunn, and that he's Lisa Miller's employer."

"I'll take it." Billy knew George well.

Becki put the call through and George's voice came over the speaker. "Mr. Grecko?"

"What can I do for you?"

"Well, I was wondering if you could help me." William leaned forward as he listened. He had dealt with George a few times in the past, mainly in assisting with various court cases. George knew that he and Brad were friends, and William guessed that the reason the man was calling him now had to do with Lisa. He was right. "I need to get ahold of Lisa, and I understand she's in kind of a sticky situation."

"Yes, that's right, George. I'm afraid I really can't go into it any more than that, though."

"That's quite all right. I surely understand the attorney-client relationship." Billy smiled to himself as he listened to the man on the other end ruffle through some papers on his desk. It sounded like George was talking on speaker as well. "I do need to get in touch with her, though. It's rather important."

William opened the bottom drawer of his desk and extracted a flask; he unscrewed the lid. "I can give her a message." He took a sip; the rum burned straight through to his gut.

A short pause from George. "It's that serious, then?"

"I'm afraid so."

"Forgive me for my ignorance, Billy." George picked up the phone and William picked up the receiver of his own phone, giving them a secure line. George's voice was clear, tinged with concern. "But what in God's name is going on?"

"You don't know?"

"I know that Lisa was kidnapped by what sounds like gang members and was sexually assaulted, but that's all I know."

"Ah." George Brooks wouldn't have found out what had really happened, not so soon. He had no idea what was going on. "Well, I'm afraid it's a little more delicate than that, George." Despite the stress he was going through, Billy relaxed a little. He had known George for twenty years, and he was one of the most reputable lawyers he had worked with. Although he knew George on a somewhat casual basis, he liked the man. Still . . . "Again, I'm sorry, but—"

"No, no, no, don't apologize," George said, sounding worried and frustrated. "It's just that . . ." He sighed. "Lisa was working on the Henderson vs. Colby case and was finalizing the deposition for an appearance in court this morning. She finished it shortly before she went on her leave, and there's another file that goes with it and we can't seem to find it."

"I see." William could detect the urgency in George's voice. Lisa's workload had probably been handed off to an associate and a clerk, and knowing from experience, anything could have happened to the file George was looking for.

"Danielle's looked all over for it and we've called Lisa at home twice," George continued. "In fact, Danielle went by there last night and Lisa wasn't in. We really need this file, Bill. If we could just . . ."

The second line on Billy's phone console lit up. The LED readout on the screen flashed: WESLEY COLLINS. Speaking of cases that needed closing, he'd been expecting this call from Wesley all morning, and the sooner he could talk to him, the sooner he could close his own affairs and get back to the Millers' personal safety issues. "Listen, George," William said, replacing the lid on the flask. "You can get ahold of Lisa at the Luxor Hotel in Vegas. They're in room 2727. And George?"

"Yes."

"Don't give that number out to anybody. Not even to Danielle." William knew that Lisa and Danielle Kwong were close friends, but he couldn't risk anything right now. He trusted George, though, and knew that the lawyer's intentions were honest.

"You have my word," George said. "I'll call you later. If

there's anything I can do to help, you know where to reach me."

"Thank you," Billy said, hanging up on George and picking up the second extension to speak to Wesley. The sooner he could finish his business for the day, the sooner he could get to the bottom of this snuff-film business. And the first order of that was the court-ordered search on the Golgotha cabin in Big Bear Lake, scheduled to take place this afternoon barring any unforeseen last-minute legal maneuvering.

"Brad?"

"Yeah?" At first Brad didn't recognize the voice on the other end of the line.

"It's George Brooks. Can I talk to Lisa?"

Recognition flooded in, and Brad turned to the bed in the center of the room. He had been in the bathroom when the phone rang, and it had rung at least five times before he managed to pick it up. Lisa had been asleep, but stirred when he picked up the phone. Now she turned over and looked at him, sleepy-eyed. "Who is it?" she murmured.

"Hold on," Brad said, placing his palm over the mouthpiece. "It's George . . . from work . . ."

"George?" Lisa looked confused, but then she recognized the name. She held out her hand for the receiver and Brad passed it to her. "Yeah?"

Brad listened in on Lisa's end of the conversation. He had been surprised at the phone call and a little scared. *How the hell did George find out we were here?*

"Oh, that," Lisa said, her voice heavy with sleep. "It's in the center file along the wall, under the label 'D.' " A pause. "Yeah." A longer pause. "You found it! Good . . . okay . . . Um . . . yeah . . . okay . . . bye." Lisa handed the receiver back to Brad.

"What was that all about?" Brad asked.

"That Henderson case," Lisa said, lying back down. "I'd forgotten all about it."

"What about it?"

"The hearing is this morning and they couldn't find my file on the addendums and amendments to the deposition," Lisa said. Her eyes were closed. "I forgot to tell Danielle where I had filed it."

"Oh." As likely as that prospect sounded, Brad was still uneasy. He liked George Brooks just fine, but if there was some way that their security was breached, Billy had to know about it.

Brad picked up the phone and carried it with him to the bathroom. He looked back at Lisa, who appeared to be falling asleep again. Then, he dialed Billy's number at the office.

Billy picked up on the second ring. "Brad?"

"Yeah. I just got a call from George Brooks. Did you—"

"He called here and I gave him your number," Billy said; he sounded busy, under pressure. "It's okay."

"Are you sure?"

"He wanted to talk to Lisa about a file, a legal case, right?"

"Yeah."

"Listen, I know how you feel." Brad could hear Billy rummaging on his desk. "I know you're nervous about this, but I guarantee you that George is okay. I mean, shit, I've known the man for over twenty years!"

"I'm sorry," Brad said, feeling his heart pound. "It's just that . . ."

"I didn't tell him what was going on," Billy said. "He knows not to let anybody at the office know where you are. He's a professional, Brad. Trust me on this, okay?"

Brad sighed and nodded. Much as he hated it, he had to put all his faith and trust in Billy right now. George

Brooks was one of the first people Brad had wanted to go to for legal advice when Lisa had originally turned up safe. No doubt George already knew the original story. Besides, the man had a wife and two children; he was involved in the community, in local charities. He wouldn't jeopardize his career, his life, for violating attorney-client privileges. Surely he'd recognize and respect that Billy was representing them.

"I'm sorry, Billy. I guess I just got a little carried away."

" 'S'okay," Billy said. "Paranoia is healthy in this case. You have nothing to worry about. George and I are the only ones who know where you are."

"And our parents."

"And your parents."

"And your security team."

"Them too. You see them this morning?"

"Yeah." Brad related the episode this morning when he had to send the room-service food away. He briefly thought about mentioning Danielle Kwong to Billy, but then decided he didn't need to. He'd only told Danielle they were going to Las Vegas; he didn't tell her where they were staying. "John and his guys are parked right across from us, and we have a hotline straight to them via the cell phone he gave us. We're fine."

"Good. John's one of the best. Plus, you're in one of the biggest, busiest hotels in Las Vegas. Nothing's going to happen to you there. You're in, like, a fort in the middle of the desert."

Brad felt a little better. He sat down on the toilet, cradling the phone. Hearing that made him feel more secure. Billy was right. John was a big man, easily over six feet, and his partner, Titan, was even bigger. Both men came from public and private law-enforcement backgrounds, held black belts in various martial arts. Plus, they were in charge of the entire security force at the Luxor. Nobody was going to fuck with them. "What's the latest?"

"I'm leaving in ten minutes for an appearance at the San Bernardino Sheriff's Station," Billy said. "The DA's in court now on the search warrant issue, and I expect to hear something on my way up. I'm hoping we get the search warrant so I won't have to drive all the way the fuck back."

"Do you think they'll overturn it?"

"No doubt of that. DA's got probable cause, which is all they need. The Golgotha people don't have a leg to stand on, legally."

"So what happens next?"

"We search the place and take it from there," Billy said. "If we find anything—and I mean *anything*—that points to foul play in that place, arrest warrants are going out to all the guys on Golgotha's board of directors. If they want to avoid going to prison, they'll talk."

Brad's mind was racing, tracking back to the story Lisa had told him. "Do you think these guys had anything to do with this?"

"I don't know. They might, but I just don't know. There's always the possibility they could have been renting it out to this Tim Murray guy and they had no idea what Tim was using it for. On the other hand, if they know something, we're going to make them talk."

"Call me first thing you find out," Brad said.

"You bet."

They hung up and Brad walked back into the room and put the phone back on the nightstand. Lisa was asleep again, curled up on her left side.

Brad watched her sleep for a moment, noting the drawn look on her sleeping countenance, the way the skin on her forehead was furrowed in worry lines. The room was dark, slivers of light escaping through the blinds that were closed against the heat of the day. Brad checked his watch. It was only ten-thirty, with the rest of the day to follow.

Brad climbed onto the bed, sat up against the headboard. He turned the television on and thumbed the volume down. He spent the rest of the morning and early afternoon channel surfing, his mind on autopilot, most of his energy going toward taking care of his wife as she slept and tried to keep the demons at bay.

William Grecko was present at the Golgotha cabin as the search commenced.

He had received the news halfway up the mountain. One of the DAs, Bruce Davis, had made the call. Billy had given a small shout of victory at the news. "The court order is being sent to San Bernardino now, so meet me at the cabin," Bruce had said.

William drove straight to the cabin, where he met four deputies and a homicide unit search team. A Golgotha representative was also present, and he didn't look too happy. He'd remained sullen as he followed the search team through the cabin, making it well-known that he wasn't pleased. Billy smirked as he caught the man glancing at him. *Fucking weasel,* he thought. *These church people are all a bunch of fucking weasels.*

There were four homicide detectives present. They made a quick inspection of the interior of the cabin. William had waited outside with one of the deputies, making small talk as the search went on. The forensics team showed up a few minutes into the search, and a trio of white haz-mat-suited figures entered the cabin. Billy turned to the deputy. "They surely didn't waste time in bringing these guys in, did they?"

"Don't get your hopes up," the deputy replied, staring at the cabin. The deputy was in his mid-thirties, with dark hair and eyes and a slim build. "We don't have much to go on in there. One of the rooms has just been repainted. If there's anything to be found, it'll be in that room, and these guys'll be the ones that find it."

Billy nodded; he had figured that the minute he saw the techs walk in with their equipment. Lisa had said the place had been barren of furniture, that Tim and that Al guy had covered the floors and walls with plastic sheets before they started torturing Debbie Martinez. They would be lucky if they found a single drop of blood in the place. And they surely weren't going to waste immediate time in digging up the grounds around the house. No telling where the bodies might have been taken. They were looking for the smallest amount of evidence they could find. Anything would do. A drop of blood, a smudge of a fingerprint, a hair. They would find it.

William was sure of it.

Six-thirty P.M.

Lisa had been up for the last two hours, staring morosely at the TV as talk shows rolled on. Oprah was conversing with the author of a new political thriller. Brad had brought Lisa a glass of water and had encouraged her to eat a couple of crackers, which she'd nibbled on. She had to get some nutrition in her, but he knew that she couldn't handle food right now. She was still in that state of nausea, and he didn't want to induce another round of vomiting. Slow and easy was the ticket.

At least she had allowed him to open the blinds a little. The early-evening sun spilled streaks of gold through the window, bringing in some heat. Brad had the air conditioner set at a comfortable level. He had spent the last few hours watching TV and reading the newspaper, which had been left outside their door this morning, courtesy of the hotel. Lisa's parents had called around noon, and Lisa had risen long enough to talk with them and assure them she was okay. Brad told them he would call as soon as he heard from Billy Grecko, which should be any minute. Both sets of parents were in a state of panic, and Brad could only imagine the anguish they were going through. It had been Billy's idea to keep the lines of communication between their parents open, including telling them the truth of Lisa's kidnapping. The best thing Brad could think of to keep their fears at bay was to talk to them every six hours or so, assure them they were fine and that they were holding up well under the circumstances.

At the same time, Brad knew that Lisa needed to get some serious professional help. She had spent most of the morning and early afternoon in a deep sleep, and now that she was awake she had been sitting in a vegetative state in front of the TV, talking only when he asked her something. The blows she had rent upon herself earlier that morning had left bruises along the right side of her face. Brad had fidgeted, torn between wanting to call somebody to help her—maybe get his parents or one of their friends back home to summon a good shrink over to Vegas to get Lisa into therapy or something—but he couldn't. They were trapped in one of the most popular luxury hotels in Las Vegas, under the watchful eye of the security experts Billy Grecko was connected to, until the people responsible for Lisa's abduction and near murder were apprehended. Until then, he felt powerless.

Then the phone rang.

Brad picked it up on the first ring. "Hello?"

"Billy here." Brad could detect the strain in Billy's voice. His stomach plunged down an elevator shaft.

"Yeah, Billy." Brad tried to keep his voice calm.

"We didn't find anything." At the confirmation, Brad's spirits sagged. He glanced at Lisa, who didn't appear aware that Brad was on the phone. "We tore that place apart. Looked through the house from top to bottom. The forensic guys went over every square inch of the room Lisa described and took some samples, but they didn't look too happy. They don't think they've found anything. Motherfuckers *painted* the goddamn room!"

"What?" Brad's mouth went dry.

"They painted it," William said again, spitting the words out in disgust. "There's a fresh coat of white paint covering the room, even the ceiling. Even the goddamn floor is painted. Motherfuckers even laid down brand-new shag carpeting!"

Brad felt himself slump. Any DNA evidence that might have been in that room was now contaminated. "What about the rest of the place?"

"Couldn't find anything. We went through the whole house. Best we could come up with were some shoe impressions left in the dirt along the driveway and the side of the house."

"The bedroom window—"

"Showed signs that suggested it might have been boarded up, but that's it." Billy sounded pissed off. Judging by the echo, it sounded like Billy was calling from his car phone. "There were fresh nail holes in the side paneling bordering the window. No signs of the boards or the nails used. One of the detectives said there's very little we can go on."

"What about the property the house is on?" Brad was trying to think of any lead they could pursue. "The surrounding area? Maybe they just haven't looked far enough."

"We searched the property and some of the surrounding area," Billy continued. "Got two sets of tire tracks and the FBI is trying to come up with a match, but that's a long shot, too. Couldn't find anything in the woods beyond the cabin. Even had a search team make the mile hike along the path Debbie Martinez normally took on her walks, but they didn't find anything."

"Shit!" Brad could feel the room closing in on him.

"Detectives are questioning Oliver Gardenia, the man whose name appears on the deed as being an officer in the Golgotha Corporation. He appears to have an airtight alibi. He's already provided documented evidence supporting his claim that he was in New York the weekend Lisa was kidnapped. Plus, he doesn't resemble the description of the men that kidnapped her."

Brad didn't know what to say. Lisa was unresponsive, still watching TV. Oprah had given way to Jerry Springer. A pair of white-trash couples began immediately verbally assaulting each other the minute the show started.

William continued with the bad news. "All the criminal checks we've run on potential suspects have turned up nothing. Tim Murray doesn't have a criminal record. A check through the DMV brings up several Tim Murrays, but they don't resemble the suspect Lisa described."

"He told her that he had gained weight and grown a beard to pull her kidnapping off so he wouldn't be recognized!" Brad hissed, now suddenly angry. Goddamn it, why were they beating around the bush on this? "He altered his appearance. Why can't you just show us some photos and—"

"We can't just pull DMV records on people without a criminal history based on lack of evidence." William sounded just as frustrated as Brad was feeling. "Besides, we got teams of detectives tracking these guys now for questioning."

"So what are we supposed to do?"

William sighed. Brad waited for him to continue. He

got up and headed to the bathroom again, where the conversation could be somewhat private. "What about the other guy, this Al?"

"We found a guy in the DMV records that matches the name and description and sent a team of detectives to question him," Billy said. "They haven't been able to locate him."

"What about the surveillance tape at the Bank of America?"

"We're working on that now," Billy said, and the first strains of optimism crept into his voice. "In fact, that's our biggest lead. Huntington Beach PD reports that they were able to get a good blowup of the man who accompanied Lisa into the bank. They're putting it over the wires today."

"Is there any way to check the description with the name Lisa gave?"

"All we know is that his name is Jeff." Billy sounded depressed again. "We've got no last name. That's not enough to go by."

The claustrophobic feeling tightened. There was no way these men were going to let this go. Even if they had no criminal records, they knew that law enforcement would be on their trail. That's why they had tried to kill Lisa after forcing her to withdraw her and Brad's life savings. Only Lisa had escaped with her life, barely. It had been two weeks since the nightmare began. Surely, if they were going to come after them they would have done so by now. Unless—

"You say you can't find this Al guy?" Brad asked.

"Yeah," Billy said. "LAPD detectives didn't find him at his home, and his neighbors haven't seen him for at least a week."

Brad's mind was racing. Wasn't Al one of the men who had threatened Lisa? "He's coming after us," he said.

"That's why you can't find him. He and the other two are coming after us and—"

"And you're safe," Billy soothed. "Just stay where you are. We're gonna get them. How's Lisa doing?"

Brad looked out the bathroom door, the sound of the television welling in the background. "Not so good. She's . . . she's all . . . she . . ." Brad's voice was shaky. "She needs help, Billy. She's so . . . so depressed and so . . . she's just so *down* that I'm afraid for her sanity. I think she's suicidal. She needs help."

"We're gonna get her help, buddy," Billy said. "Don't worry about that."

"No, I mean she needs help *now.*" Brad gripped the receiver, trying to control his emotions. He described Lisa's outburst this morning, how she wished it had been her who had been killed instead of Mandy and Alicia. How the thought of what Jeff had probably done to that baby tore her up inside, how she wished she were dead because of her actions. He described the pain he felt as he watched his wife punch herself in the face repeatedly, punishing herself. "She's really, really in a deep state of depression, Billy," Brad said, and now his voice *did* crack. "She's been sleeping all day, and now she just sits in front of the TV like a goddamned vegetable. She looks like she's in shock or something. She won't talk and I . . . I'm trying to give her space to work it out, but . . . I'm afraid it's gone beyond that. I really think she needs to be in a hospital."

"Let me make some calls," William said, "and if I can get her in somewhere nearby I'll have her admitted. Okay?"

Brad nodded, fighting the tears streaming down his face. "O-kay, Billy. Th-thanks."

"And hang tight," Billy said. "We're doing everything we can. We're gonna find these guys."

"Okay, Billy."

"I'll call you later if I can get Lisa into a hospital somewhere, okay? In the meantime, stay put. You need anything, you let John know."

When Brad hung up he sat on the toilet seat for a moment, still fighting back the tears. Then he stood up and carried the phone back into the room. Lisa was still sitting up in bed, staring at the TV, her eyes glazed over. He set the telephone on the nightstand, looked at his wife. "I love you, Lisa."

Lisa stared at the TV; it was as if she had never heard him.

And then Brad *did* break down and he sank to his knees, arms cradling his head as he slumped against the bed, and he cried heart-wrenching sobs at Lisa's feet. Lisa stared at the TV in a daze, watching as Jerry Springer encouraged familial violence to take place on his show.

Sunsets in the deserts were beautiful.

Tim Murray had just reached a crest in the hill he was hiking, and he paused to watch the sky turn red on his way back to where he had parked his SUV, which he had gotten at the scrap-metal yard the night they disposed of Al, where it had been marked for destruction. A light breeze ruffled his hair, now cut closer to his scalp. He had shaved his beard off last night, revealing a face that was slightly cherubic, with pinkish skin. He had also changed eyeglass styles, wearing a pair of wire-rims that helped accent his face. He looked like a very different man from the one who had kidnapped Lisa Miller two weeks ago.

The SUV was another quarter of a mile south along a remote trail. There was still enough sunlight left in the day to get him back to the vehicle. Then it was a trip back to Las Vegas and the motel he was staying in for the night near Circus Circus, on the other end of the strip. All his equipment was back at the room, behind locked doors. He wouldn't need much for the job tomorrow. Just one camcorder and that was it. No lights, no boom mikes, not even any plastic tarp to roll away the body and catch the flying blood.

The weather forecast for tomorrow afternoon was calling for a storm.

Tim Murray grinned. Today's late-afternoon drive had been a scouting expedition. When he had gotten the call early this morning to get his ass to Las Vegas and prepare for filming, he knew he had to do some fast thinking. Rick Shectman had warned him that if he blew this one that he would end up worse than Al. Tim believed him—hell, he'd seen what Animal had done to Al, and knew the sadist wouldn't care about doing the same to him—but he wasn't afraid. He was confident in his abilities; he knew that the desert outside of Las Vegas was the perfect stage for a snuff film, and it was just a matter of doing some exploring to find the right remote spot. The weather report only boosted his confidence. Not only was rain expected, but wind as well. It could very well turn into a sandstorm. What better way to fuck up DNA evidence and scatter a body?

Tim laughed. He looked back down at the boulders, where he decided they should film tomorrow. He had found this spot twelve miles away from a secondary road; the dirt trail had led northeast, and there had been no signs of civilization. When Tim had seen the small rise he had pulled over and begun the hike, telling himself he would only go out for a mile or so. A quarter of a mile in, he had come upon the little canyon. Away from prying eyes. Tomorrow they wouldn't have to hike this far back—they could bring her here in the SUV. The storm would erase tire tracks, too. Ha!

Tim Murray clambered down the rocks, heading back down to the desert floor. He didn't think Rick suspected that he was planning on leaving the business. Tim had made the decision last night after his meeting with the producer and hearing his indifference to the fact that he'd produced a film in which Animal had murdered an infant and was thinking of using the sadist to indulge in similar atrocities for the pedophile underworld he'd sold the film to. Tim knew from experience it would only get worse. Twenty years ago, producing a snuff film was something he thought he'd never be involved in. Sure, he'd heard the rumors before. When you worked in underground pornography you heard the stories, but you never saw the actual product. Then, fifteen years ago, he'd actually seen his first one, at a private party. It had been old, an 8 MM reel shot in Mexico. Not too long after that, the party's host had asked Rick Shectman if he could make him one, and Rick had agreed and asked Tim for his assistance. And being that Tim knew so many people nobody would care about if they went missing, and because the money dangled in front of him was too good to pass up, he'd said yes.

But I never agreed to kill innocent babies, he thought as he trudged through the desert, the warm wind blowing at his back. Junkie fuckups that cause nothing but trouble to society are one thing . . . babies are another. That was something people like Rick Shectman didn't understand. And that was why Tim Murray wanted no part of it. *Maybe I'm getting too old for this shit,* he thought. *Fuck, twenty years ago you couldn't find anal scenes in mainstream porn, and now it's a mainstay. Nowadays people are paying to watch videos of chicks throwing up. People are getting more bizarre in their fetishes. And the underground is getting more hardcore.* That first snuff film he'd seen had merely shown a woman being raped and strangled by two men on camera, their faces hidden by masks. Violent, yes, but not perversely so. Now Rick wasn't satisfied with a snuff film unless Animal sadistically tortured the person. Now the bar was being raised even higher by using chicks that looked like models, by using babies and children, and the fact that Rick was entertaining the thought of having Animal do a necrophilia or cannibalism film. Tim wanted no part of it. After this job was over, he was finished.

The rays of the dying sun beat upon the back of Tim's neck. As he reached the desert floor, he heard the light *churr* of rattlesnakes rattling their tails, agitated that he was nearby. Tim stepped carefully down the path he had taken, being careful not to step near rocks or plants or gopher holes. They wouldn't have to worry about wildlife tomorrow afternoon in the heat of the day. It would just be the three of them: he, Animal, and Lisa.

He still didn't know how they were going to get Lisa out here. Rick had told him he was working on that now, but to stay by the phone in his room; there was a good possibility his services might still be needed in assisting in the actual abduction. All Rick had asked of him in his original phone call was to make sure Animal was in Las Vegas by tomorrow morning. "Choose a location, then have Jeff picked up at the airport tomorrow morning at eight. When you've picked out the location, call me. Make sure you and Animal are ready." Tim had assured Rick that he wouldn't let him down.

Tim was glad he wouldn't have to worry too much about abducting the bitch this time. Rick didn't elaborate, but Tim guessed he was relying on his contacts on the East Coast to fly somebody in to assist in the actual abduction. How they were going to do it Tim didn't know, but it was out of his hands. He had one job, and one job only. Running the camera.

And by tomorrow evening at this time they would have it. On film.

And if the weather held up, everything else—including what was left of Lisa Miller after Animal was finished with her—would be washed away. By the following day, Tim would have his money, including his share of the bonus Rick had gotten out of the pedophilia group in the Pacific Northwest who had paid for the footage of the baby, and then he would begin thinking about his next plan.

First item on the agenda: Completely disappear. Change his identity.

Then, when he felt safe and set up in a location nobody in the business would even think of looking for him, start thinking of a way to snare Rick Shectman and Animal under the cross-hairs of the federal authorities.

He could do it. He was pretty confident that if the cops could get to Rick, surprise him somehow, they would have all the evidence they needed in Shectman's records. They could find the clients who had bought the baby snuff film, and sweeping arrests would be made. Tim would make a deal—he'd spill the beans on the whole operation in exchange for total immunity from prosecution and witness protection.

But he'd only do it if he was one hundred percent confident he could get such a deal. He'd do some sniffing around first under his new identity. If it appeared that he couldn't make such a deal, he'd find another way to expose the group. Make an anonymous call or something. Maybe in the next day or so, if he was able to, he would get close enough to Rick Shectman's office to get the information he needed. He knew that was next to impossible—Shectman was extremely secretive about his clients, and rumor was he had the backing of the Russian mafia to protect him—but it was worth a try. He had to do something to stop the memories of the screaming going on in his head.

The wailing screams of pain that sounded so much like the wails of an infant . . .

. . . or a rabbit . . .

Tim Murray took a deep breath. He felt a little better about himself now that he had made up his mind to expose the group. He thought about this as he walked back to the SUV. Tomorrow was going to be a good day; he was going to go through the job, do it good to win back Rick Shectman's confidence in him, and then he was going to return to Los Angeles to get ready for the next step. He was looking forward to it.

Twenty-six

Morning.

Brad sat on a chair at the desk, his back to the curtained window. Lisa was asleep, a snuggled form beneath the thick blankets. He watched the slow rise and fall of her chest as she breathed, ever vigilant in monitoring her behavior and health. Every time her breath hitched just a little Brad would jump, wondering if she was in the throes of another nightmare. She had screamed herself awake three times last night, clawing at the air, scrambling to run away as if someone was chasing her, and each time she shot out of a dead sleep Brad would grab her, shake her out of her dream-state until she finally snapped out of it, looking around the room wide-eyed, uncomprehendingly, until she saw where she really was, that she really *was* safe, and then she would collapse into Brad's arms, crying fitful tears.

For the past three hours, though, her sleep had been calm. Brad watched her as she slept, his own fatigue weighing heavily on him. He hadn't gotten much sleep last night at all—four hours tops maybe. Even then, what sleep he had gotten was in fits and starts. He had spent most of the evening pacing the floor of their room, watching mindless television programming with Lisa, trying to talk to her while she still sat unresponsive. He had ordered room-service dinners, had tried to get her to eat some soup, but the most she would do was look at it with disinterest. He had eaten the soup after he had finished his own food, then set the tray back outside their door.

He had tried to talk to Lisa, but she wouldn't respond. He'd told her that everything was working out, that Billy told him the authorities were closing in on this Tim Murray character and that they should know by tomorrow morning if he was in custody. He also told her that he was going to get her help, they'd get through this together, do whatever it took. And then he would wait for some kind of reaction—anything—and be greeted with that same blank, unresponsive look.

He tried to take solace in calling his parents. He gave them the latest news, expressing his anguish that Lisa wasn't getting any better. His mother informed him that they had found Lisa a good psychiatrist in California, that they had called him after talking with William Grecko, and that William was working on getting Lisa transferred to a maximum-security hospital for her own safety under this psychiatrist's care. "Billy thinks he can have her in by tomorrow evening," his mother had told him, and Brad felt a little better upon hearing that. His father was obviously still reeling from the shock of all that had happened in the past forty-eight hours and kept mostly silent, listening in on the extension, voicing his support and hopes that things concluded soon. Talking to both of them had made him feel a trifle better.

He had called Lisa's parents and informed them of the latest, making special effort to let them know that they were close to not only catching the scumbags who had done this, but getting Lisa psychological care as well. Lisa's mother, Emily, had burst into tears when Brad tried to get Lisa to talk to her mother; Brad had heard Emily break down as he sat on the bed, trying to get Lisa to talk. Lisa's father, Dean, came on the line and asked Brad to call them tomorrow morning. "Even if nothing happens, just call," he'd said. Brad had agreed, and that had been the end of the phone calls for last night.

Around eleven-thirty, Brad decided that Lisa had had enough TV and turned it off. He had skimmed down to his boxer shorts and slid into bed beside her. Lisa had still been sitting up in bed, her eyes still staring ahead of her at the blank TV. Brad had gently taken her shoulders and said, "Come on, honey, let's try to get some sleep." Moving her to a lying position had been like moving a mannequin, and once he'd gotten her to lie down, Brad lay down himself. He'd faced her, noting her still-open eyes, her blank expression unmoved. Then the floodgates opened and he bawled. He cried and sobbed, reaching out blindly for Lisa, who didn't resist or react, and that made him cry harder. And as Brad cried, the frustrations and anger and sadness welling out of him, tapped from some deep well within his soul, he felt yet another pang of rage toward the men who had done this, and that had dried the well of his tears. That anger had kept him awake most of the night, lying in bed beside Lisa, both of them staring up at the ceiling; Brad feeling the twin emotions of rage and sorrow, Lisa trapped in her own private hell, battling her own demons.

At some point, Brad must have gotten some sleep. He remembered coming to awareness and glancing at the clock on the nightstand and seeing that an hour or two had passed. On the third sense of wakefulness, he'd turned to check on Lisa and saw that she had drifted off to sleep finally. He'd watched her for a while then, lying on his side until he fell asleep for another hour and a half.

He woke up again at six-thirty, then closed his eyes, trying to fall back to sleep again. Sleep didn't come back, though, so he got up after thirty minutes. He took a peek outside; it was overcast but not yet stormy. The news report last night reported that Las Vegas was in for a torrential rainstorm that was expected to arrive this afternoon. Brad had slipped into a pair of sweatpants and a T-shirt, then sat in the chair by the bed, watching Lisa sleep.

He glanced at the clock again. Seven thirty-five. He yawned. He wasn't going to get any more sleep, but maybe Lisa would. He hoped so. He mentally added up the numbers of when he figured Lisa might have fallen asleep, guessed that it had been around four-thirty or five. He hoped she slept in till at least one, and with that in mind he got to his feet, walked over to the desk, picked up the phone, and called room service.

William Grecko had been in his Santa Ana office for only fifteen minutes when his private line rang. He picked up on the first ring. "Yeah?"

"William? It's Detective Orr. How are you this morning?"

"That depends on what kind of news you've got for me," William said. He felt like shit. He'd cut himself shaving, and his head pounded from a hangover. The coffee in the percolator was still brewing, and his stomach churned. "What's up?"

"You know that the surveillance photo of the suspect

known as Jeff went out over the wires yesterday evening, right?"

"Yeah. Anything yet?"

"Nothing." Detective Orr sounded frustrated. He was the only investigator on the case who William felt was taking it seriously. "We got no ID yet. FBI has been checking their records, and so far nothing on that end, too. We're discussing putting the photo on the FBI Web site, maybe some other places."

"And what's keeping you from doing it?" William felt his jaw clench.

Detective Orr sighed, and William could sense what was coming instinctively. "Listen, we're hitting dead ends everywhere on this. Golgotha personnel have been questioned extensively, including all the board of directors. They're really pissed, and the Orange County Sheriff's Department is double-pissed. The Golgotha people are talking lawsuits, and so far we have nothing on them. No DNA evidence, no material witnesses, no nothing on this thing. You were at that cabin yesterday with us, William. You know there's not much else we can go on without—"

"So what am I supposed to do?" William asked, his voice breaking. "How am I supposed to protect my client from—"

"Listen, I'm sorry. But there's not much to go on except for Lisa Miller's word that she saw the Martinez woman being kidnapped and abused. We have no suspects, at least none we can name. We've turned up nothing in all the databases. We've—"

"What about the FBI?" William said, feeling his head pound. He closed his eyes, trying to control himself and get past the pain. "I've read a lot of shit about snuff films the past few days, and everything keeps pointing to the

FBI, that they've been investigating illegal pornography for years."

"They've been investigating it for years and they've turned up nothing," Detective Orr said. "There's lots of rumors about it, lots of people say they've seen them, but the sightings are all once-removed. The FBI's been on this since the mid-seventies. Their official position on it is that snuff films don't exist."

"You believe that?"

Detective Orr paused. "I don't know what to believe."

"In 1970, if I had told you that there were a group of guys that got their jollies off by trading pictures of grown men having sex with little boys and that there was an underground market for it, would you have believed me?"

An awkward pause. William had him. "No," Orr admitted, his voice wearing a tinge of defeat.

"And why not?"

"People just . . ." He hesitated. "People didn't just believe that kind of shit existed back then."

"Same rules apply here," William said. He leaned over his desk, resting his elbows on the mahogany surface. "Remember that thing in the news not too long ago about that woman who was convicted of cruelty to animals? She'd been stomping on mice with high heels for a series of porno films. Remember that?"

"Yeah," Detective Orr said. The tone of his voice told Billy that the detective remembered the incident clearly. For all he knew, Orr had inside information on the case.

"A guy was busted with her," William continued. "They had been making what are known as 'crush videos' for a select number of clients. People pay anywhere from fifty to a few hundred bucks to collect videotapes of women crushing small animals with their high heels. Don't you think that if there are people that get their sexual jollies off on that, there might be even sicker people out there who get off on watching people die?"

"I understand your argument, William, but—"

"I know it's hard for you to believe, but this shit is real. I believe Lisa Miller. She's not the type of person who takes to flights of fancy. I believe that what she saw, that what almost happened to her, really happened. I believe that what happened to her is odd, yeah; I admit that. By all accounts, these guys target runaways that people won't miss. They don't go after people with families, people that will leave behind loved ones. I think the reason why the FBI is saying snuff films don't exist is because they can't penetrate the subculture that deeply. I believe the real audience for this stuff is less than a few thousand worldwide. When you stack that up against those crush films or bestiality films or other hardcore S&M films, that's nothing. I think that's why the FBI says they don't exist—the market hardly registers on their pulse. Know what I mean?"

"In other words, the market's so small it's not worth pursuing."

"Exactly."

"That's bullshit, and you know it," Detective Orr said. "If people are being killed—"

"Who's being killed? Some junkie in Harlem who's been living on the streets for ten years who has no family, no place to go? There's thousands of people like that in this country with no family, no parents, no support system. They come from foster homes, from institutions, whatever. Nobody gives a shit about them and you know it. Whatever family support they might have had is gone when they get into the streets. Maybe some of them do have somebody out there who loves them, who wonders where their son or daughter is, the wayward child who was perhaps a little too rebellious at home and left one night after a fit of anger. Happens all the time. Not all of these people get ground up and spit out for the camera; most of them OD, or they die of hypothermia, or they get knifed in a mugging or something. Or they die of AIDS. Some of them do get cleaned up. But there's probably a small number of them, say one percent, who simply disappear, never to be seen again by anybody."

"You're talking about the kinds of people who fall prey to serial killers," Detective Orr said.

"Serial killers and hustlers out to make a buck off their misery." William flipped through the papers on his desk, searching for something. He found it. "Listen to this. I printed this off a Web site yesterday. It's an article that details the illegal pornography industry, as well as the child porn market. And it stated here that something like seventy-five percent of the kids that wind up in low-budget porn—"

"I'm not interested in statistics, William," Detective Orr said, his voice becoming curt. "Look, I'm sorry, but there's nothing much I can go on. We've got a blowup of the suspect who kidnapped and stole Lisa Miller's money. That suspect and the Tim Murray character are being sought for kidnapping and extortion, and that's it. Same with the Al Pressman character. We can't make a case for murder until we get more evidence or if one of them confesses."

William Grecko sighed. His head was pounding. He needed coffee and he needed it bad. "Okay," he said. "What's on the agenda for today?"

"Just hang tight. We're still running a vehicle check on the van. We're also doing some checking on the homeless woman, the one Lisa identified as Alicia. We had a sketch artist work up a composite based on Lisa's description, and we're putting that over the wire. We're also working with the broadcast news media and some of the local papers in running the photo. Maybe somebody will recognize her and we can get a positive ID. If we can find her, that might answer a lot of questions."

"And what if you don't find her?" William asked. He got up and walked to the coffeepot, poured himself a cup. "What if Lisa's story checks out? What if this ex-boyfriend of Alicia's decides to grow a heart and calls and everything he tells you checks out? Then what?"

"We'll cross that bridge when we get there," Detective Orr said.

Titan was resting his muscular six-foot-six frame on the king-sized bed, a cup of coffee within easy reach on the nightstand. The Jets were on, pounding the hell out of Philly, and he had three hundred bucks on the game. He was following the game, his mind mostly on the last twenty-four hours. The reports that had come back from security had been negative. There was no news of anybody resembling Tim Murray, Al Pressman, or Jeff. Their descriptions had been given out to all of hotel security, and the spooks that manned the cameras in the casinos were also instructed to keep their eyes peeled for them. So far, nothing.

That was fine with Titan. As long as the Millers stayed in their room, they were safe. Titan or somebody else from the security team was always on hand, twenty-four seven, right across the hall. And somebody was always armed. Titan knew that the minute anybody resembling the suspects walked into the hotel, he or John would get a call. He'd gotten five calls between yesterday morning and last night, all of them turning out to be false leads. In each case, they had dispatched one of their men down to intercept the suspect and tail them. The report always came back the same: "Guy looks like the dude in the sketch, but it isn't him. This guy looks like a tourist, and he's got a wife and five kids trailing along behind him."

So much for that.

Titan yawned and reached for his coffee just as there was a knock on his door.

He looked at the door, annoyed. John Panozzo had gone down to the kitchen to bring the Millers their room-service breakfast three minutes ago. The knock came again, light yet persistent. Titan swung his legs over the bed and got up, ambling toward the door.

When he peered through the spyglass he saw a little old lady, looking forlorn and lost. She looked like she could be between sixty-five and ninety, and was wearing a blue plaid dress, had short, wispy white hair, her thin frame looking both grandmotherly and kind.

Titan opened the door. "Can I help you?"

The old lady turned to him, her watery blue eyes wide with confusion. "I'm sorry," she said, her voice wavering. Her hands were shaking, as if she were a victim of Parkinson's. "I got separated from my . . . my church group. We took separate elevators and . . ." She licked her lips. She looked terrified—and no wonder; for an old white lady like this one, confronting Titan—six foot six, muscular, shaved head, ebony skin—was probably giving her a heart attack. ". . . I'm lost. Can I . . . can I use your phone, please?"

Titan glanced quickly down the hall. No sign of John. The old lady trembled beneath his gaze. She clutched a small white purse in her liver-spotted hands. There were senior citizens' groups staying at the Luxor all the time. No doubt the group this poor old woman had been with had neglected to check to see if all of their party were together. Maybe this lady wanted to call a church member on their cell phone. If so, too fucking bad. "Sorry," he said. "Try the room next door."

"Please!" The woman began to cry, and Titan had almost shut the door on her when he paused. *You can break this woman in half by breathing on her. What the fuck is she gonna do?*

Feeling like a shithead for slamming a door in the face of an old lady, he opened the door. The old woman stood in the hallway, looking lost and in tears. "Come on in, but be quick," he said, already hating himself for letting a crying little old lady get to him.

The old woman sniffled back tears and hobbled in, her gait wavering. Titan closed the door and followed her into the room and then bumped into her as she suddenly stopped and whirled around toward him. He felt her face brush his chest as he tried to stop the forward momentum of his stride, hoping he hadn't hurt her, and that was when he felt the pain in his abdomen.

He looked down at his belly, his mind trying to figure out how a knife had been thrust into his stomach. The hands holding the handle were small, birdlike, skin wrapping bones. They jerked upward, opening him up, and Titan gasped, looking in wide-eyed horror at the old lady, who now wore a different expression. Gone was the look of elderly confusion and meekness and tears; it had been replaced by a look Titan had seen before only on people much younger than she—namely, male street criminals. Her blue eyes reflected a sense of malice as she grinned. "Fooled you, didn't I?" She pulled the knife out of his gut, and Titan felt the lower part of his body grow numb and wet. His belly exploded with sharp pain.

He staggered back, eyes still on the old woman, than looked down at the blood spattering on the carpeted floor. He could feel the blood soaking into his jeans. He looked back up at the woman, still trying to comprehend why she had stabbed him when she lashed out again with expert precision. He saw the blade flash below his field of vision in a delicate swoop, felt a line of pain blaze across his throat, and then a sudden sense of warm wetness as his shirt was soaked. He opened his mouth to scream, but his vocal cords refused to take the commands. "That's what I like best about being elderly," the old woman said, her voice still possessing that same brittle tone but now strong with conviction and purpose. "You can catch so many of your victims off guard."

Titan made an attempt to lunge at her, to try to get the knife away from her grasp, just as his body went completely numb. He collapsed to the floor on his knees, his belly a pit of fire, his throat singing with pain, the scent of his own blood filling his nostrils, chasing him into darkness.

Mabel Schneider didn't waste time. She wiped the bloody knife blade on the comforter, then approached the door, peering through the eyeglass.

She knew another man was due any minute now with the room-service tray. The plans they had made earlier this morning had been hasty, but they were working beautifully. The best part of it all was they were actually going to let her take a souvenir! "One of her eyes," she'd told Rick Shectman over the phone yesterday when he'd spoken to her about coming out to assist in the abduction of a snuff-film victim. "If that animal you use in those films doesn't pop them when he sticks his dick in her eye sockets, I want one of them. Maybe both of them if they're unruptured. I haven't had boiled eyeballs in a while."

Shectman had agreed, only on the condition she prepare her meal on this coast. "I can't risk airport security finding body parts when you board your plane on Friday," he'd said. "If I can't get you the eyes, I'll arrange somebody to get you a kid. How's that sound?"

"I can get my own children," she'd spat out at him. "That's easy. Children flock to me because I remind them of their grandmother. If I can't get her eyes, I'll think of something else. Maybe you can convince that beast of yours to fuck me in the ass or something."

"I'll do what I can," Shectman had said.

Mabel replaced the knife in her handbag, leaving it open enough so that she could retrieve it quickly for the next one. She examined herself quickly in the mirror. She hadn't gotten any of the big man's blood on her, which was good. She glanced back at him, her eyes lighting on his chest. It was still. He was deader than shit.

With that, she turned back to the task at hand. She opened the door slowly, peered out to make sure the corridor was deserted, then slipped out, closing the door behind her.

Then she waited.

When John Panozzo rounded the curve in the corridor he saw an old woman wandering the hall, glancing at the numbers on the doors as if she were searching for something. He dismissed her from his mind as quickly as he had taken her in, and pushed the room-service tray ahead of him, the scent of fresh pancakes and coffee creating his own pangs of hunger. *I didn't realize how fucking hungry I was until I smelled this shit. Man, that smells good!*

John pushed the tray to Brad and Lisa Miller's room and knocked on the door. He was wearing the official uniform of the Luxor room-service employees. John had thought it was a good idea to have his team dressed as hotel employees to avoid suspicion. If somebody was out to get Brad and Lisa Miller, they wouldn't have a clue they were being watched by hotel security as well as the best private security team in Las Vegas. They would be lulled into a false sense of security. Of course, that wouldn't work if—

"Excuse me. Sir?"

It was the old woman. She had noticed him and approached him tentatively. John glanced at her. She looked lost. He turned to the door as he heard footsteps approach.

"Sir?" Her voice was more persistent, wavering on brittleness and tears.

He turned back to her just as he heard the deadbolt being thrown open. "Just a minute, okay?"

He turned back to the door as Brad Miller opened it. "Room service," John said, pushing the cart past Brad.

"Hey!" he heard Brad exclaim. John pushed the tray to the center of the room, taking only quick notice that the TV was on and Lisa Miller was still in bed, lying on her right side, her back away from the door. He turned around and was surprised to see that the old woman had followed him into the room.

"Uh, can I help you, miss?" John said, stepping toward the old woman.

"I'm lost," she said, her voice sounding as brittle as dead leaves. "My church group lost me on the way to the elevator. Do you have a phone I could use?"

Brad was still standing by the open door, obviously stunned that the old woman had blundered past him into his room. John took a step toward the old lady, his training taking over. "I'm sorry, ma'am, I'm going to have to ask you to leave."

"Please!" she screeched, and then she started crying. She clutched her purse in her brittle-looking hands, and John reached her just as Brad closed the door. "Let her use the phone, John. She's not gonna hurt anything."

John was just turning to answer Brad when he felt the knife punch into his throat.

* * *

The first thing Brad saw when he came back into the room after closing the door was John was clutching his neck trying to stop the geyser of blood that was gushing out of him like a fountain. A knife with a seven-inch blade was sticking out of his throat where his Adam's apple should be. His eyes bugged in his face, his skin turned white as he grabbed for the knife unsuccessfully. The image hit Brad like a sledgehammer, shocking him with the brutal intensity of it. He felt frozen as the old woman reached for the knife handle and wrapped her brittle fingers around it. She tugged, and Brad could see the tendons along her upper arm tense as she pulled the blade out of John's throat. When the blade slid free, blood shot out of his neck with a sudden ferocity; it was like turning on a garden hose in the summer at full blast. It spattered the floor and the bed, some of it hitting Lisa.

This can't be happening, this just can't be happening, he thought. He tried to command his limbs to move, to do *something,* but he remained frozen in shock at the hideous scene. John Panozzo fell to his knees, his fingers clawing at his throat, trying to stem the flow of blood. Brad felt his chest constrict as the room became increasingly claustrophobic, and then the old woman was standing in front of him, her features twisted in a mad grimace, the bloodstained knife in her left hand. Brad was so shocked, so frozen in horror, that his reaction was like moving through a sea of molasses. The old woman reached into her purse with her right hand and brought it out, and even when she pulled the trigger on the object Brad still didn't believe this was happening. How *could* this be happening? They were under protection, with an armed security team looking out for them! And as the old woman shot him with the Taser gun and Brad felt his body go numb with pain, he slumped to the floor, hitting his head on the desk. He tried to move, tried to turn over as the woman cackled, "Fooled you, didn't I?" She pressed the trigger of the Taser gun again, sending thousands of volts of electricity through his system, paralyzing him, and the last thing Brad Miller saw before he lost consciousness was the wide-eyed face of his wife on the bed, frozen in fear, and it was the first hint of emotion he had seen in her since they had gotten to Las Vegas.

When it was over, Mabel Schneider put the Taser gun and the bloodstained knife in her purse and pulled out a cellular phone. She glanced at the woman on the bed, watching to make sure she wasn't faking unconsciousness. She'd been instructed to stun the woman with the Taser gun too, but she didn't need to do that—the woman had fainted. She lay on her side limply, tongue lolling out the corner of her mouth, her hair hanging limply across her face. Her breathing appeared shallow, and Mabel had reached out cautiously prior to putting the knife away, touching the woman's face. If she had been faking it, the woman would have jerked with a scream at her touch. Mabel had caressed the woman's cheek, then lightly slapped it. No response. Mabel smiled. She wondered why Rick wanted to take such big risks in securing this woman as a snuff-film victim, but then, he was paying well for her work. What did she care for what Rick had in mind for her?

Mabel turned her attention to the cell phone. She turned it on, hitting the speed-dial button for the number already programmed. "It's done," she said when it was answered. "I'll be waiting." Then she hung up, pushed the antenna down, stepped around the bloody mess on the floor, and hovered by the door to wait.

* * *

The minute the elevator doors closed, Tim Murray hoped it didn't stop for other hotel guests.

He glanced at Mabel Schneider out of the corner of his eye as the elevator made its descent. She looked like a harmless old lady, the kind you saw at church picnics or old folks' homes, hobbling along in grocery stores and malls like turtles. Tim didn't know where Rick Shectman found her, didn't even know the old bat had existed until last night when he'd told Tim the plans for abducting the Miller woman. At first Tim couldn't believe that Rick had access to an eighty-one-year-old psychopath like this. *How the fuck does he know so many fucking sadists?* Rick had explained to Tim that Mabel was an old friend of his father's. "She used to run an S&M dungeon in my father's neighborhood in Pennsylvania in the forties," he'd explained. "And it was rumored that after she accidentally killed a client she developed a taste for dishing out extreme torture. That it didn't bother her to hurt people. I happened to make her acquaintance by accident ten years ago on a business trip to New York. She had requested a torture video of a child, and when I made the delivery we had a . . . how shall I say it? . . . a nice talk." The tone of Rick's voice had chilled Tim, and he quickly accepted the fact that he was to be working with an eighty-one-year-old female version of Animal. He wondered where old fucks like Mabel Schneider came from and then he dismissed the thought. If Animal lived to be eighty-one, he'd probably wind up just like Mabel. An old doddering man who appeared harmless. An old doddering man with a taste for the grotesque and inflicting extreme pain on other human beings.

Remarkable how the old bat had avoided getting any blood on her. It had been soaked into John Panozzo's clothes. After verifying that he was dead, Tim had quickly trussed up Brad Miller with the duct tape he had brought, slapping a strip over his mouth as well. Then he'd turned his attentions to Lisa, securing her tightly. Mabel had waited calmly by the door, and he had slipped into the room across the hall quickly without being seen. He had given the room a quick inspection, once again amazed at how quickly and precisely everything had gone down. Then he had quickly changed into the clothes he had brought along in the light tan canvas bag he had toted upstairs: brown slacks, brown shoes, and a beige shirt; now he resembled a hotel staffer at first glance. He had placed his own clothes in the bag, then had turned his attention to the large cardboard box he'd brought up with him, unconstructed. He had quickly assembled the box, then gone downstairs to the lobby and snagged a luggage cart. He had placed the box on the cart, then spent a significant amount of time and energy hauling Lisa's trussed-up form to the box. He had injected some morphine into her to keep her unconscious, and once she was limp she was easier to move. He stuffed her into the box, folding her arms over her head, her knees folded against her chest. Then he closed the box, sealing it with duct tape. There were enough holes in the box to provide for ventilation, but that wasn't a major worry either. She wasn't going to be alive for very much longer.

Tim Murray watched their descent to the lobby on the indicator above the door as the car plummeted downward. They had left Brad trussed up in the room with the door locked, per Rick's instructions. By the time he got himself free, wifey would be meat for Animal.

As if reading his thoughts, the old woman spoke up. "Rick said I could have an eye."

"Huh?" Tim looked at her, for the first time noting her watery blue eyes. She looked crazy. Insane.

"Her eyes," the old lady said, her voice reedy and brittle. "I like to eat eyes. Rick said I can have one."

"Fine by me, lady," Tim said, turning his attention back to the door. He also had to drop this old bat off at a motel on Spring Street, on the outskirts of Vegas. He wasn't looking forward to that.

"I like eyes the best," the old lady said in a matter-of-fact tone, as if she were discussing the preparation of apple pie. "I've found that the eyes of children are the best, though. I also like asses. I like to boil the eyes in a broth I make from the blood, but I like to baste the asses in the oven with onions and bacon strips."

Tim looked at her, feeling a sense of revulsion. "You shittin' me?"

"Why, no," she said, in a tone of voice that seemed to say *Why would I lie?*

"You fucking *eat* people?"

"When I can," she said, looking indifferent to it. She clutched her purse. "I'd eat this cunt you have in the box if Rick would let me, but he's saving her for that pig you use in those snuff films. I told him I wanted the eyes, though. I like eyes."

"Shit!" Tim shook his head in disgust. And he thought Animal was a sick motherfucker.

"Of course, if her pussy's still intact when Animal is finished with her, maybe he'll let me have that. I do like the taste of pussy."

"Here we are," Tim announced as the elevator car stopped. Listening to this old fuck talking about eating pussy in the literal sense was making him sick. The doors opened to the lobby, where a crowd of tourists was waiting to get on the elevator. Tim mustered a smile and waited for Mabel to get off, then pushed the cart off. "Car's in the parking garage," he said, staying abreast of

Mabel as he maneuvered the cart down the lobby toward the exit that led to the garage. "Third level."

"Fine," Mabel said, walking briskly for a woman her age.

As they made their way to the parking garage and threaded their way past tourists, Tim couldn't help but glance at the old woman, whom he kept in front of him. Where the hell did Rick Shectman find these freaks? It was bad enough there were weirdos out there who got their jollies by watching films of people getting raped and sliced up, but to think that there were old people who were just as sick as Animal was something Tim couldn't comprehend. What was wrong with these people? Why did they enjoy doing this shit? Tim didn't understand it; the only reason he was involved in this shitty business was that the money was pretty good and he always got free blowjobs from the whores they used in films. His mind went back to the night he'd gotten rid of Al's body at the scrap yard, and how Animal had had one more go at him, raping the lifeless body, using the neck stump as a sexual orifice. He'd seen Animal use all kinds of things as a sexual orifice—gaping knife wounds he'd made in abdomens, empty eye sockets gushing blood and optic fluid, you name it. Until the last snuff job with the baby, though, he'd never known Animal to eat anybody. That was just too fucking gross.

Tim Murray kept his eyes peeled for anything resembling cops or security people as they approached the SUV. The coast appeared clear—it was obvious they weren't looking for a guy escorting his grandmother! He motioned to Mabel Schneider. "White SUV's mine." Mabel acknowledged him with a nod as they approached the vehicle, and Tim disarmed it with the remote, getting the side door open quickly. Mabel waited calmly, clutching her purse demurely in her hands while Tim hauled the box into the van. When it was secure, he closed the door and pushed the cart aside. Mabel opened the driver's-side door and climbed in while Tim slid into the driver's seat and started the van.

They drove away from the Luxor, heading to the outskirts of Las Vegas.

Twenty-seven

There was a loud humming in his ears.

That was the first thing Brad Miller was aware of when he became conscious of his surroundings.

He opened his eyes. His vision was blurred and he blinked, trying to focus. He became aware that he was tied up, that the skin of his arms was itching, and when he opened his eyes again his vision focused. And what he saw was red.

The cream-colored carpet of their room was deep red.

The smell hit him next, along with the electrifying sense of numbness that was still echoing through his limbs, making his skin ultrasensitive. His mouth was dry and he felt a metallic taste in the back of his throat. He struggled, and that was when he realized he was tied up with duct tape.

He opened his mouth to scream, but he couldn't; his mouth was taped shut too.

Brad rolled around on the floor frantically, his adrenaline pumping. The sight of the lifeless body of John Panozzo, his pale flesh looking like the underbelly of a dead fish, sent him into a frenzy. He struggled against his bonds, and when his thrashing caused him to lose his balance and fall on the floor, his cheek landing in the wet carpet, he went ballistic. He jerked up, rising to his knees, and managed to hobble to the side of the bed. There were blood spatters on the bed and the wall over the headboard, and his heart leaped in his chest. The rumpled bedsheets told him what he feared.

They've got Lisa, oh my God, they've fucking got Lisa!

One quick look around the room brought it all back, told him everything he needed to know. They had been outsmarted. Billy had instructed his security team to look for Tim Murray and that Animal guy, probably Al Pressman as well. They hadn't expected a crazed old woman.

How the fuck did they find us? How the hell did they know we were here?

While he tried to backtrack how their security could have been compromised, Brad hauled himself up on the bed and rolled across it to the other side where the phone was resting on the nightstand. He tried to wriggle his arms out of his bonds but could only manage to move them a quarter of an inch from his body. He wasn't going anywhere. In a desperate lunge, he fell toward the phone and managed to get his face next to it. Then he knocked the receiver off the cradle and felt elated when he heard an open dial tone. *Thank God thank God. Thank God.*

Now if he could only dial the operator.

Brad stared at the keypad for a moment, the dial tone echoing in the room. Then he reached out and moved his face over the buttons. He moved his nose over the O and felt his stomach roll as he pushed it, hoping he was pushing the right button. Hoping and praying that this would work.

And then the hotel operator came on and Brad felt such a rush of relief at the sound of her voice that he almost sobbed. He had no idea how long he had been unconscious, but he knew that every second counted.

He did the only thing he could do. He grunted through his duct-taped gag.

The operator's voice was clear and questioning. "Can I help you?"

Brad screamed through the gag; his voice, though muffled, sounded panicked to his ears. He hoped he was loud enough to convey this over the phone.

"Is there anybody there?"

"MMMMmmmmmmm!"

A short pause. Muffled conversation in the background. Then: "Do you need help?"

"MMMMmmmmmmm!"

"I'm sending hotel security up," the operator said, all business now. "They're on their way."

And with that, Brad Miller collapsed on the bed and sobbed in relief and fear, hoping against all odds that time was on his side.

They had been on the road for only ten minutes before Mabel Schneider started getting on Tim's nerves. Her presence was irritating; she smelled of dusty mothballs, sour sweat, and bad breath. Did this old bat ever take a bath?

"Have you ever eaten pussy?" Mabel asked him innocently. She had put on a pair of glasses and was looking out the passenger-side window, looking very much like a grandmother.

"Lots of times," Tim answered, reaching into his breast pocket for his cellular, not even thinking about what she meant. Then it hit him, and he shook his head. "No," he said, trying not to sound too grossed-out.

"Raw pussy can be quite good," the old lady said. "All of a lady's parts are good. So are all of a man's parts. You know, the testes . . . the nuts."

"Um-hm," Tim said, dialing Rick Shectman's number

by memory. Listening to this old bat was driving him crazy.

"Testes are nice. They have a nice crunch to them. Especially if they're deep-fried. I like to batter them in flour and seasonings and and fry them in a vegetable oil—"

"You know, I don't want to listen to your culinary tastes right now," Tim said as the line on the other end began to ring. *Come on, pick up, you fuck.*

The old woman looked at him, realization dawning on her face. "Oh, don't worry, young man. I have no interest in *you.* I like my men young. The best age for nice crunchy man-balls is boys that are teenagers. You know, boys in their sexual prime, when their balls are full of *spunk*. Eighteen-year-olds are the best!"

"So are eighteen-year-old girls," Tim said automatically, trying to be funny.

"I agree. Eighteen-year-old pussy is tender and sweet."

Rick Shectman answered the phone, and Tim Murray got his reprieve. "Yeah?"

"Are you shittin' me that you told this old bitch that she could watch?" Now Tim was letting his anger out and he couldn't help it. He had been looking forward to dumping the old crone off at her hotel when she insisted on coming along to the shoot, informing him that Rick had told her she could watch.

"I get the eyes!" Mabel chimed in.

"Shut up!" Tim barked.

Rick laughed. "I see that you've made Mabel Schneider's acquaintance," Rick said, chuckling. "Very good. She's good at what she does, yes?"

"You won't get any argument from me about that," Tim said. "This old bitch killed both those guys in less than two minutes."

Rick sounded pleased. "I knew she would work out. Nobody was expecting her."

"Where the fuck did you find this old cunt?"

"It's a long story, and I already told you the short version yesterday," Rick said. He sounded bored. "And I don't have the time to go into great detail of how dear, sweet Mabel Schneider came to my acquaintance."

"I know she flew out from the East Coast, so what's her story? She know the outfit in New York or what?"

"You've just answered your question," Rick said.

"She's tied in to the scene in New York, then?"

"In a way, yes," Rick murmured. "She was around when the scene in New York was fucking invented." Beat. "Listen, I gotta go. Why don't you let Mabel Schneider illuminate you to her sordid history. Let her watch Animal work, and when he's done she can have an eyeball if Animal hasn't completely fucked any up. Make sure she eats it there, though. We can't risk her boarding a plane with body parts."

Tim felt his stomach flop in his belly. "So she wasn't shittin' me, then? She really gets off on eatin' people's eyeballs and shit?"

"I do like shit," Mabel said matter-of-factly. "I like fresh shit out of a nice tight asshole."

"Shut the fuck up!" Tim barked at her.

Rich Shectman laughed. "Oh, you crack me up, Tim. You act as if the grotesque acts you've participated in the past five years are morally repugnant to you now."

"Animal doesn't *eat* people's shit!" Tim yelled into the phone.

"No, he doesn't," Rich Shectman said. "You telling me that you'd rather watch Animal skull-fuck some bitch to death or side-fuck 'em rather than eat the shit out of her ass?"

Tim didn't know how to answer to that. The question pissed him off. "Forget it. Okay, so I take this wrinkled-up old Miss Hannibal Lector fuck with me. Then what?"

"When she's finished, take her back to her room to get some sleep. Old people need their sleep, you know. Animal has his own transportation. Put Mabel on her flight tomorrow morning at 8:30 A.M. sharp. She leaves on US Air into Philadelphia, flight 135. Your own flight leaves two hours later into LAX. I'll meet you back here at my office for the transfer of the product."

"You'll have my money for me then?" Tim had gotten Rick to advance him twenty-five grand for the next job, which was already lined up. What he didn't know was that Tim already had his bags packed at home and was leaving for parts unknown that afternoon as part of Phase One of his plan to blow the whistle on Rick and the whole scene.

"I'll have your money, you greedy fuck. Just make sure you have the tape. You fuck this one up, your ass is mine." He chuckled. "I might even feed you to Mabel Schneider."

Mabel cocked a look of revulsion at Tim. "I heard that. You don't look like you'd be very good. You'd be too fat and buttery-tasting."

"Fuck you!" Tim barked at her.

Rick Shectman laughed and hung up.

Tim Murray jabbed the OFF button on the cellular, and when he braked for a red light he replaced the phone in his breast pocket. Mabel Schneider was grinning. She looked excited. "It's been a long time since I've seen anybody get done live."

"You've done plenty yourself, right?"

"Oh yes. Of course."

Tim didn't want to talk to this old crone. Not really. But he was dying of curiosity and he couldn't help himself. "How many people have you done?"

"I don't know," she said, looking out the window as they drove through the city to the outskirts. "Thirty maybe. I stopped keeping count around then, so it's probably been more like sixty."

"You've killed sixty fucking people?" Tim would have found it hard to believe that this old woman killed the two people at the Luxor this morning if he hadn't seen her results, let alone sixty. Still, Rick Shectman wouldn't have sent her if there wasn't some verifiable truth to her claims. "How long you been killing people? How'd you meet Rick?"

"I've known Rick for ten years," Mabel said, not looking at him. Tim stole a quick glance at her. No wonder she fooled a lot of people. She really did remind him of a grandmother—the kind that baked pies and knitted blankets and kept all the pictures of her grandchildren in nice little frames perched on a shelf in her living room.

"You in the New York scene, then? It's true what Rick said?"

Mabel Schneider turned to look at him, and now she bore a different expression. Now she was all business. All trace of the meek little old lady were gone. "I was first introduced to the pleasures of pain from my father, back in the 1920s. He used to whip me and my brothers. I grew to like it. He was a Catholic, and he felt guilty every time he beat us, so he would get us to punish him for his sins. My brothers and sisters, they were too scared to do it. I wasn't, though. I grew to like whipping my father. We had a . . . relationship." She smiled. Tim got the message and nodded. "By the time I was twenty, I was working a dungeon in Philadelphia. That's where I met my first husband. We went into business together and did very well. He . . . he misused me too much and I left him in '43. I had saved up some money, though, and met my second husband a year later. We married, and that's when he tried to force domestic life on me."

"He forced domestic life on you?" Tim chuckled, shook his head. "What, he knocked you up or something?"

"Yes. I bore that sonofabitch three stinking kids." Mabel's tone of voice had taken on a tinge of disgust at the mention of childbirth. "I never did adapt to motherhood."

"You ever whip your kids?"

"No." Her fingers closed over the clasps of her purse. "For a while there, I . . . I tried to be a good wife to Marlon. Even though he was a whipped dog."

"So what happened?"

"When the kids were in school and Marlon was at work, I started entertaining clients again," Mabel resumed. "It started innocently enough at first. I had a couple of affairs with people in the neighborhood. I got involved with a man who liked to be beaten. He introduced me to the scene in New York. There wasn't much of a scene in the town we were living in at the time."

"Where was that?"

"Lititz, Pennsylvania."

"Where the fuck is that?"

"Lancaster County. Two hours west of Philly."

Tim nodded for her to continue.

"My husband didn't suspect a thing for three years. I never left Lancaster County; my lover brought people from New York with him, submissives who were into whippings. We played out scenes in my basement, or in his. I started to make some money." She paused. "Then it happened."

"What happened?"

"I accidentally killed a client." Mabel looked at him, her features calm, serene. "A salesman had paid me to whip him and then mutilate him. He was overweight and . . . well, he had a heart attack. Jerry, my lover, freaked out. The guy's eyes were bugging out of their sockets and I was still wrapped up in the scene. I plopped one of his eyes out and ate it."

"You fucking ate the guy's eyeball?"

"Yes."

Jesus, fuck me! Tim gripped the steering wheel tighter as they reached the outskirts of the city. "So that's how you got the taste for it."

Mabel nodded. "A few months later, I almost got caught. I lured a high school girl to my house for a scene. I'd seduced her a month or so earlier. She was sweet. And her eyes were beautiful. I . . . I couldn't help myself."

"You ate hers, too?"

"Yes." Mabel's fingers were clasped over her purse protectively. She looked out the window, reflective. "I couldn't control myself and I just gave in to my urgings. Jerry had to come over the next day to help me get rid of the body. He was scared. He was afraid I was . . ."

A fucking psycho? Tim thought. "So what he do? He talk some sense into you, or what?"

"Jerry made a deal with some of the New York people," Mabel said. "He emphasized that I was . . . special. That I wasn't like other dominatrices. He made it clear that I could play out extreme hardcore scenes, that I had the stomach for them. Believe it or not, there were just as many hardcore freaks back then as there are now. They were just harder to find in those days. The ones we did find . . . well, they paid handsomely."

Tim nodded. "You do snuff films back then?"

"No. The technology wasn't available. We didn't even think of snuff films back then. What we had were live shows."

"Live shows?"

"Yes." Mabel looked at him, an elderly grandmother instructing the young. "If you wanted to watch, you paid two thousand dollars. We'd get around ten people, maybe twenty tops. And they would sit around and watch while I tortured some kid until they died. We'd do a show like that maybe once a year."

"Fuck! Your husband know?"

"No. He never knew about the live shows. He did find out about the lighter S&M, though. At first he was furious. Then I showed him the money I made and he had a change of heart."

"How much you make?"

Mabel looked at him, grinning. "For the regular S&M? In one year I'd made ten thousand dollars."

Tim nodded. Ten grand in the fifties would be like sixty now. "What was the scene like then?"

"Same as it is now," Mabel said. "Rich businessmen wanting to explore the forbidden. Pain freaks that got off on having pins being inserted in their scrotums or having their penises split in half and pierced. Same sick fucks."

Tim chuckled. "Aren't you a sick fuck?"

Mabel snorted. "And you aren't?"

Tim shrugged. "I just do this shit for the money."

"You don't enjoy it?"

"No."

Pause. Mabel turned back to the passing scenery. They were on the outskirts of the city now. "Waste of time if you don't enjoy it. You don't know what you're missing."

"What am I missing?"

Mabel looked at him. "If you knew, you wouldn't be asking me."

Tim glanced at her, turned his attention back to the road. He had asked Animal the same question once. The sadist had remarked: "I like the feel of brains on my dick when I'm skull-fucking 'em." That had been his answer. He wondered what Mabel's answer was. "I'm asking you now," he said. "You ain't got a dick, so I know it's not a sexual thing the way it is with Animal."

"What makes you think it isn't? Women climax just the same as men do."

"So you get off on it?"

"Yes."

"You get off on torturing and killing people?"

"I wouldn't do it if I didn't like it."

"And you really like eatin' people?"

"Yes. I do." Mabel Schneider's eyes gleamed. She licked her wrinkled lips. "You really don't know what you're missing."

They were in the desert now, cruising the last remaining suburbs of Las Vegas. "How long you been doing this shit, then?"

"Over forty years."

"And you never been caught?" He realized it was a dumb question the minute it slipped out of his mouth.

"No." She grinned. "Things were the same then as they are now. The people I was allowed to . . . to wallow in . . . they're the same kind of people we use now. Nobody wants them. They're throwaways. Homeless people, runaways, vagrants. Rejects of society. Nobody missed them then, nobody misses them now."

Tim thought about it as he drove. It was hard to believe that the hardcore scene had been around for so long, but then he supposed that, in a way, it always had been. The Romans used to have stadiums erected for the singular purpose of torturing and killing people in front of an audience. Man may be more civilized in social aspects, but he hadn't really changed in two thousand years. People still lived for blood sports. Look at boxing. And they called *that* a sport. Watch two men pound the crap out of each other for the sole purpose of trying to knock the other unconscious. And audiences cheered for the winner. The more mayhem, the more blood, the better.

Tim nodded. "Do your kids know you do it?"

"No." Her knuckles were bone white as she gripped the clasps of her purse.

"They never suspected?"

Mabel Schneider looked at him. "I never once let them even think I was involved in the scene. It's . . . it's my private thing. Do you understand? It's my private pleasure. It's something nobody can take away from me."

Tim nodded. That was the excuse patrons to the hardcore scene always gave. They participated in this in the privacy of their own homes. They didn't hurt anybody. They just liked to watch other people be tortured, raped, and murdered in the privacy of their own homes, where they weren't hurting anybody. Yeah, right.

They were ten miles from the secondary road he needed to take to get to the location. From there it was another thirty miles. They would be there in about forty minutes. "So back in the forties and fifties there was a thriving S&M scene, right? And as far as underground hardcore, there were no snuff films."

"There were no snuff films. At least as far as I know."

"You ever been in one?"

"A snuff film?"

"Yeah."

She nodded. "A few. The first one back in sixty-nine, maybe 1970."

"You wear a mask?"

"Yes." Mabel pulled herself up a bit. "I was playing the role of the madam dominatrix. I was in my late fifties then, and I still had my looks. I had quite a body back then. You would have wanted to fuck me."

"I'm sure I would've," Tim said, prodding her to go on. "So what happened?"

"I played the role of a madam dominatrix. The film was commissioned by a rich businessman. A homosexual sadist. He wanted to watch a young man get raped and tortured by a woman. Strange, don't you think? Usually queers like to watch men get done by other men. Not this guy. He wanted a woman. An older woman. He had a thing for older women, even though he was queer. It was probably a mommy complex. What do they call that?"

"Oedipus complex."

"Right. This guy, this client, obviously had one. The slave we used was some kid from New York. A hustler. He'd been kicked out of his home a few years before when his father, who was a minister, found out he was queer. He was into light S&M . . . nothing too daring. He started appearing in B&D loops that Rick Shectman's father produced as a bottom."

"So Rick's dad was into all this then? That's how Rick knows you?"

Mabel Schneider nodded. "Yes. I've done a lot of work for Boris Shectman."

"What kind of work?"

"The usual. Hardcore S&M stuff. Fetish stuff."

"He used you even when you were, you know . . ."

"So old?"

"Yeah."

Mabel chuckled. "What are you, naive, boy? Don't you know there's a big market for films showing us old folks fucking? It's *huge!*"

Tim nodded. That much was true. Rick Shectman had produced a few commissions for clients that catered to this fetish. "So you been working steadily for Boris, and now you do stuff for Rick. When was the last time you did a snuff film?"

"The last one I did was in seventy-eight or nine."

"What was that of?"

"A boy. A runaway. Maybe thirteen, fourteen years old."

"You ever do girls? Women?"

"Oh yes."

"And you still like to eat people?"

"Oh yes." Mabel grinned at him. "I haven't lost that passion."

"And you haven't been caught because nobody will believe that an old fuck like you can be a sick fuck, too."

"Look who's talking, doughboy."

They were approaching the secondary road. Tim checked his rearview mirrors, made a right, and they trundled down the road. Now it was time to start watching traffic around them. He couldn't afford to be spotted by cops now. "Doughboy. That's a good one. Nobody's ever called me that before."

"Would you prefer fat ass?"

"Fuck off, granny."

Mabel laughed. "I like you, doughboy. You're just as fucked up as I am, even though you don't want to admit it. You're going to get a good thrill out of watching her die, too."

Tim grinned and nodded. Maybe Mabel Schneider was right. He knew she was correct in that last statement: He *was* going to have a good time watching Lisa Miller die.

It took all of Brad Miller's willpower to not bolt for the door and undertake the search for Lisa by himself. He was sitting in a chair in the office of Head of Security at the Luxor, being grilled by two FBI agents. The cops and feds were crawling all over the place. Security was tight, and the last Brad had heard they were conducting a room-to-room search of the entire hotel and casino.

He didn't want to admit to himself that they were too late. It had taken a few minutes for hotel security to free him, and forty minutes had passed since then. The feds had just arrived, but he had to beg to get them to even show up. Once Luxor security informed the feds on what was happening, the mood changed. Now everybody was racing around the Luxor like they had fire up their asses. The clock was ticking.

"How old do you think the woman was?" one of the agents asked. Both agents looked to be around Brad's age. One was white, the other was black.

"She looked over seventy. Close to eighty. I've told you this five times already!"

"I'm sorry," the agent said. He looked flustered. "We just . . . I've just never heard of . . ."

You've never heard of an old lady psychopath slashing people like she was Jack the Ripper. Is that what you want to say? Brad closed his eyes, trying to stave off the headache that wanted to creep up into his brainpan. "I swear to Christ, the woman was fucking old. She looked like an old fucking grandmother, for God's sake! Now—"

One of the security team held out a telephone receiver to Brad. "Excuse me, sir? Guy on the other end says he's Mr. Miller's attorney. A Mr. Grecko?"

Brad leaped for the phone; he hadn't even heard it ring. "I'll take it!"

"Brad?" It was Billy, all right. He sounded on the verge of losing it.

"Billy, they've got her!" Brad yelled. He had called Billy twenty minutes ago and left a message, sobbing frantically into his voice mail that they had gotten Lisa again, that they had slipped past security using an old woman as their assassin. Then he'd called his parents. His mother had been shocked; she'd started to cry. His dad had gotten on the line and didn't say much. He was probably shocked, too. His dad usually clammed up when he got too emotional. Brad was the exact opposite. "They've got her, Billy, they slipped right past the fucking security and—"

"Paul told me everything," William said. His voice was even, controlled, yet with the faintest hint of strain beneath it. "We're doing everything we can, buddy."

"How the fuck did this happen?" Brad shouted. He could feel that he was on the verge of crying again and he tried to hold it in.

"I've just talked to Paul, and I told him that I just found out that there's a commercial printer in the City of Industry, a guy by the name of Rick Shectman, who might be a possible suspect. They're sending a team of agents to question him right now."

"They've got somebody? Is this a—"

"It's a credible lead," Billy said, overriding him. "Listen, Brad, my source says that the feds have been investigating this guy for years, but they've been unable to come up with much of anything. He runs a commercial print shop in Industry that is believed to also produce child pornography. My source also told me that there's speculation he's tied into the production of other forms of illegal pornography. No hard proof, though, just speculation. But get this: His father, Boris Shectman, was convicted in 1979 of producing child pornography and bestiality publications and served six months. Boris also ran a lucrative porn business, providing loops to porn shops across the country. He also ran coin-operated booths, prostitution rings, the whole nine yards. My contacts are still trying to dig his name up in connection with their snuff-film investigation in the seventies, but he's confident Boris was partially responsible for at least one snuff film that was made in seventy-eight or seventy-nine. That's what my contact tells me. His source claims that Boris was deep into the whole hardcore industry, and that—"

"They're going to get this guy? Is that what you're telling me?" Brad was excited; he wanted to get out of here *now* and help!

"They're after him now." He could tell Billy was trying to sound hopeful. "I don't want to . . . you know . . . get your hopes up, but—"

"I just want her found," Brad said, trying to control the stammer in his voice. "I just want her found."

"I'm doing everything I can, buddy. We'll find her. Now, can you pass me back off to the agents you're with?"

Brad handed the phone to the black agent, who took the phone. "Yeah? Paul Orr from the field office? Okay. Thanks." The agent gave the phone back to the Luxor security man, who hung up.

Brad leaned forward, cradling his head between his hands. He still felt weak from the Taser. Weak and sick. "Mr. Miller?"

Brad looked up. The African-American agent was looking at him with soft, brown eyes. "Mr. Miller. I have something I want you to look at."

"What?"

Another security agent had stepped into the room while Brad had been talking to Billy. He was holding a videotape. He inserted the tape into a VCR and as he got the tape ready, the head of security at the Luxor addressed him. "We questioned some of the guests and gave them your description of the woman who attacked you. We were able to verify that a woman fitting that description was seen with a man in the lobby, and that the man was pushing a luggage cart with a large box on it. Naturally, it was assumed they were guests. When I got the description of the woman from you, I ran it through security and we checked the tapes and came up with footage of the suspects leaving the hotel. We also checked the parking lot security tapes and were able to identify their vehicle. We got a blowup of the plate and alerted the state police and the DMV. They're on it now. We also gave them a description of the man seen with the woman. I'd like you to view the tape and tell me if you recognize him." He turned to the TV and VCR, pressed the Play button, and stepped aside.

Brad moved toward the TV, watching the black-and-white images of hotel patrons in the lobby hurrying to and fro. He recognized the old woman the minute she stepped into frame. "That's her!" he said, feeling his skin crawl.

The security agent slowed the speed of the tape down. "Take a good look at this guy," he said.

Brad watched the tape, his heart racing. When the man stepped into frame pushing a luggage cart, Brad didn't recognize him at first. The gold rungs of the luggage cart partially obscured the man's upper body, but as the tape progressed frame by frame, the man's figure moved into a more prominent view in the film. Brad felt his breath draw in as the man's face loomed closer. He wasn't wearing sunglasses and he was clean-shaven, his hair cut shorter, but there was no mistaking it. The man in the film pushing the luggage cart was the man who had had him arrested outside Ventura over two weeks ago. "*That's him!*" he cried, pointing at the TV. "That's the guy who called himself Caleb Smith. That's the guy who had me arrested and kidnapped Lisa!"

Twenty-eight

Animal was waiting for them at the precise spot Tim Murray had told him to be.

He was also dressed and ready for action.

Tim had piloted the SUV off the secondary road over

the bumpy terrain to the hilly area at the foot of the incline. He parked behind a large outcropping of rocks. A four-door Saturn with a rental-car decal affixed to the rear window was already parked there and Animal was waiting, leather bondage mask over his head, his upper torso bare. Mabel took one look at him and grinned. "I've seen two films you were in. I love your work."

Animal didn't say anything. His eyes were wide with surprise at the sight of the old lady. He looked at Tim.

"Relax," Tim said, as he opened the door to the SUV. "Rick hired her to take care of getting rid of their security. You ain't gonna believe the shit I seen this lady do."

"I want the eyes," Mabel said. She walked up to Animal, looking at him as an elderly schoolteacher might look up into the face of the school bully as she chastised him. "Rick Shectman said I could have an eye!"

Animal looked at Tim. "What the fuck?"

"She's cool. I'll tell you all about her later. Now, come over and help me get Lisa out."

Animal joined Tim, and together the men hoisted the box out of the SUV. Tim produced a box cutter and sliced the tape that bound the box shut. He opened the flaps and grinned. Lisa Miller lay curled inside, still knocked out. "I'll carry her out to the site if you carry the equipment. Camera and stuff is in the back." He reached into the box and grasped Lisa beneath the armpits and hoisted her up.

Animal reached into the rear of the van and grabbed the tripod and the black leather carrying case that contained the camera.

"You bring what you need?" Tim asked. Lisa was out of the box now, and he threw her limp, unconscious form over his shoulder.

"Yeah." Animal motioned to the Saturn. "In my car."

"Go get it."

Tim and Mabel waited while Animal retrieved a duffel bag from the backseat of the Saturn. The hooded sadist slung the strap of the carrying case over his shoulder, picked up the tripod with his left hand, and the three of them trudged up the hill.

It was slow going. They had to stop halfway up when it became obvious that Mabel was going to have a hard time making it up the incline. Tim felt a flash of irritation as he marched behind her. Finally, he stopped and put Lisa down. "Why don't you go over the incline and set the shit down and then come back for us," he called out to Animal. "I can't watch after this old bag and carry this bitch at the same time."

Animal nodded and trudged up the hill.

He returned ten minutes later and, with Tim's help, the three of them made it over the incline into the little valley. Animal helped Mabel step carefully down the incline, guiding her down by gripping her arm, steering her down a safe path. Mabel talked to him the whole time, relating the same background she had given Tim on the way over. Several times Animal glanced at Tim as if to say *this woman ain't shittin' me, is she?* And each time Tim had nodded. *She ain't bullshittin' you, buddy. She is what she says she is.* By the time they reached the bottom of the incline, Animal was treating the old lady as if she were his grandmother.

Tim motioned to a rock set against a small rise. "Why don't you have a seat and enjoy the action, Mrs. Schneider."

Mabel maneuvered herself to the rock and sat down. She was perspiring, and she looked happy. "My pussy's getting wet just thinking about this."

Tim tried not to show his distaste at the image she'd just presented to him, and helped Animal set up the camera. Lisa lay slumped on the ground, her hands and feet still bound together. Once the camera was set up on its tripod and Tim had checked to make sure he had a fresh tape, he turned to Animal. "You ready?"

Animal nodded. He opened up his bag, brought out a large hunting knife. He grinned. Tim nodded, catching the rise of the sadist's penis from the open crotch of his leather chaps. Why Animal chose to wear leather chaps at these gigs, Tim could never understand. He always got blood on them, and blood was hard to wash off of leather.

Tim moved Lisa into position, then went back and checked his camera angles. Animal stayed out of camera range, poised and ready. Tim lined up the shot, made some adjustments, then hit the Record and Pause buttons. The tape was set. Now all that was needed was to wake their star up.

Tim reached into his bag and pulled out a syringe and vial. He filled the syringe, being careful not to draw too much of the Narcan in, and then lightly tapped it with his forefinger to get the air bubbles out. "I fixed this stuff up before I set out this morning. Should wake her right up."

"What is it?" Animal asked.

"Narcan. It reverses the effects of morphine-based drugs. They use it in ERs when people OD."

Animal was watching intently. "That needle doesn't look big enough. Aren't you supposed to jab her in the chest? You know, put that shit into her heart?"

"Nah," Tim said, finding a vein in Lisa's forearm and injecting the drug. "That's only in extreme cases, when somebody's flatlined. They use adrenaline shots for that. This'll wake her up fine." He pulled the needle out and waited for a reaction.

The three of them watched Lisa, waiting for her to wake up. After thirty seconds, Animal said, "Well?"

"It could take about five minutes," Tim said.

"My flight leaves in four hours," Animal said. "The faster I can fuck this bitch up and kill her ass, the quicker I can clean up and get the fuck out of here."

"Okay, okay, hold on." Tim Murray felt the time pressure, too. He fixed up another dosage of Narcan, measuring out two milligrams' worth, searched for a vein, and slid the needle in. He injected it into her system and then sat back, waiting.

"You gonna untie her?" Mabel asked, grinning.

"What the fuck for?"

"Not much fun watching her die tied up," Mabel responded. "At least loosen the knots a little. Make it more exciting. After all, isn't he going to fuck her first?"

Tim turned to Animal. "What do you think?"

"What's this shit supposed to do to her?"

"It's supposed to block out all the effects of morphine-based drugs," Tim replied. "I only gave her enough morphine to knock her out a little. The Narcan should wake her up long enough for our film. She'll be conscious, but she might still be fucked up from the smack. She won't be much of a fight. Your call."

Animal nodded. "Untie her. I can handle her."

Tim set the syringe down and leaned over to untie Lisa. He laid her arms down at her side, her legs lightly spread. "You want her clothes off?"

Animal shook his head. "No. That's what knives are for."

Lisa's eyes flew open and began blinking rapidly as she began taking rapid breaths. Tim stepped back, picking up the syringe and his bag. He moved behind the camera to get started. He wasn't even able to start the film rolling before he heard Lisa Miller's first piercing scream.

When she came awake it was with a sudden rush.

She'd been swimming in a syrupy lake of deep, clogging sludge. She didn't know how she'd gotten there, but she knew if she stayed down much longer she'd never wake up. She had been struggling to break to the surface, fighting to break free and breathe, but her arms were pinned to her sides and it had been hard to break through the current. The lake she was in was so thick, so resisting, it was like fighting quicksand.

And then she was suddenly shot out of the quicksand and her eyes were open, the sunlight glaring in her eyes. She felt the heat of the sun on her bare skin, felt the air caress her body, felt the sting along the inside of her elbow, and for a moment she didn't know where she was. Her eyes watered in reaction to the sudden light. Her heart raced madly as she tried to remember what happened. She had been sitting in front of the TV vegging out, trying to stay out of the dark place that was the memory of that awful weekend when she had been kidnapped by that perverted psycho and almost murdered. That weekend she had seen Debbie Martinez horribly violated, then she'd lost her baby. The images of that weekend flashed through her memory as her eyes adjusted to the light and she was no longer swimming in that deep pit of quicksand. She was aware, she was conscious, and she was being confronted with what had happened for the first time since she had been knocked out. And what she saw brought it all back to a screaming reality.

And then her vision swam back into focus and the first thing she saw was the man in the leather bondage hood, standing bare-chested in front of her. She recognized him immediately as the man who had raped and tortured Debbie Martinez in that cabin in a time that seemed like a thousand years ago. The same man who told her how much he liked inflicting pain on other people, and how he enjoyed killing them. The same man who had later killed Debbie, Alicia, and Mandy after she'd escaped. She saw him standing there, brandishing a large butcher knife, sporting a huge erection, and she screamed.

She screamed, scrambled back, and fell, not even aware of the rough dirt that bit into her flesh. She heard laughter and it was all coming back to her. Her escape from the snuff-film makers, how she and Brad had been lulled into a false sense of security at the Luxor, how she thought they would never find her. And then how they had been fooled when that old woman had come in looking so helpless and lost, asking to use the phone because she had been separated from her church group, that old seemingly harmless-looking woman. The same old woman she had seen slitting John Panozzo's throat . . .

The old woman in question was sitting on a rock, grinning in anticipation. Lisa screamed again, her heart racing. She felt suddenly hot, flushed with adrenaline. She and Brad had been fooled! They had sent an old woman, an old woman that nobody would have guessed to be a killer, and they had done it under the noses of a hotel full of expert security people.

A shadow loomed in front of her and Lisa blinked, her eyes adjusting. A clean-shaven, familiar face grinned at her. Lisa recognized him instantly, even without the beard: It was Tim Murray, the man in the red van who had kidnapped her. "Remember me?" he asked, grinning. "You didn't think we'd let you get away, did you?"

Lisa felt her panic rise as she looked around. Tim Murray was getting behind the camera. The old woman was rising to her feet, her features a mask of gleeful anticipation. Animal took a step toward her, his penis bobbing like a divining rod, the sun gleaming off the blade of his knife. She scampered backward, whimpering. "No!"

"Try to make it last, Animal," Tim said from behind the camera.

They were going to make her suffer; that much was clear from that statement. If that was the case, she was going to go down fighting.

Animal was on her swiftly, pinning her down. Lisa tried to scramble back again, but she only succeeded in scraping her knees. Animal grabbed her hair and shoved her to the ground. She pushed herself off in an attempt to make a run for it and she felt him grab her again. Then she was slapped across the face, the blow hard enough to send her to the ground. Her cheek stung, and the slap awakened her. Her face was in the dirt, and she pushed herself up in an attempt to run for it when Animal pinned her down from above. He grabbed her from behind, his forearm getting her in a headlock. She felt his body over hers and she could feel his erection probe against the back of her thighs. She screamed and bucked, trying to throw him off, but that only made him tighten the pressure around her throat. She saw stars, felt her body grow warm, her heart racing. Her breathing was fast, panting. *He's going to kill me! He's going to rape me and kill me!*

She felt Animal's fingers and hands ripping at her nightgown, tearing it off. A rough hand moved between her thighs, pushing them apart. She struggled, trying to throw him off her back and scramble away, but he had her down. She could feel his penis against her buttocks as he pushed her to the ground, his forearm releasing his grip from around her throat. She used the opportunity to scream, and then she felt the weight off her back disappear and she took advantage of it. She bolted and felt a crash at the back of her head, spilling her to the ground. She tasted a mouthful of sand and grit, her eyes watering. Rough hands ripped her panties off, cool air caressed the back of her thighs and buttocks. Then she felt his bulk over her again, pinning her to the ground. She slapped at him, her fingers clutching leather, and she pulled. She heard a grunt, felt a blow to her chest, her face, and she batted at his face, grabbing his mask again. She pulled the mask off his head just as she felt a blow land on her throat. She fell back, gagging. She dropped the bondage mask, clutching her throat, breathing heavily, and then she was pushed back to the ground on her belly. She caught a brief glimpse of the man she had met back at that cabin, that handsome man who looked like he could have been a young doctor or a lawyer in her firm, the perfect image of the young, good-looking, urban professional. That face now wore a mask of blood lust. She gulped for air and she was realizing that when she pulled his bondage mask off, her arms had probably helped deflect the blow to her throat, otherwise she'd probably have a harder time breathing. She took a deep breath, mustering up her strength for another round of struggle, when she felt the hardness of his penis seeking entry from behind, moving into the rough region of her dry vagina.

No! Fight him! A warm flush flowed into her body; she felt highly agitated, her breathing coming in harsh pants in time with her racing heart. She felt the presence of his body over hers, not as pressed down as before, still holding her on her hands and knees, her belly resting on the ground. He was straddling her, his hips over her ass, his penis working its way between her legs to her sex while he tried to force her legs apart with his hand. His face was six inches from hers, to her right, and she felt him grip her hair with his left hand, tilting her face to his. His eyes gleamed, his All-American boyish features frightening. "You like it, bitch?"

Lisa panted, meeting his gaze. She could feel her anger building as she grew more agitated; she felt like a bundle of live wires. She wasn't going to let these bastards take her down without a fight. The adrenaline pouring through her system was reawakening her; no longer did she have the luxury to cower in fear. She *had* to fight. She had to be ruthless. She had to survive at whatever cost.

Animal's grip on her hair tightened, the pain in her scalp exploded. He was gathering fistfuls of her hair in his hands as he moved her head close to his, his eyes narrowed slits. "I asked you a fucking question, *bitch! Answer me!*"

All she was aware of was that blinding pain in her scalp along the back of her head. She could barely feel the presence of his body over hers, didn't even know if he had entered her with that vile thing that hung between his legs. She wasn't aware of anything except that loathsome face in front of her, that loathsome face that probably made women swoon. It was an inch from hers, leering at her. "You fucking listening to me, cunt?"

Lisa answered him the only way she could. She reached out and grabbed ahold of his nose . . . with her teeth.

And she bit down as hard as she could.

Animal screamed and instantly jumped back, dislodging his position over her. She held on, pulled up by his flailings, and she could feel her teeth slice through skin and cartilage. He bellowed and swung with his fists, striking her side, her back, but she refused to let go. She felt her energy surge, felt that she could run a thousand miles with all this energy, so she used it to her advantage. She brought her hands up to his head and moved her thumbs over his eyes, pushing them in.

This time, Animal howled.

She pushed Animal's eyes as hard as she could, and now she was actually on her feet; he had pulled her into a standing position in his flight to get away from her. She concentrated on one thing: killing this sadistic sonofabitch who had given her nightmares and made her afraid. She focused her mind on trying to hurt him, using her rage and hate to propel her past the pain from the blows he was raining down on her body. She moved into position, still clutching his nose with her teeth, her thumbs still pressing his eyeballs in their sockets, and then she blindly brought her knee up into where she hoped his crotch was.

It connected.

Lisa felt her teeth rip the flesh of his nose as he was driven to the ground from the blow. She tasted blood and snot. She stumbled, almost fell back, but fought to catch her ground. Animal was doubled over, howling in pain, and the adrenaline was running through her, prompting her to rush him and hurt him again, when she felt strong arms grab her from behind and pin them to her sides.

She yelled and twisted her body, trying to throw her attacker to the ground. She fought so wildly, so ferociously, that she caught him off guard. She sensed his surprise and didn't even hesitate to proclaim victory. She used her weight to offset his balance, and they fell to the ground. She landed on top of him. His grip on her loosened a little, and she slithered away. A grasping hand reached out and grabbed her. She kicked back with one bare foot, the heel hitting the side of his chest. She jumped to her feet, eyes darting around, trying to collect her bearings. Tim Murray was getting to his feet, his features twisted in an angry grimace. Animal was on his side, doubled over, writhing in pain, still howling and yelling. And the old woman was hobbling toward her, a large knife in her hands, her face twisted in madness.

Lisa turned and ran, scrambling up the incline, her bare feet slapping the rocks and hard sand. The highly agitated state she was in helped propel her forward, and she ran like she had never run before, quickly leaving

Tim Murray and the old woman behind her. She didn't look back even when she reached the top of the incline. She simply continued running, heading down the hill toward the SUV.

"*You bitch!*" Tim Murray yelled behind her, and she heard his pounding footsteps as he gave chase. She pressed on, flying over rocks and foliage as she reached the desert floor. She paused, looked over her shoulder, saw that Tim was twenty yards behind her and quickly gaining, and she pressed on.

When she reached the SUV she fumbled with the door, got it open. The keys weren't in the ignition, nor anywhere she could see. Her panic rising, she slammed the door shut and checked Tim's progress. He was ten yards away and gaining. She darted around the side, keeping the vehicle between herself and Tim.

"I'm going to kill you, you fucking bitch!" Tim huffed. He was five yards from her, circling around the other side of the SUV. She could hear his labored breathing clearly. Her own breathing was rapid, her heart still hammering in her chest. Her energy level was high, her senses incredibly sensitive. She felt warm. She moved to the right, trying to see where he was. She caught a glimpse of him through the windows. He glared at her. "You're going to wish you had never done that," he said. "You are going to suffer."

She quickly dropped to the ground in a sudden burst of inspiration and scooped up a handful of sand, coming back up in a flash. Tim dashed to the rear of the SUV and she ran around the front. They pinioned off each other. The incline was at her back now. Something scratched at her ankle and she glanced down: a bundle of twigs, blown by the rising winds.

Footsteps around the side of the SUV.

She backed up, heart pounding. A moving cloud

blocked the sun, plunging the desert in shadow. Tim appeared at the end of the SUV, his features a twisted grimace. *"Bitch!"*

And then she plunged forward, throwing her arm back and pitching the fistful of sand she clutched in her right hand the way a baseball pitcher throws a curveball. She threw the sand directly at Tim's face.

Tim flinched and howled, hands shooting up to his face, doubling over. "You *bitch!*" he screamed. *"You threw sand in my eyes!"*

She stopped, torn between rushing him again and beating him and turning to run. She glanced around. The SUV was still there, as was a four-door Saturn parked nearby. Both vehicles were useless without keys. And since she was pretty certain she had been transported in the SUV, Tim probably had the keys on his person.

She took a step forward and heard a scream. It didn't come from Tim Murray.

She looked up.

Animal was standing at the crest of the incline. He looked terrifying, larger than life, more monstrous somehow than she had ever seen him before. His left hand was covering his left eye. He was screaming and moaning in pain and anger.

His right hand clutched a huge butcher knife.

Lisa rushed forward, knocking Tim to the ground. He went sprawling, landing on his back, hands still covering his face. She fell beside him and her left hand grabbed a rock.

The sound of footsteps and falling stones to her left as Animal ran down the hill toward them. His footsteps were erratic, his voice tinged with pain.

She shifted the rock to her right hand, brought her arm up.

Tim Murray, as if sensing the blow, raised his left arm to protect himself.

Scurrying footsteps growing closer, accompanied by Animal's voice. "Fucking bitch, I'm gonna kill you . . . fucked up my eye . . ."

She shifted her position over Tim, grappling with him.

The sand she had thrown in his face had helped her more than she had thought it would. His eyes were fluttering, tearing profusely; he was fighting disorientation and irritation.

It made it easier for her to get the upper hand and get a good aim.

And bring the rock down on his head.

Tim crumpled like a limp doll, and she hit him again for good measure. Both blows to Tim's head sounded like a watermelon being split open.

The running footsteps were growing closer, along with Animal's yell of rage.

Another burst of adrenaline exploded in Lisa's system. She rose to her feet.

And met the challenge head-on.

Twenty-nine

Despite the fact that William Grecko was completely shit-faced drunk, he was thinking very clearly.

Learning shocking news probably helped keep his mind operating in a more-or-less sober manner.

William Grecko sat behind his desk, nursing a bottle of 151. No use drinking out of the flask now. Why hide it? His staff knew he was an alcoholic. He'd been in rehabilitation centers six times for his alcoholism in the past twenty years. He'd lost two wives, three partnerships, and most of his friends to the disease. He'd been pulled over ten times for DUI, arrested once. When he began gaining notoriety as a high-profile criminal defense attorney, the cops who pulled him over usually let him off with a warning for some strange reason. But one thing he hadn't lost was his ability to reason when it came to protecting his clients. And right now he had to use his mind to the best of his ability to think and strategize this latest tragedy.

What the hell am I going to tell him? William thought, running a hand through his greasy hair. *What the hell am I going to tell him?*

It was two P.M. Lisa Miller had been missing for five hours. The last report he had gotten from the Las Vegas PD was a whole lot of nothing. The feds were at least doing somewhat better. A team of detectives had questioned Rick Shectman very casually, and naturally Rick Shectman had maintained his innocence. Mr. Shectman not only didn't know the Millers, he had never seen the people in the photographs the agents showed him. "Best picture we had was the one with that guy at the bank, the good-lookin' dude who escorted Mrs. Miller inside," William's FBI contact, Phil Krider, reported. "Shectman takes one look at him, says he never saw him before."

That was the official story. Phil related that he was pretty confident that Rick Shectman had been lying when he denied knowing the men in the photographs. "I could tell by the way he looked at those photos. He didn't even give them a real look. Just glanced at them, looked back at us, and said, 'Nope, don't know these guys.' The man didn't even give the pictures the time of day, like he knew what they were of. That tells me he knows something."

Besides, as Phil Krider and the feds reported, Rick Shectman had ties with the underground pornography market. One of his associates had been busted for producing bestiality films, and Rick's father had an illustrious history that stretched back to the early seventies. Old man Shectman was even rumored to have been involved in the production of a snuff film, so it stood to reason that his son was following in Dad's footsteps. After all, the print shop the younger Shectman now operated had been run by his father. And Boris Shectman had been convicted twice of producing child pornography out of that very shop. Talk among the underground porn world was that the younger Shectman had his hands in the business, despite a lack of hard evidence. "The print shop's been raided at least three times that I know of and we never found anything," Phil told William. "He hasn't been raided in five years because of lawsuits. Also, Rick Shectman has been contributing to various political figures lately and that's helped keep the heat off of him, if you know what I mean."

William Grecko knew what Phil meant, but that wasn't what was worrying him this afternoon. Not by a long shot.

He took another sip from the bottle. He had sent Marilyn, his secretary, home at lunch. He couldn't stand hearing her outside his office. It wasn't as if she was particularly annoying, it was just that hearing her perform her normal duties was distressing to him. Listening to her was reminding him of Lisa. And Lisa was reminding him of Brad, and Brad was reminding him of—

He gulped down another shot and sighed as it spread through his system. The warmth flooded through him. He closed his eyes. First things first. Sift through what you've just been told, then make an educated decision based on the evidence. No need in getting Brad worried and riled up now.

Shortly after noon, while Marilyn had still been in the office, William had taken a call from one of the detectives working on the Golgotha angle. They had finally questioned all of the board members of the Golgotha Multimedia Corporation and all their alibis and backgrounds had checked out.

William had been expecting that, but he still had to ask the detective a little more about the board members themselves. *What had they been like?*

Rich country-club executive types, the detective had said. *Smug, pampered bastards. Oh, not smug in the sense that any of them were suspicious—they all really* did *check out fine. No criminal records, their stories and alibis checked out, the whole nine yards. But you know they've got money. It's like they all had fucking Teflon coated to their skins, y'know?*

William had nodded, feeling a little dejected at the news. *Yeah, so what else is new?*

The detective had given him the rundown. The cabin was used as a retreat for business functions, usually meetings. Sometimes they had weekend retreats, where they drove up for the weekend, went skiing, talked shop, the usual bullshit. The cabin was primarily a tax write-off. *Did they ever go up for personal use?* Billy had asked.

Oh yeah, all the time was the reply. *They all had keys to the place. It's just that the weekend your clients went missing, all twelve board members were at other locations; none of them were within a hundred miles of the cabin. We checked. Their alibis are tight.*

Billy had just been about to ask if the men had family members that perhaps used the cabin when the detective beat him to it. *Of course we questioned friends and family members. That's only following the logical trail, you know? And everybody's story corroborated. Each man had only one key to the place. That key was on that member's person, and since each member was away that particular weekend, far from Big Bear Lake, it makes it impossible that any of them could have been involved.*

The detective had been rambling, and Billy had had to steer him back to the question he wanted to ask: *Did family members have their own keys? Was it possible a family member had used the cabin that weekend?*

No, family members don't have their own keys to the cabin. Everybody we spoke to denied using the cabin that weekend. Some of them had used it before, of course, but—

Billy had leaped on that statement. *Like when? Who?*

And that's when the detective had come back with one of those revelations that in thrillers always brings a chill to the audience. It brought a chill to Billy when he first heard it, and it gave him a chill now just thinking about it.

One of the board members, guy named Larry Allen, said he had a copy of the key made for a buddy of his a few years ago, but his friend hadn't been at the cabin either. In fact, the board had been meaning to have renovations done to the place and Larry had mentioned it to this guy. His buddy said he'd take care of it for him, he knew a general contractor who would do the work, and he set it up. We sent another team of detectives to question this friend of Mr. Allen's and he checked out too. And . . . well, this is where it gets weird. His story really does *check out 'cause he was with the California Highway Patrol in Ventura County pretty much the entire weekend your client went missing. You ain't gonna believe this—*

Who the fuck is it? William had hissed.

It's Brad Miller's father. Frank Miller.

That was what had sent William Grecko over the edge.

Now William sat in his office drinking Bacardi 151 and thinking about what he was going to tell Brad.

I've known Frank Miller for ten, fifteen years, he thought. *This has to be some kind of weird coincidence. I* saw *the guy that weekend. He looked like he was a wreck. He was going through the same amount of anguish and grief as Joan and Brad were. He was elated when we found Lisa. And he's going completely batfuck now at home, waiting for word of the whereabouts of his daughter-in-law.*

Or was he?

William had been trying to play connect-the-dots with this for the past hour now. The alcohol had helped unlock a lot of the barriers he normally wouldn't have been able to get past. He wondered if the alcohol was what was now making him paranoid.

It was perfectly logical that Frank Miller and Larry Allen would know each other. Larry was an executive at Fidelity, while Frank was an executive at a competing firm. They'd both been with their respective firms for twenty years, so it was only natural for their paths to cross, being that they both worked in the financial industry. They'd probably met at a business function, became friends. No problem. Larry Allen was also a Christian, and by virtue of his stock in Golgotha, one would think he'd be of the squeaky-clean type. No alcohol, no drugs, and surely no pornography, not even of the *Playboy* variety. Although that image surely didn't provide guarantees. Lots of religious guys were closet freaks. Frank Miller was no heathen, but then he wasn't a terribly devout religious man either. So where was the bond formed? The golf course? The country club? Perhaps. It made sense.

William had formulated the relationship in his mind over sips of 151, trying to make the connections. And the connections he made weren't pretty.

Suppose they became pretty good friends. Maybe Larry tried to convert Frank at one point but Frank passed. I can buy that. But suppose there was still something they built their friendship on. Maybe Larry told Frank about the Golgotha retreat and it intrigued Frank enough that Larry had a key made. Told Frank that if he and his wife ever wanted to use the cabin, he could. And Frank took the key. There's no evidence that suggests he used it . . . I'll get to that later. But suppose . . . just suppose *that Frank later palmed the key to somebody else who used it for the snuff film?*

William shook his head. That wouldn't have worked. Frank had been a nervous wreck that weekend. He was a nervous wreck now. Billy had seen him, spoken to him. Joan was flying off the wall and Frank was . . .

Strangely silent.

William took another sip of rum. Admittedly, he'd never seen Frank upset or emotional before this mess started. And he knew from experience that people handled stress and traumatic experiences differently. Some people, like Joan Miller, wore their hearts on their sleeves. Others, like Frank, kept their emotions close to the bone. That's what he'd figured was going on when Lisa Miller first turned up missing. Frank was trying to be the rock for his family, was holding his emotions in. And he was doing that now, not saying much, being quiet, but still visibly shaken. But then . . . suppose he was shaken because he was nervous?

William didn't want to consider that. It was absurd. Completely against the character of the man he knew. Frank Miller was a good guy. He was successful, he had a good family, and Billy had never known Frank to be even a purveyor of mild S&M pornography. There was no way that Frank would have commissioned a snuff film. And for what purpose?

What did William Grecko know about snuff films, anyway? Not much. Like most people who worked along the fringes of law enforcement, he was of the opinion that they were urban legends. In all his time as a criminal defense attorney, he knew of no case in which a snuff film had been found. There had been a case ten years ago in Anaheim in which a furniture maker had been convicted of murdering two prostitutes; it had been suggested they had been slaughtered for the purpose of producing such a film. However, no snuff film ever surfaced during the investigation. From what William remembered about the case, the killer had lured the two women out to the desert where he had stashed video-camera equipment and various items of torture. Their bodies had been found a few months later, scattered across the desert. A pair of undercover female detectives, who had been hoping to bust the man in an undercover sting, had testified that the suspect told them numerous times that he'd wanted to produce a snuff film to sell to the underground extreme hardcore market.

The underground extreme hardcore market. The very name conjured images of black leather and whips, people tied to chains in basements or empty warehouses, strung up by their wrists as they were flogged or burned with cigarettes or cut with knives or razor blades. Brad had told him that the people who were into this stuff took their S&M fetish way beyond the extreme into bizarre torture and mutilation, near death. William knew that there were people into auto-asphyxiation, where they achieved orgasm at a near-death state. What he found hard to grasp was the inflicting of extreme pain and torture for sexual gratification.

Well, didn't serial killers get their kick from killing? Wasn't it all a power trip for them? Isn't that what rape was about? It wasn't so much about sex—that was a part of it, but it wasn't the primary focus. Rape was the fantasy of the perpetrator who sought to achieve a feeling of power over his victims. Taken to the extreme, wouldn't it be safe to guess that one who got their jollies watching somebody being raped was a rapist by proxy? And weren't snuff films nothing more than rape films in which the victim was later killed?

William drained the bottle. He set it down on the desk with a clink and sighed. There was no way that Frank Miller was involved in snuff films. The man had a good life; he had a loving wife, a successful child. He had a great job. He wasn't like those assholes William defended in court, those sexual psychopaths who—

Stop it! he thought. *You were going to equate Frank with the clichéd image that the public has of a rapist, the seedy-looking guy with the stubbled chin, the low-wage common day laborer, the animal who can't control his sexual urges. That's bullshit. You know that a lot of these perpetrators look like the guy next door. Hell, you just defended a kid a few months ago who was accused of raping his neighbor.* The defendant in question was a nineteen-year-old student at Fullerton College who had broken into his neighbor's home and raped the thirty-eight-year-old victim while the woman's infant son slept in the next room. The defendant had been convicted of first-degree sexual assault. William's client hadn't come from the wrong side of the tracks. If anything, he looked like a model citizen, the kind of kid any parent would want as a son.

In a way, he resembled the man Lisa described who had attacked and mutilated that woman Debbie Martinez. The guy she had called Animal. She'd said the guy looked like he could have been a lawyer or a young executive.

And if that was the case, then why do you find it so

hard to believe that Frank Miller couldn't be involved in this shit?

Because Frank Miller isn't a fucking pervert! I know *the guy! If I had known he was into weird porn, I would have known! If I had known he got off on watching women being raped and killed, I would have been tipped off years ago. Jesus fucking Christ, we talked about our sexual conquests enough times and leafed through those porn-shops on Harbor Boulevard enough after work for me to get an idea of what turned him on. And not once did I see him venture into the leather-and-chain crap in the back of the store. Not* once!

So what to do?

His private investigator was waiting for a call back. William had told him he had some thinking to do before he made his next move. The cops and the feds were looking at Rick Shectman and a few other individuals he was connected with in the illegal pornography world. His FBI contact hadn't been able to tell him much, just that they were chasing down leads, talking to people in the S&M world about the extreme hardcore element, hoping to get a lead on that. Most of their leads kept returning to Rick Shectman as a man who had a hand in producing specialty product: mutilation films, some specialized fetish stuff, usually by commission. So, naturally, the focus of the investigation was centered on him.

William knew that if Rick Shectman was involved, he'd be crafty. He'd have to be if he was involved in producing snuff films. How else could he have been involved in this underground world and not be caught? He'd be very careful now in the next few months, William was sure of it. Therefore, he wasn't going to do anything to tip the cops his way. What was the phrase Phil told him? "The guys that partake in this stuff, both the sellers and the buyers, they stay as far away from each other as possible." William believed that. Therefore, if Rick Shectman were involved in any way in the snuff pornography market, he'd be living a double life. He wouldn't be associating with anybody in the extreme hardcore scene, especially with any possible customers.

That decided it for him. William picked up the phone and dialed Phil's number. The detective picked up on the third ring. "Yeah."

"Phil, it's Billy."

"What's up?"

"I'm gonna give you an address," William said, reaching for his address book and flipping through it. "I'm also gonna give you a name and a description. That's gonna be the guy I want you to tail."

"So you don't want me to look at Rick Shectman?"

"No." William found what he was looking for. "The guy I want you to tail is named Frank Miller. He lives at 3589 Snow Lane in Irvine. He's in his late fifties, five foot seven, one hundred and seventy pounds or so, dark hair turning gray, thinning a little at the top. He wears glasses, has a ruddy complexion. Favors slacks and polo shirts; conservative business attire Monday through Friday. He drives a tan BMW, late model. I don't have a license-plate number, but you should have no trouble getting that. He—"

"Isn't that Brad's father?" Phil asked.

The realization of what he was asking Phil to do settled in the pit of his belly and burned a fire. "Yes," he said, closing his eyes, hoping to God he was making a big mistake in this. "Yes, it is."

Rick Shectman was pissed.

He was sitting in the living room of his sprawling ranch home, perched in the foothills of the San Gabriel Mountains. It was a warm day, in the mid-eighties, typical weather for Southern California, especially the San Gabriel valley. The windows were open, allowing a cool breeze to blow through. Rick had been reclining in his La-Z-Boy flipping through the cable channels blindly, waiting for the confirmation that the job he had given to Tim Murray was completed.

He had gotten the call, all right. But it wasn't the call he wanted.

Rick was seething. He wanted to break something, wanted to throttle somebody, preferably that fat fuck Tim Murray. He hoped Tim was suffering right this minute, slowly dying from his head injuries.

Provided, of course, the information he got was correct.

Rick Shectman took a deep breath and closed his eyes, replaying the phone call in his mind. Admittedly, he couldn't make out much of what had been said—the connection had been really bad—but he did make out Mabel's voice and a female in the background—Yelling? Screaming? It was hard to tell. At first it had sounded like a wrong number; a woman had started screaming, "Hello? Who is this?" Rick had answered, asking if this was Tim—the readout on his caller ID had identified the caller as Tim Murray, and he had been thrown off by the woman's voice. There had been static, then the woman came on the line saying that Tim Murray was dying and that Rick was fucked. "You're *fucked!*" she'd screamed. Then there had been the sound of wind blowing and something else in the background, as if whoever was carrying the phone was trudging through rough terrain, and then the voice came again, bellowing in the background. And what Rick thought she'd said was "Let him hear you, granny!" And then he had heard the high, reedy voice—an old woman? Mabel Schneider?—wailing. *"The eyes! Rick said I could have the eyes!"*

Then the woman's voice came through loud and clear. "Who are you?"

And Rick had shouted. "Who the fuck are you, bitch? Where's Tim? Where's—"

Then a click. She'd hung up.

Rick sat trembling in rage. He'd recognized Mabel's voice well enough. And Tim . . . if Tim was dead or dying, that meant—

No, he thought. She couldn't have escaped. She fucking *couldn't* have! They'd fucking *drugged her!* It was supposed to have been quick and easy, slice and dice and a quick romp with Animal, and then the film was supposed to be in the can. He was supposed to have the product no later than six tonight. Which meant—

Rick took a deep breath and composed himself. He'd tried calling Tim on his cellular three times and he kept getting Tim's voice mail. Rick didn't have a cellular number for Animal for security reasons, and Mabel wasn't answering her cell phone, which meant Rick had no idea what the fuck was going on. It was well past two P.M.; the film should have been done by now. Tim should have at least called to tell him it was completed.

I have a feeling he fucked this one up, Rick thought, a sense of dread settling in his system. *Now what?*

First things first. Contact the buyer. Tell him there's a problem. Warn him. Then retrace your steps, make sure you have no paper trail that will lead to Tim Murray. The phone number Tim Murray had was listed under somebody else's name, some poor victim of identity theft. If the cops did come poking around, they'd find that Rick was calling somebody named Sergio Melendez from Canoga Park. Since he'd only called Tim at that number three times, he could easily plead that he kept forgetting he was getting the wrong number. Easy. That was a lie that would hold up easy, since all three calls were made within the past day.

The buyer was the hard part, though. Sam Bash had arranged it. Sam was an old mainstay in the scene. He knew Rick's dad from way back, and he arranged the parties, private functions, slave auctions. The buyer knew Sam through the scene. It had been Sam who had come to Rick with the job, explained what the buyer wanted. Rick had agreed. The money offered up front had been twice the normal amount due to the risk. Rick had given instructions to Sam, who'd made separate arrangements with Al and Tim. After the fuckup, Tim had called Sam, who had called Rick immediately and told him, "You're on your own. You don't know me, but the contact does. He'll be in touch."

A week later, the buyer had paged Rick. The number Rick dialed rang to a pay phone. The client *had* been pissed—he didn't give a fuck about what had been delivered. He wanted what he'd paid for. And if he didn't deliver . . . well, he told Rick certain information Rick didn't think anybody was privy to. That had gotten Rick royally pissed.

He'd been tempted to send somebody after the buyer, but Sam had assured him if he did that it would ricochet back. "Finish the job," Sam had advised. "The buyer will contact you with more information." This had started Rick's plan in getting the Miller bitch, which had led to this.

Rick would have to leave the house and contact the buyer at a pay phone. First he had to make sure he wasn't being watched. A couple of detectives had come poking around yesterday and this morning, trying to dig up that old second-degree-rape charge. That had stemmed from an incident five years ago when Rick was brought up on charges that he had filmed the sexual assault of a drunken college student at a frat party. Cops never found the tape—it had been quickly sold to a purveyor—but the girl, despite her inebriation, had remembered Rick and provided a description. And because Rick's father, Boris, had been involved in the extreme hardcore scene, it only stood to reason that he should get scrutinized by law enforcement. Yeah, so what if he made a few legitimate pornos for the amateur market? Big deal! Well, it was a big deal now. He'd always had to step carefully before in this business; he'd always assumed that law enforcement had heard of his involvement in the illegal porn industry, which was why he always took pride in being as careful as possible. He had been careful in this latest job as well, employing the usual methods of setting up multiple barriers between himself and his contacts. But the customer obviously knew the ropes and was a member of the scene himself, otherwise Sam wouldn't have been involved. And he'd had the money too, in cold, hard cash. What had surprised Rick had been the customer's request of the victim. He'd actually given Rick a name!

Rick leaned back on the sofa and closed his eyes. That had never happened before in all his years in the extreme hardcore industry. Usually when a purveyor of hardcore commissioned a film, the only criteria they had in the victims were age and race. Tim Murray had a steady supply of potential victims from the circle he ran in, kids who ran away from home and got into the hardcore scene for the money and shock value. Kids like that wouldn't be too surprised to walk onto a hardcore S&M set and see Animal in his leather bondage hood. Hell, they always thought they were just in for a little rough stuff for a few hundred bucks! What the fuck did they know about the real world, where rich perverted pricks got their rocks off watching cheap little whores get snuffed out? Tim always made sure to check into their histories before making his selection. Sometimes he even found his subjects on the streets. He'd pick them up, show them some feigned kindness, buy them drugs, food, give them some shelter. Tim had his fun with them too, no problem with that; he liked his dick sucked as much as the next guy. Once they passed the screen test, and if Rick had a client who requested a particularly bloody film, Tim was perfectly happy to pass them off. And true to form, the cops never came looking for the missing person in question. Why would they? Both Tim and Rick were two and three steps removed from the victims. They protected their tracks expertly.

But this client . . . he was different. Sam had explained what he wanted to Rick, and at first Rick hadn't liked it. Too risky. Chick like that, a lawyer at a big firm, even if you don't miss her the parents will go bugfuck looking for her. But Sam had assured Rick in that smooth voice of his that the buyer had been planning this for the past year now. The buyer would make sure everything would work like clockwork. He would even pay double Rick's normal fee. That had aroused Rick's interest, and he had quickly called Tim and discussed it with him. Tim had agreed to the job after discussing the plan and, in turn, Tim had contacted Al and Animal with the usual setup. The first transaction was made through Sam. A second transaction was made in the restroom of a Mexican restaurant in Whittier, after Sam was out of the picture. When Rick saw him for the first time, he'd relaxed; he'd seen the guy at a few extreme hardcore parties in the past dozen years or so. He was one of the quiet ones, one of the purveyors of pain who enjoyed sitting back in the shadows watching scenes of blood sports and torture.

So what had happened? Al had fucked up royally and

the bitch had escaped. Tim had been freaked out, and even Animal had been a little nervous. But at least they had gotten the money they'd extorted out of her, and Rick had earned some extra money. The tape of Animal and the infant had fetched a nice price from a wealthy pedophile in Seattle, and that had almost made up for Al's fuckup. The client had been royally pissed, of course, and demanded they get the bitch back and do what he had fucking paid them to do. During that first phone conversation he'd had with him in a phone booth after the fuckup, Rick had told the guy to fuck off—didn't he see that they'd almost been caught? The numbfuck didn't get it, and actually threatened to expose him. "I'll bring you down, Rick. I'll fucking expose you, I've got shit on you that'll have the DA on you so fast it'll make your balls burst." Rick had responded accordingly: *Oh yeah? What about you? You commissioned the fucking film, you goddamn pervert motherfucker. It takes two to tango.*

And the client . . . that rich, smug, corporate bastard . . . he'd fucking *laughed.* "You think the police are going to believe you? You're a convicted criminal! Your father was a peddler of child pornography and bestiality films! The cops know you make hardcore S&M films, that the so-called mainstream stuff you do straddles the line. They know you've produced child porn, that you've trafficked in other shit. You're a fucking convicted sex offender! You think they're going to believe you? You out of your fucking mind?"

"Yeah? Big fucking deal! Tim will back me up, and so will Animal and—"

"And you'll squeal on them to get me busted? Listen to yourself, you cheap bastard! Nobody's going to believe you. You can't pin me to this. There are no records, no witnesses, nothing! Nobody even knows we met. All of our phone calls were done at pay phones. We've had all our meetings in public places, at restaurants in the fucking men's room. As far as the cops go, we don't exist. This transaction doesn't exist. There's no way to tie us together because, by the very nature of the product you produce, you have to stay as far away from people like me as possible. Am I right?"

And Rick had nodded, wanting to reach out and wrap his fingers around the man's neck and squeeze until he couldn't see his knuckles. He'd had to restrain himself. So he'd nodded, said he'd do his best, and the guy had said, "Don't just do your best. Just *do it.* I'll give you a few weeks to collect your bearings and I'll call with a new plan. And don't even *think* about having somebody come after me, either. If I go missing, or if I get hurt, I've already made sure that the cops will find you and you'll be fucked."

"Oh, and you're willing to disgrace your family? Is that it? You gonna hurt your family's memory of you by exposing yourself for the perverted motherfucker you are?"

The client had laughed, and it was a laugh devoid of a soul. "I won't give a shit, Rick. I'll be dead. Won't I?"

Rick stood up and retrieved his keys from the table in the living room. He had to call the client. It was the least he could do . . . tip the client off to what was happening and lay low. Well, Rick would make a few other calls to New York, to a certain family he knew in the old neighborhood that was tapped into the scene. Fill them in on what was going on. And if the cops came nosing around, Rick would know that the client had spilled the beans. Then one phone call would be all it would take to get Eugene and Maxwell out from New York to pay a visit to the client. He'd think of a way to distance himself from the job he'd done.

He left the house, locking it behind him, and got in his

car. As he drove to the liquor store on the corner of San Gabriel Boulevard and Foothill, he replayed in his mind what had happened next. Rick had agreed to follow through with the client's plan, but he had been pissed over the fuckup. Somebody had to pay, and if it wasn't the client then it would have to be somebody else. So he had called the meeting at the shop, telling Animal to ready himself up for some torture and bloodshed. Rick figured Tim or Al had fucked up, and he didn't really care which one went down—he had been growing rather tired of both of them lately. Still, Al was a cocky sonofabitch, and things had played out naturally that night when he'd immediately started denying everything. Tim had started squealing the minute he got to the shop, and Rick knew the shit had gone down exactly as Tim described. He already knew from Sam that Al had never called him. Al had had explicit instructions to deliver a product to Rick. He'd delivered, all right—and he'd lied to Rick and Tim when he told them Sam had OK'd it. Guy was a fucking weasel. That just made it easier to kill him right there, that night, on the floor of the print shop.

Well, Animal had done that part, of course. But it had been Rick's decision. And he'd felt better after having made it.

Rick pulled into the liquor store parking lot by the bank of pay phones. He turned off the ignition and climbed out of the sports car, hurrying to the phones. He'd committed the client's phone number to memory, and now he dialed it after dropping a quarter in the slot, waiting for him to pick up after two, three, four rings—

"Hello?"

Rick had been poised to hang up if somebody other than the client answered, but he recognized the voice. "It's me. There's a problem."

"Now what?"

Rick could tell that the client had an idea something was afoul. He had that tone of voice that seemed to suggest he was bothered by something.

"I just got a call," Rick said. "It didn't sound good. You never saw me, you've never met me, you've never heard of me before. Furthermore, you've never been involved in the circle. I'm going to call a few people we both know and ask them to deny they've ever seen you. Do you understand?"

The client tried to sound tough. "What the hell happened? If you—"

"She got away," Rick said, more firmly. "Remember. We've never met. My guess is that the cops *will* start knocking at your door. You know what to tell them, and you know what to expect if you start singing." He hung up, closed his eyes, his breath harsh in his ears.

For some reason it felt like a tremendous weight had been taken off of his shoulders. Rick sighed, picked up the receiver, and dropped another quarter in the slot. He couldn't relax now, even though he felt better about warning his client. He had to be on guard, lay low. With that in mind, he dialed the next number he had in mind from memory, beginning the process of covering his trail.

Thirty

Her mouth was dry; she was thirsty.

She could feel her energy draining . . . her body growing light with sleep.

And each time she felt herself weakening she shook her head, reawakening herself, then trudged on ahead, concentrating on piloting the SUV over the rocky terrain.

The pain in her side had dulled to a slow throb. She kept her right hand pressed to the gaping wound, trying to ignore the slickness of her flesh as she felt something slosh inside. She knew she was probably holding her intestines inside her abdomen, but she didn't look. She couldn't. If she looked she knew she would faint. And if she fainted she would lose control of the vehicle and would either crash it into a cliff or drive herself off one. The impact might not even kill her outright; she might lie pinned in the wreckage for as long as it took her to die of shock and blood loss. That was all there was to it.

So she drove.

The Nevada sky was overcast, dark with rain clouds. The wind had picked up, blowing through the open windows. It blew Lisa's hair back over her face. She licked her cracked lips, ignoring the nausea in her belly, the pain in her lower right abdomen, and concentrated on driving. Zigzagging between boulders and rocks. Steering the vehicle around cacti. Homing in on her target, her goal. The road that she could dimly see in front of her, now a good five hundred yards away. If she could make that road, she would try the cell phone again.

She should have killed Animal outright. Her mind raced over that now as she struggled along, one hand holding her guts inside herself, the other clutching the steering wheel. Animal had been weakened by her initial attack on him and he'd charged at her, swinging the knife wildly. His left hand had been covering his wounded eye, and it was obvious he was half-blinded. She'd taken advantage of his handicap by ducking and charging him, barreling into his exposed midsection, knocking him down. She'd still been clutching the rock she'd used to bash Tim Murray's skull in, and she'd swung the rock down on the sadist's head. She'd knocked him out cold first time out.

Her first instinct had been to flee, and she'd almost started running blindly, when she realized that she could probably get the keys to one of the vehicles from either Tim or Animal, who were both lying on the desert floor. She'd gone back, heart thudding in her chest, her nerves aware and jumping, anticipating the slightest twitch. She'd knelt by Tim Murray, noted the shallow rise and fall of his chest and the blood congealing out of his ears, and begun rummaging through his pockets, turning up a wallet, a cellular phone, and a set of keys, including one attached to a ring from a car-rental agency in Las Vegas.

Ecstatic, she'd started heading toward the SUV, when she'd realized the cellular phone was still by Tim. She'd doubled back for the phone, got it turned on, and tried dialing 911. She'd put the phone to her ear and started screaming for help, hoping that whoever heard her was recording her frantic cries for help. She thought she could hear somebody, but she couldn't be sure if what she was hearing was a person or static from the rising wind. Frustrated, she'd hung up and tried again. And again. Each time, she got nothing.

Then she heard a voice. A thin, reedy voice, floating from over the incline, coming from the other side. "Tim? Animal? What's going on?" The old woman.

Lisa didn't know why she did it, but she started trudging up the incline, clutching the cellular phone. She hit a button that displayed a series of phone numbers and she hit the first one, not knowing whom she would get, just trying to get a connection to the outside world. She was as surprised as shit when somebody picked up on the other end and his voice came through loud and clear.

"Hello?" She thought she'd heard him reply, but the connection disintegrated into static again. She kept saying "hello" a few times, thought she heard the man on the other end asking for Tim, and then a sudden inspiration seized her. A flare of hatred and anger erupted from deep within her and she screamed. "You motherfucker . . . you want to talk to your pervert buddy. Tim? Listen to this!" And she held the phone up toward where Tim's prone body lay, then brought the phone back to her ears. "Hear that? The reason you didn't hear anything is because Tim's close to being dead. I just bashed his fucking brains in, motherfucker! How do you like *that?*"

She didn't know how much of what she said got through, but some of it must have; the man's response was immediate. "What's going on? Tim?"

Lisa had reached the pinnacle of the incline now, and this time she saw the old woman on the other side, standing up and looking around. When the old woman saw Lisa, she let out a wail of despair. "Listen to *this,* asshole!" Lisa yelled into the phone, and held it out toward the old woman. *"Here you go granny ! Let 'er rip!"*

"The eyes! Rick said I could have the eyes!"

Lisa brought the receiver back to her ear as she started back down toward the SUV. "Your two buddies are dead, and I'm leaving the old woman here for dead too, motherfucker. Now you're fucked! You hear me!"

This time the man heard her. "Who the fuck are you, bitch? Where's Tim? Where's—"

She'd hung up on him, and when she got to the bottom of the incline she stopped, feeling a burst of triumph and pride rise within her.

I've fucking got 'em, she thought. *Whoever he is, he's on the run.* Lisa didn't know who the man was, but she had a gut feeling that whoever it was he had something to do with the illegal hardcore industry that Tim and Animal worked in. The cellular phone Tim was carrying was a cheap Minolta, and there were only three phone numbers programmed into it, which told Lisa it was a pickup job, procured probably for the weekend. She had heard of the practice in her law office, of people getting cellular phones for brief periods of time and then ditching them when they weren't needed anymore. Perhaps the guy who commissioned this particular snuff film was the person she'd talked to. If that was the case, she was keeping the cell phone. And once she got to a point where she received better reception from a cellular tower, she'd try 911 again.

She had approached the SUV and was trying to dial 911 again when she'd seen something out of the corner of her eye. She had looked up and seen Animal's twisted visage reflected in the SUV's windows a moment before she felt cold steel slide into her right side, spilling warm blood down her belly and thighs.

She didn't even know she was fighting him until she heard him scream and lean forward, clamping his jaws on her left shoulder. She screamed, trying to knee him in the groin again. She felt the knife slide into her again and she fell back against the vehicle, his bulk bearing her down. Her right fist rose and fell over his left eye, pulping it as he loosened his jaws from her shoulder to scream. The knife slid out of her and adrenaline burst through her system, propelling her fight instinct to a level that was beyond fury. She felt his grip on her weaken slightly, and she took advantage of it by driving her fist into his exposed throat. He'd fallen back, gagging, left hand clutched at his throat. He'd dropped the knife and she had pounced on it, grabbing it by the blade, feeling it slice through her hand and fingers. She'd grabbed at the blade with her right hand and lunged, driving it into Animal's midsection to the hilt. His eyes bugged out and he'd gasped suddenly, as if he'd been shocked. Then he'd fallen backward, the knife sticking out of his solar plexus, his one open eye glazing over in death.

She didn't remember how she got into the SUV, but the

next thing she remembered she was backing the vehicle along the terrain. She realized what she was doing, realized she was driving backward, then stopped. The incline they had parked at was a good hundred yards away, and she could dimly make out Animal's and Tim's bodies lying there. That's when the pain reeled in, bringing the stunning reality to everything into clear, sharp focus.

She'd risked only one glance down at her midsection. That had been enough to tell her that she'd lost a lot of blood. And that she might not last long.

Somehow she'd grabbed the cell phone when she had climbed back into the SUV. She had tried it again, her fingers slipping on the keypad as she dialed 911. She could feel herself panicking, and she closed her eyes, repeating to herself *you will not faint, you will not faint, you will not faint.* She'd taken deep, even breaths until she felt herself calm down. Then she'd placed the phone in the cup holder above the gearshift, clamped her left hand over the wound in her side in an attempt to stop the bleeding (*and keep my insides in,* she had reasoned. *I feel something trying to slide out and I've got to keep them in . . .),* shifted into drive with her left hand, then steered the vehicle around so that it was facing in a direction she felt safe to go in.

Now she was rolling along, not even sure how far she should go, knowing only that she had to put some miles between herself and the fiends she had left behind. And try to find a spot where she could receive decent reception for the cell phone.

She could feel the wind buffeting the side of the SUV as she piloted it over the rough sand. The clouds in the distance were getting darker, and she wondered briefly if she would be swept away if it suddenly rained hard. She'd heard that sometimes desert thunderstorms were like that. One minute it would be barren and dry, the next the desert would be transformed into a rushing river. Whatever. It was best not to think of that now. Concentrate on one thing at a time. Get the fuck out of here.

She drove on, trying to keep the vehicle in a more or less straight line. She had no idea if she was going north or south, east or west. Just knowing she had to find a road, a path. Anything resembling civilization. She wondered how far off the beaten path the incline they had picked for her murder was. It had to be at least a mile off the nearest road. Maybe even more. Less chance of finding her body after they were finished. Which meant she had a few more minutes of driving, if she was lucky. She'd already been driving for . . . what? Ten minutes? Fifteen?

Her side throbbed and she felt nauseous again. She fought the urge to throw up and almost brought the SUV to a halt. She took a deep breath, swallowed, and released her foot off the brake. *Move*, she thought. *Just drive. Just get the hell out of here*.

She thought she could feel her blood coagulating beneath her hand. But then every time this thought entered her mind she would feel a fresh warm squirt, and her hand would feel drenched again. She tried to focus back on the task of driving, looking out the windshield at the tumbleweed blowing across the desert, watching twigs and brush blowing as the wind picked up even more, hearing the wind howl and moan as it raced across the desert floor. She didn't even bother steering now, just kept the vehicle on a steady course. The tires bounced over rocks, rolled over cactus. She felt a shock jar her system and shake her guts, and a fresh wave of pain erupted in her side. She screamed and took her foot off the accelerator. Something had slapped the underside of the vehicle; it sounded like something had broken off, and now the vehicle was making a *chug-chug-chug* sound. The

SUV was vibrating, and she had her foot off the gas. She closed her eyes, fighting to battle the pain down, feeling her lifeblood slip away. *How much blood can a person bleed out and still live?* she thought. *A pint?* She'd lost at least that much, maybe more. The seat was drenched with blood; it was pooling down on the floor of the vehicle, near the pedals. Her back was sticky with it. No telling how much she had lost outside during her fight with Animal. She pressed her hand against the wound, reawakening the pain again, and gritted her teeth. She opened her eyes, her vision blurry, and gripped the steering wheel tighter. She put her foot back on the accelerator and focused her mind back on driving.

She managed to stay focused on driving for what seemed like five minutes. But then again, it could have been five seconds. Five hours. She wasn't counting the time. The clouds were still dark, the wind was still blowing, and now it was starting to spit rain. She knew some time had passed because the scenery had changed somewhat. She glanced in the rearview mirror, and now she could hardly see the incline. It had receded to a small thing in the background. How far had she driven? A mile? Two miles?

Then suddenly the tires rolled over smooth pavement. She stopped, looked back and forth. It was a narrow road, roughly paved, but it was a road nonetheless. And where there were roads there were people.

She took her hand off her side quickly and put the vehicle in park, then reached for the cell phone again. It slipped from her grasp from the blood that had dampened her hand. She had to hold it with two hands as she dialed 911, her tongue sticking out in concentration. A lank of bloodied hair hung over her forehead and she put the receiver to her ear, hoping and praying that the call would go through. *Pleasepleasepleasepleaseplease—*

Nothing.

She wanted to scream. She wanted to cry. She fought the urge to do both. Instead, she replaced the phone back in the cup holder, put the vehicle back in drive, looked both ways, decided to turn right, and started heading down the road.

She wondered if Animal and Tim were dead now. How hard had she really hit Tim? Maybe he was only knocked out. Maybe he just had a really bad concussion. Didn't people who have concussions bleed out of their ears? Maybe he'll come out of it, and when he sees Animal's body lying there he'll realize what's happened. *Maybe he'll get Animal's keys and come after me. Maybe he's driving after me right now, maybe he's coming after me right this minute and—*

She banished the thought completely and gritted her teeth. Her left hand went back to trying to staunch the flow of blood from the wound in her side.

And she drove.

She peeked in the rearview mirror occasionally, seeing nothing. The road ahead of her was barren, now growing dirty from the blowing wind. The clouds loomed darker, solid black where they met the horizon. A crack of thunder reverberated in the air and the sky lit up with lightning. To her right she could see that it was raining far off in the distance. Judging by the way the wind was blowing, the storm was heading her way.

She drove. And concentrated on keeping her mind off the pain of her wounds by driving. She thought about Brad, her parents. She thought about winning, about beating the bastards who had set this all up. And the more she thought about them, the angrier she got. And the angrier she got, the more determined she became to fight the drowsiness that was now threatening to envelop her. She shook her head, forcing herself to stay awake. *Keep driving. Just keep driving, keep the vehicle on the road and keep dr—*

And then she was on another road, this one a much larger highway. Two lanes, freshly paved.

She stopped the SUV, looked up and down the road, fighting drowsiness, trying to reach a decision of which way to turn.

She turned left.

When she pulled onto the road she saw a flash of light in the distance. As she pulled into the lane she squinted, fighting to stay awake. The lights loomed larger, and when she recognized them for what they were she felt such a rush of excitement that she almost collapsed over the steering wheel in joy. She fought the urge and continued on, the plan springing to mind as easily as the decision to fight for her life back in the desert. The headlights were far enough away that she could simply steer the vehicle into the opposing lane, blocking its path. Whoever was driving the vehicle would stop. Whoever it was would help her.

She turned the steering wheel sharply to the left, feeling the tires skid across the pavement. She thought the SUV was going to tip over and she automatically grabbed the steering wheel with her right hand, a fresh wave of pain exploding through her abdomen. Her foot was pumping the brakes and she felt herself spinning, as if she were on an amusement park whirligig.

When the SUV stopped she was facing the headlights, which were now looming larger; she had made a complete three-sixty in the opposing lane. The headlights were blinding and now she could see the vehicle clearly. It was a tractor-trailer truck, one of those long-haul eighteen-wheelers. She could hear the hiss of its air brakes as it began slowing to a stop.

With a gasp of relief, Lisa fumbled for the driver's-side door and got it open. She spilled out onto the pavement, screaming in agony as her side exploded again. She tasted dirt in her mouth. The hiss of escaping air from the huge truck's braking system was loud in her ears, and she tried to ignore the sensation of her guts sliding out of the hole Animal had made in her side with the knife. She tried to move her arms, to position herself to move forward, but she was feeling herself fall down into a dark hole. She fought the feeling, shook her head to clear the blackness that was rapidly engulfing her from the inside out, and the last thing she was consciously aware of was a rapid plummet toward darkness, strong hands grasping her, and the sound of a male voice.

His parents had arrived at the hotel a little before four P.M., and it was now closing in on five-thirty. Brad Miller was slumped in a chair in his room, staring out the window. His mother was sitting next to him; his dad was pacing the floor, running a hand through his thinning hair, looking worried. The head of Luxor security was in the room with them, along with two Las Vegas detectives, trying to keep things calm.

Brad closed his eyes, trying to get past the sense of dread he was feeling. Thirty minutes ago Mike Hall, one of the detectives, had gotten a call from the Nevada Highway Patrol. The thunderstorm that was currently wreaking havoc on Las Vegas was hindering their search efforts. All roads going in and out of Las Vegas were closed and there were flash-flood warnings. "We won't be able to get out there until tomorrow morning at the earliest," the detective had told Brad.

It'll be too late by then, Brad thought. He closed his eyes, all the tears long since drained out of him from crying all day. He was staring at his future, and try as he might, he simply could not imagine it without Lisa.

Then Mike Hall's cell phone rang.

He answered. "Yeah." The long pause made Brad look up at the detective, and what he saw brought a burst of hope through him. The detective's features had brightened. He was actually *smiling*. "That's good news, sir. Yes, I'll tell him." He hung up.

Brad sprang to his feet. "Where is she?"

"They found her," Mike Hall said, beaming like a proud father. "She's at Las Vegas County, undergoing surgery. A trucker found her on Interstate 15. She—"

But Brad wasn't listening. He was scrambling out the door, his mother and father trailing after him. Joan Miller was crying in joy, calling out to her son to wait up for them. Mike Hall could only follow, trying to keep up with the mad caravan to the hospital.

William Grecko was both ecstatic and filled with dread.

He grew happy every time he glanced at Brad, who was sitting next to his mother, Joan, talking to Mike Hall or one of the other detectives. Frank Miller was always in close proximity, either sitting near them offering smiling words of encouragement and occasional laughter, or he was pacing the floor of the waiting room, pausing every now and then to glance out the window at the dark rain-filled Las Vegas cityscape amid all the glittering lights.

The dread filled him every time he laid eyes on Frank Miller.

William had been trying to get a read on Frank ever since he'd pulled in to the hospital. He had received a call from Brad on his car phone when he was just outside the city limits on his way in to assist in the vigil, informing him that Lisa had been found. William hadn't asked questions right away. He'd simply told Brad he was happy she'd been found, then pulled over to the side of the road and hunted up the number to his FBI contact and given him a call. After relaying the news, he'd given the agent the number to his car phone and resumed his drive. When the agent called back thirty minutes later, William was pulling into the parking lot of the hospital. He'd sat in the car talking to the agent, getting the latest information.

A long-haul trucker had found Lisa just after three P.M. on Interstate 15. She'd been driving a white SUV and had swerved into oncoming traffic. The driver suspected something was amiss, and that was confirmed when he saw Lisa's bloodied form on the pavement. He immediately went back to his rig and raised a distress call on his CB. Fellow truckers responded by calling 911 for him and relaying vital information on their location. Between then and the time it took for emergency personnel to arrive, the trucker had covered Lisa up with a thermal blanket and tried to control the bleeding. Lisa was airlifted to Las Vegas County, where she was immediately whisked into surgery.

Because her description had been broadcast to the Nevada State Police, the FBI was immediately dispatched to the scene. Under fierce wind and rain, they managed to recover the cellular phone in the SUV. They immediately traced the vehicle to a rental agency where it had been rented by a man bearing a California driver's license identifying him as Carl Whitman. William's contact told him that when the DMV faxed their field office a copy of the license he was stunned. "It's him," he'd said as William sat in his car, rain pelting down on the windshield. "It's the same guy Lisa identified as Tim Murray. Beard's shaved off, but it's the same guy. He must've gotten a false ID."

An APB was out on Tim Murray, as well as the still-unidentified man seen in the bank surveillance video with Lisa. In addition, a still taken from video cameras at the Luxor was now being distributed. Brad's description of the events of Lisa's abduction were fantastic but certainly credible. "An old woman would be the perfect ruse," one of the agents told William. "Nobody expects somebody who looks like their grandmother to be a cold-blooded killer. I mean . . . even criminals get old, Billy. This old lady's probably been involved in this shit for years."

The rainstorm was hindering search efforts, but the authorities were certain they would make progress by tomorrow. Meanwhile, Lisa was in surgery, and once she regained consciousness and was able to talk, various law-enforcement personnel wanted to meet with her. William would be present, and he wanted to question Lisa himself on certain things. Once he got her by herself, he wanted to ask her questions about Frank.

William had received only one call from Phil, the private investigator he had hired. Phil had told William that the minute he had pulled into the neighborhood where Frank and Joan Miller lived to begin his surveillance, the couple left their home. "I'm following them now," he'd said. "Looks like they're heading out of town. What's up?"

That report had come in shortly after two. William had been sure Frank would leave the house, maybe meet up with Shectman. That hadn't happened. Instead, the Millers had gotten into their vehicle and driven straight to Las Vegas. *Maybe Frank doesn't have anything to do with this,* William thought. *Maybe I'm just . . . being paranoid.*

If he was being paranoid, he was doing a good job of it. He watched Frank out of the corner of his eyes, noted how the man was standing quietly at the window, looking out at the dazzling lights of the Las Vegas strip in the distance. William watched him, wondering what was going on in the man's head, trying to retrace his steps. Then, telling himself it was now or never, he rose to his feet and approached Frank.

Frank turned around, smiled when he saw William. "Thanks for being here, Billy," Frank said.

William nodded. "It's the least I could do." He grasped Frank's elbow and motioned him away from the window. "Listen, can we talk in private?" His voice was lowered, serious. "Just the two of us?"

Frank's expression became serious. He nodded. "Sure, Bill."

The two men headed out of the waiting room. Joan called out: "Frank?"

Frank turned to his wife. "Bill and I are just taking a quick walk. We'll be right back, dear."

William waited until they were out of earshot. He motioned toward the snack bar. "I could use some coffee. How 'bout you?"

"Sure."

Coffee purchases were made from the dispensing machine, and once the cups were in hand, William nodded at Frank. "I've got . . . well, I've got some concerns I want to talk to you about, Frank." He started feeling nervous and he licked his lips, hating himself for it. Normally, he was fine when it came to confronting people. He did it all the time as a lawyer and he thrived on the atmosphere in the courtroom. But here? At the hospital, with Lisa Miller undergoing emergency surgery to save her life, he was going to confront her father-in-law with suspicions that he'd arranged her murder?

Was he losing his mind?

"I've been helping Brad deal with this the past few days," William began, taking a sip of coffee. "When Brad told me everything, I was . . . well, I was shocked. It's just—"

"It's just so unbelievable that people would be into such things," Frank Miller said, shaking his head. "I know. It sickens me."

William glanced at Frank, noted his expression. Was Frank's expression of shock genuine? It was hard to tell. William pressed on. "Anyway, I . . . I employ the services of a lot of private detectives. I'm sure you know that. And I gave the details of the case to one of them and he went to work on it. I've also been working with law enforcement in California in helping to find the people that . . . you know . . . abducted Lisa in Ventura. Of course, we had no idea that what happened today was going to happen. I had Lisa and Brad sent out here for their safety, not knowing that—"

"How the hell did they find them?" Frank looked at William, open shock and horror in his features. "How the hell could these . . . these *freaks* find my son and Lisa and try to do what they failed to do in California?"

With rising doubt, William shook his head. "I don't know, Frank. That's what I'm trying to find out."

"It just makes no sense," Frank continued. He took a sip of coffee. William noted that, as usual, Frank looked impeccable in his Gucci loafers, his polo shirt, his dark gray slacks. His wavy hair was slicked back, speckled with gray. A gold bracelet dangled from his wrist. *He should be a criminal defense attorney,* William thought, rubbing self-consciously at his own gold chain bracelet. "The only people that were supposed to know about Brad and Lisa being here were your people, us, and Lisa's parents! Who else could have found out?"

"I don't know," William said quickly. "That's what we're trying to find out."

"I know Brad hasn't talked to anybody in California since arriving here a few nights ago," Frank continued. "He asked us to start looking into getting psychiatric care for Lisa. I just don't see how anybody outside of our little circle could have—"

William tuned him out as a slow, dawning realization came to him. Lisa's boss, George Brooks. He had called just yesterday, wanting to get ahold of Lisa. Something about missing files. He'd needed to speak to Lisa desperately. And what had William done?

He'd given George their room number at the Luxor.

It can't be George, William thought. *I know him. He's no more a sadist than I think Frank is. And as far as I know, he has no connection to Golgotha. The only way I can pin him to anything is that he had knowledge of where Lisa and Brad were holed up and—*

"You okay, Billy?"

William started, looking at Frank. "Yeah, I'm fine. Why?"

"Looked like you were letting your mind wander. I know this looks bad, but we're gonna nail these bastards. Don't worry about it. I've been talking to one of the lead detectives on the case and—"

William spit it out. "I know the FBI hasn't questioned you yet, Frank, but I'm guessing they will soon because of your affiliation with Golgotha. That you know one of the board members, that he gave you a key to his place. I know all about it."

Frank stopped talking, mouth gaping open in shock. He looked stunned.

William pressed on, feeling inspired. "Why didn't you come to me with this information before? When we found out?"

"When you found out?" Frank asked. "What do you mean, when you found out? How was I supposed to know that a man I'm friends with would be linked to a crime scene that my daughter-in-law was a victim of? My God, Billy! If I had known—"

"You would have told the authorities? If so, why didn't you?" William could feel himself getting on a roll now. He felt very much the way he did when he was in court cross-examining a witness. "You would have found out about the Golgotha cabin the same time Brad and I did, which was shortly after the FBI took Lisa up to Big Bear and she identified the place. I got her and Brad out of Orange County that evening, and here it's been over two days and you haven't said a word about it."

"Are you accusing me of setting this up? Is that what you're getting at?"

William stared at Frank. "I'm not accusing you of anything. I'm just saying that the circumstantial evidence is—"

"What? Overwhelming?" A red flush crept up Frank's neck. He looked pissed off, but there was something about his eyes that gave off a hint of panic. Was he panicked because he had been found out or because he was scared that he was being framed?

"Yes. It's overwhelming."

"Bullshit!"

"Frank, listen to me." Frank had stood up and was walking back toward the waiting room. William caught up with him, their coffee cups left behind on the snack room table. "Just listen to me. If you aren't involved, fine. But the police are already nosing around. If they catch this Tim Murray guy and he corroborates any of the evidence they've found, there could be some serious implications—"

Frank stopped, whirled around so that he was facing William. "You *are* accusing me of arranging this, aren't you? You think *I* had something to do with it! You think *I* set up the murder of my daughter-in-law, that I hired a snuff pornographer to capture her rape and murder on videotape for whatever reason you've dreamed up in that sick little mind of yours. And you're coming to this conclusion because in Lisa's confusion and fear she misidentified the place she was taken to as the Golgotha cabin. That's it, right?"

"The FBI is still running tests on the evidence they found at that cabin," William said, "and you know it. If they don't find anything, great, but if they do, it might be wise for you to start thinking now about retaining the services of—"

"Of a lawyer. Right, Billy. I take it you're going to recommend your services to me, huh?"

He wasn't listening. William could see that Frank was furious. His face was beet red; his eyes were blazing pits of anger. He could feel the tension in the air, thick as butter. "You and I know that you were nowhere near that cabin that weekend," William hissed, meeting Frank's gaze. "I *saw* you that weekend, Frank. I *saw* how Lisa's disappearance affected you. I saw how worried you were, and how worried you are now even though she's been found. I know you're not anywhere capable of—"

"Then why are you accusing me of setting this up?" Frank shouted.

William started, the loudness of Frank's voice ringing in his ears. He looked around, saw a nurse coming down the hallway glance at them with a frown. William turned back to Frank, his heart pounding. "I'm not accusing you of anything! I'm just saying that the evidence that points to you is—"

"Overwhelming. There we go again!" Frank threw his hands up in the air, and there was something about his demeanor now that William would look back on later as odd. For despite Frank's obvious anger, William detected a hint of genuine fear coming off the man. It was a fear that said *I've been caught.* William had seen this behavior thousands of times in his career. He'd defended thousands of people in various criminal cases, and most of them were guilty—he'd known that going in. Yet he never coerced his clients into revealing their guilt or innocence; his job was to defend his clients, to ensure them a fair trial as outlined in the U.S. Constitution. And even though William had never outright asked his clients if they had committed the crime in question or not, they always volunteered their plea anyway: *I didn't do it! It wasn't me!* And they always made that plea with the same look and telltale body language signs that told William they were lying. Frank Miller's speech, the way he reacted to everything, told him all he needed to know. And with that epiphany came a sudden burst of revulsion.

William stared at Frank, mouth gaping open in horror, which he tried to rein in. "Oh my God," he said.

"What?" Frank barked.

As quickly as the feeling came William shook it off, hoping Frank didn't catch it. He didn't want Frank to know that he had gotten a sudden revelation.

That he was looking into the eyes of a man who was not only afraid but was lying.

He was lying to save his skin.

William stood straight, injecting a calm purpose in his voice and mannerism. "I'm sorry if I've offended you," he said, forging ahead with a new plan. "I just thought I would let you know and be honest about it. I don't want the police to see you as a suspect, Frank. But if you don't know what you're up against, how are you going to defend yourself if they come after you?"

That question spiked through the armor Frank had erected around himself. For a moment, the Teflon that Frank Miller wore slipped down briefly and William saw a scared, confused man standing in front of him. A scared, confused man who was afraid of being exposed for the monster he was.

Frank looked at him, the fear a faint hint in his eyes, and then it was quickly gone, the mask slipping back comfortably into place. "They won't come after me because you won't encourage them anymore, will you?"

"I'm not encouraging anybody, Frank, I'm trying to help your son and Lisa!"

Frank's mouth was open to say something, and he stopped. He nodded, his shoulders slumped slightly, as if he had seen his fate and was accepting it. "You're right," he said. For the first time, he looked embarrassed. "I'm sorry I made a scene. I know you're just trying to help. I just—"

William treaded carefully, choosing his words with precision. "That's all I'm trying to do. Help your family. All I've done is help the police and the detectives with certain information I've been able to uncover. They're already investigating the underground S&M market, trying to get people to talk. I know they've talked to one guy already who they're considering a suspect."

Frank's head snapped up. "They do? Who?"

"A guy named Rick Shectman." William watched closely for any sign of recognition on Frank's face; if Frank knew Shectman, he didn't show it. "He's got a record for peddling child smut, and it's rumored he'll film anything if the money is there. Including snuff films."

"Really." Frank's tone of voice was tinged with an inflection that suggested he had prior knowledge of Rick Shectman.

"Yeah," William said, trying to keep Frank calm. "And of course they're still working on identifying the guys who actually kidnapped Lisa. My guess is that they'll find them soon. Once Lisa comes out of surgery, she'll be talking. Your son's already given a good description of the woman who killed John and Titan, and we have witnesses that saw her with a guy that matched Tim Murray. The pieces are falling into place. I'm sure Lisa will be able to tell us more by tomorrow. We're going to get these guys. You can trust me on this."

Frank smiled, laid his hand on William's shoulder, his grip firm. "I know you will, buddy. That's why you're one of the best damn lawyers I know. Even if you do defend scum." He smiled.

William smiled back. As genuine as he wanted to believe Frank's smile and demeanor were, that sixth sense was telling him that there was something lurking beneath the surface. Something that had a dark soul and dark desires. "It's a dirty job, but somebody's got to do it."

Frank laughed.

They began walking down the hall toward the waiting room. Frank put his arm around William's shoulders. "Listen, I'm sorry about the way I reacted back there. I don't know what got over me. I guess . . . all the stress is just getting to me."

"It's okay," William said.

The waiting room was still another hundred yards away. Frank stopped and motioned toward the men's room door ahead of them, on the right. "Listen, why don't you go back to the waiting room and see what's up. I gotta pee and wash up. All that yelling made me sweat." He grinned. William laughed. Sweat dotted Frank's brow and was shining in his hair. He hadn't noticed how badly Frank had sweated; it was literally beading on him like water on a freshly waxed car. Dark wet patches had appeared along the underarms of his shirt.

Another sign of guilt? William nodded. "Yeah, sure, Frank. Take your time. And listen, I'm sorry if I came across as being . . . well, accusatory. I didn't mean it."

They shook hands, Frank's gaze meeting William's.

Frank's smile was pensive. "I know you didn't." Then he turned and headed to the men's room.

William walked to the waiting room, his heart racing. He felt the flesh along the back of his neck ripple in gooseflesh. A shudder of cold fear enveloped his system. Something about Frank's demeanor was really bothering him. He had defended a lot of bad people in his life: gang members who didn't care that they had inadvertently blown the head off a three-year-old while they had been aiming at a rival; child molesters who feigned repentance but went right back out again and committed other heinous acts upon children when they were released from prison; rapists who took delight in terrifying and abusing their victims. It was a dirty job, but somebody had to do it. Those accused of crimes had the right to defend themselves in a court of law—anybody who had cruised through a course in U.S. government knew that. William had defended his share of clients who he knew in his heart were innocent of the charges brought against them. It was this motivating factor for being involved in criminal defense—to protect and defend the wrongly accused. Yes, there were times when he had to defend scum; it was part of the territory. But of all the people he had defended that he had the feeling were guilty of the crimes in which they had been charged, none had ever creeped him out as much as Frank Miller just had. Looking into Frank's eyes was like looking into the face of evil itself. He thought he had known Frank Miller; he had been proven wrong.

Halfway back to the waiting room, William got the sudden urge to head to the men's room. He didn't have to relieve himself; instead, he had the strong feeling that something was going to happen, that Frank was going to do something and that he had to somehow stop him.

William raced back down the hall and entered the

men's room, and at first what he saw was so surprising his first reaction was to gasp in surprise. He felt his breath freeze as Frank Miller, who was standing with his back to the lone urinal with a gun to his head, looked up at William's sudden intrusion and, seeing him, took the gun away from his head and pointed it at William.

"Frank, no!" William cried, barely aware of the door to the restroom closing behind him. The look on Frank Miller's face before he pointed the gun at him was one of surprise and despair. He was breathing heavily, his arms trembling as he held the gun on William.

"Get out!" Frank said, his eyes wide and scared. "Go on, *get out,* this has *nothing* to do with you!"

"It has everything to do with me," William said, his mind kicking into overdrive. "Please put down the gun. Let's talk about this."

"What is there to talk about? You've already spelled it out for me. You think I had something to do with Lisa's kidnapping and attempted murder. You think I set this up based on all your circumstantial evidence."

"That's not true, Frank, and you know it. I only want to help you."

"You've already helped me by telling me all I need to know, okay? I've learned enough to know I'm fucked."

William could tell that Frank was just as nervous as he was. When he'd entered the bathroom and saw Frank pointing the gun at his head, he could tell that Frank was trying to muster the nerve to pull the trigger. If he was that reluctant to pull the trigger on himself, maybe he could be talked into putting the weapon down. "I can help you," he said, holding up his hands. "I know it looks bad and all that stuff I said . . . that might not even happen. I just wanted you to be aware in case it *did* happen and—"

"Oh, it's going to happen, I can guarantee that," Frank said. He was sweating profusely. His eyes were wide and panicked. "They're going to find out, and you aren't going to understand when that happens. I don't want to be around when it happens, because I don't want to see the look on Joan's face when she finds out . . ."

"When she finds out what, Frank?"

Frank tightened his grip on the gun and leveled the weapon at William, who raised his arms higher and backed up. His back touched the bathroom door. If somebody came in now, they'd bump into him and Frank might squeeze off a shot in surprise. "Please put the gun down, Frank. Let's talk about this."

"We are talking," Frank said. He looked crazed and desperate. "You need to listen."

"Okay, I'm listening." *Please, just put the gun down!*

"You already told me everything I need to know. I'm fucked. My life is over, it's gone, it's fucked. They're going to find out everything, and I don't want to be around when that happens."

"What are they going to find out, Frank? Are they going to find out that you really *were* involved?"

Frank's face trembled; he looked on the verge of tears, as if he was trying to hold his emotions in. He struggled to compose himself, still pointing the gun at William. "I never wanted them to find out. You've got to believe me. I've kept it secret for so long . . . nobody knew. Not even you. Joan certainly never knew, and she never would have understood. She would have left me in a second if she'd found out. I knew I could never show her that side of myself . . . she never even indulged in light bondage with me. You know what I mean, William? The bitch never even consented to just a little light B&D, a little slap and tickle, a little role-playing. Know what she called it? She called it sick fantasies for sick perverts."

William didn't know what to say. He could only stand

there silently, hands raised in surrender, hoping Frank would calm down.

"I kept it to myself," Frank continued. "I . . . it hurt me to hear her say that, so. . . . I kept it to myself . . ."

William licked his lips. "I'm listening, Frank. Go on . . . you can tell me everything."

Frank looked up at William again, his eyes wide, panicked. "Why should I tell you everything? You're just going to tell Joan that—"

"What's the harm in her knowing now?"

Frank's grip on the gun tightened. "If I shoot you now, nobody will know!"

"That's not true, Frank. On the way over here, I talked to one of my investigators. He's the one who found out the information on you." William paused briefly, hoping this would get to him. It did; Frank's face paled. "How else would you think I found out? Why else would I bring this subject up to you?"

"Oh . . . God . . ." Frank moaned. His back was leaning against the tiled bathroom wall. He still had the gun pointed at William, but he was loosening his grip. "I'm . . . so . . . fucked . . ."

"It doesn't have to be that way, Frank! I can get you help. Please put down the gun!"

"You can't help me. They'll still find out and I'll be ruined. Everything I've worked at to keep that part of myself secret . . . it'll all come out and I'll be called a monster, only I never actually *killed* anybody! I just liked to *watch!* It'll be just as bad—"

As William's suspicions bore fruit, he tried to fight down his revulsion. "You liked to watch? Why? I don't understand, Frank, what led you to this. Why . . ."

"I don't know," Frank moaned, tears pouring down his face. "I don't remember how it started, it just happened! I just . . . found myself attracted to it . . . found that the hardcore imagery turned me on sexually and . . . the more I got into the extreme hardcore scene, the more I *liked* it. It just . . . it just kind of *grew* from there."

William was regaining some of his confidence in controlling the situation. If he could keep Frank talking, keep talking to him in a smooth voice and get him to let down his guard, he would rush him. "Why Lisa, though? I can accept you had . . . that you were living this secret life as . . . as a voyeur of . . . of this stuff, but . . . why Lisa?"

Frank wouldn't answer at first. He kept the gun pointed at William, his features displaying the range of emotions that were battling to the surface. William could tell he was losing it. "I couldn't imagine what Joan's reaction was if she'd known I was into heavier stuff than just the light bondage, which she was so . . . so *repulsed* by. I kept it secret. I *had* to. I needed Joan, *needed* that security of a wife and a family and a job. I needed that . . . that *respect* that comes from doing well in business. But I also . . . needed to *indulge* every once in a while. I . . . I didn't like to . . . actively *participate* . . . but . . . I just liked to *watch* . . . and . . . and . . ."

"How long have you been into this, Frank?" William asked calmly.

Frank wasn't looking at William now, although he still kept the gun trained on him. "A long time," Frank said, looking at the tiled wall in front of him. "I was fortunate enough to keep it hidden, to live that other life so nobody knew. It was like . . . any other thing. Some guys get turned on by normal pornography, others get turned on by fetish stuff . . . all that never did anything for me. What I liked was . . . very *extreme* hardcore S&M. At first it was okay that it was all an act, that . . . the people in the videos were all consenting adults. I could fantasize that the bottoms were being taken by force. But . . . after a while that wasn't enough. Can you believe I was actually asked to leave one of the bondage groups I was involved with?" He looked at William. "When they found out I wanted to watch a scene where the slave was really being taken by force, that she was an unwilling participant, I was told to leave and not come back. They looked at me like I was a freak. That's when I knew that . . . something was wrong."

"Why didn't you get help?"

Frank ignored the question. He was looking back at the wall in front of him, still holding the gun. "I did some more searching, was able to find out through one of my contacts about a more select group, and I got in. That . . . made me feel better. Knowing there were others like me, who just liked to watch . . . who were just as outwardly normal and were professional people on the outside in their everyday lives and contributed to society, even though it was a very small group of people. At least I knew I wasn't alone. I still contributed greatly to society; I rose up in management, I provided for my family, gave them everything they needed. But when I needed release, I knew I had an outlet. I was . . . fortunate enough to gain the trust of this group. I was good at keeping my mouth shut, at just showing up at the gatherings and watching, paying any amount of money they asked for to watch and then go away. But then—"

"Why Lisa, Frank?"

Frank had slumped down into a sitting position on the bathroom floor, his back still against the wall. The arm that held the gun was less in control now, but William still didn't dare take a step forward to try to take it from his hands. He hoped to be able to talk Frank out of it. "The minute I saw her, I knew that she was the one."

William paused. "What do you mean?"

"When I saw her, I couldn't get her out of my mind.

Every time I saw her, I . . . I imagined what it would be like being with her . . . doing to her what . . . what I saw in the few . . . snuff films I saw. I kept fantasizing over and over what it would be like to . . . torture her and see her suffer. Maybe that's how it works for . . . the people who are into this. I know that's how it was for me. I didn't pay to see some . . . some anonymous whore get snuffed and imagine I was the one doing it to her. I always pretended that it was somebody else and . . . in the last few years that somebody I visualized was Lisa."

William felt cold listening to this. To think that it wasn't malice or greed or some monetary reason that had driven Frank to arrange for Lisa's murder, but the simple desire to watch her suffer and die left William reeling.

"For a long time it was just something I could fantasize about," Frank said, panting. "I could fantasize about it and it was okay, but then . . . then when Brad got engaged to her and they started coming to the house more she . . . she became part of the family and they got married and then . . . then I . . . started becoming more . . . emotionally *attached* to her . . . more . . . I couldn't control the thoughts, they got *stronger* and . . . I didn't want her . . . didn't want to someday lose control and . . . and be alone with her one afternoon or something and lose control of myself and make an advance towards her. That would have been trouble and . . . Brad and Joan . . . they would have hated me forever. So I kept trying to suppress those feelings, but they wouldn't go *away!* They just wouldn't go away, no matter what I tried to do!"

"So you did it," William said, barely able to control the revulsion he felt for the man who was sitting in a crumpled heap across from him. "You didn't even try seeking psychological help, did you? Instead you raised the money and tried to have her raped and killed so you could own her, because you felt she owned you! The only way you could control your sick feelings over her was to control her, and the only way to do that was to watch her suffer and actually possess a visual documentation of that! Isn't that right, Frank?"

Frank turned to him. "So you do understand?"

"No, I don't. And I'm not even going to try to pretend to."

"I knew you wouldn't. That's why I have to do this." And with one swift motion he stuck the barrel of the gun into his mouth and pulled the trigger.

The gunshot was loud, and the suddenness of the act made William yell and jump. His back hit the bathroom door and he felt wetness in his crotch as he peed himself. The force of the gunshot rocked Frank's head back against the wall and he slumped down, eyes open and staring at the ceiling. Twin fountains of blood gushed out of his nostrils like water shooting out of a faucet. The handgun that he had shot himself with lay in the clutches of his limp right hand, now resting on the tiled bathroom floor. A puddle of blood was slowly seeping outward from the body; more blood stained the wall and mirror in erratic splatters.

Then William's stomach convulsed and he threw up, not even aware he was yelling and crying at the same time.

Thirty-one

"How can I help you today?"

The ticket agent at the US Airways desk was young and blond. She smiled sweetly at Mabel.

"Yes," Mabel said, handing over a dog-eared US Airways envelope that held her travel information. Her hands shook, and she tried to keep the shakiness in her voice to a steady level for dramatic effect. "I was supposed to fly out yesterday morning at eight A.M., but I missed my flight. I was visiting my sister and she had an accident yesterday. I couldn't make it to the airport because I was in the hospital for most of the day, and I couldn't get my nephew to drive me out here because—"

The agent took the ticket. "Let me see if I can help."

Mabel nodded, looking crestfallen. It wasn't hard to act her way through that; she was tired. She'd gotten some much-needed sleep last night, but her body was still bruised and sore from that long hike around the desert pass yesterday. She'd gotten so much sleep that she'd snoozed right past her originally scheduled departure time. She sniffled. "I really hope I can make it back," she said, her voice low and brittle. "I had to call a cab to take me out here because we still can't locate my nephew, and I need to get back home to get the proper papers for my sister's will if she . . . you know . . . if she . . ."

The ticket agent was typing information into the computer while Mabel talked, and now her smile widened. "Don't worry about anything, Mrs. Schneider. We can put you on the next US Airways flight out of Las Vegas into Philadelphia."

Mabel looked up, trying to act hopeful. "Really?"

"Really." The woman typed more keystrokes into the computer. "We have a flight leaving in thirty minutes. Flight 293. It gets in at ten thirty-six P.M. Is that all right with you?"

Mabel nodded. "Oh yes, that would be lovely. Thank you."

"No problem." The blond woman was all smiles as she went about preparing Mabel's ticket. Mabel smiled. If she'd made it this far, she was going to make it home. It had taken her three hours to pick her way around the low hills where they had intended to kill the Miller woman, and by the time Mabel reached the area where they had parked the cars, it was pouring rain. The SUV was gone, but the Saturn had still been parked by the large rock. Mabel had taken the set of keys that Animal had left with his clothes, and she had given his body a quick inspection. He'd still been alive; he was unconscious, a knife stuck in his gut, and Mabel had seen the weak rise and fall of his chest. She'd pulled the blade out, then stuck it into his right eye, bringing slow, shuddering release. Then she'd licked the blade clean and gone to where the fat guy lay slumped on the ground, thick blood congealing out of his ears. He'd still been alive too; at least she thought he was. It had been hard to tell with the pouring rain and her own shot nerves, which were screaming at her to get the hell out of there. She'd knelt down beside him and slit his throat for good measure. Then she'd gotten into the Saturn and, after resting up for a moment, she'd started the engine and driven away.

It had taken her four hours to get back to her motel. Maneuvering through the rain had been terrifying, the only time she had been scared in a long time. She drove slowly, trying not to drive over large rocks if she could help it, and tried to remember the path Tim had taken them down. It had taken her an hour to find the road, another hour after that to find the main highway. By the time she found the first road, the rain had flooded the desert. She had felt panicked, hoping that she wouldn't be washed away in a flood. Once she'd reached the main highway, she'd felt better. The Saturn had three quarters of a tank of gas, plenty to get her back to the Strip. She'd headed back to Vegas, taking her time, and once she reached the city she tried to remember where her motel was. She remembered the name, but not the location, and one phone call to information services was enough to put her in touch with the front desk, who gave her implicit directions. She was safe in her room by eight P.M., and after a hot bath she fell into bed, exhausted.

Now it was almost twenty-four hours after they had attempted to revive Lisa Miller and begin the filming of her torture and murder. That surely hadn't happened, and Mabel didn't give a shit about it, either. She'd already been paid for her part; she'd made sure Rick Shectman had paid her in cash before she'd boarded the plane to Las Vegas a few days ago; he'd actually had it sent to her by courier from New York. The cops hadn't come nosing around her motel room, and she'd slept soundly last night. Once she had woken up she'd taken another hot bath, packed up, checked out of her room, driven to a Denny's, and ordered herself breakfast: scrambled eggs, pancakes, sausages, orange juice, and coffee. Then she'd gotten back into the Saturn, double-checked to make sure her ticket was in her purse, then driven to the airport. She'd left the Saturn in the airport parking lot after wiping the steering wheel, gearshift, dashboard, and doors with a rag. If the cops found it, they might be led to believe that there was a third accomplice in Lisa Miller's attempted murder, but with any luck they wouldn't have her description. And in case they did . . . well, she was just a little old lady. Whom could she possibly hurt?

The ticket agent smiled as a printout of Mabel's new flight itinerary spit out of the printer. She pulled it out, tore off a strip of paper, folded it up and scrawled the gate number in red ink. "There you go. Gate number fourteen, US Airways Flight 293. It leaves in about thirty minutes."

Mabel smiled, trying to look grateful. "Thank you, dear. You've been such a big help."

"No problem, ma'am. Would you like to check any bags?"

"No, thank you." Mabel picked up her carry-on bag, which was a small duffel bag she had packed with her overnight clothes and toiletries. "This is all I have. Thank you." She smiled at the ticket agent and shuffled away, down to the security checkpoint.

Mabel smiled as she hobbled down the gateway. She smiled and nodded pleasantly to the airport security checkpoint people as they ushered her through. She smiled as her carry-on bag was placed on the conveyor belt as she went through the metal detector. She picked her bag up on the other side, smiled at the young black girl who handed her bag back, then hobbled along, smiling pleasantly at those who looked at her and nodded. Those who saw Mabel Schneider on her flight home would think she reminded them of their elderly grandmother.

HUMAN BODY PARTS, BONES, AMONG HORRORS FOUND IN HOME OF RECENTLY DECEASED GRANDMOTHER

September 15, 1998

Lancaster, PA—AP

In what has to be one of the most bizarre cases in the annals of modern crime, authorities in the small Pennsylvania town of Lititz are puzzling over the discovery of the partial remains of several human beings found in the home of a recently deceased grandmother.

Sources say the woman, identified as eighty-three-year-old Mabel Schneider, lived alone on the quiet tree-lined street, often entertaining her children and grandchildren in her two-bedroom cottage. The woman was also known for contributing cakes and pies to church fund-raisers, and was known throughout the neighborhood as quiet and neighborly. When her oldest daughter Miriam, 57, discovered her dead last month from natural causes, she had no idea she and the rest of her family would be plunged in a whirlwind of media activity.

Found among Mrs. Schneider's possessions in a basement room that had been sealed off was a cardboard box containing mason jars filled with the pickled remains of various human body parts. "They aren't discarded lab specimens," remarked Detective Barney Hillman. "We did a routine check with medical centers in the area, and a DNA check on one of the remains came back with a match to an unsolved homicide from five years ago." That homicide, the murder of eighteen-year-old Doug Sawyer of Spring Valley Road, had puzzled investigators. Sawyer went missing on May 2, 1993, around eight P.M., when he was last seen by his mother when he left the house for the Weis Market on Broad Street. He never returned. Partial remains were discovered in a ditch on Route 772 outside of Brownstown, but no solid leads had yet emerged. Until Mrs. Schneider passed away last month.

"I'd hate to think that Mrs. Schneider had anything to do with Doug's death," her neighbor Claire Ellerwood said yesterday. "She was such a nice lady, always happy and cheerful. She mostly kept to herself, but she was such a nice person."

Forensics investigators say some of the remains may be as old as forty years and may have come from children. Some match other missing persons going back to at least 1955. A Lititz high school jacket from the class of 1956 was among the items found in the basement; it's been positively identified as the jacket worn by Bonnie

Febray, a teenager who went missing in November of 1955. Mabel Schneider and her husband George, who died in 1989, lived a few doors down from the Febray family in the early nineteen fifties. So far, none of the human remains discovered have been identified as those at Miss Febray.

Also found among the deceased woman's belongings were various sexual devices and pornographic material, including child pornography. "All the pornographic materials we confiscated at the Schneider residence are on the extreme side," Hillman said. "It's very sick and graphic in nature, and I will find it hard to believe that the people depicted in the stills and videos we found actually lived through the brutality."

Meanwhile, Mrs. Schneider's three adult children are reportedly shocked at the findings and allegations and are refusing to comment on the matter. All inquiries directed to them have been referred to their attorney, Joseph B. Lockerman, who also refused to comment on the case.

Epilogue

Six Years Later
April 12, 2004
Laguna Beach, California

It was a beautiful spring day when Brad Miller got out of his car, a brand-new Saturn LS, and walked over to the plots that he had picked out for the girls five years before.

He had chosen a spot beneath a shady oak tree, near the far eastern corner of the lot. In the summer the massive branches and leaves provided ample shade, and Brad and Joan had bought a small concrete bench for visitors to sit on when they came to visit. The final resting spots themselves were lined up rather nicely; Lisa had picked out the stones herself, and when Brad had Lisa's stone picked out he chose one that was similar to what she had picked out for Alicia and Mandy. It was only fitting. He didn't know if it was what she would have wanted, but it made him feel better. It had made him feel good to take care of her—to take care of *them*—during those dark years.

Brad paused when he reached the grave sites. The late-afternoon sun shone high in the sky, casting rays of warmth across his face. He looked down at the headstones and read each one, savoring it, committing them to memory.

Alicia Lynn Stevens
May 8, 1971–August 5, 1998

Amanda Beth Stevens
June 4, 1998–August 5, 1998

Between both names were the following words: *Mother and daughter, always in our hearts.*

Then the next stone:

Lisa Ann Miller
December 8, 1967–June 22, 1999

Below Lisa's name, Brad had added a line from Psalms: "*Yea, though I walk in the valley of the shadow of death, I shall fear no evil.*"

Brad closed his eyes as tears pooled out and dripped down his cheeks.

Then, mustering up his courage, he took a deep breath and opened his eyes.

He sat down cross-legged on the grass so he could talk to Lisa.

"I know that . . . well, I know you probably know about what's going on with me, Lisa. I mean . . . sometimes I can't help but feel you're still with me, you know? Even though you're. . . ." He paused, feeling the tears sting at the back of his throat. He swallowed, gained control of himself. "I still can't believe you're gone. Despite all that's happened . . . I still can't believe you're gone."

After his father's sudden suicide and the revelation that he had been responsible for the horrors he and Lisa had been embroiled in, Brad had plunged into a deep depression. He couldn't eat, he couldn't sleep, and he couldn't work. He lost fifty pounds in two months. On the flip side, Lisa seemed to bounce back stronger than ever. She had undergone four hours of surgery to repair extensive damage to her intestines and stomach, and was laid up in the hospital for three weeks after infection set in. Those first few weeks when she was recovering seemed to be a battle for her; she'd been determined to live, just to spite the men who had done this to her. Brad had visited her every day, slept at her bedside, and she'd seemed to draw on this for her strength. She'd bounced back improved as news of the investigation unfolded. When the bodies of Animal and Tim Murray were found, she identified them; a month later, when Mabel Schneider was discovered dead in her home in Pennsylvania and the news of the horrors that had been found in her home reached her, an FBI agent had flown out and shown Lisa photographs of the woman. Lisa had identified her as the woman who had killed John Ponozzo; Tim's murder was also pinned to her officially.

"Anyway," Brad continued, pulling up tufts of grass. "I know I haven't been by in a while. Hell, it's been almost a year. That's the longest I've been away from you, if you know what I mean."

In the weeks that had followed the discovery of Animal and Tim Murray's bodies, more revelations were unveiled. Rick Shectman had been brought in for questioning and he'd denied everything. While Shectman was in jail being held on other charges, one of William Grecko's contacts, who had been quietly working the extreme hardcore S&M angle, came back and revealed more pieces of the puzzle, confirming the disjointed confession Frank gave before he blew his brains out. According to the informant, Frank Miller had been a longtime devotee of the circle. He was known as a voyeur. "It's like he told me: He liked to watch," Billy had told Brad six months later at a small bar in Huntington Beach. "He especially liked watching women get cut with knives or burned with cigarettes or branding irons. He was into what is known as blood sports. It's like . . . people getting off sexually at the sight of blood or getting off in the act of cutting or mutilating people."

"My mom's doing pretty good," Brad continued, the first hint of a smile breaking his stoic features. "She's . . . she's actually starting to have a life again. It was hard for her—you remember that. It was hard for all of us. But she's finally been able to put it behind her." He shook his head. "It's weird to hear me say that. When I think back, I realize she's been getting her shit together far longer than I have. She bounced back pretty quickly, actually. I guess the fact that she's seeing somebody made me realize that she's gone on with her life." He looked at Lisa's headstone. "You'd like him, Lisa. His name's Robert Walker and he's a writer and a musician. Total opposite of what Frank was." Brad still couldn't refer to the man that had fathered him as *Dad*.

At some point during the nine months Brad and Lisa spent in therapy, recovering physically and mentally from the ordeal, William Grecko had come to the house and, with Joan Miller present, he'd told them everything; he'd kept most of what Frank told him a secret from them, but that day he told them all of it, including the corroborating evidence his investigator uncovered. How the S&M acquaintance had revealed that Frank liked to watch people being sexually tortured and abused; how he had fantasized similar scenarios with his daughter-in-law in mind. Telling them the truth about Frank's sickness was the hardest thing he had ever done. Joan had reacted visibly to the news. "I'm sorry," Billy had said while Joan cried.

"You'd really be surprised if you saw Mom now, Lisa," Brad said. "She's . . . well, she really shines now. You'd be happy for her."

He remembered how Lisa had reacted two months after she had come home from the hospital, when Billy told them that cadaver-sniffing dogs had located the remains of Debbie Martinez, and Amanda and Alicia Stevens. DNA evidence found on the bodies matched with Jeff Sheer—Animal—pointing to him as the killer. Unfortunately, Lisa's testimony wasn't enough to have Rick Shectman arrested for murder. There was no record that he was involved with Frank Miller. Phone records showed Rick had frequent contact with Tim Murray, who, in turn, had contact with Jeff Sheer. But there was no evidence of Jeff and Rick ever coming in contact with each other. Al Pressman was never located. William surmised he either disappeared on his own or was bumped off.

Lisa took solace in taking care of Alicia and Amanda Stevens. After Alicia's father was informed of his daughter's death and he refused to have her body shipped to him, Lisa had arranged for the woman and her daughter to be cremated. She'd also arranged a small ceremony. She had broken down and wept at the service, and Brad could only allow her this time to grieve. Lisa's grief had been a great release, mourning for a woman and child whose deaths she felt responsible for. Her taking care of them after death and seeing that they were honored and remembered in a memorial service was her way of making it up to them, however small it was.

Lisa bought the plots herself, at Forest Hills Cemetery

in Laguna Beach. She visited the grave sites regularly for a while. Brad visited them with her too, and could only feel a sense of numbness as he sat beside Lisa while she cried, her grief still great and immense. He understood where it was coming from, but he could not share her grief at that time; he had his own turbulence to go through: the betrayal of his father.

Brad rocked forward a little, a light breeze ruffling his hair, which he'd allowed to grow longish. "So much has happened in the past six months. You already know that Elizabeth and I have gotten married. I told you about that a year ago, right on the eve of our wedding. I'd hardly think you'd forget that. I was bawling like a damn baby when I told you."

He had met Elizabeth Robles in Santa Fe, New Mexico, where he had stayed with an old college friend during his two-year ramble around the greater North American continent. Following Lisa's passing, he'd come dangerously close to following in her footsteps. He'd spent two months in a drug and alcohol fog until he'd pulled himself out of it with William Grecko's help. William had gone into rehab six months after Lisa was discharged from the hospital—his sixth stint in twenty-five years—and he'd emerged not only sober but with a sense of triumph, an outlook that he admitted was one he never thought he'd have. "I'm not going down that road again, buddy," Billy had told him. "From now on, I'm choosing life."

William had helped Brad make that choice nine months later, when Brad realized that Lisa's choice had been that: her choice. It had been a hard one to make, but he really couldn't see her taking the alternative. "She would've been a mess for the rest of her life," he told Billy later after an AA meeting, which Brad began attending for a while and later dropped out of. He'd never had an addiction problem previously, and the meetings had merely been a form of support for him following his own rehabilitation and therapy. More therapeutic were his private meetings with Billy, which the two lawyers had at least weekly. And when Brad was on the road on one of his rambles, he always talked to William via cell phone or through letters, which he posted in whichever town he was in—from Anchorage to Belize. By then, Brad had quit his position with Jacob's and Meyer's and was living off of the money that had been recovered during the theft of their life savings. He knew he would have to return to work eventually, but for a time he couldn't. He had to find himself, had to find peace, and the only way he could do that was to stay in motion. His travels by car were wide-ranging and in some cases adventurous, and in seeing the natural beauty of the country he began to feel beauty again in life.

But it was a long, slow process. And there were setbacks along the way. More than once, Brad had gasped awake in some strange hotel room in some state he had never been in, alone, the memory of Lisa's voice, her touch on his mind, and he would collapse in uncontrollable sobs.

"We're doing very well," Brad said, feeling in touch now with Lisa's spirit. "We finally sold the house. Can you believe I was able to sell it for almost half a million? I mean, we paid two seventy-five for it when we bought it, and five years later I get double for it. Elizabeth and I were able to get a nice home outside of Santa Fe, where we live now. You'd love it, Lisa. Five bedrooms, on two acres of land, with a little lake in the back. I mean, it's a gorgeous house! Easily a two-million-dollar home in Orange County. And I paid three-fifty for it. A steal."

Officially, the FBI had kept the case quiet. With Lisa's testimony they began monitoring Rick Shectman more closely. And when he was finally caught in an undercover sting operation involving a worldwide child pornography ring two years later, he was brought up and convicted on various charges that resulted in a life sentence. Brad regretted that Lisa never lived long enough to see that happen.

In November of 1998, two months after Lisa emerged from the hospital, she returned to work, but she was never the same. For the six months that followed, she and Brad lived lives mired in depression, grief, and uncertainty. Brad was able to pull himself out of his own quagmire of guilt to focus on helping Lisa, who continued to beat herself up over Mandy and Alicia's deaths. They both underwent therapy, individually and group. Life became a routine of work, sleep, visiting the grave sites, crying, and therapy. During the few times Brad was able to get Lisa to talk about it, she told him that she didn't know if she could ever forgive herself for what she'd done. Her therapist was trying to work her through the guilt, but it remained. "I feel like I'm a traitor," she told Brad on the rare occasions when she did talk about the incident. "I feel that no matter what I do, no matter what I try to do in their memory that will somehow make it better, it will never *be* better. They died because of what I did. And no amount of money donated to charities in their names or organizations founded for homeless women or whatever is going to bring them back and undo the pain they suffered. They died because of a selfish act. They died because for a split second I decided I was better than they were, that I deserved to live more than they did. And once I got those freaks on that train of thought, there was no stopping them, even though I *did* try to save Mandy and Alicia. They were still killed."

Her depression affected her work performance, but she wasn't let go. George Brooks put her on light duties, and when she wasn't at work or therapy, she slept. Brad constantly worried that she would turn to self-abuse, and he monitored her medication and was hesitant to leave her alone. Gradually, when it became apparent that she wasn't a danger to herself, he began to allow himself brief sojourns out of the house to cope with his own problems and issues. During the spring of 1999, Lisa began to show strides in her therapy. It appeared that she was making great progress; she spoke less of her guilt, began entertaining thoughts of the future. There was something about the way Lisa carried herself, the look in her eyes, her demeanor, that told Brad she was getting past the worst of it. "I may never forgive myself, but I can try to move on, right?" she said one evening while they lay in bed talking about their individual therapies. Encouraged by this, Brad began pulling himself out of his own funk. They began doing the kind of things they used to do together: shopping at Triangle Square and taking in movies (light comedies, mostly), followed by dinner. They even went out with friends one night.

And then, as suddenly as it had begun turning good, it nose-dived. One balmy June Saturday afternoon when Brad returned home from running errands, he entered their bedroom and found Lisa in bed, the two urns that contained Mandy and Alicia's ashes clutched to her bosom. An empty box of her sleeping pills was on the nightstand, along with a note, which Brad didn't read with any clarity until three days later: *No matter what I do now to make it better, it will never be better. Even though I made a horrible mistake, and my actions were deplorable and I don't deserve forgiveness for them, the fact of the matter is I fought for them. I fought for us when we were pulled over in Ventura, and I fought for my life back at that cabin. I fought for Alicia and Mandy even after my own selfishness took over, and I fought for my life again in Nevada because after being dragged all that way I didn't want to go down without a fight. I wanted to hurt those who had hurt Mandy and Alicia. And I hurt them. I hurt them bad, and I'm glad they suffered before they died. But I can't live knowing the one who is the cause of Alicia and Mandy's deaths is allowed to live her life, be happy, possibly have children and see her babies grow. That was denied Alicia and Mandy, and I know that I would be a miserable wife and mother and human being for the rest of my life if I continue on. Therefore, it is with great sadness that I leave. Know this, Brad—I love you, and I will always love you. Go forth and do what I will not be able to do. Live life. Enjoy life. And more importantly, appreciate the beauty in life. Do this for me. Don't beat yourself up because of what your father did. Your father was the monster—NOT you. He did this, NOT you. Don't let him drag you down. I only wish I could be strong enough to resist the urge to end it all, but I can't. I've tried to look at things from a different perspective the past few weeks, but I can't stop thinking about them and what I did. There is no other way for me. My path has led me to here, and I would rather chose this path than the one of life, which I know will be wrought with pain for the rest of my life. Maybe I deserve that, but I don't deserve the possibility that I can rise above my grief and misery and be happy once again. I don't deserve the possibility of happiness and all that can come with such happiness, such as our love and marriage, our getting pregnant again and having children. I don't deserve it, and I know this and accept it. Please understand Brad. And please remember that I will always love you. Love, Lisa.*

He still had that suicide note, and he read it again as he sat at the grave site, the paper it was written on now lined and creased from constant handling. Brad folded the paper again and wiped the tears from his face. "I understand now," he said, as he held the note in his hands. "I understand."

He paused for a moment, eyes closed. The late-afternoon sun was warm, and the breeze that blew in from the ocean was tinged with salt spray. Brad sighed, feeling in touch with himself again. Ready to go on. "You know, the past year I've never felt better," he said. "I mean, I'll always miss you, and Elizabeth knows that you'll always remain special in my heart. In fact, it was her idea for me to come out here and tell you this, so . . . well, I better get to telling you."

He paused; he had been rehearsing what he wanted to say all day, and now that he was here he felt awkward. In a way, he felt the same as he did in the months after meeting Elizabeth on a stop in New Mexico and falling in love with her. He felt a slight edge of betrayal that he was stepping out behind Lisa's back. But he also felt that Lisa was smiling down on him, was telling him *It's all right, Brad. She's wonderful, and you deserve her. Be good to her. Be good to each other.* And hearing her voice whisper those words in his mind brought a smile to Brad's face. The two years he had taken off of work after Lisa's death had been dark years, and many times he wondered why he even bothered to continue living. But it was his travels, meeting new people, keeping in touch with Billy and his mom, and Danielle Kwong and George Brooks and the rest of their friends, that had kept Brad going. In their own way, they had helped Brad find beauty and wonder in life again, and when he and Elizabeth Robles fell in love two months after meeting at a dinner party given by an old college friend, Brad finally felt he could end his solitary rambles and try to appreciate life again.

That had made it easier to uproot from California to New Mexico. Orange County held too many memories of Lisa, and the trips he made back to visit his mother and Billy became less painful as the months flew by. When he and Elizabeth wed in September of 2002, their wedding was held in the foothills that surrounded Santa Fe, the city he now called home.

"You know, I understand now why you did what you did," he said, fingering the note. "Checking out, I mean. It's taken me the past five years to come to peace with that, and I suppose that if I'd been put in the same situation I would've done the same thing. I would've checked out too.

"Because life's worth living. You don't forfeit others' lives for your own. You fight for life. For your own, for others. You made a horrible mistake, and you regretted it and . . ." The tears came again. "I still wish there were some way you could take it back, but you can't. You can't take it back, and I can't take it back, and life has to go on, you know? So I'm going on and it's been hard. But as you know . . ." He sighed. "The past year or so has been great, considering all that's happened. I've gone on with my life. I have a new life, a new home. I'm working for a small firm in Santa Fe now, and Elizabeth is a journalist for the local paper. We do pretty well, you know?"

He took a deep breath, looked down at Lisa's suicide note, then at her grave. "Elizabeth's pregnant," he said, sobbing as he spoke those words. He was sobbing out of a mixture of pride and regret that it wasn't Lisa who was going to bear his child. "We're already past our first trimester, the hardest part. When we found out, I was so scared. I mean, I couldn't believe that it could happen, and it did, and I didn't want anything bad to happen, you know? So we kept quiet about it and hoped and prayed everything would be all right, and we're past the first hurdle. The last two ultrasounds we've heard a nice strong heartbeat." Tears blurred his vision. "We're gonna be okay."

The breeze died down. The sun felt warm on his face. Brad wiped the tears from his cheeks and thrust the suicide note into his pocket. He'd thought about destroying the note for the past few months; it was the only thing he had that represented that horrible time in his life. He had gotten rid of other personal things that brought the memories back to that fateful weekend, and even now he tended to avoid the news and he no longer enjoyed psychological thrillers the way he used to. He'd kept the note because he felt he still needed that connection with that part of his life, despite how awful it had been. He never wanted to forget it despite wanting to. He didn't want to forget it because he didn't ever want to forget Lisa.

Brad shuffled to his feet, brushed the grass off his jeans. He looked down at the grave sites, reflecting on Amanda and Alicia briefly, wishing them well and hoping they were at peace, hoping they knew that he loved them and would always love them. He straightened himself up and turned to Lisa's headstone, swallowing a dry lump. "I know I'll be back soon. My mom's still in Orange County and . . . well . . . she'll want to see her grandchild. Maybe someday . . . if it's okay . . . we can come up? If it's okay?"

A light breeze rustled the leaves of the oak trees and whispered over his hair, caressing him. Brad closed his eyes, feeling comforted in what he knew was her positive answer.

"I'll never forget you, Lisa," he said. "And I'll always love you. I love Elizabeth . . . I never thought I could love another woman, but you helped me to love her. You . . . helped me to see the beauty in life again. If it weren't for you, I never would have made it this far. This baby is as much yours as it is Elizabeth's and mine."

Brad smiled down at the headstone, feeling strong, feeling more pure and good than he had felt in years. "I'll be seeing you soon, honey. Be good to yourself, okay?"

Then he turned and walked back to his car and drove off to his new life.